T0065472

TRUE LOVE
AND BROTHERS
LASTS FOREVER

Volume 1

DAVID L NISWANDER

authorHOUSE

AuthorHouse™
1663 Liberty Drive
Bloomington, IN 47403
www.authorhouse.com
Phone: 833-262-8899

Published by AuthorHouse 04/06/2022

ISBN: 978-1-6655-1112-4 (sc)
ISBN: 978-1-6655-1111-7 (e)

Library of Congress Control Number: 2020925148

Print information available on the last page.

This book is printed on acid-free paper.

CHAPTER 1

It was a clear early spring day, warm, but surprisingly not cold. There were fanfares, marches, and overtures heard from many directions. The city park's band shell was packed with tall slender men holding various instruments. At the cue from the director's wand, the musicians began to play. At the city park, there was food, beverages, entertainment, and much fun for every one of all ages. The city had the celebration twice yearly.

JB was never late, but due to the various parades and activities, he had to navigate through narrow-winding streets which were packed with cars and people. This reminded him about doing the same in Afghanistan, but there he had to watch out all the time to keep from getting shot. He walked toward the band shell. The band was playing, and people were standing around the bandstand having a festive time dancing and listening to the band.

JB was almost to the bandstand when a loud bang, an actual explosion was set off causing people to yell and running in all directions. But not JB, he ran right into the center of the explosion. He recognized that it was a flashbang, which only makes a lot of smoke and noise, but does not damage anything. He looked around at all the people and saw a man with a satisfied look on his face. JB knew the look he had seen it often in ten years.

He ran over to the man with the look of satisfaction on his face, and said, "You did this, didn't you?"

The satisfied look eased away, and now it was fear that covered his face, he looked around for a place he could hide.

He replied, "I didn't want to hurt anyone, only to scare them. I did it, to make people worry about an attack from terrorists; JB was bigger than this man and as he watched fear appear on the man's face.

JB asked, "What is your name?"

The stranger replied with a shaky voice, "It its Henry sir" and fear was all over his face.

"Henry get some soap and water to clean this area. If any reporters come around, tell them someone threw a cigarette into the fireworks and they went off. Then, there won't be a story." JB Instructed.

"How do you know this stuff?" Henry asked.

"I have been fighting terrorists for the last six years of my life. If this gets out the terrorists will think they may have an easy time hurting people here," JB clarified to Henry.

"Why are you here? Are you with the government?" Henry asked in confusion.

"Now, get this mess cleaned up to keep you out of trouble," JB demanded.

Henry looked over the mess that he created. *I was really stupid to have done this he though.* He turned to say that he was sorry, but JB had already left.

JB took out his phone and called his Dad. His dad answered and said, "What's up." JB: "Some idiot made a flash bang and set it off at the park in the city while the band was playing, trying to make people aware of the danger of terrorists, if some reporter makes a big deal out of it and it gets on the wire and some big city picks it up, we could have terrorists coming here as it might look like an easy target." Dad: "I hope not." JB: "I don't think we can rule it out, you need to call the hospital and have them put out an ad for an ER Nurse, from a big city and this nurse should be here in at least 3 weeks from now." Dad: "why an ER Nurse?" JB: "Big city ER Nurses see things smaller towns don't, Burns, gunshot wounds, knife cuts, missing body parts, the average nurse does not see those kind of things." Dad: "I will call them tomorrow and get them on it." JB: "I am going back to the base, and touch base with my guys and let them know we might have a little more trouble than we thought, I will see you in 3 weeks, bye." He headed for the airport to get a flight back to the base. Tomorrow would be a busy day.

Henry got done with his cleaning and was getting ready to leave when a reporter came by and ask about the explosion. Henry said, "Someone dropped a cigarette in a box of fireworks, lots of noise but no damage, no big story here just dumb luck, not worth your time." The reporter with a thoughtful look said "are you trying to hide something." Henry: "No, and a government or military man, a scary guy said it was nothing to worry about, he knew all about Terrorists, forget this as it was nothing." Henry turned and walked away.

The reporter though this is my big chance to make the big time, I heard that a Navy Seal was coming home to take over the Park. I can put this in a story that will get me noticed.

The next morning JB's Dad called the Hospital and talked to the administrator and told him what JB had said "about hiring a big city ER nurse, and told them the nurse should have experience with gang violence victims." The administrator said," we have been thinking along those lines, we will get a wanted ad out right away, and thanks for calling." Dad hung up and though I hope we really don't need an ER Nurse.

Jennifer sat down at her computer and checked for any openings at the hospital in her old hometown as she had done every day for the last six months.

There was an opening for an ER nurse in the Hospital she was waiting for, she filled out the application and attached a copy of her resume. Then she shut down the computer and went to put Ben her son to bed. Jennifer said, "Ben have you brushed your teeth and washed your face?""Yes mom I am all ready for bed, will you read another chapter before I fall asleep." "Yes," she said and sat down in a chair and opened the book and started to read. Ben fell asleep quickly and she got up and got ready for bed. She hoped she would get an offer later this week.

The alarm went off at 6:00 and Jennifer got up and went to the kitchen and put on the coffee. Then she woke Ben up, and laid out his clothes and went to the kitchen, she fixed two bowls of cereal and packed two lunches for the day and she got ready for work and made sure Ben had what he needed for school and they left and she locked the door.

She started the car and took Ben to his school and then fought the traffic to work. She finished her rounds and it was time for her break.

She got a cup of coffee from the pot and went to the exit and went out. She hoped to get a call from the application. She had listed her breaks as times she could get calls. Two sips into her coffee her cell rang. It was the hospital; they ask her why she wanted to leave her present job? She said, "I want to get to a smaller city, where there is a nicer atmosphere and a better school for her son." The voice at the other end said: "how old is he?" Jennifer replied "11." The voice on the phone said, "we like your qualifications, when can you start." Jennifer said, "I can give my 2-week notice and it will take a week to get things packed and then I can be moving in four weeks in total as I will have to look for a house." The voice on the phone said "we would like you to start in 3 weeks; we will get you a discount at a motel where we send families when they are visiting a loved one. Also, we will send movers there to help you pack and we will store your belongings until you find a place to live." "The movers are local people we know, they will take good care of all your things as if they were their own and we will pay the movers." They set the date the movers would arrive and Jennifer said "goodbye" and went to turn in her two-week notice. She was starting a new chapter in her life. *Now how was she going to tell Ben's father he has a son or maybe not it would depend on his situation?*

Jennifer now had to break the news to Ben about his new home, school and new friends and all the new wonderful things he would discover in his new home.

CHAPTER 2

James Benjamin Jones Known to his friends as JB, some people asked why do they call you JB instead of James, and JB would reply over there we seals have a bounty on us so we used initials instead of names so they would have trouble finding out our real names. JB though about the things he would do first when he went back home. He had not seen his father and mother much over the last few years. The seals had been on call at a 24 hr. notice or less and they could be any place on the planet. And that made it very hard to have a life outside the Military. The service was just not the same as when he joined up, time to go home and start a new chapter in his life. The Doctors said his dad could spend no more than two hours a day and only 2 days a week at the park, as the stress was killing him and it was too much for his mother by herself, so his enlistment was up in three weeks. He would be home the next day after that, He had put some thought into things he wanted to change when he got home. So he started his list, he liked to set up a list of mission objectives, and then he and all his men would work out the mission and when they all were agreeable, they knew what they must accomplish.

He was glad that his main squad was going with him as he knew their good points and bad and given a job they would finish it or die and he could trust them, they had each other's backs. They all had a lot of the same skills to survive but each had special talents that he could use to improve the park and the city. The world has changed and he felt not for the better, people were not responsible for their actions, so they would do things that were not in the moral code he had been brought up with.

His Dad had written that they had some gang trouble and the security and the local police had not handled it well. He knew that **LJ (Larry John Nelson), CR (Charles Robert Young), JR (Jose Rodriquez)** and himself could fix that in short order. The Grounds had to be maintained, better communication for Security, start a survival school for local kids to help get them get off the street, self-defense classes for boys and girls, Setup a First-Aid Station, Set up a 300 yard gun range for the Swat team the city wanted to start. All his men would help with that to start with, they would join the police force part time until it was fully functional.

List for the Park

Task	Start	Finish	Person	Out come
Gang control	1st to ·3rd month		JB-LJ-CR-JR	
Grounds	1st week		LJ when he arrives	
Maintenance	End of 1month	JR		
Security	1st month		CR-JR	
First Aid Station	1st-2nd month		CR-JR	
Long range	1-3 month		JB-LJ-CR-JR	
Survival School	1-4 month		JB-LJ-CR-JR	
House Clearing	1-6 month		JB-LJ-CR-JR	
SWAT Training	3-6 month		JB-LJ-CR-JR	
Self Defense	1-3 month		JB-LJ-CR-JR	

That should keep them busy for the next 6 months. He was excited to see his Mom and Dad, it had been way too long, Dad really had some time off coming as the park was a full-time job for 3 or 4 people and dad had worked way too hard. It was time to get him into some hobbies for relaxing. That should be a good start to get things going for the next 6 months, and hopefully that flash bang at the city park would not change things for the worse.

CHAPTER 3

MONDAY WEEK 1

Jennifer checked into the motel and unloaded the car.
"Ben," she said, "Are you hungry?"

Ben said, "Yes and could they have pizza with the round things on top?"

Jennifer said "you mean pepperoni".

"Yes," he said.

Jennifer said, "I saw one a few blocks from here."

They got in the car and were off. Jennifer though then we will go to the hospital and I will check in and get my schedule.

JB arrived home and unpacked. Then sat down and talked to his Dad about the list he came up with.

JB said, "Dad is there any things you are working on that I can finish for you."

Yes, his dad said one of the restrooms was vandalized and that needs to be fixed tomorrow.

JB said, "Ok I will take care of it first thing in the morning."

They talked a little more and JB said: "I think I will go to the park and walk around and have a look, it has been a long time since I have seen it."

JB got up and said, "See you later."

Jennifer got directions to the park from the clerk at the pizza place; the town had changed quite a bit in 12 years. She and Ben got in the car and drove to the park.

They started to walk and Ben said: "I want to see the animals."

Jennifer asks a Security Guard that was walking by and he said: "the park is actually closed but I don't think they'll care, I will show you the way."

The Security Guard walked them to the petting zoo.

Jennifer and Ben went in and started to visit with the animals. Jennifer watched Ben having a great time but she needed to go to the restroom. Ben was having such a great time she asks the attendant if he would watch Ben until she returned and he said "sure, he won't get in my way, so it will be fine. Jennifer got directions to the nearest restroom and left.

As she was walking around a bend in the path she came on to 3 Security Guards and they kind of surrounded her and ask if they could help her.

She said "I have directions and I will be fine, but they got to arguing with each other about who would walk her to her destination.

Just then a man came around the bend in the path, Jennifer looked at him with a rescue me look.

JB walked up and said, "Is there a problem here?" One of the Security Guards said, "This does not concern you."

JB said "Yes it does, now one of two things is going to happen, you are going to go about your duties or you are all fired."

The mouthy Security Guard said, "Who do you to think you are that you can fire us?"

JB said, "I run this place as of this morning." "Now get back to your posts all of you except the mouthy one, you will come with me as we take the lady to her destination."

They walked to the restroom and Jennifer went inside.

When Jennifer disappeared from sight the Security Guard said with a worried look on his face. "Am I fired?"

JB turned to the Security Guard and said: "no you get two mistakes but I don't like it when you make a second, and you tell all of the Guards they are to come to a meeting at the office day after tomorrow one half hour before your shift starts, can you do that?"

The Guard said "Yes", and then quickly left.

Jennifer came out and said, "Thank you for the help."

JB said, "Not a problem and I am sorry you had this kind of a problem but it is not going to happen again."

"May I walk you to your destination?" JB said with a smile.

Jennifer said, "Ok, my son is at the Animal Zoo." They started to walk. JB said, "Do you come here often?"

Jennifer said, "I just moved here this week, I am a nurse at the Hospital."

They arrived at the Animal Park, Ben came running over.

Ben said: "Mom I am having a great time I think I am going to like it here."

JB smiled and said, "I guess we are doing something right, Kids are a great source of information if you just listen to them."

Jennifer smiled and said, "From the horse's mouth."

JB said, "Yes, have you found a place to live yet."

Jennifer said, "No the hospital has us staying at the motel until we can find a place."

JB said, "That could be expensive."

Jennifer said, "Yes but the hospital is covering half."

JB said, "It could take a while, I don't want you to think I am being forward but my dad has had some heart problems and he has trouble staying away from the office, Mom and I are trying to get his mind off the park and find other things for him to do."

"We have a spring house for guests. You could stay there until you find a place at no charge, and my dad would have someone to keep him busy until Mom gets home; I bet he would take your boy fishing or for a walk in the woods above the house, He loves kids and they like him."

"It would be good therapy for him and you would not need a sitter; take a day or two and think about it, call the office and ask for JB and let me know."

Jennifer said, "I will do that and I thank you very much."

JB said, "I like helping people, God put us on this earth to get along with each other and help each other and the human race is failing at that."

Jennifer said, "I bet you protected the smaller kids when you were younger." JB said, "Yes I did." Jennifer though *I had better watch what I say, he may recognize me.*

Jennifer said, "We must start back to the car as it is getting dark."

"Do you mind if I walk you back I don't want you to have any more trouble?" JB said.

Jennifer said "OK." And though *I think he is interested in me.*

"In the short time you were in the park did you see anything we could do to improve it?" JB ask.

Jennifer said, "You should have signs with a map saying you are here, it would make it easier to find where you are."

As they got to the car Jennifer said, "I will think about your offer and let you know tomorrow." JB waved goodbye and then entered the suggestion into his phone.

JB turned and went back home, his Mom said "supper is ready." they all sat down to supper.

JB said "Mom there was a little problem with some Security Guards with a lady at the park. She just moved here with her young son and I offered her the spring house as a temporary place to stay while she finds a place to live, I thought Dad could use a diversion, and he could take the little boy fishing up in the old pond or walk in the woods, dad it would give you something to think about instead of the park. The little boy seems to be a nice kid about 10 or 12, I told her to call me in a day or two, you would not mind would you?"

Mom looked at dad and said, "You know how long it has been since the Spring House has been used?"

"Quite a while I will have the cleaning girls clean it tomorrow it should be done anyway." Dad said.

JB finished his supper and said, "Dad lets go play some pool I have not done that in a long time." JB's Dad said, "go on down and I will be right along."

JB left, Dad turned to Mom and said: "that may be fun; I wish we had a grandkid or two.

"JB still likes to help people just like he did when he was younger, he makes me proud", his mother said.

Dad turned and said, "I better go and see if I can still beat the boy

I don't think he loses very often now." Dad went down to the game room, JB had the game all set up and they begin playing, it was nice having his son around. They played for an hour and then they went to bed morning comes awful early.

Jennifer drove back to the motel and thought to herself, this would be a good way to have them meet their grandson and not even know he is their grandson. I don't want them to think I am trying to get anything from them, and James could be married, and that may be a problem. I did not come here to cause him a problem but I am still in love with him.

CHAPTER 4

TUESDAY WEEK 1

JB got up at 5:30 am and put on his running suit and went for a 3-mile run, when he got back he did 50 pushups and 100 crunches. Shaved and showered brushed his teeth, went down and got some breakfast and went off to the park.

He got there just as the office assistant got there and they went in together, she was a nice lady about 50 and had worked there from day 1. He thought *she will be a lot of help getting me up to speed, and probability knows all there is to know about what needs to be done.*

JB said "tell me about the Security Guards do we hire them or are they leased.

Betty said "we lease them from a local Security firm."

"Do you know what kind of training they get as Dad said they had a little gang trouble last year and the police were called and it took a while for a response?" JB replied.

"Yes it took them about 25 minutes before they got here." Betty stated.

"That is not good enough; a lot of people could be hurt or dead in that time frame." JB replied.

"Yes we were lucky it was just a brawl and only the gang members were hurt none of the other guests were involved." Betty stated.

"How many were there?" JB inquired.

"There was four in one gang and five in the other." She replied

"If my squad had been here we could have taken them down and had them under control in two minutes." JB stated.

"I had a little trouble with three of the guards last night and a guest, and I am going to have a meeting tomorrow morning a half hour before we open. What time do they arrive?"

"about a quarter to 8:00." Betty said.

"I did not see any radios or Tasters on them?" JB said.

"No they just have a stick and I don't think they know how to use it." She replied.

JB thought a minute and said, "how far from here is their office?"

"About a half a mile from here." Betty replied

"Get the owner on the phone and I will talk to him, we can't have things like that happening a second time with a response like the first." JB said with disgust in his voice.

JB thought a minute and said "I want to talk to the police chief as I think I went to school with him, and see if we can hire some of his guys after hours until we get our security upgraded; see if you can set up an appointment with him for this afternoon; also order 10 Level 5 bulletproof vests and get them here by Friday."

Betty went to her desk and called the Security Guards office and got the owner on the phone.

"Hi this is JB from the park; I have some questions about your guard's training."

The voice on the phone said "they get a couple of holds with the sticks and how to block attacks with objects such as clubs and sticks.

"What if we train your guys in hand to hand combat for you?" JB asked

The voice on the phone said, "I don't know if I want the extra liability if they have to subdue people."

"We will get that added in our liability policy so you will not have that extra exposure and expense." The voice said, "Then it is ok by me."

"I will want the same guards all the time once they are trained unless you would like all of your guards to be trained."

The voice said, "That would be fine."

"At the end of the training I will pick the ones I want in the park as not all of them will be as good as I want."

The voice said, "OK we can work that out later."

"I am going to buy Bulletproof Vests for them so they have better protection." JB said.

The voice said, "<u>That</u> is great we were thinking we might get some for our guys maybe we could buy together and get a better price."

"The ones I planned to get are 500.00 apiece." JB informed him.

"That is a little more than I can afford." The voice replied.

"They have some level 3 for 300.00 and with a bigger order they may give us a discount." JB stated.

The voice said, "That is a little better as I would need 20."

"Ok I will see what I can do and my assistant will get back to you before we place the order."

The voice said, "OK let me know and we will go from there."

JB said "Goodbye" and hung up. JB said "Betty when you get the Vest Company on the phone see if you can get a discount. We want 10 level 5 and 20 level 3, are you good at haggling prices?"

"Yes I do it all the time." She replied.

JB smiled and though *things are going very smooth, I hope it continues.*

JB said "The lady I helped last night gave us a good idea. She said if we had maps with you are here so people could know where they are and make it easier to find their way around, and we should mark the restrooms, and concessions, and a first aid station."

"that is a good idea I will have the printer make some larger maps and we can put them up and mark them. I will get maintenance to start work on them when I get the dimensions." Betty replied.

"Dad says we have some repair work to take care of in one of the restrooms."

"One of the sinks was broken and leaking so we turned it off; and it is on the list to get fixed this morning." Betty said.

JB started to get up and go and meet his employs when the phone rang.

Betty answered the phone and said "it is for you."

JB said "OK" and picked up the phone.

JB said, "Hello this is JB."

The voice on the phone said, "This is Jennifer I thought about your offer and I would like very much to take you up on it."

"They are cleaning it up today, you can move in tomorrow and if you need any help I would be glad to help." JB said and smiled.

"That would be nice I have a couple of things in storage I would like to get. But is there a wife that would get upset with you helping a single woman?" Jenifer asked.

"No wife, call me when you go to storage and I will meet you there." JB replied, *she wanted to know if I was single, that's good.*

"Thank you very much, well bye." Jennifer replied, *this is good she thought.*

JB said "Betty I am going to walk around and introduce myself to the workers. Call me on my cell and let me know when I can meet with the police chief."

"OK I will let you know." She replied.

JB left the office and walked around looking for people as the park rides were not ready yet, the animal exhibit was open, and the grooming had started and they were handling the new animals so they were not afraid of people. As he walked around he noticed the shrubbery was really greening up and introduced himself to people he found along the way, then his phone rang, it was Betty.

She said "The chief said to come over in half an hour and you can talk and then go to lunch and catch up on old times.

JB stopped at another ride and then headed back to the office to get the company car and head out to the police station. JB got the keys from Betty and left.

The sun was out and the day was a beautiful spring day and he observed that the town had changed a fair amount while he was gone, some of the old things were gone and new things were in their place and he was pleased how things were going so far but it can't last forever.

The police station was newer than when he was a kid and a lot bigger, Hank had done all right for himself becoming chief. JB went in and told the cop at the desk who he was and he had an appointment with the chief.

The Sgt. said right this way and took him to a door in the back of the building, with Chief on the door. The Sgt. knocked on the door and a voice said "come on in." The Sgt. opened the door and JB walked in.

Hank got up and came around the desk and shook hands with him and said: "You have grown some since I saw you last, what was it 10 or 12 years."

"12 years and I am back to stay because I am sure you know Dad has some medical problems."

"Yes, I always liked him; we had some good times on our little outings." Hank reminisced.

"Dad said you were still thinking about starting a swat team?" JB inquired.

"Yes we were going to get a 6 man squad, and your Dad said the park would help with some of the cost." Hank replied.

"Yes I am putting in an order for 10 level 5 vests, 4 vests for myself and my squad that is going to work at the park the other 6 are for your swat team. And one of my guys might be interested in joining your swat team on a permanent basis, and we would be available on a part time bases." JB replied.

"That is great and I gather that you are all snipers?" Hank said.

"Yes and we have some other skills that maybe helpful, like room clearing for one and we will set up a 300-yard shooting range at the park to go along with the pistol range. I was also thinking of putting up a building for training house clearing." JB stated.

"That would be great I think we might get some grant money to help with the cost. Hank said.

"That is great, I was also wondering if we could give some of your off-duty officer's part time work?" JB inquired.

"I don't see that being a problem, I know some could use the extra income." Hank replied.

"I also want to put up a building to have self-defense classes for boys and girls, also some survival classes on survival training and outdoors skills and see if we can get some of the gangs to disband." JB said.

"Yes that is a great Idea as the gangs are getting to be a problem, you could use our gym and they could get to know the police are really their friends." Hank replied.

"Great, let's go get some lunch, I'm really hungry." JB said.

"OK me too." Hank said with a smile.

JB and Hank got up and walked out of the room. They walked the 2 blocks to the diner and had lunch and talked about who was still around and what they were doing with their lives.

Hank got up and said, "I have to get back for a meeting; it has been great getting together."

JB said, "Yes it has and I will get back to you when the vests come in, and when you put your sign-up for volunteers mention that women should apply also."

Hank said, "That is a good idea as I think a woman would help with small children, and I am working on a grant for some of the cost, I am glad we had this talk, I can see we are going to help each other out."

JB said, "Yes we will and you have a good day and keep in touch."

They walked back to the station and JB got in his car and went back to the park.

CHAPTER 5

WEDNESDAY WEEK 1

JB went into the office and Betty said "Did you know the paper ran an article on you with a picture?"

"That is bad; you know what I did in the service?" JB asked.

"Not sure, I know you were a Seal." Betty replied.

"Yes we did secret missions, and the terrorist have a bounty on us, mine is 500,000 and my squad is 250,000 each." JB stated.

"Wow I didn't know that; that's bad." Betty replied with fear in her voice.

"Yes crooks and terrorist would like that kind of money, which puts us all in danger." JB said. "Would they bomb us?" Betty inquired.

"I don't think so, they need a head for proof of death." JB stated.

"What kind of animals are they?" Betty inquired with a worried look on her face.

"They are living in the stone age, might makes right, the best fighter rules. Would you get the police chief on the phone?" JB asked.

Betty called the chief and put the phone on hold. Betty said "chief is on line 2."

JB picked up the phone and said "chief we may have a problem, the paper ran an article on me, and they used an old picture from school so it might be nothing, but we need to watch for tails and surveillance. You know they have bounties on us."

"Yes we know about that, but you look a lot different now; then you did when you were in school." The chief said.

JB thought then said "I was thinking what if they though my guys all look like they were men in your police department, and were in police departments elsewhere so they could hang around and look like they had been police a long time but were new to the department. If we could get some of your single women to work undercover pretending to be wives or girlfriends. No funny stuff, it would be just for show to give them a different identity, the park will pay them for their trouble."

The chief thought for a minute: and said "that could work I have a good friend in a city in another state and I am sure he would fix up new identities; I will get our wives looking into the girls and let them pick out the guy they will be working with."

JB said "Thanks that takes a load off my mind."

"What about you, won't you need one too?" The chief inquired.

"Yes but I have someone in mind. So I will let you know if it doesn't work out." JB stated.

"Goodbye" and JB hung up the phone.

"Have you got a girlfriend?" Betty asked.

"No but remember the lady I said had trouble with the guards?"

"Yes." Betty replied.

"I offered her the spring house to stay in until she found a home."

"I don't know if someone you don't know and with a child might not want to do that." Betty said.

"Yes I thought of that, but there is a passageway underground to the big house, I could go over there and no one would know I was not there with all with the shades closed." JB said.

"That might work." Betty replied.

"I hope so, there is something about her, and it feels comfortable being around her." JB said.

"Didn't you have a girlfriend in the service?" Betty asked.

"Not really, with being on call 24/7 I didn't think it would be fair to her as I could be gone for a day or two, or a month or two and I can't say where I was or what we did or call." JB said.

"I see what you mean."

"To change the subject, how are the repairs on the restroom going?" JB inquired.

"They finished it about ten minutes ago."

"Is there anything else I don't know about that needs to be taken care of right away?" JB asked.

"No. go to the dinner and take a break." Betty said.

"I think I am going to look at how someone could fire at us and see what we could do to fix it." JB thought out loud.

JB left the office and looked all around to see if there were any good advantage points for a sniper, there were a lot of trees in front of the windows that faced the entrance to the park so that side was fairly safe. The other sides were blocked by buildings and rides so they should be fine. So he started to walk all around the park to find good spots to conceal a shooter. He found 3 that looked like they would work so he thought he would fix two of the sites so they would be unusable and set up a camera to see if he got any bites on the other site.

It was getting late so he went back to the office and he and Betty looked on the internet for some camera's and he though there should be some surveillance on the rest of the park.

He decided to go home and have some lunch with his Dad and talk about what he had planned so far. When he got home his dad was walking around and looking like he was going stir crazy.

"Dad lets have some lunch, we can run into town I am sure you know of a place we can talk and eat." JB told him.

Dad said "sure" and they got in the car and left.

They stopped at the dinner and went in. They looked around and saw the chief just finishing so they went over and JB told him about what he was going to do about stopping snipers.

The chief said "he was working on finding some girls for the undercover work, one girl was already on patrol and she said she would volunteer."

JB said "one down 3 to go."

The chief left and he and his Dad sat at a table in a corner of the room where JB could watch the rest of the room and the door.

JB asked "Dad are the people in here regulars or a lot of strangers?"

"I have seen just about all of them here before. I know the owner and he has a surveillance system, I am sure he would let you look at the files." Dad replied

"That's a good idea; before we leave I will talk to him." JB said.

The waitress came and took their order and JB's dad told her to tell Bill to come over for a minute.

She said she would and left.

Dad said "You know there are a couple vantage points up on the hill where you can see the whole park, it is quite far but with these new guns you are looking at ½ to ¾ of a mile away.

JB said "let's go up there tomorrow afternoon."

His Dad thought it was a good Idea.

Their food came and they ate. When they were done Bill the owner came over and they talked and Bill said he would be happy to let JB look at the files.

JB said "fine and he would set up a time and 1 or 2 of his squad from the service would come along 6 eyes are better than two."

They thanked Bill and left.

JB took his dad home and went back to the park.

Betty said "the bulletproof vest company confirmed the order and it would be in on Monday next week."

JB said "that was going to be good as he would like to start wearing one."

Betty said "The restroom has been cleaned up and open to the public."

JB:"Good and we need to order radios for the security guards and the rest of the employees." JB and Betty went out on the internet and looked at radios from different manufacturers, JB picked out what he liked and Betty put 50 sets on order to be delivered by Tuesday next week.

JB sat down and *thought about what he would say to Jennifer about pretending to be his girlfriend or wife.* Well he would cross that bridge when it comes. JB thought, *I got a lot done today I think I will go home and visit with Mom and Dad.*

He got up and said "I am gone for the day, I will see you tomorrow, and remember I am going to meet with the Security Guards early in the morning."

JB left the building and headed home. On the way Betty called his cell and said "a girl named Jennifer called and left her number, and would you call her about tomorrow."

JB put her number in his phone and thanked Betty and hung up. He called the number and three rings later Jennifer answered.

"Hello this is Jennifer."

"Hi this is JB returning your call are we still on for tomorrow?"

"Yes I am getting off at 3:00, and I can meet you at the motel about fifteen after as I have to pick up Ben, is that OK?"

"Yes that will be fine, how much do you want to get? You Know the spring house is completely furnished, all you need is clothes." JB informed her.

"OK I have 3 suitcases at the motel, which will fill my car; I want to pickup 3 or 4 boxes at the storage center." Jennifer replied.

"That would be fine, would you like to have supper after we unload, that way you can spend the evening unpacking instead of fixing a meal and doing dishes." JB asked.

"Sure that would be nice; see you tomorrow."

OK, goodbye." JB said with a smile.

"Goodbye." Jennifer said and though *he really gets to the point.*

JB pulled up at home and got out of the car. He went in and started to run over what he had gotten done today.

Mom said "supper is ready shall we go eat."

"Sure." JB replied.

They went out to the kitchen and sat down at the table and had supper.

"Tomorrow I am going to help Jennifer get some of her things from storage and help her move in. Then take her and her son out for dinner."

"You kind of like this girl even though you just met her once." Mom asked.

"Yes for some reason she just seems nice to be with; the paper printed a picture of me in the paper, and it was picked up by a big town paper, and they mentioned that I was a Seal, which is a bad thing, all us seals have a bounty on us, I was afraid this might happen. Terrorists might see it and come to town to collect, so I am taking some steps to prevent it. I talked to Dad earlier today. I talked to Hank and we are going to have some women go undercover and pretend to be wives or girlfriends and my guys are going to be dressed as policemen and pretend to be newly hired cops as a cover, that way I will be the only one in danger." JB informed them.

His Mom and Dad gave him a strange look his dad said "Why are you the only one in danger?"

JB said "I can't watch everything at once and I am the only one with a picture out there. The guys can watch my back just like they have been for the last ten years." We all have our own weapons and we are crack shots at 300 yards, 600 yards, and 1200 yards and close up and personal. The distance here will not be over 600 yards, but I think it won't be any place closer than that; they will have someone close to grab my head. I am going to set up surveillance cameras around the park and home and have full time monitoring on the screens 24 hours a day. We really need it at the park as people will steal anything now days to get drugs."

His Mom said "he has a point."

JB: "LJ will be here on Thursday, CR and JR next week then my back will be covered." They can cruise the park as policemen and they are the best there is, believe me I know what they can do."

"Dad do you have a topical map of the area?" JB asks.

"No but we can use the internet and get a rough Idea what I was telling you about." Dad replied

They went off to the computer for some research.

CHAPTER 6

THURSDAY WEEK 1

JB got up and put on his running clothes and did his daily exercise routine. Then he shaved, showered and went down to have breakfast. His Dad was sitting at the table and said: "You got a busy day." JB said, "Yes, I got a meeting with the Security Guards early this morning and then I will be back and get you so we can look over the hill." They ate and JB left.

JB got to the office before the Guards did and he went over in his mind what he was going to say. The Guards started to come in three of them were five minutes early, two more four minutes three more two and a half minutes early one more one minute before the deadline. That made nine of the ten; he put his gun on the table and said "you nine are going to be my main core of guards around here. I don't think your employer gives you the training you need in today's environment."

Number ten walked in the door JB picked up his gun pointed it at number ten and said: "bang you are dead." Number ten looked at him and said: "I am sorry I got stuck in traffic."

JB ask "is this the first time you came here." Number ten said: "No." JB replied "In my old job if you were late you usually ended up dead; I give everyone two mistakes and then there gone from my squad, mistakes are what get us killed; If you didn't do your job, you let the team down and we cannot trust you." Number ten said,

"Nobody is going to get shot here." JB said, "How do you know that." Number ten said, "We are not at war." JB said, "Do you have Gangs in this town?" Number ten "Yes we do." JB: "Do you think they might have a gun or knife." Number ten: "I didn't think."

JB: "Well in this park I want you thinking all the time, you have one of the most important jobs in the park. You have all the guests in your care. Have all of you thought of your job this way?" They all said "NO." JB; "One of the most important jobs is taking care of others and sometimes it is the most boring job there is. You may go weeks with nothing ever happening, and when it does then someone gets hurt or dead. I want you all to know that I think your job is very important, if not the most important. Now I have ordered bulletproof vests for you to wear and your employer thought it was a good idea also and he is paying for them, so he thinks you are important too. The next thing I am going to do is train you in hand to hand combat so you can defend yourself if you have to, also I have ordered radios which you will be carrying with you at all times. Put your radio on the charger when you leave at night, if you don't and your radio dies on you that is a mistake, you can't help your team and they can't help you, putting your radio on the charger is important.

Now if you think you see a problem coming, get on the radio right away so help gets there quick. And when I say:"quick I mean run if I hear the radio I will be coming as fast as I can and so will my team from the Seals, and they will help, they will also help in your training. We are a team. Also, we have a gun range and we will be teaching you how to shoot and gun safety. Now I will give you my rules. 1, don't make mistakes you only get two. 2, if you don't know, ask. The only dumb question is the one you didn't ask and that is the one that gets you killed. 3, other members of my squad are coming in the next week and they will help you the same as I will and they can fire you the same as I can. Their rules are the same as mine, the four of us agreed on them. And don't think they are not as good as I might be because they are the best. "Now are there any questions?" Number three asks "When will this training begin?" JB: "in about three weeks." It will be in the evening two nights a week and last for at least one hour, longer if you want." Number five "are we getting paid while we are in class?"

JB: "No and I don't get paid to teach it and neither do my guys. If you don't care enough about your job and your own safety to put in the time we will get someone else. Once we are done with the training you will work here, only guards who pass the course will work here. Don't pass or don't come or are late or don't complete the course you will be replaced. And when you are done the park will also supplement your pay because you are going to be better than the rest of your employer's men. We will open the training up for any of the other of your boss's employees so we will have people that can replace you when you are sick, hurt or take a vacation. You do not hit on the quests this job is to not get a girlfriend; it is take care of people so they have a good experience here. A couple of faces got a little red. Now what you do on your own time is up to you.

Remember while you are here you represent the park and me and I don't like being misrepresented. Now you all start with a clean slate, but do not be late I expect you to be on time or early being late is a mistake." JB said "the vests should be here by next week and the radios to, we will let you know and we will give you training on them when you get them. JB looked around then said "Are there any more questions." No one said anything.

"If you have a problem come and talk to me or one of my men they will all be here by the end of next week. Remember there is strength in numbers and you are a team and teams work together. Look at it this way you are forward observers and you call in your back up so when the S hits the fan you are not getting it all by yourself a larger force will usually make a smaller retreat. So call when you need help and remember, better to have it and not need it, than need it and not have it.

JB left the meeting and went to the office and told Betty he and his Dad were going up on the hill to look it over, and then he left the office and got in his car and went home. His Dad was ready and he got in the car and they left.

The drive to the hill took about 15 minutes and was a pretty drive; the side on the park was a sheer wall one hundred twenty feet straight up was rippled like a giant cutter had just sliced off the side and haled everything away, was gray with light streaks in different places running horizontal, and it hadn't changed much in the 12 years he had been gone, about the only thing that hadn't. They drove out of the park, turned left, the road had a gentle curve around to the left and up the hill they went until it leveled off. His Dad said "take the next road to the left." JB made the turn and they drove down a narrow drive with brush on both sides all most like a narrow tunnel, then it opened into a small clearing, JB parked off to the right and got out of the car and opened the trunk and took out a gun case.

His dad said, "Wow you came loaded for bear." JB: "I have to know what a sniper is going to see for the best type of shot." JB saw a faint path on the left side of the clearing and he and his dad walked about 100 feet and came to the edge of a small opening in the forest there was a few bushes on the edge of the clearing near the edge, the clearing was about 10 feet across and didn't look like anybody had been there for quite some time.

JB opened the gun case; it contained a 308 sniper rifle. His Dad said, "You have ammo in that." JB said "in the clip but not in the chamber, the clip is in the case." JB lay down and stuck the barrel through the brush and looked through the site at the view below. "Dad you do get a very good view of the park from here, I could hit any target from here, and I will put a marker on the left side that we can see from the park to sight in."

"You would have trouble seeing this spot from down below." His dad said.

"No Dad it will shine from the marker will be hard for someone to find up here but easy down there." JB went to the left and found a small tree and hung a 2-inch disk that had a flective surface on each side, he shoved it as close to the tree as he could and when he backed away it was all most invisible. His dad got up and looked at the tree and said "I can't see what you did, that is slick."

JB: "Yes they would have to look very hard; we used these on some of our missions when we staked out places." JB put the gun back in the case and said "let's go to the next site." They went back through the path and came out to the car. JB put the gun back into the trunk and shut the lid. Unlocked the car and they both got in. JB turned the car around and they went back to the road.

His Dad said, "Turn left and go about a ¼ mile and there is another spot." The road was windy and turned right then left then right then left straightened out and 200 yards ahead there was a road to the left, JB turned and the road was similar to the last one, a narrow Tunnel like road, they drove about three hundred feet, then it opened to a larger area than the last and there was trash all over the place, the kids must come here to party. JB said, "I don't know about this spot it looks too used."

His dad said, "I don't think they leave here, the brush is really thick and very few people use the path "OK let's look." JB opened the trunk and took the gun case out and shut the lid and locked the car. They walked to a small opening in the brush and pushed through and walked about three hundred feet and came to a smaller opening in the trees smaller than the last place they had been. JB look around and the brush was not as thick as the last spot but it was good enough. JB took the gun out of the case and lay down and crawled to the edge stuck the gun through the brush and sited in on the park. JB: "Dad this is a clear shot a little closer than the last, the other was more secure than this but this is a better spot. You would need a couple of people at the car to keep people from coming here. If the gun was silenced they would not know there was someone out here, I will mark this spot. And we will go."

JB found a tree on the left he could use to mark the spot and hung the reflector in the same manner as the last one. JB put the gun in the case and they went back to the car. When they got there they put the gun in the trunk and got in the car. JB turned the car around and drove to the main road. Dad said, "There is one more spot but I don't think it is very good, go left again." JB turned left and went about a quarter mile; there was another road to the left. JB's Dad said, "Take this one." JB turned left and this road was real narrow the branches rubbed the sides of the car, and hit the windshield the road was about 400 feet long then stopped. They got out of the car and opened the trunk and got out the gun case and took the gun out and closed the trunk. They went around the car and found a small break in the brush and followed it about hundred and fifty feet and there was a space about eight feet across with thick brush. JB lay down and inched forward sticking the gun barrel thru and made a small opening for the gun site and looked at the park.

Dad if I was going to shoot someone in the park this is where I would do it from, I bet it is almost imposable to see from the park and the view is the best of the three." JB got up handed the rifle to his dad and took out another reflector and hung it on the left side about 5 feet from the site, then he went 5 feet to the right and found a good tree and hung it up and smoothed the brush back into place at both trees. Dad said 'I can't even see what you did." JB: "I hope no one else can either, I am hoping they don't think anyone has a clue that we think someone will want to shoot us." They went back to the car, and put the rifle back in the trunk, closed it and they got back in the car and slowly backed up to not break any branches so it would look like no one had used the road. JB said "Let's get some lunch and then we will go back to the park and scope the hill for my markers.

They stopped at the diner and ate then went back to the park to check the markers. When they got to the park JB said: "I need a place we can get to and not being exposed and not seen in the process, we need to be able to shoot out of cover without the rifle being seen." His Dad said, "There might be a place above the animal barn or in the office." JB: "Let's go look, we will start at the office." At the office, JB opened the trunk and got the gun case and they went into the office. Betty gave them a funny look but didn't say anything.

His Dad opened a door and went up the stairs there was a small area with a few boxes stacked around for no apparent reason, there was a space about six feet wide that you can walk from one end to the other and there was a window at each end. JB looked out the window that faced the hill and said: "this could be one spot let's see if I can see all of the markers."

JB knelt down and looked thru the scope and started to scan the upper rim of the hill, and then he said "there is the first one. Now, where is number two, there you are; now for 3, there is 3 and 4. We should be able to spot all of them."

JB: 'Let's go look at the next sight", JB put the rifle back in the case and they went down stairs.

Betty said "Jennifer called to confirm your meeting this afternoon."

JB said, "Would you call her back and tell her I will meet her at the storage area at 3:15."

Betty said "OK."

JB said "Thank you", and he and his Dad left the office. They got in the car and Dad said "to take a right and go two blocks and turn right."

The animal area has a barn with a window that looks right toward the hill." They got out of the car and got the suitcase out of the trunk and they went into the area and into the barn. Inside on the back wall was a latter going up to the loft, they climbed up and there were bales of hay stacked up in neat rows on both sides all the way to the roof with a walkway about three foot wide in the middle.

JB went to the window facing the hill and opened the case and inside was a spotters scope, he went to the window and looked up to the ridge of the hill and found the first marker, then the second. Then he had all four." This is a better spot than the office but we should build a closet that can be locked so no weapon is seen going in and out. His Dad said, "We sure can do that, I will get maintenance up here 1st thing in the morning."

JB said "OK Dad I will take you home as I have to help Jennifer get some boxes from storage and help her move in. JB dropped his Dad off at the house and drove to Town. He got to the Storage area a little early so he waited at the gate." Jennifer got there about five minutes later.

JB said "HI."

Jennifer said, "I hope you didn't have to wait long, it took longer to get Ben out of school than I thought."

Ben said "Hi from the back seat. Mom said I was going to live next to you."

JB smiled and looked at Ben and said "yes you are and I hope you like it."

JB and Jennifer went to the storage box and she opened the door. She looked at the boxes and found one and JB took it to his car, and when he got back she had another for him. JB picked it up and took it to the car, she had two more and he loaded them and shut the door.

Jennifer Closed the Storage stall and they went back to their cars and Jennifer said "I will follow you so I don't get lost.

JB got in his car and they headed toward the park. It took about fifteen minutes to get to the spring house. He pulled up to the spring house and unloaded the boxes and took them into the spring house. JB: "Where do you want them?"

Jennifer: "These two go in the bedroom and the other two in the kitchen.

JB took the two into the hallway and then the other two to the kitchen.

She opened the boxes and put things in the cabinets and put the boxes in a closet so she would have them to repack when she found a place of her own. She said "would you show Ben around while I unpack the other boxes."

JB with a smile said "sure I will take him up to meet Mom and Dad Come up when you're done, just walk in and holler and we will find you. JB and Ben walked up to the main house.

"Ben meet my Mom and Dad." JB said.

"Hi my name is Ben." Ben said shyly.

JB's Mom said "Just call me Bea."

His Dad said, "Just call me Uncle Ben."

Ben said "OK Uncle Ben" They talked for a while and Jennifer came in and called "I am here."

"Straight ahead and you will find us." JB replied.

Jennifer came into the room.

JB stood up and said "Mom this is Jennifer, Jennifer this is my mom Bea and my dad Ben."

Jennifer said "Hi I am Jennifer and I want to thank you for letting me stay in your spring house."

JB's Mom smiled at Jennifer and said, "It is a pleasure; you stay as long as you want or until you find the perfect house."

JB said, "I am taking Ben and his Mom to supper, see you later." They left and JB opened the door for Ben to get in the back of the car then opened the Front door for Jennifer, she got in and he closed the door and went around and got in, started the car and off they went.

There was a nice family restaurant and JB drove there and parked the car and opened the car door for Jennifer and Ben and they went into the restaurant. They got a booth and Jennifer and Ben sat on one side and JB on the other side across from Jennifer. They picked up the menus and JB said:"get anything you want my treat." Jennifer said, "But you have done so much already. JB said "You are going to help me by being here with Ben, I think it will be great for my dad and I have to run the park and I can't spend time with him so I look at it like this. You and Ben are saving my dad's life." She smiled and said, "OK if you put it that way." They ordered and talked small talk and laughed and had a good time. *Jennifer was very happy things were going better than she thought they would.*

JB paid the bill and they went to the car JB opened the front car door for Jennifer and the back for Ben, they got in and JB took them home. JB parked the car and walked Jennifer and Ben to the spring house and said "Good night and thanks for the evening I really had a nice time"; JB turned and went to the big house.

Jennifer thought to herself, *I think he likes me; this is going to go better than I thought it would.*

His Dad and Mom were sitting and watching a movie, and they turned off the TV and ask if he had a good time?

JB looked at them for a minute and said 'Yes I did, I really did, I guess that was what I have been missing all these years and I didn't know it."

Dad said, "I think I am going to enjoy having little Ben around, It will remind me of some things you did when you were little, and maybe I will see some of the things I missed because I was working."

JB smiling said "Dad do you want to play another game of pool?" Dad looked at JB "You let me win last time." JB shook his head and said "No I am out of practice; I haven't played in 12 years." Dad: "OK let's get you some practice." They went down to the game room and Mom went back to her movie.

CHAPTER 7

FRIDAY WEEK 1

JB got up and dressed and did his morning routine, and went down and ate breakfast; his Dad came and joined him.

They finished and JB said "are you coming with me, I am going to get some cameras to put on the hill to monitor the shoot sites."

His Dad said, "Sure I wondered if you had more in mind than I did."

JB said, "We should be able to find something to hide and still give us pictures if anyone is using the sites. I am going to call Hank and give him a heads up on our plans, and fully explain what we are preparing for and why."

Dad said, "Good plan he won't want any surprises." They got up and left the house and got in the car and left.

They went to the police station and went in and ask to see the chief. Three minutes later they were taken to the chief's Office.

Hank with an inquiring look said, "What bring you here today?"

"You know that article about me in the paper."

"Yes." Hank said.

JB: "Dad and I went up on the hill and found 3 spots that a Sniper could shoot from on the park, I plan to hide some cameras at these sites and see who visits them. If we see someone that looks like they are sighting in to shoot we will have proof if things go bad, any footage we get, you will receive a copy, as you know locals and strangers, and it might be of use to you as well."

Hank looking serious said, "That is a good Idea we want to stop things before they happen if we can, I would hate to lose a friend when he just got back."

"Well I don't want to take up any more of your time. Can you tell me what store might have what I am looking for?" JB inquired.

"You should go to Bill's sporting goods; he was telling me that some of the hunters have been having the cameras stolen, so he is stocking some covert models." Hank informed them.

"Thanks that will save us some time, Have a good day and I will get back to you."

JB and his Dad left the office and got back in the car.

JB s dad Said, "Go to the end of this Block and take a right." JB started the car and pulled out into traffic, at the end of the block he turned right.

His dad said, "Go 5 blocks and take a right, it is a block and a half on the right."

JB did as instructed and they arrived at Bill's Sporting Goods. They got out of the car and went in.

They ask for Bill.

The man said, "That's me, what can I do for you?"

"We would like to buy four or five of the covert cameras you have as we hear that some people are stealing them."

Bill: "Yes some people are like that, we have two that people seem to like, It will record eight hours and then you must plug in a flash drive and download the files, the battery will last for forty-eight Hours and then need to be replaced, it comes with two rechargeable batteries. The other one has a 200-foot transmission area, you take a laptop and set it up to receive a signal and you can download your files without touching the camera at all. That way you do not disclose the position of the device, The battery charge on that one is only twenty-four Hours that is recording, and download time; you will need six AA Batteries for each camera. The 1st one is 199.00 and the 2nd one is 239.99 ea.

JB said, "I want six of number 2, do I get a volume discount, this is for the park."

Bill: "Sure I will give you a 10% off on the total."

JB paid for the cameras and thanked Bill and he and his dad left the store. They got in the car and went to the park. JB parked in front of the office and they went in.

Betty said "HI" you have a visitor; he said to tell you LJ was here."

JB said "I didn't think he would be here until tomorrow. Come on Dad I want you to meet one of my right-hand men."

They went into the conference room and LJ stood up and said: "Hi surprise I got done early so here I am." JB' said "Am I glad to see you, Dad I want you to meet Larry John Nelson, he will be working here at the park with us and call him LJ.

LJ with a big smile said "I am glad to finally meet JB's Dad.

Dad shook hands with LJ and said "It is a pleasure to meet one of the men keeping my son safe; you 3 are my adopted son's now."

"I am honored, Sir." LJ replied.

They sat down and JB said, "Where are you staying?"

"I don't know yet." JB said.

"You will stay at the house until you find a place to live." JB's dad informed him.

LJ said, "Thanks a lot that will make it easy."

JB said "let's see how these cameras work", and he took one out of its box and they spread it out on the desk. In fifteen minutes they had it working. JB said "it also has night vision. We can go out and download what was seen the day and night before. I think we should set all the cameras up and get them up and doing their jobs", JB "Hopefully we are ahead of anyone after us."

LJ stood up and said "I am ready when you are".

JB: "we are gone." They headed out the door and JB said: "Betty we will be back in three or four hours if you need text."

Betty replied. "OK."

Dad said "I am going to walk home so I can be there when Ben gets there, You two don't need me, this is your area of expertise."

They got in the car and off they went smiles on their faces, they liked the action.

As they drove JB said "The first two sites you can drive a car most of the way, the third you have to walk all the way. I thought we should put two cameras at each site one facing out to catch a face or license plate in. one facing toward the park to catch a face leaving."

LJ said "that sounds good; we will go right down the line should take no more than half an hour each."

JB said "I agree." They got to the first site and pulled in and it was empty. JB drove down the narrow road to the end they got out and JB took the spotting scope

LJ grabbed two cameras and they started down the trail. After about 25 feet LJ said "I like this spot and this tree for the first camera, we should be able to hide it behind that vine going around the tree."

JB replied "looks good to me, I will keep going and look for a good spot for number two." JB got to the site and it looked the same as it did yesterday, so it looks like no one had been there since he and his Dad were there. JB looked around and saw a great place to put the other Camera. Bushes were grown up high up in front of a tree and there was just enough room for the lens to see through. JB carefully attached the camera to the tree and made sure the bushes hid it and then he walked around to set off the camera, then they could download and see what they got.

LJ came into the clearing and said "I got good pictures from number one."

JB: "check number two, I have been walking around."

LJ said I don't see it so talk to me computer." The pictures downloaded and looked great.

JB said "On to site number two."

They headed back to the car, got in and turned around and head back to the main road. JB turned left and they went to site two. JB turned left and entered the dirt road and drove to the large opening and there was a car there. It looked like a rental.

LJ whispered "I don't like this."

JB whispered back "me either." JB: "I will take a camera and the rifle and slip into the trees; you take the Binoculars and act like you are bird watching."

LJ said "OK", and set on the left front fender, that way he could roll off and be behind the car if any shooting started.

JB slipped into the trees where he could not be seen and levered a round into the chamber, lock and load. They waited, about fifteen minutes later a young boy and a girl came out of the trail and got their pictures taken.

They saw LJ sitting on the car and stopped in surprise, they didn't think they would be seen. They started walking again and LJ said "nice scenery here. Is it better down the trail?"

The boy said "Not until you get to the end, there is a small area and you can see the valley

LJ said "thanks, I like to watch birds I can see in different places and thank you for the tip

The boy said "good luck and bye. They got in their car and left.

When JB could not hear their car any more he came out of the bushes and set the cameras on the hood and released the magazine from the rifle and levered the bullet out of the chamber and pushed it back into the magazine.

JB said "caught with his hand in the candy dish,"

LJ smiled and replied "ah to be young again."

JB: "let's get this one done JB put the rifle back in the trunk and off they went down the trail.

About 60 feet later LJ said "I like this spot, you go on JB kept going and soon he came out into the open area. It looked a little more messed up than yesterday. He saw a good spot and set up the camera and though we are going to get some X-rated pictures. He turned on the camera and walked around and LJ came into the clearing.

LJ downloaded the pictures and they looked good. LJ said "if we had been here a little sooner we would had some X shots/"

JB; "Yes I was thinking the same thing. They left the clearing and got back to the car and left. JB turned left and they went to the last spot Pulled off on the side of the road and got the last 2 cameras out and walked down the narrow trail.

LJ said "I think this is a good spot see you in a little."

JB keep on walking, when he got to the small opening he stopped and looked, it looked a little different than it did yesterday. He carefully looked at everything, it looked as if someone had been lying down and set up a rifle and did a little sighting in.

LJ came in and looked and said "Company?"

JB: "Looks that way we may be a little late."

"They will do a little sighting and planning. We should be able to come up late or drop off at three or four in the morning. Then see what comes along." LJ replied.

"I didn't think it would be this fast." JB said.

"You just never know, but we are better than they are." LJ said with conviction

"I came home to get away from this." JB said regrettably.

LJ replied "Yes I know and so did I, But we can handle it and keep your family safe."

JB thought about Jenifer and said "I met a girl two days ago and I like her and she has a nice son, I was going to see if a relationship might develop."

"We will keep her safe too." LJ said with conviction.

JB finished setting up the camera and made sure it worked and they left no sign that they were there. They went to the road and carefully checked to see if anyone was around, after twenty minutes they got in the car and left.

"Where is your stuff?" JB asked.

"I left them In the conference room." LJ replied.

"Let's go get it and if we park up front it is fairly shielded from the hill, and I think they are done for the day," JB said

"I agree." LJ replied.

JB drove to the park and they got LJ's gear and loaded it into the car and drove to the big house.

They took LJ's suitcases in and put them in one of the guest rooms and came down and introduce LJ to his Mom.

Mom smiled and said "It is a pleasure to finally meet you,"

"I have heard a lot about you and it was all good," LJ said with a grin.

They laughed and Mom said "Why don't we have supper."

They sat down and there was a knock at the door.

JB got up and so did LJ.

Mom looked worried and said "what is wrong?"

JB: "I will tell you later, if it gets loud go to the basement and don't come out until one of us says it's all right. They went into the other room and opened the door and JB was ready to jump away.

LJ was ready to slam the door. There on the other side of the door was Jennifer and Ben.

JB said "Jennifer come in."

Jennifer looks at LJ and said "is something wrong?"

JB smiling at Jennifer said "Not now but we have to have a talk, have you two had supper?"

Jennifer "No but we don't want to Interrupt you if you have company."

JB: "you are not interrupting anything we were just going to eat, this is my brother from the service, there are four of us and that is the way we think of each other. We have been through a lot together, and that makes us close, I don't know of any other way to put it."

LJ: "You said it all."

Jennifer: "I was going to see if you wanted to go to supper was all."

JB: "I would have been happy to go, but you come in and have supper with us and I won't take no for an answer."

Jennifer smiled and said "Come on Ben we are eating here."

Mom had already added two more places as she knew her son and she liked Jennifer and Ben anyway. They sat down and ate supper.

JB and LJ cleaned off the table and put the dishes in the dishwasher then JB and LJ sat down at the table.

JB said "I am sure Mom knows what I am going to say, so Mom you and dad can stay or leave if you want to

They said "no they were going to stay."

JB looked at Jennifer and said "LJ and myself and the others are X Navy Seals, we have been fighting terrorists for the last six years, they have put bounties on all of us that were over there, The local paper put an article about me in the paper with a picture. If a terrorist saw that, or a crook figures out who I am they will try to kill me and my brothers if they figure out that they are here. I have talked to the local police chief who I went to school with, and his department and the four of us are working together on this. We think there is a minimal danger to anyone other than us. To collect the bounty they have to have a picture of a head and themselves to collect so bombs are out, there is nothing left to show, to many people and there is chaos and they do not like to be seen, which means few people around. LJ and I put cameras up on the hill and we hope to get pictures of them scoping out a way to get us. If we see anyone up there we call the police and at least two of us will go up there and take them down. The police chief is going to find two or three women to volunteer to be wife's or girlfriends so we don't fit the profile which is single guys and my guys are going to be listed as cops for the last five years in other towns and they were just hired here to be the basis of the new swat team. This leaves me as the primary target though my profile states that I am single. I was going to ask you if you would pretend to be my wife or girlfriend since you were living here anyway or you can go back to the motel. We think there is someone already here as we found a sniper setup on the hill. That's a bad thing and a good thing as we know where they are and can stop them before they can do anything. With the cameras set on the hill we will have pictures of them in a day or two and then we can grab them, and an anti-terrorists unit will take them away never to be seen again."

"I was going to ask you if you would be my pretend wife since you are already in the spring house, I could come there every night and not come out until morning, when in reality I won't be there at all. As there is a passageway to the main house, so you can go between the two houses without having to be outside in bad weather. I will understand if you want to leave. I want you to know that I did not know about this problem until you were already in the house. You owe me nothing. So you know the situation please don't repeat anything I have told you to anyone." JB informed her.

Jennifer sat there for a while, *this might be a blessing in disguise*, and asks "How are you going to protect both of the houses if someone comes here?"

"We are having a surveillance system put in, also spy cameras that are not going to be seen." JB replied.

LJ will be watching the main house, and I will be watching the spring house."

Jennifer: "I would feel safer if you were in the house with Ben and me."

JB said: "I can do that, LJ and I are very light sleepers and we are armed and I will take you to the shooting range this weekend and teach you to shoot. If anything does start. You, Ben, Mom, and Dad will all be in the passageway with the steel doors locked and there is also another way out and Dad knows the way."

Jennifer: "OK I will do it, are we going to start tonight?"

"Yes I would." JB replied.

"I would feel safer." Jennifer said, *and thought now we will get to spend more time together.*

JB: "Ok I will get some things and I will bring them through the passageway, then I will come back and we will walk over together." JB left the room got his sleeping bag, Pistol, 3 extra clips a shotgun and a shell belt with 20 rounds in it for the shotgun.

He carried them downstairs and went to the game room and went to a section of the wall and pushed a section of the trim and a door opened revealing a steel door four feet ahead. JB walked to the door and typed a four letter code and the door opened and he reached in and switched on the lights, they were not as bright as the house lights as they were run from batteries and they were dim to help with night vision if you came out the other end in the dark.

JB carried his things to the other end but did not open the door. He went back to the house and he closed the steel door and the secret door and came back upstairs and rejoined the family.

They were all talking about what was happening.

JB said "I am going to have a couple of Security Guards here when the surveillance people are here, and LJ and I am a phone call away." JB: "Jennifer I will take you to work and Ben to school and set the school to keep Ben inside until I pick him up, and no one else but LJ, he will come with us tomorrow, and you stay in the hospital until I call you and I will let you know I am outside and which door I am at. From now on LJ and I will be armed at all times."

JB got up and he, Jennifer and Ben walked over to the Spring House went in and locked the door.

JB said "Jennifer and Ben I am going to show you a secret, do you know what a secret is?" as he looked at Ben?

Ben said "Yes."

JB: "OK tell me what a secret is?"

Ben said "It is something that I can't tell anyone but Mom."

JB: "Very good so you two come with me." They walked and went to the door that opened to a stairs that went down to the basement. JB turned on the lights and they went down the stairs. At the bottom JB ask do you see anything that looks like a door.

Jennifer and Ben looked and looked and said "we don't see any'.

JB said "Ben come here, and they walked to a wall that faced the big house. There was paneling on the wall with strips every 4 feet. JB said "Ben go to the end of the wall on the left side."

Ben did as he was told. When he got to the end he turned and looked at JB.

"Ben do you see the strips on the wall." JB said.

Ben walked four feet to his right and pointed at the strip.

"Very good now go to the third strip, you are at the first strip now." JB informed him.

Ben touched the strip in front of him and said "one and moved to the next and said two then went to the next strip and said three."

"Now push that strip." JB said.

Ben pushed and the secret door opened in front of him.

JB said "Ben you cannot open this door unless you are very afraid do you understand."

Ben nodded his head yes.

JB went through the door and said "come in here;" Jennifer and Ben came through the door.

"You must shut this door before you turn on the light so no one on the other side of the door knows where you are; Do you understand?" JB asks.

Ben and Jennifer both said "Yes."

"Close the door but look at the switch so you know where it is." JB said.

Jennifer closed the door then felt around until she found the switch and turned it on.

JB said "The reason is so you have time to get thru this other door before they find the door you came through. JB said "See this Panel and the sixteen buttons."

Jennifer said "Yes."

JB: "the code is my birthday 0815."

Jennifer typed it in and there was a click and JB said "turn the handle."

Jennifer turned the handle and the door opened and the light went a little into the darkness.

JB walked in and said "come in and turn on this switch Jennifer hit the switch and the tunnel lit up in a soft light. JB said now you must turn this switch off so the light on the other side of the door goes out, then you pull this lever to the right and he pointed to a lever in the door.

Jennifer grabbed the lever and tried to pull it to the right it didn't move, she look at JB and he said "you can't pull it, there is a plate on the floor and if you pull the lever and are not on the plate nothing happens. Now stand on the plate and push."

Jennifer moved left and turned to face the lever and pushed and it moved very easy.

The door clicked and JB said "the door will not open from that side it would have to be cut open with a torch. So when you are in here no one can hurt you. If you think you are in danger you come down here and stay here until I or LJ come to get you. Now follow me, we are going to the center between the two houses." As they walked down in the dim light Jennifer saw that the walls looked as if they were concrete and they had been painted gray.

When they got to the middle there was a large space with Padded benches all around the walls. There were cabinets above the benches, JB opened a cabinet door and there were cans of food and behind another door were glass jugs with water. Another had a small stove with a propane bottle connected to it.

JB said "Only run this until the food is warm as canned food was cooked in the canning process. The air will circulate all by itself so you will not run out of air. The tunnel that is straight across from the one we came down goes to the big house.

The one in the middle goes to a door that will let you out away from the houses You can't open the door neither can I it is covered by dirt so no one can find it. There is a hand pump that will open it but it takes a while, we use it once a year to make sure it will work, then the dirt is put back on and the sod is fixed and everything disappears."

"Do you feel a little safer now?" JB asks.

"Yes I do, but for some reason when you are around I feel real safe." Jennifer replied.

"I am glad, let's go back to the house." JB said.

They went back the way they had come, and Jennifer opened the doors and closed them again.

JB had her open everything again until he was satisfied she could do it if he was not here. JB carried his sleeping bag, pistol, and shotgun up the stairs.

Jennifer said "I don't want Ben to get hurt, I am afraid of guns."

JB took the pistol and ejected the clip, and pulled the receiver on the pistol back and it locked in the open position. JB said "I don't keep a bullet in the chamber, and I don't think Ben is strong enough to put a shell into the chamber." JB released the receiver and it slammed shut, JB pointed the gun at the floor and pulled the trigger, the pistol made a click." JB said "Ben come here."

Ben came over to him and stood in front of him.

JB said "Here I want you to pull this back just like I just did."

Ben tried and tried and it did not move.

JB took the pistol and put the clip back in.

"Jennifer I will carry this on me at all times, so there is no chance of him getting it. But if I am gone I want you to have protection. So we are going to get you a pistol and then I will teach you how to use it. I will talk to the hospital and have them let you off, and we will pick one up that you like and will fit your hand."

Jennifer said "All right but I am still worried about the gun."

JB said, "Ok we will work it out because I want you ok with what you are doing."

Jennifer said "OK." And she squeezed his arm.

JB smiled and he said: "I will fix my sleeping bag on the couch but first I will close the blinds, I don't want people looking in and knowing where we are."

Jennifer said "You get the blinds and I will fix your bed, I need to practice being a wife."

JB smiled and said, "It is time for me to go to bed as I get up at 5:30 and run and exercise."

"OK, Ben come it is time for bed." Jennifer said.

"Can I sleep out here to?" Ben asks.

"Not tonight, maybe another time." Jennifer said, She though, *not too much too soon, and he still has that gentle side.*

CHAPTER 8

SATURDAY WEEK 1

JB opened his eyes and though must be time to run, then he felt movement at his feet and he felt very carefully and there was a small body at the end of the couch. Ben must have sneaked out and fell asleep. JB lay back down and went back to sleep. JB got up and picked up Ben and carried him back to his bedroom and covered him up, then went downstairs and through the tunnel to the big house. JB came up from the game room and started up the stairs and LJ was coming down. "Give me a minute to change and we will go together." JB said.

LJ said "OK."

JB came down they started their run. As they were going "We should check the cameras today and see if we have any pictures." LJ said.

"I was thinking the same thing, and if the last site is being used we will come at 3:00am LJ tomorrow." JB replied.

LJ: "Sounds good to me." They continued the rest of the run in silence. They finish their pushups and crunches. They got back and they went in to clean up.

JB said "I have to take Jennifer to work and Ben to school, you come with us and we will go right up on the hill." LJ: "OK." JB:"Give me 15 minutes." LJ: "OK." JB headed to the game room. He opened the door to the basement and he could hear Jennifer getting Ben ready for school. He went up the stairs and said "I am coming in."

"OK." Jennifer said.

JB opened the door and came into the room; Jennifer and Ben were sitting at the table having breakfast.

"Would you like some?" Jennifer asked.

"No I will get some later, (JB said smiling.) LJ and I will be busy this morning checking on things."

"We will be ready in 10 minutes." Jennifer replied.

JB said "OK I will get LJ and meet you at the car." JB left and went to the big house. LJ was ready and he had his Pistol in a shoulder holster. LJ was pulling his jacket on and the pistol was now out of site. They went to the car and got in.

Jennifer and Ben were coming to the car.

JB got out and opened the door for them, in they went, and he shut the door and got back in the car. He started the car and drove off. They took Ben to school and set the permission for JB and LJ to pick Ben up and they left. JB opened the door for Jennifer and she got in he closed the door and got back into the car and they left. He dropped Jennifer off at the front door and said "I will pick you up at the Emergency Entrance when I come back."

Jennifer said "Okay at 3:00 pm."

JB: "Right bye." He and LJ took off for the hill. They stopped at the 1st road, no cars were around so they checked the 1st camera just a few animals, and the 2nd camera was the same. They got back in the car and turned into the 2nd road. They got to the open area and parked. This camera had people in it, Kids partying and having fun; the time stamp was last night, nothing this morning. They changed batteries in this camera so it would always have a full charge; better spend money on batteries than lose pictures. They went down the path to the small clearing at the edge of the cliff. There were pictures on this camera also. They deleted them so no one would get in trouble. They changed the batteries in this camera also rehid it and left. They went back to the car and left for the 3rd site. They got there and a car was parked there, the same one as yesterday. JB keep going up the road until he came to another road and pulled in and put the car out of sight. They got out and opened the trunk and got his pistol and belt. Checked the clip and put a round in the chamber. They started back on foot and stayed on the side of the road so they could slip into the woods if anyone came along. When they got to the narrow road they went in to stealth mode and went down the path very quietly they came to the 5th camera and downloaded the pictures. It was very interesting; the 1st pictures were stamped at 8:00pm when it was dark. And all they showed were the backs of two people, leaving the site. But no faces, they were leaving for the day both carried cases large enough to hold a sniper rifle. The next pictures were stamped 8 AM and gave faces, two men one was Arabic. The other was white, looked like someone they knew, they were talking but the camera was set up to take pictures instead of video. LJ changed it to video. LJ said "maybe we can hear what they are saying" JB: "If we are lucky they may convict themselves." They changed the batteries and LJ said "it looks like we have quests at this site and they are armed, we will have to come up here to get the pictures off the last camera I don't know if the camera will make noise downloading from a distance." JB replied. They walked back to the car and saw no one. JB opened the trunk and ejected the clip and took the round out of the chamber put it back in the clip and put it back in with the pistol and closed the trunk. They got in the car and pulled out and went back to town and got some breakfast. When they finished they went to the police station to see the chief. They had to wait 15 minutes before the chief could see them. They showed him the pictures from the last camera the chief said "it looks like they are armed with those cases."

"That's what we thought, and because of the stamps they are out there right now." JB replied.

The chief said "should we go up and check them out?"

"No we need a few days of pictures to call Home Land to come and get them; I am setting two sniper sites up in the park to monitor them. And we will not give them any easy shots at that distance the vests will stop them unless they got Teflon shells; I want to get the rest of the pictures and then your guys can go to the gun shops and see if any rifle ammo was purchased by the men in the pictures, and here is the license plate from the car. I don't think they know they are under surveillance." JB said.

"We will know better when we get the last camera tomorrow morning." LJ replied.

The chief said "Ok let me know what you get."

"Here give your people a copy of these; we will wait while you do that." LJ said.

Chief said "Thanks", and he called the SSgt and said copy this and brings it right back. The SSgt was back in two minutes.

JB and LJ got up and left. They got back in the car and headed for the diner and had coffee and pie.

"What is the plan for the day?" LJ asked.

They are building a gun case in the loft of the animal area as it is a great spot for us, you can get a wheelbarrow and hide your rifle in to transport it to the site and then lock it up. We will by a lock and you will have the only keys, I would buy a new rifle but we don't have a good place to sight it in and you already know your rifle." JB replied.

LJ comely said "I don't mind using mine we are not ready to start a war yet, we are still in recon mode but we can respond if necessary."

"The white guy in the picture he looked real familiar, didn't you think?" JB asked.

"Yes I am trying to place it; I know I have seen him before, I just don't remember where." LJ said.

"Me too I just can't place him." JB answered. They went to a hardware store and got a lock. Got back in the car and headed back to the park.

"Our vests should be in Monday, I think we should be wearing them from now on, and I am going to get 3 women sizes and 3 children for the kids. I am going to overnight them." JB said. They got to the park and pulled up to the office and walked quickly to the office and went inside.

Betty said "Hi, the vests came early just a bit ago; they are in your conference room."

"Thanks, now I want you to order 3 women's and 3 children's sizes and have them sent overnight." JB instructed

"OK." Betty replied.

"What do we have in the way of medical supplies?" JB inquired.

"A box of Band-Aids and Antiseptic." Betty replied.

"Order a complete med kit, like splints, tourniquet, raps, like an ambulance would carry. If you are unsure call Jennifer and ask her what they have in the ER. I want something on hand today if possible. Also when are the radios due to arrive?" JB asked.

"They said the order was shipped this morning." Betty said.

"Have them shipped over night if they can. JB said with a serious look on his face.

"Why don't we check up on the case in the Animal Area, as I would like to take a look up on the hill." LJ stated.

JB and LJ went out to the car and got in, and drove to the animal area, and parked where they could not be seen from the hill. JB and LJ got out of the car and opened the trunk; LJ grabbed his rifle case and his range finder. They went into the shelter and climbed the latter. The case was built and attached to the wall and JB grabbed it and tried to see if he could rip it off the wall but it did not move at all.

LJ looked at JB and said "Looks real good, you must have some good people working here."

"Most have been here all their lives, Dad was good to his people and they work hard for him." JB replied as he took the spotter scope and moved close to the window but back far enough to not be seen. JB looked for about a minute and said "I see a little bit of a barrel, they are carless, Range 540 yards. An easy shot for you."

"I will set up a spot." LJ stated as he moved some bales of hay over and made a platform to lie on and sited his rifle up the hill. "Got him, you are right I got the tip of the rifle, I could take him right now." LJ informed.

"To much paper work, we will let them shoot first." JB replied.

"What do you mean?" LJ ask.

"We need a little more recon and then I am going to give them a shot at me." JB informed him.

"No I don't like that, not at all." LJ replied.

"I don't want to be hiding the rest of my life, I want this over with and done. You are going to be in here and CR will be in the office.

You take the one on the left CR takes the one on the Right you keep shooting until they stop. JR will be on the hill with the police and attack when the shooting stops down here we will have radios and we will need to test them to make sure they are powerful enough to reach the top of the hill. Then JR and the police can slip in and mop up, or catch them if they are able to walk out, the radios should give us a good coordinated takedown." JB replied.

LJ backed off the platform, and said "that should be good it is softer than most of the ones I have used." He put the rifle in the case, shut the door and put the lock thru the hasp and locked it up. Then JB and LJ climbed down the ladder and went back to the car and left to go up the hill to check the cameras and change batteries.

"I am hungry why don't we eat first and see what is going on up there later in the day." JB said.

"OK with me." LJ replied. JB drove the car to the diner and parked, as they started to get out LJ said "I know who the white guy is, he was the Seal that got Rodgers killed remember, you Court Marshaled him and he got kicked out of the Navy. He said "he would get us because we turned on him, he was lucky we didn't kill him."

"And you are right, now it is coming back; he was the poorest Seal I had ever seen." JB stated. They went into the diner and ordered the Beef Sandwich with mashed potatoes and gravy. Thirty minutes later they were on their way up the hill. The first site look deserted, they stopped and checked no pictures so they went to the next road. It looks used like the day before; they downloaded the pictures from both cameras and put in new batteries. Then headed to the next sight and the car was hidden in the bushes, like the day before, they drove a half mile farther past the path and parked in the bushes, They walked very carefully back to the car took another picture of car and license plate then went to the path stopped and listened for noise of any kind but heard none after 15 minutes they went to the first camera and downloaded the videos, and changed the batteries. They looked at what they had downloaded and they got a new face and the same two as before.

LJ said "I wonder who this new guy is; it is starting to get interesting." They left to go to the car. And as they were almost to the car when they heard someone coming and they slipped into the woods. The car stopped by their car and looked at it for a while and then drove on.

"Quick let's get out of here." JB said and they ran to the car and jumped in, and turned around and shoved the gas pedal down and got out of there fast. They went to the Police Station and went to check in with the chief. They told him who the white guy on the first video was and that there was a 3rd new guy today. They showed the chief the pictures and called the SSGT in to make a copy of the flash. JB and LJ said "goodbye" and left the Station; and JB took LJ back to the house and said "I have to go get Ben and Jennifer; I will be back as soon as I can.

He turned the car around and headed for the school to pick up Ben. At the school he had to go into the office and get Ben, The teacher checked him and saw he was one who could take the child. She said "sign here and pointed to a line on a paper. JB signed said "Thank you, and left with Ben. JB opened the door for Ben to get in the back seat, and made sure Ben buckled up and closed the door. JB got in and away they went to pick up Jennifer.

JB drove to the Emergency Entrance and called Jennifer and told her they were at the Emergency Entrance." Then got out and opened the back door so Jennifer could get in, after she got in he closed the door and got back in, and drove off. JB said "We will drop Ben off with Dad and LJ until we get back." And he took them to the big House opened the door and Ben got out and ran to the house looked back and said: "see you later", then ran in the house.

JB came back to the car and opened the back and said "Jennifer would you like to sit up front?" Jennifer said "I got a headache maybe we shouldn't go. And loud noises make me nervous."

"I was wondering if you would back off at the last minute, as for loud noises, you will have ear protectors on." He said with a smile. You will hardly hear any noise at all. But if it gets to be too much I will bring you home. I can't be with you 24/7 all of the time, and I don't want anything to happen to you, I am getting fond of you and I don't want to lose you now."

Jennifer stood still for a minute then, and though *he is starting* to care for me, then she got into the front seat. JB drove on to the gun range.

JB opened the door for Jennifer and she got out, JB opened the trunk and got a box out, and closed the trunk. They walked to the door and went into the range.

"HI can I help you?" said the man running the range.

"I am from the park, I want to teach her about guns, do you have an open stall. "JB asked.

The manager said "yes", and took them to one of the stalls, and said "do you know how to work the target?" JB said "yes could you bring me 2 or 3 targets." The manager said "Yes." And he brought 3 targets over to them.

JB pushed the button to bring the target holder to them, and then he put a target up. He sent the target about 12' down the stall. Then he opened the box and took out a pistol. He released the clip and pulled the receiver back and showed her the inside of the pistol where the bullet fits into the barrel. JB said "When you put the clip into the weapon and take this safety off (he showed her the safety lever) the receiver moves forward and a bullet is pushed from the clip into the barrel." Now I am going to release the receiver but no clip in place" He moved the lever and the receiver slammed forward. Jennifer jumped and moved up next to him. He said "I am sorry I should have warned you it is empty because the clip with the bullets is not in place. She said 'I thought it went off."

"I would not do that to you, I will let you know when the bullets will come out." He said, then he put the pistol out in front of himself in a shooting stance pointed down the barrel and squeezed the trigger and it went click. JB said "I want you to hold the weapon just like I did and aim down the sight, there is a v shape at the rear of the pistol, and a site bar on the front, and he pointed at the bar. You line the V with the bar and squeeze the trigger slowly with your finger until it clicks. Now pull the receiver all the way to the rear of the weapon and let it go."

Jennifer did as she was told and the pistol was cocked, and JB said "aim again and squeeze the trigger slowly as you aim." She did the routine again. He had her do the routine for ten minutes. JB said "now we are going to fire a round." He handed her an ear protector to deaden the sound. Then he put a bullet in the clip and had her put the clip in the pistol. Then he had her release the receiver. Now the pistol is live you squeeze the trigger the bullet comes out the front." JB said "Now take your stance and look down the site and line the v with the bar then the center of the target, then squeeze the trigger, don't move just relax and squeeze."

Jennifer did as he said, bang the shot went off and the pistol moved up and she look around with fear on her face. JB said "That was great, and took the pistol then said "look at the pistol see how the receiver has locked in the open position."

Jennifer looked and said "Oh now what happens JB said "The pistol is empty, you are out of bullets to fire again you must reload." He put another bullet in the clip, and said "Take the clip and slip it into the pistol." Jennifer did as she was told and the clip clicks in. " Now hold the pistol so it points away from you toward the ground and strait ahead of you, toward the target now push the receiver lever and reload the pistol"

Jennifer did as she was told and the receiver slammed forward, the pistol was reloaded. JB said put the pistol on the shelf in front of you." She did as she was told. JB came over and said "This is the safety and shoved it. Now he picked it up and squeezed the trigger nothing happened, He said now you squeeze the trigger, she did and said "it doesn't move."

"Good you know how to put the safety on, now release the clip." She released the clip and laid it on the shelf. JB said "Now Point at the target and squeeze again."

Jennifer did as she was told and the pistol fired again. JB came up and took the pistol and set it on a shelf and hit the button to bring the target back.

"When you fired the 1st bullet where did you point the gun. She said "I am not sure." JB took a marker and circled the 2 holes. He said now when you shoot again we will know if you are hitting where you are aiming" JB put the clip in and released the receiver and reloaded the gun. He released the clip. He pushed the button and moved the target back where it was. Now he took a pair of binoculars and gave them to Jennifer and said "look at the target."

She did and JB said "Do you see the 2 holes, she said "Yes."

"OK put the glasses down and pick up the gun, sight down the v bar and aim at the center of the target. She aimed and squeezed the trigger bang the gun bucked and JB said "put the gun down and pick up the classes and see if you see a new hole in the target."

She picked up the Binoculars and looked; and said "there is a new hole." JB asked her "Where is the hole?" She said "Below the center 2 circles." JB said "you are shooting a little low; you must move the bar higher on the V." JB said "Try again." She picked up the gun slipped the clip in, she started to remove the clip but JB said "Leave it in." She took aim and squeezed the trigger. Bang. "Put the safety on." JB said. She did. JB: "put the gun on the shelf and pick the glasses up and see where you hit." She looked and it's up on the ring below the middle. JB took the glasses and looked, he said "you are a good student, I am proud of you." He pushed the button and brought the target back, released it and got another target; it had the shape of a person on it. JB said "You see the center of the chest?" She said "Yes." JB said "that is where you aim for" he put the clip in and she got ready to shoot. She released the receiver and aimed at the target and started to shoot. Bang, JB: "Again." Bang. "Put the gun down and look at the target."

She looked and they are below the center."

"I want you to try again and shoot all the shells, and then we will bring the target in, try to get the shots a little higher."

She took aim again, bang, bang, bang, bang and bang, the receiver stayed back gun empty. She laid the gun down and JB brought the target back and released it. They looked and there was a small group below center and a larger group a little above center. JB said "I think that is enough for now I know you could hit a man, and stop him, the hard part is to really pull the trigger when a person is coming at you. Remember it could be a man or a women, each is capable of killing you and Ben. So pull the trigger.

The ten commands say though shall not kill. There is a lot of passages in the Bible where God told the Jews to kill everything when they took over a country. The disciples carried swords, Paul cut off the ear of a roman soldier, and the soldiers were well trained so Paul was real good. I think that they did not give us the full passage, I think it should be thou shall not kill for personal gain, remember King David sent a soldier to the front line so he would be killed because he wanted to marry his wife Bathsheba, and god sent a messenger to Rebuke him. So I will not hesitate to protect my friends, family or anyone that is in my care. I hope you are all right with that, I don't want anything to hurt you."

Jennifer "I did not know that was in the bible"

JB; "Yes I had to look in there to know I was doing the right thing." They folded the Target and picked the shell cases from the floor. JB said "Jennifer I am really proud of you, you just stepped out of your world into a world you never dreamed of and really did a good job."

Jennifer smiled and said "Thank you."

JB paid the man and they left, Jennifer held on to his arm and they walked to the car. JB opened the door and Jennifer got in and closed the door, and JB walked around and got in, started the car and they left. They got home and went to the big house. JB's Mom said you two are just in time sit down and we will say grace. Mom said grace and they began to eat. LJ said "How did she do." JB said "Very good for a beginner, look at her man target when you're done." Jennifer smiled *he is taking up for me*. They finished and JB an LJ cleaned the table and put the dishes in the dishwasher and turned it on.

LJ said "Where is that target?"

Jennifer said "right here" and pulled them out of her purse and handed them to LJ. He opened them and looked at them and said "You do this for her?"

Jennifer proudly said "No I did it myself."

"Yes she did." JB replied.

LJ smiling said "We will see next time if it was beginners luck or is she a natural." They all laughed, and Ben said "What is so funny?" "Your Mother did great at the shooting range." JB said with a smile.

Ben: "My mom is the greatest."

"I won't argue with that." JB replied.

Jennifer said "I need to go home and do some Laundry Ben needs clothes for tomorrow.

"I will walk you home." JB told her.

"Come back we have to talk a little." LJ said.

"OK." JB and Jennifer got up and left. Jennifer went to the basement to start the clothes and Ben went to the bathroom to get cleaned up for bed.

JB went back to the big house; LJ and dad were sitting in the living room.

JB said "We were tailed on our way home."

LJ; "This may be moving faster than we think."

JB: "I know Jennifer did real well at the range but on a real person I don't know, I did tell her that if she did not shoot they would kill her and Ben, her body language changed a little so it's 50/50 maybe 52/48, 52 she will, another week and I give her 80/20 but I don't know if we got another week, though this might be just round one."

JB: "how about 2:00 we go to the hill and get the other pictures from camera six, I got two night visions in the trunk plus 2 Glocks and a shotgun that should be good and 2 extra clips. I will come over through the tunnel and we will leave from here.

"Ok." LJ replied.

"I will show you how to operate the tunnel so you can come over and not be seen, I showed Jennifer so she can operate it and hide, let's go." JB said, and they went to the basement and Jennifer was just finished separating the clothes and started the washer.

"I am going to show LJ the tunnel, I will be back in 5 minutes don't answer the door until I get back." JB informed her. JB took LJ and showed him the strip to push the code and the lever to push so the door would lock. Then he sent him on his way and went back to the spring house.

Jennifer was finishing with Ben and he was ready for bed, he came over and hugged JB and said "I am glad you like my Mom." Jennifer blushed and said "I am sorry he said that."

"That's all right because I do." JB said with a smile.

Jennifer blushed again. And she grabbed Ben and disappeared. She came back and said "I really am sorry about that, I didn't know he was going to say that."

"He came out last night and got under the covers on the end of the couch, and when I got up to run I put him back in his bed, sit down Jennifer we need to talk; I am really sorry about the situation I have gotten you into; because we were followed on our way home tonight. I didn't want to tell you earlier and spoil your supper. I don't know how good the local police are and I plan to help them get better, but that will not be soon enough to help and CR won't be here until Monday so we have to get thru the weekend. I know that the 4 of us can take on ten to twenty of them if this was a military operation, but this is a little different, there are a lot of civilians involved, and they do not understand the danger of the real world. Those people are worse than the worst thing you can imagine, they strap bombs on little kids younger than Ben and tell them to walk to the Army men and push the button. Boom no kid no army men. I think they are going to try to bomb the park, after they finish with me. I am going to try to get the loan of a couple of bomb sniffing dogs from the Navy or buy them from another source. I am telling you this so you don't get blindsided. If you want I will give you money and hide you some place where no one will find you and I will send JR and his family with you that way you will be beyond safe."

Jennifer said "I will do what you want but I would rather stay here with you thru all of this and I like you too. She got up kissed him on the cheek and said "I really have to get some sleep, that shooting took a little out of me, I didn't think I could do something like that. Good night see you in the morning." She went to her room. JB got in his sleeping bag and went to sleep.

CHAPTER 9

SUNDAY WEEK 2

JB got up at 2:00 and put his shoes on and went to the basement and thru the tunnel to the big house, LJ was waiting for him by the door.

LJ opened the door and out they went and, LJ made sure it was locked and they slowly went to the car making sure to stay in the shadows.

JB touched LJ and pointed to the car at the end of the driveway. JB: "I think it might be my shadow from the police dept., maybe we should take him with us so he does not give us away?"

LJ: "Good idea." They moved slowly from shadow to shadow until they got to the car. LJ went to the rider's side door and JB went to the driver's side.

JB knocked on the window and with his hand in his pocket like he had a gun said "can I help you?"

The man in the car jump up in the seat and said "I am your tale don't shoot."

"Put your hands on the steering wheel and don't do any fast moves, where is your badge?" Said JB

"In my pocket." The man replied.

JB said "reach very slowly and bring it out so I can see it."

The man moved very slowly and brought his badge out for JB to see.

JB said "Ok you can relax were not armed yet." JB: "I guess you are going to follow us."

The policeman said "Yes that is my job."

JB said "Get out of your car and lock it up, we are going to check out a site and we don't want a lot of commotion to give away our location."

The Policeman said "I don't know if that is proper?"

"Don't worry. JB said. "I will fix it with Hank and you can sit in back and after all you are still following us right."

The policeman laughed "I like you guys." He got out of the car and locked it and they went back and got in JB's car and off they went. The trip to the hill was uneventful and when they got close to the first road JB said "we are going to the 3rd road and we will go farther and double back on foot, you can come with us or stay in the car.

LJ said "what is your name?"

The Policeman said "Everyone calls me David."

JB: "Ok David you can come or stay?"

David: "I will come."

JB and LJ got their gear out of the trunk; each took a Glock and a spare clip, and the night vision glasses. The 3 of them went carefully back down the road, looking for anything out of the ordinary. They reached the narrow road and started down JB on the left, LJ on the right, with David in the middle.

JB said "stay behind us we are looking for booby traps."

David whispered "Ok."

They moved very slowly down the trail until they came to the 1st camera, LJ downloaded the pictures and changed the batteries, then they went a little farther down the trail.

JB whispered "David slip in the bushes here and guard the rear, if you see anything whisper on the radio. LJ give him your radio we won't be that far apart."

David took the radio and clipped it to his side, JB and LJ disappeared down the trail. They went very slow looking for trip wires and other types of traps. They finally got to the open space and didn't see anything that could harm them so they entered the site, and JB went to the spot where he had hidden the camera, it was there undisturbed. LJ downloaded the pictures and put new batteries in and put it back and then he checked to make sure it was still hidden. The downloading was very quiet and LJ said "we could download from back up the trail but we won't be able to change batteries. JB said "the battery meter said they were 40% charged so we would not have to change batteries for at least 2 days maybe 3."

"I will make it 2, I don't want to lose anything." JB replied. They went back up the trail, met up with David and went back to the car. They put their equipment in the trunk; they got in the car and went back to the house.

JB said "if you want you can come in, it would be a lot more comfortable."

"That would get me in trouble, but thanks anyway, it was fun." David said and unlocked the door and got back in his car.

JB and LJ went back to the house and JB went to the game room to get back to the spring house. JB went to the couch and Jennifer was there asleep he sat down beside her and touched her hand to wake her up.

She leaned forward and hugged him and said "I am glad you are all right." JB put his arms around Jennifer and kissed her and said "I am glad you are here." They held each other and JB said "you better get back in bed before we get in trouble."

Jennifer: "Ok but would that be a bad thing."

"No it wouldn't if all this stuff was not going on." JB said with a smile. Jennifer got up and went to bed. JB lay down on the couch, smiled and went to sleep.

At 6 o'clock Jennifer came out of the bedroom and smiled at JB looking at her and he smiled back. Just then Ben came running out of his bedroom and jumped up and said "what are we going to do today?"

JB said "I am not sure but the surveillance people are coming to put up cameras today."

"Can I help you." Ben replied.

"Not today, that could be dangerous; we will do some things when the situation gets better." JB told him.

"Ok." Ben said a little sadly.

Jennifer asked "is it okay if we go to the store and get some things."

"Yes, but we need to be quick we want as little exposure as possible, and I will go with you and LJ can make sure the cameras are where we want them." JB replied.

LJ came over and knocked on the door.

JB let him in and they sat down on the couch and LJ said "I called CR and told him the situation and he will be here today, it should be before noon. That will take some of the strain off." LJ: "I have looked at the pictures and we have a few more players than we had before." "The Arab, X Seal, another Arab and two more that might be gang members; they were all dressed alike and have the same tattoos. I downloaded all the pictures to my laptop and I put all the pictures on a disk to give the police." LJ said "We will go up and download the other cameras and replace batteries'.

JB: "Jennifer needs to go to the store and I am going to take her. You stay here as the surveillance people are coming and you know where we want to put the cameras. When I get back you can take our shadow to cover your back and download the rest of the cameras, unless CR gets here, and then when I get back you two can go."

LJ: "Mom is going to have a house full."

"Yes, and she will love it." JB replied, "and as an after though LJ would you go and check the hill and see if they are there." He left and went upstairs to his room and got his rifle out and put a round in and scanned the site, there was the barrel, they were watching." LJ called and told JB the news and said "Ok stay there until we get in the car, if the barrel starts to cover us take him out, and when we get back I will call and you can get on watch again."

JB went to the spring house and went in.

Jennifer said "when can we go?"
"right now if you want." JB replied.

Jennifer: "Ben come on we are ready to go." Ben came running out and they shut the door and locked it and headed for the car. They got there with no problems and JB opened the rear door for Ben and made sure his seatbelt was fastened, shut the door and was going to open the door for Jennifer but she was already in the car so he got in and away they went.

Jennifer said "I got in quick so you would not be out there so long." JB: "That was very thoughtful of you, where do you want to go first?" JB asks. "I need something from the drug store. Jennifer replied. JB drove two more blocks and turned right and there was one a block down on the corner. JB parked in their lot and started to get out and Jennifer said "don't get out I will only be a minute." JB "Ok." He and Ben waited about 5 minutes and she was back. Jennifer got in and said "To the grocery store." JB drove to the big grocery store, parked in the lot, turned off the car and got out. He opened the door for Ben to get out and shut the door. Jennifer was already out so he locked the doors and they all went inside. There were a lot of people inside the store and JB thought it must be a busy day for them; he followed Jennifer up and down the aisles and watched as she put things in the cart, so this was what it is like to be a family. He though I have been in worse places. Jennifer looked at JB and said "you never went to a store with someone else?" JB: "no this is a first time." And smiled at Jennifer, she smiled back. Ben was looking at everything and you could see his mind working. JB though I bet I know what he wants cookies. They keep going up and down, more things in the cart, JB though this is like getting ready for a mission. They were going past the bakery section and Ben darted out and headed to the cookie section and started to look then grabbed a box and went around another table so his mother could not see what he had, then he came up behind them and tried to put it in the cart, Jennifer grabbed the box and said "you didn't ask so you take it back."

Ben look at JB with a help me look and JB said "you should have asked before you took it, I would do what your mother says, Good little boys do that."

Jennifer gave him a thank you look.

Ben took the cookies back, and they continued on until Jennifer seemed like she had everything she wanted, then they went to the check out and unloaded the cart items to the conveyer belt, where they put them in bags and back in the cart to go. The cashier said that will be $65.89 and JB got out his wallet and gave the man $66.00. Jennifer said "you can't pay for that."

"Why not, am I not the husband." JB said with a smile.

Jennifer just stood there for a moment and JB said "we are holding up the line and he took the change from the cashier and gave it to Ben." Then he grabbed the cart and walked out. They got to the car and he opened the trunk and put all the bags inside, unlocked the car opened the door for Ben made sure he that his seatbelt was fastened and then took the cart to the area for empty carts and got back in the car. He looked at Jennifer and said "you look like you want to say something?"

"I could have paid for that." She said with a frown.

JB said "yes I know you could but we are supposed to be married and the husband usually pays doesn't he?"

"I have never been married so I don't know." Jennifer replied.

"I have never been married and I don't know either but we have to keep up appearances don't we?" JB stated, "I have never been in a situation like this but I thought I should pay so I did. Are you mad?"

Jennifer "No I am just not used to having someone do that for me."

"Well it kind of felt good to me." and JB reach reached over and squeezed her hand. He started the car and drove away;"Is there any place else you want to go." He asked.

Jennifer said "No."

When they got home; the Surveillance crew was there and LJ was watching everything they were doing, so JB drove down to the spring house, backed up to the door hit the trunk button and got out of the car opened the door for Jennifer and she got out and opened the door for Ben while JB was caring the bags in and putting them on the kitchen table.

Jennifer said "I am sorry I acted the way I did."

"That's all right Ben should ask before he takes something." JB replied.

Jennifer came over and hugged him, and said "I could really like this marriage thing."

JB: "I kind of thought you did." She started to laugh and so did he. He said "I am going to check on things, so stay in the house. If you or Ben want to come out call me." JB opened the door and ran to the big house. Jennifer started to put things away.

JB went around and LJ was watching. "I thought you were going to call when you got here?" LJ said.

"I got sidetracked and forgot all about it." JB replied.

"That is your 1st mistake." LJ replied.

"It won't happen again, I am new at this husband thing and she is new to the wife thing." They both laughed.

"CR called and said he is about an hour out." LJ said.

"Did you tell him to be on alert and not to expose himself to the hill." JB asked.

"Yes I did." LJ replied.

"You guys are great, the best thing I got out of the Navy is you three." JB replied.

"We feel the same way brother."

"As an after though have you contacted JR?" JB asked.

"Yes but I told him to keep to his original schedule, and to keep his eyes open, we don't know what they know. I would like to get my hands on one; we would get all he knows." LJ stated.

CR arrived 45 minutes later.

JB went out to help him bring his things into the big house. They put him in the room next to LJ's; they were ready to spring the trap.

JB called the police dept. And told them his name and asked to have Hank call him right away. Five minutes later Hank called. JB said "Hank my third man is here and I would like you to come to the house so we can lay out a plan."

Hank said "He would be over in 20 minutes."

JB laid out a rough drawing of the hill and the three sites and how they would take down the terrorist; they all agreed it was a good plan as they waited for Hank.

LJ went back out to watch the progress of the surveillance crew.

Hank arrived there ten minutes later. There was a knock on the door and JB opened the door and let Hank in. After JB introduced CR to Hank, they sat down.

CR moved the map in front of Hank and pointed to the 3 sites and said "this is where they are now as far as I know there are no more sites on that hill".

Hank:"there is one farther past the 3 site but it's very hard to get to and most people don't know that it is there."

"We will have to go up there and scout it out in the morning." JB said.

"Show me on the map about where it is." CR replied.

Hank extended the drawing to include the new site; which was about 200 yards past the third site. "As best as I remember it is grown up lot and has many more rocks on the path than the other three, but you should be able to get there without making too much noise."

"Hank how much leeway do we have?" JB asked.

"If they have not fired a shot we can't arrest them." Hank replied.

"That's what I thought so I am going to have to give them a shot at me"

"What"!!!! said Hank and CR, with a startled look.

JB said "I figure it this way, a minimum of 540 yards, and that next site is over 600 yards, and the way these guys are waving their rifle around I don't think they're very good; maybe on a still target but not so good on a moving one, I also think they might be planning to plant bombs in the park, and I can't let that happen, we are presently trying to get some bomb sniffing dogs in here to patrol the park disguised as service dogs. I will even hire handlers and dogs if I have to, and I want to have one in the park from now on."

"The world is a crazy place now and there is a lot of sick in the head people out there." CR replied.

"Amen to that." Hank said with seriousness in his voice.

"With CR leading your men you should be able to take anyone that tries to escape." JB said.

"I have to be honest with you my men have never been in a firefight, I don't know what they will do." Hank said.

"As long as they don't shoot me I can take out anything that comes our way, LJ will be in a sniper set up in the animal area barn, and when the first shot is fired he will take out the sniper and I will shoot the sniper just in case and then scream don't move, and hopefully the spotter will freeze and we will have people to interrogate, if they have a 2nd site I doubt there will be that many at either site and if armed men come out just shoot first and ask questions later. CR said.

JB: "I think we need JR here tomorrow tell him to leave his family where they are and get here as quick as he can, get the best hotel he can to keep his family happy, I will reimburse him whatever it cost, and if he needs me to pay for the hotel call the office here at the park and give Betty the info and she will pay the bill. He is on the payroll as of right now, same as you two."

"Then we have two squad leaders that know what they are doing." CR replied.

"That sounds a lot better, but if you get yourself killed I will never forgive you." Hank said in a worried voice and they all smiled and the meeting was over.

"We will touch base tomorrow in the afternoon." JB said.

After Hank left, JB and CR went over the plan again. "2:00 am tomorrow up the hill." CR said.

JB said "I wonder If Bills Sporting Goods has Night Vision." JB looked Bill's up on his phone, got the number and called.

Bill said he had two with the specs JB was looking for and he had them in stock;

JB told him "I will be down to get them so hold them for me ok."

Bill said "Yes."

JB and CR went out the door, told LJ what they were doing and left. JB and CR jumped into the car and went to Bill's they arrived there in10 minutes. JB parked in front and they went in and looked the Night Vision Goggles over and were pleased, JB said "wrap them up." He paid for them thanked Bill and left" They drove back to the house in ten minutes and only stayed five minutes at Bill's, he was only gone for 25 minutes, and Jennifer was in good hands with LJ there.

LJ was watching the surveillance crew, CR went to join him, and JB went to the spring house to see how Jennifer was doing and to see if she needed anything. JB opened the door and went in the spring house; Ben was watching TV and Jennifer was doing things in the kitchen.

JB said "Hi how is everything going?"

Jennifer "not too bad, I am fixing supper for us, I hope you like it."

JB "I thought we would eat over at Mom's."

Jennifer: "If we are going to look married I figured we should eat here to make it look good."

JB: "You are right I was not thinking. I have so much on my mind with all that in going on. I ordered bulletproof vests for you and Ben to wear they should be in today."

Jennifer: "Is that necessary?"

JB: "I want to give you both all the protection I can." JB: "You are in my care; I will die to protect you."

Jennifer: "Wow no one ever said that to me before."

JB: "I mean it."

Jennifer came over and hugged him and said "You are the nicest man I have ever known." And went back to the kitchen and continued fixing supper. JB went back out to check on the surveillance crew and told LJ to show CR the firing site in the animal area. LJ and CR left. The cameras were going up right on schedule, JB was pleased.

LJ and CR went to the animal area and climbed up the ladder. LJ opened the gun closet and got his rifle out, and gave it to CR. LJ said there 4 markers up there the first two did not work out, the third site is between the last two markers in the middle." CR: "I see what you mean, that barrel should be out of sight, and unless they are trying to fool us and have another site we haven't seen." LJ: "That is to night's mission. We are going to pull the cameras on the 1st marker and check out another site." Tomorrow they are going to be putting more cameras up in the park." The Surveillance crew would work the rest of the day and come back tomorrow and finish, then put in the secret cameras after midnight. JB went in the office and one of the Surveillance crew was showing LJ and CR how the system worked and how to zoom in for more detail, also there were four secret cameras and they had a map with their location along with all the regular cameras. JB said, "Jennifer is fixing supper for us, so I will not be joining you." LJ said, "You are really getting into this married thing." JB: "Yes it has to look real." The rest of them laughed and JB blushed. JB: "I am going down to the spring house and play husband, I have a lot to learn in that profession." CR said, "Don't we all, I guess that comes for us on Monday."

JB left and hurried down to the spring house opened the door, went in and quickly closed the door. Jennifer said: "Hi are you here for a while." JB said "I am all yours", and smiled. She laughed and said, "How did your day go honey?" With a twinkle in her eye, JB smiled and said, "just great but better now that I am here with you." Jennifer came over and hugged him and said "I guess we have to start somewhere." JB: "this could get habit forming." She said, "Would that be a bad thing." JB: "No I don't think so." Just then Ben came up and said: "could you read to me?" JB: "Yes, what book should I read?" Ben ran to his room and brought his book. JB and Ben sat on the couch and JB began to read. Jennifer watched them and hoped that this could go on forever. JB read until Jennifer said supper is ready. Ben and JB got up and sat down at the table. Jennifer reaches out and grabbed Ben's hand then she reached for JBs' and he grabbed hers and then Ben's. Jennifer said grace and then they started to eat. JB took large portions and passed the food to Jennifer and she filled Ben plate then hers. They ate in silence until JB was half done, then he said: "Jennifer this is really good, thank you for a very special supper."

Jennifer smiled and said, "Thank you I am glad you like it." They finished supper and JB helped with the dishes and put them in the washer while she put the leftovers in the refrigerator. They sat down and JB said, "The team is going up on the hill tomorrow morning we leave at 2:00 I will try not to wake you when I leave and when I come back." Jennifer said, "Be careful I would hate to be a widow in the 1st week." JB said, "It should be very quiet, the last time we went up there we were the only ones up there, this time there is 3 of us instead of 2." Jennifer said "That was very nice of you to read to Ben." JB: "I like him he is a good boy and learns fast, that is a good trait to have, it is hard to teach that to someone." Jennifer: "He is an only kid, so I have tried not to spoil him; I have seen only Childs and they don't mind or throw tantrums, and I think that hurts the child when they get older." JB: "I had more trouble with men that were brought up that way." JB: "What do you want out of life?" Jennifer: "I want a loving husband, that loves and wants' 2 or 3 children and treats me and the children nice and with respect." JB: "I think you have the right idea." Jennifer: "What do you want out of life?" JB: "I want a loving wife that I can trust and takes good care of the children and disciplines then and is kind."

Jennifer "I think you and I want the same things out of life." JB: "I think we do too." Jennifer: "Please don't get killed, OK." JB: "I only take risks that are 80 to 90% in my favor, and with my 3 brothers that all most makes it 98%. They are the best in the Navy, though they're not in the Navy now." JB "Though we could be called back up if a war started, I thought you should know that." Jennifer: "Why is that?" JB: "Because it ruined a relationship I once had, I wanted to marry my high school sweetheart, and she left me because of the Military." Jennifer looked at him and said "Why are you telling me all this?" JB: "because I am interested in having a real relationship with you, its' been a long time since I have had the feelings I get when I am around you and I don't want you to think I am just using you until this is all over, I would never do that, I would like a real relationship with you. I will never lie to you, or hit you, I may make you mad but it will not be on purpose, we men look at things a little differently than women do."

Jennifer: "I have never had anyone be this honest with me as you just have." JB: "If we were married I would not keep any secrets from you that has anything to do with our relationship." JB: "remember what I said, I will die to protect you and Ben, while you are here that is my job." Jennifer grabbed him and hugged him and cried. JB held her until she stopped." Jennifer: "I am sorry I cried." JB: "you don't have to be sorry you are going through something you have no control of without any training to fall back on, I hardly can believe how you are holding up with all this, you did not ask for it, it just fell on you, and that's because of me. You are one in a million." Jennifer sat there and just looked at him and said nothing. JB said, "I don't think you could live any place else now that they have seen you, I would have to fix up fake ids and hide you across the country, and I will do that if you want." Jennifer: "no I am here to the end." Then she kissed him and got up and went to put Ben to bed. Ben said his prayers and jumped in bed and said "I like JB mom." Jennifer: "I do to." She turned off the light and closed the door and went to her bedroom and came back out and said: "Good night, see you in the morning." Then she turned and went to bed. JB spread out his sleeping bag and crawled in and went to sleep, Seals sleep quickly because they never know when they will be able to sleep.

CHAPTER 10

MONDAY WEEK 2

JB woke at 2:00 and got up dressed and headed for the basement and Jennifer came out and gave him a kiss and said "You be careful", and went back to bed. JB though *this could get to be a habit, but a good habit*. He went through the tunnels and LJ and CR were ready to go and LJ said "right on time." They opened the door very slowly and went out, LJ said in a low voice 'are we going to take the shadow?" CR: "who is the shadow?"

JB: "It is a police escort to give us a hand if we need it and to back our stories." CR nodded that he understood. They went out and ask the shadow if he wanted to go and he said "Sure I wouldn't miss this for anything." He got out and locked the squad car and got in the back with CR. LJ introduced CR to the shadow and they shook hands and they were on their way up the hill. When they got to the first road they all got out of the car, JB said "LJ you and David take that first camera and CR and I will get the second, and we can download in the car as we go to the next site, and give David one of those new night vision goggles." They went and got the cameras downloaded and put in new batteries and came back to the car. JB said "just some small critters" and deleted them off the cameras and replaced the batteries.

They pulled up to the second road and got out and LJ said "should we take these down to." JB: no let's monitor these kids one more day and make sure our targets are not visiting with them." LJ

"Ok let's download and change batteries. They quickly download the cameras and changed the batteries and went past the 3rd road and to make sure there was no car parked anywhere close and they stopped half a mile up the road and walked very carefully so they were not surprised. They came to the path and CR took the left and LJ the right and they went slowly down the path looking for trip wires or cords. They got to the first camera LJ started to download. JB whispered to CR come with me and we will put batteries in the next camera and then LJ can download." JB went to the left CR to the right and they went slowly down the path. They got to the end of the path and slowly entered the open space, they could see that it was being used and they figured more than two people were using this space JB very careful went to the camera and changed the batteries, the indicator said they had 6% life in them CR said: You cut this one close." JB: "yes, I am very curious what we will see and hear on this camera." LJ and shadow came and LJ download the camera and they turned and went back up the path. They slowly went to the car, some thought they were overly cautious, but some of them were not around anymore, better safe than sorry. They got in the car and went to the next road to the left and went past it and a half mile down the road saw nothing and drove back to within a quarter mile of the road and got out of the car. They opened the trunk and took out 2 Clocks and a shotgun' LJ took a Glock JB took a Glock and he gave the shotgun to CR. They closed the trunk very quietly and went slowly down the road to the path in the woods JB took the left, LJ the right. CR and the Shadow took the middle of the path and slowly went looking for trip wires booby traps and mines. About 100 feet down the trail they found a spot to put the camera where it could not be easily seen and set it up then they went farther down the trail to an open area and you could see that it was being used. JB whispered: "good thing we checked this site or they would have been one up on us." JB gave CR a reflector and he set it about 5 or 6 feet in and on the rim and take my night vision and hang this. JB took out a flashlight and stepped back and shined at where the camera was and he could not see it. JB: "Well I hope it is not seen, this is our edge over them." They went back down and went to the car. Opened the trunk and put the weapons back and closed the trunk, and got back in the car and started down the road and went back home.

Shadow got back in his car and the other 3 went in the house.

They went down to the game room and started to view the video and on the 3rd camera they saw kids being kids. LJ started the number 4th camera and got some critters and that was all. The 5th camera showed the Arab the X Seal and a new face. LJ said "it is going to be interesting to see the video on Monday." They started to watch camera 6 and it got real interesting, the audio was full of their plans to kill JB an LJ plus they talked about bomb placement in the park and the sequence to set off the charges. LJ said "we got them now." JB said "yes we do, but I don't want some lax judge letting them off because they are just talking, or some future president to let them loose I want the Arabs and Henry dead. I am not going to spend the rest of my life looking over my shoulder." LJ: "me either." CR "That goes for me too, and I know JR will agree with us." They said let's sleep on this and JR will be here tomorrow early he figured around 8:00 am and CR and I can pick him up at the airport. CR: "That's fine with me."

JB smiled and got up and went to the secret door to the tunnel and opened the door, and looked back at LJ and CR and said "LJ show CR how the tunnel works." LJ "will do." And JB went thru the steel door and back to the spring house, went thru the basement and up the stairs and went to the couch and there was Jennifer sleeping waiting for him to come home. He sat down next to her and took her in his arms and kissed her and she kissed him back, they sat there and held each other for a long time and said "you better get some more sleep tomorrow is going to be a long day." She kissed him and said "I could do this forever." JB: "me to." Jennifer got up and went back to her bedroom. JB got in the sleeping bag and went to sleep dreaming of kissing Jennifer.

JB got up went to the big house and the 3 of them did the morning routine came back and said "See you in an hour, and you eat with Mom and Dad as Jennifer is probably going to make breakfast for me. JB went back through the tunnel and Jennifer and Ben were just getting up and JB said "I am going to take a shower while you make breakfast, OK." Jennifer said "I thought you were going to make breakfast", with a smile on her face. JB replied "If you want it to taste good you better make it or I will make it out of all I know how to fix, which is C-rations. "Jennifer: "That does not sound good, but I was only joking I was going to fix it, that's my job in this relationship." JB went to the bathroom showered and shaved and put on new clothes. Then he went to the kitchen to see what Jennifer was fixing. She was making pancakes, because Ben liked them a couple times a week. JB sat and ask "Ben how do you like your new school?"

Ben said "It is a nice school but some of the kids pick on me." JB: "How do they pick on you?" They tell me I am a loser." JB: "How do you feel about that?" Ben: "I don't let it bother me as I got the best Mom in the world and they don't."

Jennifer said "Ben why didn't you tell me about this sooner?" Ben: "Because I told them my dad was a navy seal and if they hurt me he would come and whip them and then beat their fathers up." Jennifer looks at JB in disbelief and then her eyes got big." JB was laughing and had a big smile on his face. Jennifer said "he should not say something like that."

JB said "Just maybe since you are pretending to be my wife he could pretend to be my son, so everything looks real, he's helping me with my problem." Jennifer: "I don't know what I am going to do with the two of you." Ben said "Just love us mom." Jennifer said "where did all this come from?" JB said "He is smart and he has been listening to us talk and figured out a solution to his problem, I for one am proud to see him use his head instead of his fists."

Jennifer: "When you put it that way I can't argue with logic like that; I will have to enlist your mother to be on my side so it's two against two." JB laughed and said "She would too, she likes you." Jennifer "I am glad she does." She said "Sit at the table as the pancakes are done and she brought them to the table and they sat and Jennifer said grace and they ate their breakfast. When they were done JB helped her clean the table off and they went in the outer room and sat down. JB said "Ben will you go watch TV so your mom and I can talk big people talk OK?"

Ben said "Ok I will go in my room." Ben went to his bedroom and shut the door.

Jennifer said "what do you want to talk about?" JB: "We know a lot about the Terrorists. From the video we got this morning and how they plan to set bombs in the park and kill LJ and me. So I am going to use myself as a goat, and get them to shoot at me." Jennifer got a very freighted look on her face. JB: "Wait a minute let me finish, I don't want to die, now that I found you but I don't want these people chasing me the rest of my life. We could never have a normal life; we would be on the run forever. Over there someone wants to kill you, you go out and dispose of them, its kill or be killed that's their way that is the second reason I left the Navy."

Jennifer still looking afraid "I guess I can see your point but I don't want to lose you." JB: "We are afraid, that is the four of us and JR'S wife and two kids, that some lousy judge or some president might make some kind of political move and let them out of Guantanamo. The American people do not understand what these people are like or they would not let them within a million miles of here." Jennifer: "In the short time I've known you I have not seen you do anything really crazy and I don't think you have a death wish, have you guys done this before?" JB: "Yes in worse places where there are not many places to hide, here I can roll and get behind shelter, also I have three excellent snipers to watch my back, The police can't arrest them until they actually do the crime, so I have no choice. From the actions we have seen they are not that good, they have bad habits from killing people that don't know they are around which is like shooting fish in a barrel." Jennifer: "I see your problem and I guess it is my problem now also, so I said I was here for the long run, I am committed to see this all the way." JB: "I could pack up, take you two with me and run I can live off the land and survive for years but that is not the kind of life I want, and I don't want you to have either." There was a knock on the door, JB went to the door and opened it, it was LJ and CR," JR is at the airport." JB said "why don't you two go and get JR. Jennifer and I are having a discussion about our upcoming events."

LJ replied "OK." JB gave him the keys and they left. JB sat down and looked at Jennifer and said "You are the best thing to come into my life in a long time; I understand how JR feels about his family, now that you are around. It gives me a different outlook on life that I didn't have before; worrying more about someone other than yourself, really makes them 1st and you 2nd but it's a good feeling. It was easy; I was in love with someone else until I met you." Jennifer said "Wow I don't know how to answer that, can I live up to her." JB replied "You already have." They sat there in silence for a couple minutes and Jennifer took his hand and arm and put it around her and leaned on him and just snuggled there. An hour later there was a knock on the door. JB went and opened it and there were the 3 of them; JB said "come on in and I will introduce you to Jennifer." JB: "Jennifer this is JR, you met the other two, and we are the four musketeers, one for all and all for one." Jennifer said "it is nice to meet you all." JB said "I am going to take you over to the big house thru the tunnel and they are going to walk over there so are friends on the hill think you and I are still here." JB: "I will meet you over there." JB called "Ben will you come here. I want you to meet my brothers." Ben came out of his room and came over and shook each one's hand, these are all your uncles, you will do anything they tell you todo, and do you understand? Ben: "Yes, if they tell me to go to my room I have to go right." JB replied "right." Ben then said "I got it, there like you are, the boss." JB said "see you over at the big house."

JB locked the door after they left. The three of them went down to the basement and JB said "Ben will you open the doors." Ben said "Yes." And he went to the panel that opened the first door pushed and it opened JB and Jennifer went thru the door and Ben turned on the light and shut the first door and then went to the steel door and punched in 0815, the door clicked and Ben opened it and they all went in. Ben turned on the light in the tunnel and then turned off the light in the entryway and pulled the door shut and got on the plate and pushed the lever and the door went click and they were locked in. Ben led them thru the tunnel all the way to the big house and stood on the plate and pulled the lever until the door clicked and pushed it open then he turned on the light in the entryway, and turned off the tunnel lights and they were in the small entry room, Ben pushed the button to open the secret door into the game room, and they went in. Ben turned the light off and closed the door and they were in the big house. JB said "Ben you did very well I am proud of you." They walked up the stairs and everyone was in the kitchen sitting around the table and lunch was set, Mom said "Sit down and eat so I can visit with my sons." Jennifer could say nothing to that, and they sat down in the three open chairs. Mom said grace as they all held hands and then the food was passed around and they ate in silence, when they were done the four brothers got up and cleared the table and when they were done, Dad said "We are going to have a family meeting, so everyone knows where we all stand on the situation at hand." JB said "what do you know." Dad: "That there is a number of men on the hill that want to kill some of us, that it was bad enough to have CR and JR come early." JB: "IF we were over there we would just go out and dispatch them, but we are here and the police cannot do a thing until they do something, we have evidence that they plan to bomb the park, if you would like to see the videos LJ can get them for you and feed it into the TV but we will let Ben go downstairs and play games or watch TV or a movie." Dad: "No we will take your word on that, how close is this to starting?" JB: "my guess is, to get me in the next two days; they might not know who CR and JR are yet." JB "The plan is I am going to be the goat as I am worth the big bounty, LJ will be in the animal barn up stairs in the loft, with one of the security guards, and his job is to take out their 2nd site we found this morning when we were out. CR will be in the office loft with another guard their job is to take out the 1st site, JR will have a team of police on site one, Hank will have a team on site two, the police have never been in a firefight so that is why Hank has site 2 as we figure they are the 2nd team or the weakest team. When JR gets all the enemies at the first site that are alive, they will cuff them to trees and JR will interrogate them, the rest of his team will be taking watch over the prisoners he will have one watching the prisoners the rest will be fanned out watching the woods on the side next to the new site in case any try to escape that way. JR will go to the new site and make sure Hank's guys are all right and they got everyone, the only one that might get away is an X Seal, but we will track him down and erase him. He a real bad guy, he has more training than the rest of them but he is sloppy." Mom asked "why you?" JB: "because my bounty is the highest, they think I am the brains of this outfit, but what they don't know is that the four of us plan together and the plan is developed by all of us, that is why we always win, our plans are better because we each contribute so the plan is balanced not leaning to one side because no one person can not think of everything. At that range the bullet has lost its main power and the vests we are wearing are Level 5 or the best we can get. There is no level 6 or I would have gotten that."

Mom:"you really got this laid out don't you?"

JB looked at his Mom and said "Yes we plan to grow old with our wives the same as you and Dad. The plan includes bomb sniffing dogs made to look like service dogs with handlers, and walking like ordinary people, when these terrorists are caught with a bomb they go to Guantanamo. We haven't located dogs yet but we might be able to borrow some from the service, some people owe us some favors I called Hank and he and his guys will be coming over later this afternoon with their wives as a decoy and you girls can visit while we go over the plan with Hank and his men."

Mom said "I suppose you boys have been in worse places than this."

JB: "the four of us have been faced with larger forces than this and we are still here."

LJ said "we all agree or we make another plan that we do agree on, always." The voices on the video put us as their first target because we fight back, the park 2nd because it doesn't." Then they were talking about a few other bombs after they get done here and if they see the FBI they will leave and come back another time."

JB's Dad said "I guess this covers it, Jennifer you have said nothing, you are entitled to ask anything you want."

Jennifer: "JB explained all this earlier before we came over and I understand why they have to do this, if they don't a lot of people are going to get hurt or killed, these people are sub human and should be done away with, and now you will have an ER nurse to patch you up if needed."

Dad said "I guess this meeting is over. Let's go down and teach Ben how to play pool." And they went down stairs. JB said we have some snacks and drinks in the kitchen, we should get them out before Hank gets here." They all went in the kitchen and Jennifer gave all of them things to do to get everything ready. 20 minutes later the doorbell rang and LJ went to answer the door. They could hear Hank and his crew come in and they came out to the kitchen and everyone was introduced to everyone else. The men went out in the other room and were gone for 15 minutes going over the plan, and Hank said "this is simple but seems to cover everything, I am impressed." JB said "we will finalize it after we get the last video." JB said any of you wives that want to see the last video we got this morning we will run it before you leave." The volunteer girls started to talk to LJ and CR, a lot of men shy away from the girls when asked what they do and they say we are police women. The women seemed to be having fun asking LJ and CR embracing questions, but they seemed to be enjoying it any way.

Hank said "they needed to go and the three girls said they would leave later as it was time for the boys to ask them questions" LJ and CR ask what kind of training they had received, how good could they shoot, what did they like to do for fun, food they liked and various other things. They also said they would teach the girls any skills that they had that the girls wanted to learn. It was getting late; the girls said good bye and the party came to an end. JB said "I think that went well, LJ and CR what did you think of the girls. LJ, "I think they have potential, we might even want to use them in the park as temp help at real busy times and as a fill in when needed when we are shorthanded." CR: "I agree they seem capable." JB: "Ok I think Jennifer and I will head home we will have a big day to tomorrow." JB and Jennifer went down to the game room, got Ben and went through the tunnel. Jennifer said "I will get Ben in bed, we can talk then."

JB sat down on the couch and waited for her to get done. Jennifer came out and said "they seem to be nice people, are they all people you know?" JB: "I know a few of them, Hank and I went to school together and two of the police men were in lower classes but I did not know them very well." JB; "I bet all this is kind of over whelming for you." Jennifer: "in the ER we don't get to plan so it is just there and you try to cover everything at once, start with what looks like the worse and work yourself down to the least, the ER teaches you do what has to be done and worry about it when it is over."

JB said "I think life is like that for every one, it's the degree that is different, do the best you can is all you can do." Jennifer: "what do you want out of life when this is over?" JB: "Run the park smoothly get married and have a family spend time with my brothers; help other people when I can. And what do you want Jennifer?" Jennifer "can I be honest with you?" JB: "Yes always I am not in to playing games." Jennifer "I don't know how to start and I don't want to lose you, I have loved you all my life." JB with a strange look said "How is that possible?"

Jennifer with a sad look said "I am Jane the girl who let you get away when you went in the service, I was too immature, I was afraid because I was mentally to young, I did not come here to get money from you or force you into anything, I would like to spend the rest of my life with you and can you forgive me for what I did to you?"

JB sat there for a while and let that sink in. Then he said "that's why I liked you right off my subconscious must have known but I didn't recognize you, you look different but similar."

Jennifer said "my nose was bigger and I always hated it, so I had it fixed and changed my name. I was pregnant with Ben, he is your son, and then I went to nurse's school so I could support the two of us." JB: "you should have told my parents, they would have told me and we could have gotten married." Jennifer: I was confused and really not thinking, I wanted you to be happy and not tie you down or keep you from doing what you wanted to do with your life." JB: "I went in to the Seals to keep busy and not think about you all of the time be cause I couldn't take that, you are the only girl I ever loved." Jennifer: "Do you hate me for what I did?" JB: "No I love you, how would I ever hate you." Jennifer grabbed him and started to cry. JB held her tight and tears came to his eyes, the girl he had always loved was in his arms, his search was over. JB said "When this is over we will get married and be a real family if that is what you want?" Jennifer said "Yes that is what I wanted, and to be close to you." JB kissed her and she him, their prayers were answered. JB said "We have been hiding from each other all these years and all we would have had to do was talk, this is a good lesson. From this day forward we talk, about anything that is on our minds so we are always on the same page." Jennifer: "Sounds good to me, I am now the happiest women in the world." JB: "We will keep this to ourselves and tell Mom and Dad when this is over and then we will tell your parents." Jennifer said "Ok my parents always said that I was crazy for not marring you because you were such a nice boy." JB smiled and said "Good then they should still like me." Jennifer: "They keep telling me that I should tell you that you had a son." JB look at her "You don't have to worry about that now." JB: "We had better get some sleep tomorrow is going to be a busy day. Jennifer kissed him and went to bed. JB got his sleeping bag out and went to sleep.

CHAPTER 11

TUESDAY WEEK 2

JB got up and stopped at the big house and the other three were ready for the run, in the navy they usually ran together and they would discuses mission if they were getting ready to go on one. They started to run JR said "Why don't we split up this morning and spy on them up close." JB: "The brush is thick between the trees and we don't want them to know that we are on to them." CR: "I am inching to go; I do not like being watched." JB: "We are not over there anymore, the rules here are way different and we don't want to get put in jail." I think we will let Dad drop us off and we spy on them with laptops and watch what they are doing live for a little while see what they do and get a better feel for our attack." They all agreed. JB said, "Ok I will have Dad drive us up there in the park van and drop us off, I have a shadow that the police has on me and I will take him with me." They finished and did the rest of their routine and JB went back to the spring house.

He unlocked the door and Jennifer was up and putting breakfast on the table. She looked up and smiled at him and said "Good morning." JB: "Hi are you ready for the day?" She said "Yes, I am very happy this is the first day of the rest of my life." JB looked at her and said, "I love you, you better stop looking at me like that or I might carry you off someplace where we can be alone." Jennifer said, "I would love that but you won't because you are on a mission."

JB: "Yes we have to download the cameras and finalize our plans and decide when to implement them. We can go on a moment's notice, I doubt the police can, they are not used to doing missions like this, we will have to teach it to the swat team when we start it." They sat down and ate and JB got cleaned up and dressed in camouflaged clothing. When he came out of the bathroom Jennifer looked at him and said: "That really makes it look all real." JB: "Don't worry it should be a quiet day." Jennifer got Ben ready for school and they got in the car and drove off.

LJ and CR went to LJ's room and took a sniper scope and looked up at the hill the third site had the gun sticking out but the fourth sight did not CR said "I guess I will have to wait for the muzzle blast that must be the best shooter they have." LJ: "we will find that out shortly." They went down to wait for JB. JB got back 10 minutes later and Dad was all ready to go. He looked at his sons in camouflaged clothing and said "I guess it is starting to be the real thing." JB: "Yes we are getting down to the real thing, it won't be long now." JB: I am going to take my Glock and 2 extra clips and you do the same, would one of you bring a rifle and we will be ready to go." They went for their equipment and went out to the van, CR said "I am glad the house shields us from the hill, it would be hard to get our rifles out." They all agreed and loaded everything in and they drove out to where the police cruiser was parked.

JB got out and told shadow what they were going to do and ask if he wanted to go." He said "Yes." JB: "Bring your shotgun and a few extra rounds just in case the crap hits the fan." Shadow grabbed the gun and got in the van. They headed off to the hill, Dad drove to the 3rd road and then a little farther and JB said: "Ok let's get out He and shadow got out and his Dad drove on' JB and shadow went into the woods and logged on to camera number3 in the small area on the rim, the Arab was laying on the ground looking thru the scope. Beside him was one of the other people they had seen before but there was a new guy sitting on the ground and he would write every time the Arab said something. JB and shadow sat and watched for about 10 minutes and his cell started to vibrate, JB turned it on and whispered "what."

It was LJ and he said "we got a real problem up here they don't have a sniper site up here they have a mortar and 5 rounds aimed at the park, you better get Hank up here." JB said "OK I will call you back."

JB: "whispered to shadow did you hear that." Shadow: "No what is wrong?" JB: "They have a mortar and 5 rounds at the other site, will your radio reach the station, we have to get Hank out here now and by himself in an unmarked car, and don't tell anyone until we talk." Shadow: "Ok." He took his cell phone out and called, he got Hanks in 10 seconds and the call lasted 20 seconds and JB'S phone vibrated it was Hank. JB answered and Hank asks "what are you going to do." JB said "Nothing until you get here unless they try to drop a shell in, CR is within firing range and if they try to load he will take them out." Hank: "this is not a war zone." JB said "If they are trying to fire a mortar it is a war zone." "I will not let them kill innocent people." Hank; "You are right I am not used to this kind of thing. JB: "get here as fast as you can no siren." Hank: "I should be there in 12 minutes." JB called his dad on the cell. His Dad said "Hello are you ready for me." JB: "No we have a real problem; they have a mortar up here." Dad: "O that is terrible; what do you want me to do?" JB: "nothing stay where you are until I get back to you. And don't tell anyone. LJ and CR will take them out before they can fire so everyone is safe right now."

JB called LJ and said "are you close enough to take them out if they try to fire?" CR is within 10 to 12 feet and I know he will stop them, you know how fast he is." JB said "Hank is on his way, but you stay right where you are, but get so someone coming up the path can't see you, wait until they pass you so no one is behind you remember there is three, once they are past you, don't move and if they do shoot first, and make sure they don't kill you." JB looks at shadow: "I will be firing into them from my position we will have them in crossfire, can you do that." Shadow said 'I have never fired at people before." JB: "You are on the range point and squeeze your training will take over, never hesitate just do."

JB moved close to the road and 5 minutes later a car came up slow, JB called Hank. Hank answered, JB said "That you in the black car." Hank: "Yes." JB ran down the road and stopped him. Hank was all hyped up and JB said "Calm down we have everything under control, if they try to fire CR will take them out. You should have no backlash, You will have a mortar and shells, even if we kill them all you will be a hero for the state, you can have all the credit, we are not here it was you and a fellow officer." Hank: "I have never done anything like this before." JB: "That's why you are just here to watch and take credit we will take care of everything, that's what we have been trained to do." Hank relaxed a little, JB said "Dad is parked at the diner so anyone leaving will not know that we are here; now you back up and turn around and go to the diner and have Dad drive you back here and let you out at the second road and go into the trees about 4 feet and walk very quietly back here and I will meet you in the woods."

Hank: "OK." And he started backing up.

JB slowly went back to shadow and said "You calmed down." Shadow: "A little." JB: "Believe me it gets better with time and repeated missions." To get his mind off what he had just seen, JB said "We will be giving hand to hand combat training and you might want to practice with us." Shadow said "I think I would like that." They waited a while then went back thru the woods to wait for Hank. He thought this might really help get Hank and his people ready for D-day. JB waited another five minutes for Hank to arrive. When he got here JB said "you are dead, I heard you five minutes ago, I said quietly." JB said, "I am not going to make a habit of calling." Hank: "I am just going to let you guys handle everything." JB: "Do you want to see the other site or wait until this is over." Hank: "Over." They slipped into the woods and went back to Shadow. JB looked at the screen and said "we are going to stay here until they leave so we know there will be no danger. You may miss supper I am not sure when they will leave and tomorrow we will be up here early before they get here; we will make a new plain that includes the mortar."

At dusk the Terrorists packed up and started up the trail three minutes later they past by JB and his crew, and walked out to the road and a van pulled up and they got in and headed to the next site. JB said "you stay here I am going to try to get a picture of the van's plate number when they leave then we will give them a half hour to get off the hill and then call Dad to come and get us.

JB called Jennifer and told her he could not pick her up but his Dad would in the park van at the front entrance then she could pick up Ben and he would take them to the big house, and they should stay there until he got there." JB then called his Dad and told him to pick up Jennifer at the front door of the hospital and then pick up Ben and take them to the big house for supper and he might pick up three or four jumbo pizzas to feed everyone." Dad said "OK I am on my way bye."

JB got to the edge of the trees and found a place to hide one of the cameras they took from site 2 and set it up where it could get a picture of the van and the plate, and then he vanished into the woods. 10 minutes later the van past by them and they were gone. JB checked the camera and saw that he had got what he wanted. He called up LJ. LJ: "empty here we are coming to you, see you in ten by."

JB went back and got Hank and Shadow and went up to the road to wait for LJ and CR. Eleven minutes later they came out of the darkness. JB said "I am going to give the terrorists another twenty minutes and I will call Dad to come and get us. What all did you see?" LJ: I downloaded all the video put batteries in both cameras. We are going to have a crew up here to take down the mortar as I think their plan is to fire mortars into the park and city when the shooting starts." CR: JR and I need to be up here, one of us at each site. The mortar site has to be eliminated to prevent any shells; we hit them hard, no survivors. Hank has any of your men been in a firefight?" Hank I have two or three that went to Afghanistan for at least one tour. These are the men you should send up here we need experience." Hank: "That sounds kind of harsh." JR: "Do you want mortars falling into the park and city." Hank: "NO." JR looked at Hank and said "I know that this is way out of your experience, if there was another way we would do it but we want no civilian casualties, if my family was down there that's what I would want." Hank nodding his head and said "You are right; I think we should maybe bring in the district attorney. JR: "Is he a family man?" Hank: "Yes he has two children ages ten and seven." JR: "He may be all right, how big a politician is he? Hank: "I think he is a good man and will do the right thing." LJ: "I hope so because a lot of people could be killed and hurt, not counting the property damage." JB though for a few seconds and said "let us talk about it when we get home, maybe have him over to the house tonight and feel him out." Hank said "that sounds like a good idea." JB said "it time to call Dad."

He got his cell out and called, and then said "He's on his way." Fifteen minutes later the park van pulled up and they loaded up and Dad turned the van and drove to the diner to drop Hank off to get his car and they went home with Hank following. They pulled up to the big house and everyone got out and they went to the house and Jennifer came out of the kitchen and said "come and have something to eat." They followed her and all sat down, the table had magically gotten bigger so there was room for everyone. They sat and ate and then Dad said "we will clear this table." JB got up to and so did CR, LJ, and JR, the table was cleared and cleaned in two minutes. They sat back down and got the laptop out and started to run the videos, they showed the sniper site. Then LJ got the other laptop, set it up and they watched three terrorists at the second site and saw the mortar and five rounds. That made some very sober faces." CR looked at Hank and said "What do you think your district attorney will think about that?" Hank: "That should scare anyone; I will call him and have him come right over." Hank pulled out his phone and called the district attorney and talked to him for two minutes and hung up. Hank said "he will be here in fifteen minutes." CR: "LJ needs to stay in the sniper site in the barn; Hank's three men and JR will hit the mortar site and wipe it out." They have the experience with a firefight; it should be over in one minute." CR: "I will stop anyone coming out of the sniper site with whatever men Hank gives me; the sad thing is they have no experience. So Hank you need to quiz them because it will get hard, they may have to shoot someone. They have only three men there on every video we got. "When the sniper fires at JB, LJ has to take the sniper in one shot or we will, the sniper must not be able to make a second shot because I don't plan on losing JB do you understand that Hank." CR said. Hank shaking his hear yes "That's good with me, I don't want to lose him either."

"We want at least one live terrorists when this is over if we can and we will find out everything he knows and Hank you and the district attorney will not be there so you don't have to worry and it will be the two of us to say he is lying, this is a war that is being waged against us whether people want to believe it or not. The video shows that but it will not make the evening news. We have to protect our country, we took an oath to protect the constitution and this country and that's what we are going to do." CR said.

"That is the plan, Hank do you have any input for us on the plan or is it good the way it is?" JB asked.

Hank replied "I don't see anything left out." They hear a car pull up and a knock on the door; JB said "Dad would you get that please? I will get a chair for our new quest." JB said.

Dad came with the district attorney and introduced him to JB and his men. LJ said "before we get started we would like to show you some videos that were taken today up on the hill."

The district attorney said "Ok I would like to see them and Hank has told me it is a life or death situation." JB, LJ. CR and JR ran the videos of the first site then the second site with the mortar and rounds." The district attorney looked a little shaken; he said "Hank is this really true?"

Hank: "Yes and I have more videos at the precinct. The district attorney said "We have to call in the National Guard." JB: "Sir as the national guard pulls up, they will make a lot of noise the mortars will come falling down, is that what you want and then the lawsuit for all the damage because the city made a big mistake and got people killed, right now they don't know that we are on to them."

The district attorney thought a minute then said "You bring up a valid point, what is your plan?"

They went over the plan leaving out the interrogation. The district attorney looked at Hank and said "What do you think."

Hank: "I think it is the best plan with the least amount of fall out, these four gentlemen have been doing this for ten years, I think they have more experience than anyone we can come up with and their families are right in the danger zone."

JB said "Do you think that I would endanger my mother, father and fiancée and son with a plan I was not sure of?" The district attorney with a sad look said "No I guess not."

JB: "We would like a few more days, as we have a new video of their van and a plate number that we want to run, we do not know if we can capture anyone one alive so if we could get some more information to track down any of them that we don't know about, Hank will show the pictures to his men and see if they know any of them, and run them thru the system, we want to get as many as possible before the word get out, this is not a good city to mess with." The district attorney said "You men are remarkable, all the details you have come up with, and it is amazing." Hank: "These are the men who are going to set up our new Swat Squad."

The district attorney: "It should be a very good one we are a lucky city, thank you very much and we will talk again."

JB: "I would recommend that you keep this to yourself, tell no one, and not even your wife, so it stays a secret."

The district attorney: "You are right." And Dad showed him out. Dad came back in the room and sat down. Mom said "When were you going to tell us the good news?"

JB: "After all this was over and things settled down." Dad said "Well congratulations and welcome to the Family Jennifer, and now I have the grandson I've always wanted." Mom went over to Jennifer and hugged her and said "We are very happy you are in the family, JB has been a lot happier since you came here and we are glad for you both." LJ and CR "we agree with everything being said sister." JB looking at Hank and said "Hank we will need two men here at 4:45 AM to go up the hill and be on watch. Give each one of them one of the vests and armed with a pistol, 2 extra clips and a shotgun and 10 to 20 extra shells, food, water, and to dress for cool weather. They will be there all day; we cannot pick them up until the enemy has left the hill and make sure you tell them there might be a firefight."

CR said "We will brief them on the attack plan on the way up." JB: "We should wrap this up, we need to get Ben home and in bed. I will see you at 4:30. Jennifer we will ride home in the car." They said goodbye and left. They got in the car and went to the spring house. They jumped out and went quickly in; JB locked the car and joined them inside. Jennifer got Ben cleaned up and to bed. She came over and sat next to JB on the couch. She looked at him and said "I thought we weren't going to tell anyone?"

JB looking at Jennifer "I did to, but I though the district attorney needed a push to get on board and I will do anything to protect you and Ben, I could have said the district attorney didn't need to know that was for show after he left, but I was not going to lie to family. Do you forgive me?" Jennifer though then said "I love you how could I not forgive you for trying to save our future together. I doubt he really understood the real gravity of this with not being in it from the start; he was overwhelmed, his whole world just turned over, he hit a wall that he never saw. I had that feeling when the first gang fight victims were wheeled into the ER, I almost fainted there was blood all over them, you have to see that a few times before you wait until you are done before you are overwhelmed."

JB said "The first few missions are like that. Most people are living in a fantasy world in their little scope of reality and to instantly have it destroyed blows their mind and some can't handle it."

Jennifer: "I bet the district attorney is going to have a hard time getting to sleep tonight, and his wife is going to question him." JB: "I hope he does not tell her the truth it will be all over the city, we may have to start sooner than I would like. Bringing him in may have been a bad move, but Hank had to cover his but; I hope it covers us as well, a lot of times they throw us under the bus." Jennifer: "I understand that, I've seen it before." JB: "we have had enough for one night." He reached out and held her and kissed her and she kissed him back and they both felt better. JB: "Time to go to bed the clock starts tomorrow, the countdown to attack in case you don't know the expression." Jennifer: "I saw that movie." And she smiled and he kissed her and she got up and went to bed. JB got his sleeping bag out and put it on the couch and got in and went to sleep, tomorrow would come quickly.

CHAPTER 12

WEDNESDAY WEEK 2

JB was up at 4:00 and got dressed in his regular clothes and put his inside the pants holster so his Glock would not be seen he would get his vest at the office and put it on under his jacket. He put 2 extra clips in his inside hidden pockets and turned off the lights and went out the door locking it. He went quickly to the big house and let himself in. LJ, CR, and JR were coming down stairs, LJ had a 5-gallonpail full of the supplies he would need for the day, CR and JR each had a Camouflaged bag with their supplies they carried a Glock and a rifle over their shoulders and they had extra clips in their belt. His Dad came out and said "you all be careful I don't want to lose any son's today."

They smiled and LJ said "today should be quite, hope for the best prepare for the worst." The other two nodded and smiled it was always easier for the ones that go, than the ones at home. They heard a car pull up and they went outside and Hank was getting out of his car and two men got out also. They went to the open trunk and got their gear and supplies. Hank introduced them to, LJ, CR and JR, CR had them put their gear into the park's van, Dad came out and got in the driver's seat and said "I will take you up and pick you up when you call I will be ten minutes away at all times." Today I am yours. They said "thank you." JB said "to keep you informed, I will expose myself and see what they do, it will be quick no more than two seconds I will do that at 8:30 when I get back from dropping Jennifer and Ben off. Change that to 8:45, in case of traffic, any change I will text."

Dad started the van CR, JR. and Hanks men got in the van and they left. They waved to the shadow who was watching the preparations, and he waved back. JB walked toward Shadow's car and went to the window, the window came down and Shadow said" is there a problem; I saw there were more of you here today. JB: "No they are going up on the hill and recon for more info. D-day is close so you hear shots come but be careful do not just run in, use caution look before you leap." JB turned and went back to the big house LJ and Hank were already inside, JB went in and they went to the kitchen and sat down to a cup of coffee that JB's Mom had made. JB said "Mom what are you doing up this early?" Mom: "making sure you got some food before you go. They ate, then JB: "LJ you get in the barn while I take Jennifer and Ben to town and then I will be back for our little test." Mom: "what kind of test?" JB: "we are going to see if they are on the ball." Mom: "You are not going to take any chances are you?" JB: "Not any more than when I take Jennifer and Ben to town." Mom: "I hope not." JB: "Well I will see you later I better help Jennifer", he got up and went to the door and went quickly to the spring house.

JB opened the door and went quietly in and closed the door. Jennifer was sitting at the kitchen table drinking a cup coffee and said: "Are you doing anything dangerous today that I have to worry about?" JB: "That is relative; I think it is no more dangerous than when I take you and Ben to town." She said, "I don't know what that means but I guess that is all I am going to know." JB: "If I thought it would be bad I would tell you." She said "Ok I will have to settle for that." She asks "do you want me to fix you something?" JB: "No I had Breakfast at Mom's she was up and had it fixed. "Jennifer "I will just have some cereal then and she got up and fixed two bowls and went to wake Ben. He came out with a sleepy look and said: "Hi dad." JB smiled, he liked the sound of that. He went and shaved and showered and got dressed for the day, it might get interesting before the day was done.

LJ left the big house and walked to the animal park and went to the barn and climbed the stairs, it was going to be a long day and he would not have a spotter to talk to, He got his rifle out of the wall case, dropped one in the chamber, and put the clip in. He went to the window in the back end of the building and blocked it with dark plastic so he wouldn't have any background light revealing his location. Then he went to his fire position at the bales of hay, opened the window and set up his rifle. Adjusted his optics in on site 3, and thought they won't see my barrel, they won't know what hit them. LJ relaxed and waited, a half hour to do nothing, the life of a sniper, hurry, hurry, hurry, to wait, wait, wait; then action. He heard a car start up and there goes, the clock is started.

JB got Jennifer and Ben in the car and they headed off to town, and their shadow followed about half a block length behind them. JB looked over at her and said "You don't have to worry the experiment will be over by 9:00. We will know that piece of information by then."

Dad drove up the hill and dropped CR and his policeman off at site three and they went in the woods with all their gear and disappeared into the darkness Dad went to the next site JR and his policeman got out and took their gear and disappeared into the woods. Dad turned the van around and went down the hill and was back at the house in ten minutes way ahead of the time the terrorists would be showing up. Ten minutes later Dad heard JB leave with Jennifer and Ben, he was happy to be a grandpa; He said a prayer "God please protect them all."

JB finished dropping Jennifer and Ben off and then he called Hank. Hank answered his phone "Hank here can I help you?" JB said "This is a have you got any info yet?" Hank: "Yes the van is register to a small conveniences store owned by an Arab sounding name, one of my men is going to stop in and buy something and see if any of the men in the pictures are there; We ran the pictures thru the state DMV and got two hits with address, we are checking to see if any are on a watch list or are wanted anywhere." JB: "Ok I will check back after our little experiment is over, bye", and he drove back to the park pulled into the office, parked the car and went inside. He told Betty what they were doing so if she heard gunshots she would not panic. He checked his watch he had fifteen minutes to go. He got a cup of coffee and took a couple sips and set it down, though what he would do. He would go out the back door of the office and headed for the ride booth they had picked out when planning the mission. He could start to walk there and stop a step away and bend over and look at something and quickly step behind the booth. He ran that over in his mind until he said 'time to go." Pulled out his phone and called LJ. LJ said "Here" JB: "Now." JB walked out the back door and started the walk to the booth. He was ready to jump if anything happened, he got one step away from the Booth looked at the ground leaned over and looked then stood up and walked behind the booth stayed behind the booth then went back to the office'. CR called and said "they jumped to take aim and then stopped you caught them off guard they were just watching when they realized the opportunity was lost, but it looks like they are ready to play." JB: "I will wait fifteen minutes and come out for a minute are they on scope now." LJ: "Yes." JB: "I'll call you back" and hung up. Next he called JR. JR answered "Yes boss." JB: "You get any action?" JR: "No they didn't seem like they know anything is going on, they must be waiting for someone to tell them what to do." JB: "How close are you? JR: "12 feet to the opening 15 to the targets, I can't miss." JB: "call you later", and hung up. JB thought they will be easy we just have to watch the snipers as I think once the shooting starts the second crew goes into action and I know JR can take them all out or wound one or two, for interrogation. We are set; we just need more info to come in. He called Jennifer and her phone went to voice mail so he hung up and sent her a text "All over."

He called Hank. Hank: "How did it go?" JB: "they were slow not watching like they should so they are sloppy, we have the edge, keep that to yourself I don't want the district attorney thinking this is nothing or he might not take this as serious as he should, he is still living in his little world."

Hank said "Ok, the more you know the scarier it gets." "I will call you if I get any more info." JB hung up and called LJ. LJ answered his phone "hello boss." JB said "CR said they were not ready to shoot, they missed the opportunity, and they are sloppy." JB: "I think I am going to have Hank put a guard on Jennifer, they could fake an accident and take her hostage to get at me." LJ: "I would if she was mine." JB: "Thanks LJ." LJ:" That's what brothers are for." They both hung up.

JB called Hank. Hank said "Hello." JB: "I am worried about Jennifer she is very vulnerable where she is at, they could fake an accident, and grab her and go and I would have to get her back." Hank: "Sure I will have someone there in fifteen minutes." JB: "I owe you." Hank: "you pull this off and I will owe you big time." JB: "Thanks, bye." JB ran things thru his head, where was the X-seal he was not in the last photos, what was he up to. JB called LJ. LJ: "Hello boss what is up?" JB: "Do you remember seeing the x seal in the last few pictures?" LJ: "No I didn't, I wonder what he is up to."

JB: "I was thinking the same thing, I am going to call the Security Company and see if he has had any x seals that have put in an application I will get back to you." JB hung up with LJ. He ask Betty to call the Security Company and see if they had any applications that were from an x Navy Seals and if they did put me on the phone. Betty called and ask the question, the answer was yes so JB took the phone, "This is JB, can you describe him for me", he listened and said could you text me a picture?" "Sure the voice said, is there something wrong with him." JB: "If he is who I think he is, he has a link with terrorists and he will be a lot of trouble, text the picture and I will call you right back." JB hung up and ask "Betty is there any more Security Firms in town?" Betty: "Yes, but they are small they usually only do small overnight jobs." JB: "he may just be trying to get a uniform or to get sent here." The text came in and there was JB's man so that's what he is up to, good try but no prize. Betty called the Security Company and got the owner back on the phone and JB said "that's the man; do you have an address for him?" "Yes" said the voice on the phone "I will text it to you and thank you very much, this business is hard enough without saboteurs from within." JB said "Did he have a phone number also?" "Yes he did I will include it in the text." JB: "Thanks for all your help." The voice said "We thank you." And he hung up.

JB: "called LJ." LJ: "Yes boss." JB: "I found our seal, he applied at the Security Company but I stopped that." LJ: "He was trying to get in the back door." JB: "The Security Company sent us a good picture so we will post it by the screens and if we see him we will pick him up." JB: "Bye." JB called Hank, Hank answered "Hello." JB: "I found the X Seal, he has not been in the latest pictures, he applied for a job with the Security Company so he could get unnoticed access to the park but I put a stop to that, and I will text a picture and his address and phone, I assume the phone is good but the address might not be." Hank: "We will get right on it".

Hank sent one of his plain clothes policemen to check and see if the address was real. Hank said 'Josh check this guy out but be discreet like checking information on an application for a job make sure he lives there, got any roommates, smokes drinks causes trouble." Josh: "I will be back in 30 to 40 minutes."

Josh left to get the information. Josh found the apartment and went in and found the manager, he showed his badge and said no one is in trouble; this is a background check on an application for employment. Josh let the manager see the picture "Is this the man that lives at this address?" The manager: "Yes." Josh: "does he have roommates?" Manager: "Yes two, one is an Arab looking man, the other is white they seem nice." Josh: "Do they smoke or drink make any trouble?" Manager replied "No we have no trouble with them and I have not seen them smoking or drinking but I don't watch all the time, they have privacy." Josh: "Thank you very much this helps, bye." Josh turned and walked out and got in his car went back to the station and gave Hank the information.

Hank called and said: "We know where the seal lives and he has got an Arab looking roommate. JB: "Well we can put surveillance on them and see who they associate with but we don't have much time to watch them I think this is going down in a day or two they are just waiting to get me then make their big move. If you do surveillance don't get seen." "Jennifer is ok my man has her in sight at all times except in the restroom." "Thanks a lot." Hank: "My pleasure." JB hung up then he called LJ and asks "Have CR and JR checked in lately?" LJ: "Yes all is quite no new faces." JB: "Next time they check in let them know the new info, also I told Hank if he could they might put surveillance on that spot but discreetly." LJ: "If they get caught things may blowup in a hurry, bye." JB that's what he liked about LJ get to the point and get it done."

Hank called the detective department and said: "Send Bill and Carl to my office right now please." Three minutes later the two detectives walked into Hank's office. Hank said I have a quick surveillance job for you, its top secret no one is to know what you are doing, I know you two and I trust both of you and what is said here goes no further." Bill and Carl both nodded yes. Hank: "We have a situation in this city; terrorists are going to try to shoot the Navy Seals that are moving here, they are going to help us setup our Swat Team. Right now they have part of them under surveillance with two of our men, but I need you two to watch their apartment and if any of the men come out get pictures of them and if you can follow them without getting spotted, let me say it again, you cannot get spotted it will drastically hurt the operation. Don't sit in one spot too long and take separate cars. We are not sure how many of them there are so if any new faces appear get pictures if you can. Let me say again not even your wives or anyone outside of this room can know what you are doing or what you know, is that clear?" Bill and Carl said "Yes." Hank said "here are the pictures a set for each of you and I hope we have all of them but we will see." Hank: "Check in with me every thirty minutes so I know you are all right, one of them is an X seal that was kicked out of the Navy; we are not sure who is boss but he is probably the most dangerous one of the group so be careful, if you think you are being watched go into a store and buy something and leave and make sure you are not followed if you are, pick a large building or business and go in like you work there." Bill and Carl said, "Ok, We are on our way." They left Hank's office and got into separate cars and drove off.

Bill drove past the Building and went around the block and came back so he parked across the road in the block before the building, if someone was coming out of the building he would not be seen but his camera telephoto lens would give a good picture. Carl had pulled up in the block past the apartment and watched from the opposite direction. They hoped that would work and Carl could get out and tail them. Twenty-five minutes into the surveillance one of the men in the pictures with a new face Bill quickly took three pictures of them, two looked very good. They turned and headed in the direction of Carl, he got out of his car and locked the door, then started to walk toward them pulled his phone out and started to talk like he had a phone call and he walked toward them and stopped at the crosswalk as the light changed and the two men started across the street and Carl went across on his side, the men turned and started down the other side of the street and Carl crossed when the light turned and he hurried across the street to catch up and Carl almost ran into them, he walked on still talking like he was so engrossed in his call and paid them no mind.

They went into a coffee shop and Carl hurried toward Bill's car, Bill got out and started in Carl's direction and slipped him the key and continued on and went to the coffee shop and bought a coffee and sat close to the two men, looking toward the street instead of at them Carl gave Bill eight minutes and called Bill and then Bill held a recorder up that looked like a phone and pretend to talk and then listen on a call but was recording what they were saying after three minutes Bill put the recorder back in his pocket and grabbed his coffee took a sip and got up and walked out and walked back to his car. He got in and he and Carl listened to the recording. One of the men was talking about the men on the hill and said they would shoot their main target and drop a mortar in the park and in the confusion get a picture of the dead guy so they would get paid. Then they said we look for a good place to place another bomb get pictures and get another payday. And that was the end as Bill had left the coffee shop. They called Hank and told him what they heard. Hank said "Watch them if you can but stay hidden.

Hank called JB and told him what they heard and they had another player in the group. JB said "That is probably all of them there is going to be; you get too many and they don't get paid as much and the more people the more things go wrong." JB said "Thanks I will tell the others." JB called LJ and told him what he had just learned. Then he called CR and then JR.

JB called his Dad and said "It looks like we are going to have action tomorrow so bring all the men to the office and make sure the inside lights in the van don't come on when you unload them at the office. I will have Betty close the blinds so no one can see in as we are going over the plan again and Hank will have to make a decision about the others. Pick up a box of big black garbage bags and wide masking tape and bring them into the office.

JB called Hank and told him to bring the district attorney with him and park where you can get out and not be seen. Hank said why don't we have it here at the station?" JB "I know no one will be listening here, I don't know that at the station, and it is my life on the line." Hank: "I guess I understand. I am new at this so we will go with whatever you say." Hank said, "Good bye see you later." JB went to his car and left to pick up Ben and then Jennifer.

He stopped and went in and picked up Ben and saw a car that was parked and had been following him and he reached under his coat and took his Glock out and put a round in the chamber, he called Jennifer and said "when you come out, go around any ambulance parked there and stay on the side away from traffic and the policeman who has been watching you have him on the traffic side of you. I will be parked in front of the ambulance with the door you are going to use open, get in and shut the door and we will go." Jennifer said "Ok have you got Ben?" JB: "Yes he is with me, I will call shortly."

He drove thru traffic and a car was back there following about 5 cars back, JB continued on like he did not know he was being followed. He called Hank and told him that he had a tail." Hank: "what kind of car." JB: "Green Chevy." Hank:"that is one of us." I thought it might be a good idea." JB: "Always tell me when you do these things, so I don't have to look out for any more cars than I have to in this traffic." Hank:"I will pull him off right away", two blocks later the tail turned off. JB called Jennifer "I will be there in two minutes." Jennifer: "Ok." JB hung up and drove the rest of the way to the emergency room door and picked up Jennifer. Then he pulled into traffic.

JB: "Jennifer I hope I didn't scare you?" Jennifer: "A little." JB: "I saw a tail on us and I was going to be safe, better than sorry and I called Hank and it was his and he never told me and I had him pull it so I didn't have too many things to watch, it was probably good practice for you in case it does happen, you already know what to do when you get in you and Ben get down as close to the floor as you can. I have some spare Panels I will put behind the seats to protect you." They got home and JB pulled up to the spring house and had Jennifer and Ben gets out the side next to the house. Jennifer and Ben rushed to the house like they were having a race.

JB got out and walked to the door and went in and locked it. JB said "after supper, I have to go to the office we are having a meeting and need to revise our plan; I want you and Ben to go over to the big house thru the tunnel, stay with Dad and Mom until I get back. Jennifer said "Ok." She took some frozen burgers out of the freezer and started them cooking and made a salad and got out some buns and Ketchup and Mustard, in fifteen minutes they sat down to supper. When it was done they went over to the big house through the tunnel and went up and talked to JB's Mom.

JB: "We are going to be real busy tomorrow so I will drop you and Ben off and you will not be able to reach me and I don't want you to worry." Jennifer: "What is going to happen tomorrow?" JB: "I don't know, Hank has new information and new faces and I will not be able to tell you any more until it is over." JB "That is the rules and we must operate by them."

Jennifer: "Am I going to have to worry?" JB's Mom "Do I have to worry too?" JB: "I don't think so, we have been in a lot worse situations on other missions, and did not have as much information as we are going to have on this one. The only weakness is Hank's Guys as we have not worked with them before, but we could do most of it by ourselves and not have a problem, most of his guys are going to be in the city doing their thing." It was dark outside and JB said "I have to go now and light proof the office, so no one can see that we are in there, see you later." JB left and Jennifer and Ben went down to the Game room. Dad and Ben played pool.

JB opened the office and walked in and turned on a light, he had put on his head, the light was red an gave just enough light and he found the bags and tape, he went to the conference room and started on the first window, he took out a black bag and put it over the top of the window and taped it down across the top then down each side then took out another bag and covered the bottom part of the window taped it bottom to top and both sides. He did that to the other 5 windows and was just finishing up when he heard the van pulling up.

JB went to the door and opened it and the men walked in single file, JB had his red light in his hand shining into the room so they could see. When they were all in, he shut the door and opened the door to the conference room and lighted the way with his red light, when they were all inside he shut the door and turned the lights on. JB said "Let's move the table up to the front and arrange the chairs in rows and get a few more out as Hank is bringing more men with him." They did as they were told. JB said "The lights are going to be out so I can let the others in like I did for you." And he went to the door and turned them off and went thru the door and closed it.

JB went to the main door and opened it, and went out and Hanks people were getting out and Hank had fixed his car lights so they did not come on. They saw JB coming in the dim light and started to come to him. JB said in a whisper "We will go single file into the office, the lights are off and I will shine a red light so you don't fall, then we will go in the conference room and then we can turn on the lights." They followed JB into the office and thru the conference room door.

JB came in last, shut the door and turned on the lights and went to the front of the room and said I don't know if you all know all of my Brothers, we were a team and when you depend on each other you get very close." "You will each have a job to do in the mission; if you don't do your job someone can get killed. With that said LJ stood up, CR stood up JR stood up. JB: "We have been thru 100s of missions together and we know what each of us will do in any situation, any of you who join the Swat training will have the same feelings and knowledge about you as teammates, on the hill do as my men tell you and we should get thru this with no problems. First I am going to be a goat and draw the first shot, then LJ is going to hit the sniper before he can take a second shot, CR will also shoot the sniper to make sure he cannot take another shot.

The district attorney said "Isn't that enticing him to shoot you." JB looked at him and said "Why is he up there." The district attorney: "I am not used to this kind of situation, yes he is up there to shoot you or he would not be there." JB: "Right we are controlling when he shoots rather than him controlling it and he does not know that is the case." JB: "That is the first mission." LJ will leave his sniper position and run to where I will be, hopefully in operational condition because one of their men will come to take a picture of himself and me to collect the bounty, and probably shoot me to make sure I am dead, LJ has to get to me quick in case I am not functioning as I should be."

CR stood up: "I will shoot the sniper as soon as he shoots and there have been a maximum of three up there in every picture we have, so we yell don't move if they do shoot them, but we would like to get some alive to interrogate them as they are Terrorists, not your standard criminal, in the second site up there is a mortar and in the pictures they have five rounds."

CR sat down and JR got up and said "My team is to ensure that the mortar never fires they can move that mortar to take out a lot of your city and cause chaos to cover their escape. I will shoot the first man to try to get to the mortar, the man with me is to yell don't move and hopefully they will do as told, but they may want to martyr themselves and take you along with them so shoot and make sure you are on target. JB:"They are not the normal criminal you are used to dealing with; they want to kill as many of us as they can to get points for when they go to their heaven." JB: "Are there any questions?" One of the new men that Hank brought said "Why are we here, it looks like you have everyone you need." JB: "You are to capture the men that are not on the hill, we have pictures of seven men and no more than five have been on the hill, and two of you have a recording of them talking about bombs in the city, they are your job to find and arrest them. Another reason you have shown an interest in the Swat Team, so you are being exposed to what that will be like to help you decide."

Hank got up and said "We would not have known anything about them or how to handle a thing like this. Who here has been in a fire fight?", LJ, CR, and JR and one of Hank's men raised his hand." JB said "It is not like you think it is, it is chaos, multiple shots and lead flying at you and it gets real crazy, and you must stay calm until it is over, you panic you die."

JB: "The hardest part will being on guard for the long time you will be waiting for the action to start and still be at peak performance." Hank: "You will all be given pictures of everyone we have seen and you men in the city, if there is a new person with one of the people in the picture they are guilty by association treat them like you do the rest, they make a move shoot, they are terrorists or they would not be with them. This is not a game."

JB asked "Any more questions?" No one said anything. JB: "You who are to be on the hill be at the diner in the morning before 4:30, my Dad will pick you up there and if you are late go home because the van leaves at 4:30. If I was going to be on the hill I would be there a little after 4:00 but that is me, take something to eat because you will get hungry, so you are not distracted by your stomach, get a good night rest you will need it; I will now turn off the lights and stand outside this door and you will slowly go out and no lights, if you have trouble seeing stop out of the way and wait for your eyes to adjust. Dad I will go with you to drop off the men at the diner or if you are tired, go to the house and get some sleep and I will drop them off."

Dad said "I took a nap in the van earlier today you can drive and I will ride." They all left and loaded up in the various vehicles, and LJ, CR, and RJ went to the big house. JB drove to the diner and parked behind and let everyone out and they said goodbye and everyone went home. JB said "goodbye to his Dad and walked to the spring house staying in the shadows, he opened the door and slipped in and locked the door." Jennifer was sitting on the couch waiting for him. JB went over and sat down beside her and she snuggled up to him and they sat that way for a while then she said "How am I going to get to work?"

JB: "I am going to take you like I do every day and drop Ben off at school." "What if they shoot you there?" Jennifer said with fear in her voice.

JB: "That is not a good place to do it, how are they going to get a picture with all those medics around me."

Jennifer: "You have an answer for everything." JB: "No I don't have an answer for everything but we went over this plan and it is the only thing that makes since, for them to get paid and get away. We have the advantage because we know what they are going to do and they don't know that we know they are here." Jennifer: "I guess you know what you are doing." JB: 'I have been doing it for ten years." Jennifer: "Can you give it up." JB: "I already have I didn't ask for this I just got it, we have to deal with life and luckily I have the training to handle it. If you want I will get you and Ben out of town until it is over." Jennifer: "That would be worse because I would not know if you were alive or dead, I will stay here and don't make me a widow." She grabbed him and kissed him hard and he her, it lasted a long time. Jennifer said "See you in the morning and I love you with all my heart." JB: "I love you with all my heart." She got up and went to bed. JB got his sleeping bag out and put it on the couch and got in and went to sleep.

CHAPTER 13

THURSDAY WEEK 2

JB woke at 3:45 got up and dressed, and went down to the basement and went to the big house thru the tunnel, LJ, CR, and RJ were ready to go. They all checked their watches and made sure that their watches were all the same time. They were all synchronized. JB said "I will get back from dropping off Jennifer and Ben and be back here by 8:45 at the latest, I will call before I leave the office, I will stop and act like I am getting a call just before I get to the barn, there is a spot where they cannot see me, I will call LJ then CR, CR you call JR, the word is GO: within two minutes I will be at the spot where I bend over and then turn and stand up with my back to the hill and I will move to my right, he may miss but the shooter is dead either way I will figure to be hit, I will try to get my Glock out before I hit the ground, so LJ hurry I may be slow, I have never been shot." LJ: "He shoots I shoot drop the rifle and drop down the ladder and shoot him whether you do or not." CR: "When the sniper shoots I will shoot him and he will not shoot again." JR: "I will move out to stop the mortar from being fired if they don't I will try just to wound one so he can't get to the mortar, so we have at least one to interrogate, hopefully, my helper will be able to get one cuffed and I will start to ask questions."

JB: "I will say bye to dad and you can all leave." JB went up the stairs and said goodbye to his Dad and Mom and his Dad left with CR and

RJ. JB's Mom said, "Be careful boys I want you all back tonight for a big supper." They said "they would not miss that for anything", and they left. JB's Mom said "Son you be really careful you have a future wife and child to worry about and they will be worrying about you." JB and LJ left to go to the barn to run thru what he was going to do. JB did his bend over and turn until they figured it looks real and not a setup, they thought he would be down if he was hit and LJ practiced how he would come out of the barn from the loft to the ground, and where he would shoot from. LJ went to the barn and climbed up the ladder and was gone. JB went back to the spring house to get a little more sleep, Seals sleep when they can.

He got up at 6:00 and Jennifer was just getting up and she came over and kissed him and they hugged. Then she went to get Ben up and ready for school. JB fixed pancakes for breakfast; he knew Ben liked them so that should be a hit. Jennifer and Ben sat down and they all ate together. Jennifer got Ben's back pack and they were ready to go, JB went out first and opened the door for Ben and made sure he had the seat belt on right, then he closed the door, and Jennifer got in the front and opened his door, JB got in and they drove off. JB let Jennifer off at the emergency entrance she kissed him bye and JB drove off. Ben was singing to himself in the back seat. JB said, "That your favorite song?" Ben: "No I heard it on TV last night and kind of liked it." JB got to the school and let Ben out of the car and walked him to the door, and said: "Be good today and learn all you can." Ben said "I will" and hugged him then ran down the hall to his classroom. JB got back in the car and drove back to the park. He parked the car at the office and went in and told Betty that "there was going to be some shooting at around 8:50 to 9:00 and to call the police, there might be an officer parked in the lot, he might come in or head for the sound."

JB: "So you stay inside and don't come out until there is a policeman to be with you, we will be down by the barn, you might not want to go down, as there may be a body and it will not be pretty." Betty: "This is what all the equipment has been for?" JB: "Yes we are going to get some terrorists that have been watching the park. Today it stops." JB checked his watch. He finished putting on his bulletproof vest and put his shirt on and his shoulder hostler and checked his Glock and put a round in the chamber and then the gun in the hostler, put his jacket on smiled at Betty and walked out the door. He got his cell phone and called LJ: "GO", then CR: "GO." JB walked toward the barn. He walked to the spot where they had put a can JB bent over and grabbed it and turned as he stood up back to the hill and moved to the right. He didn't get far and he was hit and flung around and he was on the ground on his back he was dazed he had his Glock in his hand down by his side, he saw a man running toward him, a with a gun in his hand and a cell phone in his other hand. It was not LJ; it was the X Seal and the gun was pointing at him.

LJ saw the flash from the hill moved his aim 1/2 inch to the right and fired dropped his rifle and ran to the ladder and dropped to the floor.

CR saw the sniper shoot and then start to reload. CR aimed and pulled the trigger and the man started to just rise up and CR's bullet hit him and blood was erupting from his back, LJ had hit him also. CR said "Don't move", CR moved toward the other two men who were staring at the Arab, CR: "Yelled again "Don't move. The policeman with him also yelled, "Don't move." The man in the middle started to reach for his gun and CR shot him and so did the policeman, bang, bang the man went down, the third man froze.

JB raised his Glock and squeezed the trigger, bang, bang the gun jumped in his hand and he wondered how it could make two bangs.

LJ ran toward where JB was lying on the ground there was a man running toward him with a gun in one hand and a phone in the other, the gun was pointed at JB, LJ fired his Glock and bang, bang the man was slammed backward and hit the ground, twitched then was still. LJ got to JB and grabbed his gun hand and said "I am here and X is down. Are you hit bad", JB: "I don't know I am numb, help me up as he kept his eyes on the body laying on the path, then they heard two shots from the hill, LJ: "I thought I heard a shot right after mine, I thought that would be CR, these must be RJ taking out the mortar, that sounds good as there should be captives to interrogate; JB was in a sitting position, LJ was taking off his Jacket, shirt, then the vest, LJ looked at JB's back and there was no bullet hole, just a large red mark and the start of a bruise.

JR saw one of the men run toward the mortar with a round in his hand and shot him twice and he went down. RJ and the policeman both yelled" don't move, don't move."

The other man froze fear on his face and he screamed "Don't kill me. Don't kill me. I know things." RJ said "you better start talking", and pulled a recorder out and recorded what he had to say.

JB: "Go make sure the X is dead." LJ got up and walked over and knelt down and felt for a pulse, there was none. LJ said, "That is the last of him." JB started to get up and said "I think my rib is broken. LJ came back and helped him up and took him to a bench and then called 911 "We need an ambulance at the park by the animal area. LJ then called CR. CR answered on the second ring. CR: "Is JB ok?" LJ: "Yes got a bad bruise and maybe a broken rib, X is dead. CR: "good I have one here and he is talking, I am going to give him a few more things to think about and we should have all he knows, bye." LJ called RJ. NO answer. LJ: "RJ must be Interrogating." JB: "He will call when he gets what he wants." They heard a siren in the distance and getting louder and louder. JB: "I am going to stand and move a little." LJ: "No if you have a broken rib you could puncher a lung and that would be bad, Just stay where you are; I will take care of things, the goat gets to sit that is his job." They both laughed and JB winced. JB: "You may be right." Five minutes later the Ambulance pulled up and Jennifer and a paramedic got out. Jennifer ran over and said: "Are you ok." JB: "I might have a broken rib so check and let me know." The medic: "What about the other guy?" LJ: "Go check, I could not find a pulse." The Medic went over checked the body out and came back, said: "He's dead; I will call the coroner to come out." The medic went to the truck and made his call. Jennifer said I don't think it is broken but we need to take you back to get an x-ray to make sure." JB: "I have things to do." LJ: "No you get checked out, I can take care of this until we know you are ok, that an order." The medic brought the gurney over and JB got on and lay down, and said "I want to set up, it is more comfortable." Jennifer raised the front of the gurney up then she called JBs Mom and said: "he is all right we are going to take him in for an x-ray to be sure." The coroner arrived and started to work on the x seal. The Ambulance left and LJ left to leave them to their work. LJ got to the office and told Betty that JB was ok and they needed to get a cleanup crew to scrub up blood and might need a pressure washer to go over it after a scrub and have a disinfectant in the water. Also have them rope off the area until that is all done. LJ said "I will be back I have something to finish: LJ went back to the barn and put his rifle in the case and locked it up. Then he went over and picked up JB's vest and looked it over and there was the bullet stuck in the vest. LJ thought that was worth every penny it cost, then he went back to the office and put the Vest in the conference room, everyone needs to see this.

CR was finishing up his Interrogation When Hank came down the path and looked things over. Hank: "What happened to his hand?" CR: "He hurt it somehow." Hank we may have to work on that one" and smiled. Hank said, "You done with him." CR: "I guess so, then turned to the man and said, how much do you know about these men from Afghanistan?" The man said "not much, they were going to pay us a lot of money." CR: "I know a lot about them and they are going to slowly take you apart piece by piece until you give them what they want then kill you to keep your mouth shut, so if you know more you better tell all so you can go into the witness protection program. The man was white as a sheet. There is a little more so CR started the recorder again and got the rest of what he knew.

RJ called JB. JB answered: "Hi what you got." RJ: "I shot the mortar guy but his buddy sang like a bird he wants protection." JB: "OK call LJ and fill him in, I am on my way to get x-rayed to make sure I don't have a broken rib." JR: "I am glad you are all right, see you later, bye." RJ called LJ and filled him in. JR: "then also this guy said they were to get the money from the brother of some guy shot in Afghanistan." RJ: "That means we are not done yet, he will come over now he knows where we are, we have one more to go, we will have to get the Swat team going as quick as we can; LJ agreed and said "bye" and hung up. RJ called CR and filled him in. CR said, "I will call Dad and have him come and pick us up."

CR said "Hank we are done with these guys if you want you can take them away and call homeland to pick them up. Hank you make copies of everything you have and hide it as they are going to take everything away from you. We may still need it because someone over there knows where we are, and when they don't hear back they will come looking for us." Hank: "So this is not the last of this?" CR "Right, we might as well go check on RJ your men can take care of this." CR and Hank left for the mortar site. RJ saw them coming down the trail and went to get them while the policeman cuts the man off the tree and cuffed him around another tree to keep him immobile. RJ: "How is JB?" CR: "He may have a broken rib, otherwise he is ok." Hank: "Has our friend here had anything to say." RJ: "Yes and it is not over yet, we know who the moneyman is and he will come, I figure four, six, or eight weeks for him to sneak into the country and get here, we will have to spread his picture around." RJ: "We need to start Swat training in the next week." Hank: "Sounds like a good idea we are not going to be so lucky next time, they know we know about them." RJ: "Remember they are very clever and smart and they do not live by the same rules we do." "They will kill us just because we are not Muslim."

JB got to the hospital and was wheeled into the ER and quickly sent to x-ray. A doctor came in and looked at him and said that was done by a bullet." JB: "Yes a sniper rifle at 450 to 500 yards from a hill." You had a vest." "Yes a level 5." Doctor: "Good choice, that the highest they have isn't it." JB: "Yes it is." The doctor: "I should have the x-ray back we rushed it for Jennifer." The doctor turned and left. LJ called and JB answered, "Hi what have we got?" LJ: "We know who the money man is, the brother of that terrorist's group we hit just before we got out and the brother was not there." JB: "You figure six to eight weeks." LJ: "That is what we think, I informed Hank and I told him to make copies of everything and hide them because homeland will confiscate everything." JB: "Good move, my x-ray should be here soon and then I can leave." LJ: "all right' bye." JB hung up. The doctor came back 15 minutes later and said: "you have a hairline fracture, so you will have a little pain for the next couple of weeks, you're free to go." Jennifer said "get into the wheelchair and I will wheel you out." JB called LJ and said, "Come and get me the keys are on the wall." LJ: "I will be there in 15 minutes. LJ was getting ready to get in the car when Hank dropped CR and RJ off. LJ: "I am going to pick up JB, they let him go, and he has a hairline fracture. They said, "We will change and get cleaned up and meet back at the office after we check out the barn."

They left and went to the barn; a crew was finishing up pressure washing the walkway down. In five minutes there would be no sign of blood and in a day or two no clean spot either. They turned and went to the big house.

Jennifer wheeled JB to the front and said wait I am going to change and we will go and get Ben from school and we will all go home" she left and was back in 10 minutes. LJ pulled up 3 minutes later and JB got in the front Jennifer in the back and she gave directions to the school. When they got there Jennifer went in and got Ben, 15 minutes later they were on their way home.

Betty looked up when they walked in and said: "Hi I am really glad to see you, looks like you are fine." JB: "Just a bruise." Betty: "the rest of the bullet proof vests are in." JB: "Jennifer you take one of the women's sizes for you and a Childs for Ben. I will fit them on you when we get home." LJ get a hold of Hank and have everyone that did anything on this mission, I think they call it a case here tonight for debriefing, and I don't think we should include the District Attorney on this one, let Hank decide."

Jennifer, Ben and I are going to have lunch, LJ you still got the keys?" LJ: "on the board." Jennifer, Ben, and JB left and drove to the diner. They got out of the car and JBs Dad pulled up in the van. Dad said, "Hi thought I would have lunch with you." They went into the diner and sat in a booth, JB put his dad on the side facing the door and Jennifer on the other side and he sat next to his dad.

Jennifer: "why do you always sit this way?" JB: "Because I want to see who comes and goes and if there is a stranger, force of habit, it has kept me alive for 10 years." The waitress came over and brought menus and water for all. JB said, "We are celebrating so order whatever you want." Ben said: "Me too?" JB: "Yes but it can't be all ice cream and cake." Ben with a sad look: "All right." He was not too happy with that but he got into ordering and all was forgotten.

Dad: "Well that went as planned did it not?" JB: "like clockwork and we were lucky none of them tried to martyr them self's, It also looks like we got a lot of information to work with." Dad said, "I am glad no one was hurt real bad." JB said, "Yes this was much better than what they had planned for me." The waitress came back and took their orders. They chatted a little and the food came and they ate in silence. When they finished their meal they left for the park.

LJ had set the debriefing for 7:00 pm. JB and Jennifer sat and started to talk about where they would live, Mom and Dad said they may move into the spring house and let us have the big house or they will just build a smaller one behind the big house instead of the spring house as LJ or CR might want to live there. And whoever is left can build close and tunnels will be attached to all of them and we will make the center space bigger to have room for all." Jennifer: "That is interesting, that way all our family will be together. JB: "What about your mom and dad, would they want to move here too." Jennifer: "No they like it where they are, they will come and visit or we will visit them." JB: "Whatever you decide will be all right with me."

Ben said "Can we go play pool." JB: "Not today but I could read to you." Ben said " I will go get my book." He was gone in a flash and then was back. JB read to Ben and Jennifer sat close to JB and thought this is what I dreamed about all these years. After reading for a while, JB said "Ben have you had any more trouble at school?" Ben: "No we are all friends now; I guess they don't want you beating up their dads." JB: "I guess I will have to go to school and calm their fears." Jennifer smiled; she thought life was going the way she wanted.

It was 6:45 and JB said I have a meeting to go to I will see you later. Jennifer: "Ok I'll be here." JB got up and went out the door and locked it, and then he went to the office. LJ, CR, and JR were there and JB said "are we on the same page?" They all said "Yes." JB: "Do we know who will be coming?" JR: "Ahmad Emir Zafir." CR: "It is a shame, I'm sorry that we were not able to get him when we got his brother." LJ: "such is life." JB: "We will get him when he gets here as he will want to do it himself since the others failed; He probably thinks it will be easier here because we do not have a compound to protect us." JB: "I think he will go to South America and come north and across Mexico, to cross the border, I don't think he will bring anymore than two or three, it gets harder to sneak across with more people in the group, and a lot of them don't speak English or any other foreign language."

JB: "I hear cars the others are here." Hank came in with shadow, the two that were on the hill and three others. Hank said "For the ones of you who don't know everyone we will go around and say your name." JB: "JB" LJ: "LJ." CR: "CR" RJ: "RJ." BILL: "BILL I am on the detective squad." Carl: "Carl I am on the detective squad." One of the men on the hill said " My name is Quincy and I am volunteering for the Swat Team." The second man from the hill said "My name is Sam and am volunteering for the Swat Team." The last man said, "My name is Curt and I am volunteering for the Swat Team."

JB: "if you are interested in how good the bulletproof vests are come up here to the table and look at my vest and the bullet in it." They all came up and looked and one said "that looks like it will do the job." JB: "that was from a rifle that is capable of doing 1200 yard shots effectively, at close range a 9 mm will knock you down but will not go through, now we will start the debriefing."

JB said, "WE will start with myself and go thru what I did during the mission." JB went through every detail up to the time LJ came into the picture. LJ started with the Flash from the barrel up to the point he got JB on the bench. CR started at the point he heard the shot and went to the finish when Hank arrived. JR started at the point when the man picked up around and went for the mortar and though everything to the time the terrorists told all he knew. Then Curt went through everything to the end of the Interrogation. Quincy went through everything to the end of the Interrogation. Bill and Carl went through everything they did on the stake out.

"it looks like we did a great job on this. What is the time frame on this next Arab coming over?" Hank, JB: "We figure six to eight week's tops. Which is bad in that the park will be filled with people every weekend 4 weeks after that every day. The good thing is we will have four to six weeks training on the Swat team, and I am trying to find at least two bomb sniffing dogs in the next two weeks. LJ, CR, and RJ will go out and look at the dogs and CR and JR will train with them before they come here." LJ said, "Betty told me she though she found a trainer who had four for sale and ready to train with a handler and how to work with them when we bring them home." JB: "LJ, CR. RJ be ready to leave tomorrow." RJ get a hold of your wife and tell her I will be there to pick her up on Friday, and the movers will be there Thursday to get all your belongings. Hank would one of your swat guys want to handle a dog, if so RJ can go to his family. I did not want to commit any of your people." Hank looked and said, "Anyone wants to handle a dog." Curt said, "I would like a dog and I can leave anytime." Hank said "I have a feeling you are going to keep two of the dogs at the park?" JB: "Yes I have to check a large area because of the number of people." Hank: "I understand I would like to have at least 4 dogs in the area and I know if we need you, you will come, so if you get any call backs let me know and I will see if anyone else is interested. JB: "Betty said there were four dogs available, so if you have somebody else have them here in the morning." RJ said "well I will leave tomorrow and take care of my family." Hank has the District Attorney said anything about today." Hank: "Yes he said it looks like we all did what needed to be done and there should be no repercussion, he is more than pleased and will be happy when Homeland gets here and takes the prisoners away." I did not tell him about the new Arab, we will let him calm down first." JB: "Hank I have two vests for the women and we can order more if necessary. There are also two vests for JR's boys and we can order another woman's if you want RJ. RJ: "Yes I want one." JB: "I will get one overnight and it will be here when you get back." JB: "anyone has anything to say or ask," no one said anything. JB: 'it was a pleasure to work with all of you I am very excited to start our Swat training next week, good night and I will see some of you tomorrow." LJ, RJ, and CR moved the table and chairs back where they belonged, while JB put notes in his phone for plane tickets and to start the 300 yard range. LJ, CR, and RJ went to the big house and JB headed to the spring house, he was feeling his back, just a little pain, and he put it out of his mind and thought about Jennifer and Ben. He opened the door and they were waiting for him to come home, Jennifer had been reading to Ben and he had fallen asleep. JB picked him up and carried him to his room, Jennifer pulled back the covers and JB put him down gently on his bed. Jennifer covered him up and they shut his door on the way out.

Jennifer took his hand and they went to couch and sat down. Jennifer said "this was a hard day I was worried all day long and I was almost hysterical." JB: "I should have told you that I was all right, I was not thinking and I am sorry, I am not used to telling other people about my condition, I will make sure that I do that because we are going to have at least one more of these to worry about. One of the phones had made calls to Afghanistan and I know who the man is and he will be here within 4 to 6 weeks which will give us time to get ready. I will understand if you would like to get out until this is over."

Jennifer: "I said "I am in this to the end, I let you get away once I will never leave you again until death do us part." JB put his arms around her she put hers around him and squeezed JB winced and Jennifer let go. She said "I am sorry I didn't think." JB: "It's all right I forgot already and it talked to me so I will be a little more careful." JB to change the subject he said "Have you thought of where you want to live here, Big House or build one?" Jennifer: "Are you changing the subject?" JB: "Yes I have had enough of it for one day, but if you would like a blow by blow tomorrow I will give you the whole mission as I controlled this, so you must never tell, my mother and dad will never hear a word of it because it never happened and if it got out I could go to prison." Jennifer: "No don't tell me."

JB: "The official story is they think someone on the hill was shooting on the hill and missed what they were shooting at and the bullet came down I just happened to be there and luckily all the energy on the bullet was gone and it just cracked a rib so no one was hurt bad, just a freak accident and the person does not want their name released." Jennifer: "It must have hurt?"

JB: "Yes it was like getting hit by a truck one second I was doing my turn away and the next thing I knew I was on the ground on my back and dazed, I saw a man I knew in the service and he had a camera in one hand and a gun in the other, for a second I couldn't move then adrenalin kicked in I raised my gun and there was two bangs and he went down LJ and I fired almost at the same time so even if I had not been able to fire the man would have never got off a shot, he was so fixed on me he never saw LJ. He was an X Seal and he made mistakes all the time and he got one of our men killed and I court marshaled him and all four of us gave testimony against him, and he was given a dishonorable discharge which ruined his life, people usually don't hire men who are discharged with that, he vowed he would find us and kill us, well that didn't happen.

We are still one step ahead of them, I am sure they are thinking we will not be looking for them, that was the only smart thing he did was leave a man behind to inform them overseas or it just happened that way and this guy is an Arab and Hank has two detectives looking for him, and we think he doesn't know we even know he is here."

Jennifer" It scares me to death that I will lose you now that I got you back." JB: "I will never take a chance that I don't have at least an 80% chance of winning and we plan very carefully and that is why we got through so many missions and because we were so good we always got the real bad guys because they knew if we couldn't do it they would have to come up with a new plan, and we never did their plan we got what we were to do and we devised our own because we did not think they were as careful as we were because they weren't going to be there and we always found holes in their plan so after a lot of missions they would give us the objective and all the info and they went with our plan. That is why we were so good and they would not disagree with any part of the plan that we came up with, I told them we are in this together so each of us likes the plan or it gets changed until, we all have something to contribute, why would I not want to use an asset, they couldn't get past the rank thing, when bullets are flying all around and people are trying to kill you there is no rank, just the man next to you who is willing to die for or with you, that is what made us the best, we very rarely took anyone else except on easy missions and only the best got to go on another. That is why we are all here between the four of us we cover all bases, and that is why we are all here, we were not happy with the way the Navy was changing so when dad got sick and I had to quit we got together and I told them I was not going to extend my enlistment.

Mine was the first to come up and we were about to all get out any way so this was as good a time as any we all said we were not going to reenlist and we sat down and made our plan I had told them that they could work at the park and that we are brothers and probability closer than most brothers and that there was room at the park to build homes next to my parents as they know how close we are and if their parents want to move here we would help them any way we could to make it happen. That was the plan I came home with a little less than 3 weeks ago as I had leave I had not used and I saw a sign about a free concert at the city park and while the band was playing some fool planted what we call a flash bang all smoke and noise no damage to make people aware of the Terrorists threat in this country, his intention was a good idea but his method was stupid, I was real close and as the people ran away I ran to the spot and looked for the person with a satisfied look all bomb makers do that, as I did I spotted him, and I grabbed him and scared him and I thought he was going to cry, but I gave him things to do and to tell anyone that asks to say some body dropped a cigarette in a box of fireworks that were to be set off later as a surprise. But some reporter decided to make a name for herself and fabricated a story to make her famous and got 3 people killed and 3 that will never be seen again. That is when I called dad to have him call the hospital and to have them hire an ER nurse that had a lot of experience from a big city as they see everything almost as much as a front line nurse and that is what happened at the park. Dad said he would call them right away and was sure they would honor his request as the park is one of their biggest donors. Then I said "I had to go back to base tell the guys what has happened here and are they coming or do I make a new plan. They said "we are brothers and we stick together no matter what, and it will keep us sharp. So we made a new plan and I canceled my leave so I would get paid for it and I have a lot of money in the credit union as I didn't really need much as I didn't go out much except with the guys and we never got drunk as we always wanted full control of our actions, no stupid stuff." I guess I am a lucky man as you answered the ad and was an exact fit for what I told them to look for."

Jennifer: "You seem to be at the right place at the right time." JB: "I think God has a plan and some time we deviate from it or maybe we were supposed to so we would make better decisions and he will always do what is best for us." Jennifer: "I had been looking for an opening here for the last 6 months because I wanted to come back here to be close to you and my parents and I hoped you weren't married, I didn't want to cause a problem in case you were married and I didn't want your parents to think I was trying to get money out of anyone I just wanted Ben to know his father if he could as you might still hate me for walking out on you, that was what was in my mind and when you offered to let me stay in the spring house, I all most grabbed you and kissed you I was so happy, but I got control and said I would think about it as I didn't want you to think I was too eager. I have missed you so much and I decided that I had to get a trade and support myself as I thought you hated me for just walking out on you, so maybe God did make this work out."

JB: "I want you to understand that this is the last I can tell you as this next one will have the government all over it but we will use our plan or there will be a problem. Tomorrow I will call my old co and inform him of the situation and who is on his way and the navy can't operate on US soil and neither can the army unless we are at war and our country is invaded, that means homeland security will want to take over and I will not let them get me killed as I know they are not as good as we are, and I am going to have him recommend that they let us lay out the plan as we have had more than 300 missions and not one failure that was our doing, it was all of the targets didn't show, and eliminating Terrorists was our job. So this is why I never dated anyone because it would not work and I was still in love with you anyway."

Things like missions I can't tell you, other things are an open book; I don't do things I might be ashamed of later. Jennifer said "I believe you were always like that my parents said you were the best young man they ever met, what you see is what you get, and my dad said if more people were like you we would not have wars; I am glad we had this talk and I am confident you will care for us." JB: "that is why I told you about the tunnel as it will survive everything that the Terrorists may build but a direct hit from a bomber and as far as we know they don't have any of them yet and all sales of old bombers is highly investigated."

JB: "I have to go to bed as I have to get up and run, the doc gave me some pain pills if it got bad and I told him I have to stay in shape because you never know when you have to perform, he said take one 20 minutes be for I start", Jennifer: "What did he give you?" JB reached in to his jacket pocket and handed her the bottle. She looked at it and said "that should work and it has no narcotic, so you can drive." JB: "I told him I had to be in full control all the time' and he said working out will take longer for it to heal, I said life is life, you take it as it comes, someone once told me if you are not falling down you are not learning anything new." Doc said "He would have to remember that, there is so much wisdom in that, thank you for sharing."

Jennifer leaned over and kissed him again and got up and went to bed after fixing his bag. JB said "The doc is real impressed with you, he said "you are the best he has ever seen, thought you might like to know." JB though someone once told me that if you put castor oil on things it made them heal quicker, he got out his phone and put a note to get some castor oil, he would need all the help he could get.

He thought about his talk with Jennifer and it seemed to go well and her mind was now at rest, so hopefully she won't worry so much, he needed her to be strong as things will get beyond their control in the future. JB crawled into his sleeping bag and tried to get comfortable, his back was going to be a pain.

CHAPTER 14

FRIDAY WEEK 2

JB woke at 5:00 am and took a pain pill then put on his running suit and then he went thru the tunnel and waited for his guys to come down. 5:20 am LJ, CR, and JR came down and JR: "How you doing boss?" JB: "We will see in a few minutes." And they went out and started to run and they got back in 20 minutes did their 50 pushups and 100 crunches. JB was sweating and looked very uncomfortable but he said nothing. JB said "I will get cleaned up and take Jennifer to work and Ben to school and meet you at the diner and we will make sure we have our bases covered on what we know, see you in 40." They went upstairs and JB went through the tunnel and took a shower and got dressed. Jennifer and Ben were eating breakfast and Jennifer said "Would you like something?"

JB: "No I am going to meet the guys after I drop you two off at the diner but thanks." Jennifer smiled and said "How was the run." JB: "Pill worked fairly well for the run, the pushups and crunches were a different story." Jennifer and Ben finished and JB cleaned the table while she got Ben and herself ready and they left. Jennifer put Ben in the back and made sure he was buckled in and she got in the front and JB started the car and they left to start their day.

Betty called and said "they have four dogs." JB: "tell them we will take all of them, call Hank and tell him that we got four, bye." JB let Jennifer out at the front door and said "We will continue to change doors in a random order as there is still one Arab we didn't get, so keep alert don't you let your guard down, you do and you vanish, I can't lose you now." Jennifer: "I love you." JB: "I love you and Ben." She smiled and turned and went into the hospital. JB drove and took Ben to school and took him to class, said to his teacher don't let him leave the room unless you all go." The teacher said "That is a strange request." JB: "There has been a threat made against the hospital employs, and you cannot tell that to anyone if it gets out I will pull Ben out of school and home school him and I will know you told because the hospital people will not tell anyone because they want to catch this person, he does not know we know about him so he will be caught, within a month to 6 weeks." The teacher: "I can do that and he is a good little boy."

JB: "Thank you very much." And he left. JB went to the diner and took the booth in the back and 5 minutes later his team and his Dad came in and sat down. One minute later the girl that wanted a dog came and joined them. LJ got a chair from another table and gave it to her, she said "Thank you" and she sat down. JB: "I think we all know each other." They all nodded yes. JB said "four of you will be gone until next week stay until you are comfortable with your dogs and you can handle them in your sleep. I will have Betty get a layout for a training area to work the dogs and I hope maintenance will have it done by the time you get back. They are working on the 300 yard range today and the target stands should be here today or tomorrow, it will be done before the end of the week. JR will be with his family by the end of the day. They will pack tomorrow." JR: "The movers got there yesterday after noon and started packing and my wife was very pleased with them." JB: "JR do you want us to find you an apartment or stay at the big house until your wife finds one, my Mom can go with her or you can have a house built near the big house where mine is going to be." JR: "I will let her decide, I would like to be next to all of you, the same as it has been." The waitress came and took their orders and left and they got back to business.

LJ: "We still don't know if the Arab has shown up yet." The girl Mary said "as of last night he has not been seen, the chief said when he does he will call right away, as he wants you all to take care of that as you have been doing it for so long and he said that mission on the hill was the slickest thing he has ever seen, and what you did was unbelievable and it worked just like you said it would." CR: "Our secret is no one person can think of everything so we all agree or we make a new plan and if we all have not come up with something we have missed something and we go back to the drawing board, we are all equal no matter the rank that was JB's rule." JB: "Is there anything we have missed?" CR: "Keep us informed on the Arab and if you need help, call us." JB: "We should be safe until you all get back and I don't think the big guy will be here any sooner than 4 weeks, I think closer to 6 weeks. I plan to wear my vest and be armed at all times, and Hank has issued conceal and carry until you are officially sworn in to the police dept., we will do that when you come back, Betty has them at the office, so don't forget them." The food came and it got quiet as they consumed their food. JB's Dad smiled, he went from one son to a daughter in law and four sons a grandson and two more on the way and another daughter, life can sure surprise you.

JB got in his car and the rest in the van and they went to the office. When they were all in the office Betty handed out conceal and carry permits, boarding times and check in. Also she gave LJ, CR, credit cards to cover their expenses. All their luggage was in the van so all they had to do was unload and go. JB said "Check in and let me know how it is going, this company had very good reviews, the police departments that had their dogs said they will buy from them again." They all said good bye and they got in the van and left. JB: "I am going to check in on the range and we need to get a price on a dog training facility to keep the dogs up to peek performance, the dog training people should have something so we know where to start." Betty replied. "I will get right on it."

JB left and got in the car and drove up to the back lots. They were near the gun range and the city had donated land to house the new additions that were going up. These had to be up and functional in four weeks. JB got out of the car and looked at the range it was coming along nicely; they were putting in the target holders. JB was pleased; it was nice to have good workers you could rely on. JB got back in the car and went to the office. He went in and Betty said "The dog people have a crew that will come out and erect a compound and it will be done when the dogs get here they just need the dimensions so they have enough material to get the job done." JB: "Did they have recommendations?" Betty: "Yes for the number of dogs you have they recommended 100 yards by 200 yards." JB: "How much?" Betty: "25,000 and that is everything including devices Instructional videos and they are on call for the next 6 months for any questions you might have." JB: "Go ahead and have them start, Hank will get the permits Issued and when can they start." Betty said "It would take four days to get the materials on site and they start the next day. And if you have people that can help it will go quicker, they are sending 6 men." JB: "Maintenance will be done with the range tomorrow so that will be done. When are they to start on the room clearing house." Betty: "The prebuilt walls will be in by Monday afternoon the footers will go in Monday morning and should be set so construction can start on Tuesday." JB got out his list.

List for Park

Task	Start	Finish	Person	Out Come
Gang control	1st-3rdmo		LJ-CR-JR	
Grounds	1st week		LJ when arrives here	
Maintenance	End of 1mo		JR	
Security	1st mo		CR-JR-LJ	
First Aid Station	1st-2nd mo		CR-JR	Building 10,000
Equipment and supplies 3,000 budget 15,000 2,000 under budget				
Long range	Started wk 2		LJ-CR-JR	
Survival School	1-4 mo		JB-LJ-CR-JR	
House Clearing	3rd wk		LJ-CR-JR	

SWAT Training	3-6 WK	JB-LJ-CR-JR	
Unexpected problem - terrorists		LJ-CR-JR	1st group eliminated
Dog training comp	3rdwk	outside	
Dogs Trained	3rdwk	LJ-CR	

The list had grown but looked good as things were getting done and new things had not got anything else out of order. JB was happy: "Betty I am going to get Jennifer and Ben, see you later." JB got in the car and went toward the hospital he saw a car that had followed his to close, so he turned and pulled over and went in to the store and got some note books. Went to the check out and paid and walked out the door and got in his car and got back in traffic he stopped for a light and called Hank. Hank answered: "JB here, have you got someone on me?" Hank: "No I wasn't going to do that until we found the Arab." JB: "Ok I have one where are your guys looking for the Arab?" Hank: "Near the apartment." JB: "I will call Jennifer and tell her to wait I will pick up Ben first so plant your guy before the school it is a green ford I will bring him buy in 15 minutes, I will make another stop and get something that looks natural for me to get." Hank: "OK he is on his way." JB pulled in to a gas station and filled it up and then went in and bought some flavored drink, and some crackers and came out with everything in a bag. Got in the car and drove off on his way to pick up Ben. He drove down the street to the school and the green ford was still behind him. He got out of the car and went in to the school, and the green ford pulled past and parked across the street and down half a block. JB though Ben will be safe as the position of the car is not good for shooting. JB got Ben and they left. He gave Ben the crackers and drink and Ben was real happy. He drove past the ford and turned for the hospital he called Jennifer and said get a security guard to walk you to the emergence exit and walk behind the ambulance I will pick you up there. As JB pulled up to the exit the ford pulled into the regular lot and drove around trying to find a spot. Jennifer got in and JB pulled out and headed for home, then he said "Jennifer you need anything from the store?" Jennifer: "Not really but if you want something we can stop." JB thought about it and decided don't push your luck he may realize you are onto him.

JB called Hank. Hank: "It is the Arab and someone else Billy got pictures and he and Carl will follow them and see where they go." JB: "What about the address we got from the terrorist on the hill has that been looked at yet? Hank: "No." JB: "Thanks let me know, bye." JB turned and pulled in to the park and drove to the spring house. Let Jennifer and Ben out and said "I will be back later." And he drove to the office.

JB went in the office and Betty said "Everything is set to go on the dog area, so things should go smoothly." JB called Hank. Hank: "Hello." JB: "Any more from our friends?" Hank: "They drove to a different apartment complex and they went in. Bill and Carl will have to make other arrangements as there is no place to park and not be noticed. But that is my problem, we will work it out, we can rent and send radio cars in to follow." JB: "Why not use the same ones we used on the hill, that way if they have a scanner we won't show up on the regular channels." Hank: "Good idea I will pick up 4 or 5, thanks." JB: "I had another thought is anybody checked on the owners of the van that they were using you know the convenience store?" Hank said " no I forgot about that I'll get some surveillance there." JB: "see what I mean about two heads are better than one, bye." JB: "Betty will you pick up a couple bottles of castor oil for me?" Betty: "On my way home, you will have them tomorrow." JB: "I am going home as it has been a long day, see you tomorrow." JB got in the car and drove to the spring house. He got out of the car and went inside and locked the door and shut the shades. He went in the kitchen and sat down on one of the kitchen chairs and looked at Jennifer and said "How was your day." She smiled "Kind of slow." JB: "I am going to have to send you some pictures of bad people and if you see any of them run to a secure room that you can barricade yourself in and don't come out until I come for you, that is for any reason, I don't care how many people they shoot you stay in the room. Understand?" Jennifer looked at him in Disbelief "you really mean that." JB: "Yes my life depends on it; If you can't do that I will keep you home until this is over, and that will include JR's family as well, I am not up to full strength, and until I do get there or the guys are back, that's the way it is." Jennifer: "I will have to think about that." JB: "You don't have to think, it is a yes or no; and you will stay here anyway." JB: "When people think about something they talk themselves out of the right answer and they end up dead, I have seen it a 100 times." JB: "Could you get me a glass of water so I can take a pill?" Jennifer: "I will fill the tub and I want you to soak in zero gravity and get the pain of your back down to a better level you have been suppressing it all day, right?" JB: "I guess I have but my decisions under pain have been good for ten years, I am still alive, I have beaten the odds."

Jennifer went to the bathroom and started to run the water and she went and helped JB up and they went to the bath room, she helped him undress and get in the tub. He relaxed and floated and she could see the pain start to go down. "If the water gets cold before I come back yell and I will make it hot again, you need 30 minutes of hot." She went back in the kitchen and thought I will have to monitor his pill taking so we don't have another one of these.

Ben came in the kitchen and said "Is Daddy all right?" Jennifer: "Yes he is just tired he had a big day and he is hurt but mommy will make him well." Ben: "I really like having a real Daddy of my own." Jennifer went and checked the water and it was cooling off and JB said "turn on the pump and heater and the water will stay warm, even get hot." Jennifer: "I don't want you to get to week as I don't think I could get you out by myself." Jennifer called his Dad and asks 'If he and Mom would come over and help with JB."

They came out of the basement 5 minutes later and she told them what happened as JB had gone into shock, and she had him in the tub as he was not taking his pills and she had to get him to relax or call the ambulance and put him in the hospital. JB was looking better when they went into check on him his face was not pale anymore and he seemed to be in a calmer state. Jennifer said "you did not take your pills today why?" JB: "I wasn't in pain." Jennifer: "You were but you suppressed it and the pills were to help you relax and help with the pain. If you are not going to take them I will have you admitted to the ER." JB: "Ok they are in my pocket right side." JBs Dad got the pills from JBs pants and gave them to Jennifer. She went to the kitchen and got a glass of water and he took his pain pills and the antibiotic also.

Jennifer got his pajamas and gave them to him and he came out with them on and he sat on the couch. JB: "I do feel a lot better I guess I went off didn't I." Jennifer: "Yes you did but I think we have it under control." JB's Mom brought some food from the big house and they ate it for supper. JB started to get up to clear the table and Jennifer said "No you don't you need to relax and let the pills work." They take awhile and JB's Mom and Dad went home and Jennifer read to Ben and JB just looked at his family and was very happy. He now had what he had been wanting and didn't know that was what he had wanted all the time. Jennifer put Ben to bed and came out and took JB into the bed room.

She said "I will come and wake you around 12:00 and give you pills and then you can sleep the rest of the night and you will not get up early and run and exercise. You need to rest a day or two and we need to see the results of your urine sample before you can push again. Are we clear on that?" JB: "Yes, are you going to be a bossy wife?" Jennifer: "Only if I have to." She had JB lay on his right side away from the damaged area and turned out the lights and closed the door and went out and lay down on the couch and covered up and went to sleep. JB woke up and Jennifer had a cup with pills and a glass of water. He swallowed the pills and drank the water and gave the cup and glass to Jennifer and said "Thank you." And went back to sleep. Jennifer went back to the couch and went to sleep.

CHAPTER 15

SATURDAY WEEK 2

JB woke up and Jennifer was coming into the bedroom with his pills and a glass of water. JB took the pills and drank the water. Jennifer asked "how do you feel today?" JB: "so far I feel pretty good but I haven't started to move around yet, thank you for taking care of me last night."

JB got up and he and Jennifer went into the kitchen Ben was there eating his breakfast Jennifer said "would you like some breakfast?" JB: "yes that would be nice thank you." They ate in silence and when they were finished. JB said "I would like you to castor oil pack me when Betty calls, she was going to get some last night." Jennifer "I will do that, when she calls." JB went over and sat on the couch while Jennifer cleaned up the kitchen. There was a knock on the door Jennifer opened it and there was Betty with castor oil. Jennifer said "thank you" and Betty went back to the office and Jennifer shut the door.

JB lay down on the floor and waited for Jennifer to come over. She brought the hot pad, the castor oil, and the pad that you put the castor oil on she pulled his shirt up and looked at his back and said your bruise is bigger. She laid the pad across his kidney and poured castor oil on it, put plastic over the pad to keep the castor oil from getting on the hot pad. 20 minutes later Jennifer took the hot pad off pulled plastic back and puts more castor oil on the pad then put the plastic back on then the hot pad back on. 20 minutes later she put castor oil on for the last 20 minutes put everything back and relaxed again. 20 minutes later she came again took everything off used a little soap and water and cleaned JB's back she looked at his back, it looked all right, she said "I'm really curious to see how quick this really heals, I know how quick I am used to seeing these heal. She went back to the kitchen and put the castor oil away and came back and Ben was sitting on the couch with JB next to him.

Ben said "mom what are we going to do today?" Jennifer said "I am going to take care of your father today so we'll have to see if grandpa wants to do something with you." Ben said "I would like that, he is teaching me to play pool just like he used to teach dad how to play pool." JB said "Dad will like that it brings back happy memories of when I was small, he and I didn't get to play as often as I would have liked because he had too much to do at the park." "I have some things I need to get done today."

Jennifer said "you are not going anywhere until I get the results back from your urine sample we need to know how badly hurt your kidney is. People die from damaged kidneys so we need to know how yours are before we go do any running around." Jennifer "I would be happy if you spent the weekend relaxing and healing." "Later in the day I will have an ambulance come over and we will take another urine sample, then we'll see how that looks to see how you're progressing." JB thought I didn't have to take chances like this over in Afghanistan but here I can see it's going to be different. I need to call Hank and see if we can rig something on the side of the hill up close to the top where the snipers were and do a little target practice with the SWAT guys when I get back because LJ and CR are going to be using the dogs looking for people with weapons and explosives JR can teach them how to shoot, the range will be open and we could maybe rig something so we could do some long shoots I think that would be a good idea to talk to him about that. Now I will have to have Betty check and see if there's any 600 yard ranges within 100 miles, so we can go out there and take a few shots so they can get used to long shots. I also need to put batteries up on the hill and the cameras and see who's been up there that's what my chores for the day were and that has to be done.

I will have Jennifer and Ben wear their bulletproof vests which would be good practice for them and then I can go armed and get dad to drive us up there and we will get that done in an hour or so. JB called Hank. Hank said "hello, how are you today?" JB: "not too bad, anymore on our friends?" Hank: "not yet we are going to rent an apartment across the street from them where we can see the front and we will get that done over the weekend and get them moved in so they can be monitoring and taking pictures, what have you got going for the day?"

JB "I am going up on the hill and change the batteries and download the pictures, we'll see if we have any new visitors up there on the hill." Hank: "good idea." JB: "I have another thought what if we hung a target holder over the hill for some long shots we could drop it down about 10 feet from the top even if they missed it would ricochet off and go nowhere that we have to worry about, but they should be able to hit that after we get them proficient on the 300 yard range." Hank "let me think about that, it might be possible." JB: "I will call you when I get the pictures and I will send them over to you and you can look them over." Hank: "sounds good talk at you later bye."

JB could think of nothing else he needed to get done today. JB called his dad and said "Dad can you drive us up on the hill to download pictures?" Dad "Yes that's not a problem, when do you want to leave?" "In about 20 minutes." Dad: "Okay see you later." JB told Jennifer to get the bulletproof vests for her and Ben and they would practice putting them on. JB got Jennifer's vest adjusted where it fit nice and then had her put on a shirt to cover it up, next he got Ben adjusted and had Ben put on a shirt to cover his up.

Jennifer said "are you going to make me wear this in public?" JB "yes there will be a time when you have to wear this in public and Ben also." "Today we are going up on the hill and you both will be wearing these, we are going to download some pictures from cameras and I want you to get into practice wearing your vests." JB "I am going to teach Ben how to walk quietly through the forest and we will sneak up on the cameras." Ben said "can I have a gun to?" JB "no not now you have a lot of other things to learn before you can carry a gun." JB's dad walked in the door and said "are you ready to go?" JB said "yes as soon as I get my pistol."

Jennifer said "is that really necessary?" JB "until this is over yes, we cannot let our guard down for a minute I don't want us to get complacent, that is when people get killed. I won't tell you how to heal me if you don't tell me how to protect you; we each have our skills, agreed." Jennifer "yes you have a point." Dad said "when are you two going to explain what's really going on here, I know there are things that we just don't know." JB looked at Jennifer how about we tell mom and dad this weekend?" Jennifer said "that is fine with me; we could do it tomorrow after lunch." Dad said "fine I will call mom and tell her and she will fix lunch for us tomorrow, are we ready to go up on the hill?" JB: "yes we are."

They walked out the front door JB locked it and they got in the van with Dad. Dad started the van pulled out and up the hill they went. Dad said "how far away from the first site you want me to stop?" JB said "about 3/10 of a mile." JB:"Jennifer you want to come with Ben and me?" Jennifer "no I'll stay here with dad." JB got out of the van grabbed Ben and they started walking down the road. 50 feet in front of the van they turned left and went into the woods Ben followed they vanished she couldn't see them anymore. She looked at JB's dad he smiled at her and said "the way they vanished surprised me just like you did, you see them and then they're gone."

JB and Ben were 5 feet into the woods it was extremely thick Ben was making a lot of noise, JB said "look where you are stepping you don't want to step on twigs and branches you want to step between" and he showed Ben how to do that. They walked about 20 feet straight ahead then turned right and they walked straight ahead again, Ben was getting the hang of it and was doing really good, he was hardly making any noise at all. Ben started to say something and JB shook his head and put his finger to his lips so Ben wouldn't talk. 200 feet farther JB could see the path heading to the cliff he stopped put his hand on Ben's shoulder and then he pointed to the trail and Ben shook his head yes he saw it. JB turned left they slowly walked beside the path very quietly making no noise 30 feet later they came to the first camera, JB changed the batteries, then downloaded the pictures closed the laptop and started walking farther through the woods toward the cliff. 300 feet farther they could see the opening it was empty nobody was there JB told Ben to stay right where he was and he went ahead and went to the left and retrieved the camera replace the batteries in the camera and placed it back up, downloaded the videos there wasn't much so it was a quick download.

Now they retraced their steps back through the woods, Ben was working real hard not to make any noise and so they came out a little bit in front of the van. They walked to the van JB put Ben in told Jennifer Ben did real good it won't take me long to make a real woodsman out of him, he works at doing things right Jennifer you've done a good job." They drove to the second site JB got out and Ben got out they went up the road about 30 feet turn left and vanished into the woods. JB watched as Ben worked at not stepping on any twigs he's also learned that he has to put his feet down very slowly on leaves or they would make noise he was doing really well JB was proud, they went about 40 feet turned left and then they could see the opening, they went down circled around the opening and came to where the camera was hidden, he changed the batteries and downloaded the video there was quite a bit of that so it took a while he closed up the laptop and they went back out the way they had come. Ben got back in the van, JB got back in the van, Dad proceeded until they came to the third site, that part was 300 yards away. JB said "Ben you sit this one out. JB got out of the van 20 feet down the road he was into the woods and gone. JB moved through the woods like a shadow came close to the path turned left and went parallel to the path all the way down to the cliff, JB changed the batteries in the camera by the cliff downloaded the videos and headed back up the path back into the woods, changed the batteries, downloaded the videos in the last camera on the site went back into the woods and came out in front of the van.

JB got back in the van and dad drove to the last site. JB got out of the van went into the woods paralleled the path till he got to the first camera change the batteries downloaded the videos and then walked to the clearing, it was empty he went to the other camera changed the batteries downloaded the video went back through the woods to the van. JB's dad drove farther up the road turned the van around and they headed home his dad dropped them off at the Springhouse and he went back to the big house.

Jennifer: "Was it fun in the woods." Ben: "It was hard but it was fun I thought I was an Indian going through the woods." JB called Hank: "I am going to download the videos I haven't looked at them yet but you go ahead and look at them if you see anything let me know and I'll go through it if I see anything I'll let you know." Hank said "sounds good I'll get back at you later." JB started the download and 10 minutes later it was done.

JB looked at the first site and the Arab was looking all over but he couldn't seem to find anything so the cleanup crew had really done a good job. There was a new guy with the Arab JB hadn't seen before but that may be the one that Hank had been talking about he would check that out later then he looked at the second camera at the second site that was nothing but kids so he passed through that then he went to the third site. The Arab was very careful about looking at everything he could not figure out why it had not worked JB could see him shaking his head and then they moved down the trail out of sight and that was the end of the video. The third site was the same way the Arab was very careful about looking at everything he could see where the mortar should have sat that there was no sign it had ever been there, he shook his head and went off back up the trail.

JB said "Jennifer I'm ready for my castor oil pack." Jennifer: "I will be with you in a couple minutes it's time for another pill round." And she came in with pills and a glass of water, JB took the pills and washed it down with water, then she had him lay on the floor she proceeded to set up the castor oil pack. JB laid on the floor for 20 minutes on his right side and then she came back put more castor oil on the pad put the plastic cover back on then the hot pad on, covered up with the towel and JB relaxed and 20 minutes later she did it all over again. 20 minutes later she came in and cleaned him up put the things away and ask how he felt? She said "that bruise is really getting smaller, how do you feel?" JB said "I feel pretty good a lot better than yesterday at this time." Jennifer said 'they are sending the ambulance over for a urine sample, the one yesterday had little traces of blood so we will see how it comes out today." JB said "Okay give me a cup and I will put something in it." 20 minutes later the ambulance came she filled the bottle and gave them the sample and they left. JB sat on the couch and Ben brought his book over and JB started to read to Ben, while Jennifer started supper. 20 minutes later Jennifer said, "Put the book down, come and eat."

They sat at the table. Jennifer reached her hands out and she grabbed Ben's and JB's and they grabbed each other's hands and she prayed. They each said "Amen" and then they started to eat. JB thought it was a lot like him and the guys having supper together but this was a little different something a little more special. Jennifer said "Go and sit on the couch and I will clean up from supper and then we can sit and talk a little bit. JB watched as Jennifer cleaned up out in the kitchen and he thought my life is sure going to be a lot different now I have a wife and child and more responsibility, JR had talked about that, you got a wife and kids it's not just you anymore now they come first and you come second, JB thought well I kind of understand now what he was talking about they become your whole world, he had enjoyed teaching Ben to walk in the woods, it had given him pride to watch Ben learn.

Jennifer came over and sat next to JB, "you look deep in thought" she said. "yes, I was thinking about teaching Ben to walk in the woods when we were up on the hill, I was so surprised and so proud he worked so hard to get it right; I've missed so much not getting to see him learn how to walk to learn to talk; there is a whole world out there I don't know about. Yes some of it's good, some of its bad, you can't even imagine how these people think over there in the Arab world, what we are going to be dealing with here in the next couple months, you have to learn how they think so you can figure out what they're going to do next and sometimes that's not a good place to be. We have been raised with a whole different set of values and until you see what they do you just can't even dream that anyone would do something like that because you wouldn't, they cut off people's heads they stone their women, for something that they feel has dishonored them, and there is a group of people that want to let people like that into our country, they have no idea and when they finally figure it out it will be too late." JB said.

Jennifer: "I will put Ben to bed and then give you your castor oil pack before you go to bed." She was gone for about 15 minutes, and then she went out to the kitchen and got the supplies for the castor oil pack. JB laid down on the floor and Jennifer pulled his shirt up and looked at his back and said "this bruise has really gone down today, Jennifer put the castor oil pack on JB's back and covered it up turned on the hot pad and over the next hour JB got his castor oil pack she then took it off cleaned him up and put the supplies back in the kitchen drawer. He went in the bedroom put on his pajamas she came in and gave him his pills he lay down on his right side and he went to sleep Jennifer went out, crawled up on the couch under the sleeping bag and went to sleep.

CHAPTER 16

SUNDAY WEEK 3

JB woke up Jennifer had come into the room she had the pills and the water, he downed the pills and handed the two glasses back to Jennifer and said "thank you." Jennifer: "how do you feel this morning?" JB: "I feel pretty good this morning, I hardly feel my back what does it look like?" Jennifer set the glasses down and came over and pulled up his shirt. She said "there is hardly any bruise left." She pushed on his back and said "how does that feel?" JB: "that didn't hurt at all." Jennifer picked up the two glasses and left the room saying "I'll start breakfast."

JB got dressed and went out to be in the kitchen with Jennifer, he pulled out a chair and sat down, and he watched Jennifer as she was fixing breakfast he felt like he was really a lucky man she had been the only girl he'd ever fallen in love with. Jennifer said "I don't want you to run until we get the results from the last urine specimen, if it's clear then you can start running again and exercising." JB: "that sounds good to me, I need to go back up on the hill and download the videos check the battery levels we should probably do that this morning and after that we can go to Mom and Dad's."

Jennifer said "do I have to go up on the hill too?" JB said "yes and you have to wear your vest and your going in the woods with me too." Jennifer: "why do I have to go in the woods?" JB: "because you need to learn to walk through the woods without making any noise in case you are caught out in the park and have to vanish while somebody's trying to catch you, you can move and they can't hear you, then you have a better chance of getting away. I can't be with you all the time, the Arabs aren't use to running through woods like we have here, and I want you to get some clothes that would blend better in the woods." Jennifer was done fixing breakfast and she went and got Ben up. They came back in the kitchen and sat down, Jennifer prayed and they all ate breakfast.

When they were done JB said "Ben will you go put your vest on and the jacket you had on yesterday, we are going for a walk." JB got up put his vest on and a camouflage shirt over it. And he put his shoulder holster and gun on and put a camouflage jacket on, and put two clips in the jacket pocket. JB said "we will be back in about 15 to 20 minutes." And he and Ben walked out the front door. As he closed the door he grabbed Ben's hand and moved quickly to the left now they were under the shadow of the tree standing next to the house. JB said "Ben do you know why we moved under the tree like this?" Ben: "no, why?" JB: "look up what do you see?" Ben: "limbs and leaves." JB: "right if you can't see beyond the limbs people can't see through the limbs at you, now you are hidden from them that way somebody who has a higher position then you, cannot hurt you, do you understand?" Ben: "if I can't see them then they can't see me."

JB: "that is close enough, if we get behind the trunk of a tree or behind a bush then we are harder to see understand?" Ben: "I think so." JB said "follow me and we'll see how it goes." JB moved from tree to Bush to tree to Bush and then stopped. JB took the binoculars and looked up toward the hill first he looked at the first site, he saw nothing there, then he looked at the next site nothing there, then he looked at the third site he thought he saw movement, I will have to check that site and see what the camera sees. Then he looked at the last site saw nothing there then he said "Ben I am going to show you how to look thought binoculars.

JB: "you have to hold the binoculars to where you can see with both eyes and only see one circle." JB showed him how to adjust the binoculars and bring them back together so he could adjust for his head size. Ben worked with it a little while and then said "I only have one circle." JB: "tell me what you see?" Ben said "I see the big hill and it's a lot closer." JB: "look for any bright or shiny things." Ben looked and looked and then he said "I see a couple of little shiny things." JB: "keep looking and then tell me how many more you see." Ben kept looking and JB could see him counting on his fingers, it made him smile. Ben finally said "I see four." JB said "that was pretty good for the first time, there are actually five, four is pretty good for the first time I'm really proud of you Ben."

JB took the binoculars and looked for himself, after about 10 minutes he thought he saw a little movement again. Yes I'll have to be careful up there on my downloading. I will not be able to put batteries in the cameras they should be good until tomorrow; I will download the video and see what's really going on up there. He and Ben went back to the Springhouse slipped in closed the door and locked it. Jennifer said "breakfast is ready come and sit at the table." They finished and JB said "I was teaching Ben how to use binoculars and I think I saw movement up on the hill so you two are not going up with me and I don't want you to leave the house and let's use the tunnel and go over with mom dad and I'll just do this alone."

Jennifer: "Okay we'll see you over at the big house when you get back, be careful." JB got his rifle put a clip in it and went out the front door slipped to the left went from tree to Bush just like he had with Ben until he got to a good spot where he could prop the rifle to hold it steady. And sit in a comfortable position so that things would not move as he studied where he thought he saw movement ten minutes later he saw the movement it was a rifle barrel moving the grass. So they are watching me again I'll have to let Hank know just in case I have to shoot one or we may want to go up and capture it.

JB called his dad and said "I'll be over in five minutes I think we got company on the hill again so it is just you and me going up, put your pistol on I don't want you up there unarmed, and I know you can point and shoot." JB got to the house and the van was running his dad was already in; JB opened the door laid his rifle down and jumped in the front seat with his dad. Dad backed up turned and headed for the hill. Dad said "you see something up there on the hill." JB: "yes I saw movement and I think I saw a rifle barrel that's why you're armed, we will have to go up real early in the morning probably between 2:00 and 3:00 but we are going to download now and see what's going on up there." They got about 300 yards from the first site, JB got out went into the woods walked about 100 feet opened the laptop and started downloading there wasn't hardly anything so it was done quickly and he went back to the van they drove to the next site. They did the same routine slipped into the woods one about 100 feet and started to download there wasn't much, so it downloaded quickly; he closed up the laptop and headed back to the van.

He drove to the third site and did the same thing all over again this time there was a lot of video, but the battery still showed 50% so we should be able to get pictures of today, he closed the laptop and headed back to the van. Dad drove to the fourth site, JB got out of the van about 50 feet down the road went left into the woods, he moved stealthily went about another hundred feet toward the rim opened the laptop started download the camera that was the closest camera and that didn't have much so it went quickly, he switched to the camera up on top there was a little more video up there which took a little longer, when he was done he closed up the laptop and went back to the van. Dad drove a little farther up the road turned around and they headed back for home.

While they were driving JB started looking at the videos when he got to the forth site there was an Arab and another guy he did have a rifle with a scope the other guy had a spotter scope but it seemed like the guy with a rifle would say things, the spotter would write down looked like time and what happened so I said well they are doing their homework I will have to tell Hank about this and we'll see if he has pictures of these people. After viewing all the video he shut the laptop up and they just pulled up to the big house.

JB grabbed his rifle out of the van and took it in the house while dad locked up the van and followed him in. JB said I'm going to call

Hank and download these pictures they will have them first thing in the morning and then I'm going to call my CO see if I can get a favor from him. JB got a hold of Hank and downloaded the pictures, and then he ask Hank to download all the pictures he had to him Hank said "yes he would connect him in about three minutes."

JB set the laptop up to receive and three minutes later the download started took about two minutes and he had everything then he closed up the laptop and called his old CO. He got an answer in three minutes he told his old CO what was going on and he would like to send pictures to see if there were any Terrorists that they had in their database that were here in his town he told him about the ones that they had taken out last week and he said that is confidential nobody in town even knows though. The CO said "they let you do that?"

JB: "they were happy to, they didn't have a clue how to proceed and we haven't set up their SWAT unit at all, homeland took the bodies and the ones we use for interrogation and they all vanished, remember when I told you the brother that we missed was coming over this is the group he is coming to meet up with so whether they have sent over some bomb makers we don't know but see if you have any of these on record and who they are and are they from over there or are they from over here or any information you might have would be fine I would like to keep homeland out of this until it's all over, I don't want them getting any of us killed."

The CO said "I will have one of my electronic guys call you tomorrow around nine and he will tell you how to start the download and I will get you all the information I can." JB said "bye." He went to visit with everybody else, he found them down in the game room sitting and chatting. Mom said "Hi we can't take this suspense anymore we want you to talk." JB said "well I guess we have time because it's an hour and a half before lunch."

JB: "you remember when I ask Jane to marry me right after I enlisted in the service?" Mom and dad both shook their heads yes. JB: "Well this is Jane." Dad said "I see a resemblance but Jane had a large nose?" Jennifer: "yes I did and I hated it. When JB asked me to marry him I was pregnant with Ben and I was scared to death we would get married something would happen to him and I'd be stuck with a child all by myself and then I had no skills. That was probably the dumbest thing I ever did but I was too immature and I was just afraid." Dad said "we would've helped you we would've taken care of everything for you." Jennifer: "I know that now but then I was an 18-year-old scared little girl, then when he told me he had joined the Navy I just couldn't think. So I ran, I enrolled in nurses training and mom and dad helped me and I got an apartment and I did well in school so they let me take breaks while I had the baby, mom stayed with me for the first year taking care of Ben, so I could put more into my nursing and helped with raising the baby. My mom and dad decided to move away because they wanted to live in a small town and there was a nice one 20 miles from here, and that is where they're living now.

About seven months ago I decided I want to move back to this town just in case JB ever came back I could see him and if he wasn't married maybe I could get to know him and see if he would be interested in a girl that had a small child. I guess it was just luck that I had everything they were looking for when the hospital decided to look for an emergency room nurse." Dad said "JB gave me all the criteria for an ER nurse because of an explosion in a park inside the city, so actually you are what he told them to get, and he even gave the timeframe of when you needed to get here." JB's mom said "we always liked you we thought you were the sweetest girl and we would've been happy to have you for a daughter-in-law, should we call you Jane or Jennifer?"

Jennifer: "no I'm Jennifer from now on and my first day here I took Ben over to the park to see the animals and the security guards were pestering me and who should walk around the bend in the path but JB, I gave him a help rescue me look and he did, he had them straightened out in less than 10 seconds, I was amazed and so happy I could have almost cried. And then he walked me to the restroom when I came out the guard was gone and he said he had to walk me back to where Ben was. I was so happy but I had to contain myself because I wanted to know if he was married or single had kids and I did not want to interrupt his life, or cause him any problems.

JB: "I came around the bend in the path and there was this poor girl surrounded by my security guards and looking scared and I thought this is ridiculous they're not supposed to be doing that so I went up and gave them my standard two options quit what they're doing and get back where they belong or get fired. Then I walked Jennifer to the animal barn. Then she told me about being hired at the hospital as the ER nurse and staying at the motel and I thought well that could get expensive, and there was something about her I wanted to see her again so I asked her if she wanted to use the Springhouse. She said she'd think about it and I gave her my number and thought I hope I see her again but you never know."

Jennifer: "I almost said yes that night but I didn't want to seem too anxious as he might think something was wrong so I didn't call till the next day." "Then he moved me into the Springhouse the day after that and shortly after that all the problems started and he said if I wanted to leave I can leave and he would put me somewhere else anywhere I wanted to go where I felt safe, and I thought I'm probably safer with him than anywhere else around and I was not going to lose him again so I said I'd stay. Then I found out he was not married no kids and I said no I'll stay through the whole thing I wasn't going to run out on him this time or any other time." "Then things were starting to get intense and I didn't want to wait too long and he not know he was a father and it seemed like he was taking a lot of chances and I thought maybe that would slow that up a little bit."

JB: "there was so much going on that I didn't want to many things all at the same time; so I said we should wait until after this was over but when we had to bring the district attorney in, it seemed like he was balking and I thought he should know that I have a lot at stake in this also and I think that pushed him over the edge so he would join the group, I didn't know how big a politician he was because that's what most of them are is politicians." Jennifer : "I am going to tell my parents tomorrow what we've told you today, as I have been talking to them and telling them that we are getting along really good so I think they kind of expect it, they knew why I came back."

JB's mom said "lunch should be ready, let's go out and eat." They went out into the kitchen and ate their lunch and visited and had a great time. JB, Jennifer, and Ben went through the tunnel back to the spring house. Jennifer said "it's time for another castor oil pack"; she went into the kitchen and got the supplies. JB lay down on the floor she put it on and they went through the hour-long routine. Jennifer read some chapters to Ben in the book and then put him to bed. JB said "I'm going to bed early because I have to get up at 2 o'clock." Jennifer: "I will wake you up at 12 and give you the pills, then you don't have to take any until in the morning and then you don't have to take the antibiotics anymore, I was reading to Ben and the hospital called and said there were no traces of blood in your urine so your kidneys have a complete bill of health, that castor oil must be good stuff because I've never seen anybody have bruised kidneys and recovered this quick." She went and got JB's pills with a glass of water he took them, and told her she should sleep in the bed tonight, he'll sleep on the couch. She said "fine and went to bed." JB lay down on the couch and went to sleep.

CHAPTER 18
MONDAY WEEK THREE

JB put on his vest, and then his holster checked the Glock and put it in the holster, put on his jacket and went outside. His dad was already in the van and had it running. He laid the rifle in the back and they left to go up the hill. 12 minutes later they were at the first site, JB got out and went away from the van turned left and went into the woods when he got close to the path he turned left and paralleled the path until he got to the camera, the batteries were still at 30% so he downloaded and then put in new batteries turned and went back out to the road, he did the same routine for the rest of the cameras they were done in 30 minutes 12 minutes later they were off the hill. JB looked at the videos on the way down and thought he could save battery life by going into single pictures on movement, they wouldn't have to change the batteries as often yet they still should get the pictures they were looking for.

Then he thought I wonder if they have an external battery pack that will last longer and is rechargeable I will have to check on that when I go into the office. His dad locked the van and he waved goodbye and went into the big house, JB headed for the Springhouse. He opened the door, went in quietly closed and locked the door and turned, there was Jennifer sitting on the couch. JB took off his jacket, took the clip from the rifle, took the cartridge out of the chamber, then he did the same procedure with the pistol and put them up on the top shelf closed the closet door and went over and sat down next to Jennifer.

Jennifer said "how did you feel up there any pain?" JB: "no pain I felt pretty good things went very smoothly." JB: "are you worried about me?" She said "yes." JB: "over there I had thousands of people that wanted me dead over here I have 8 to 12, I had the best team the Navy SEALs had, JR will be back Wednesday the other two Friday or Saturday then the team will be complete again. If you would like I will show you the videos of what they're doing up on the hill and I will explain to you what they are doing and then you can better understand what is going on. They are in what is called the information phase where they try to get my movements so they can predict where I'll be at any point in time, but that won't work real good for them because everything I do is on a different schedule because I do different things every day the only thing that is constant every day is when I take you to work and drop Ben off at school and then come and pick you both up."

Jennifer: "maybe you shouldn't take us to work and school, and pick us up." JB: "that makes you too vulnerable they can stage an accident where a car pulls in front of you where you can't miss them, a van pulls up people grab you and Ben jump back in the van and they're gone now I'm really vulnerable because they know I'm going to come for you and they now control the situation." She says "they would do that?" JB: "yes they would, these people drive themselves in cars and blow themselves up to kill lots of people, and do you understand what I am saying?" Jennifer: "I think I do it is just this is all so new."

JB: "they would not do that with me because they know I will shoot back and I will have the advantage, they need to be able to show my head so they won't blow me up and in heavy traffic there's too many people around so that really won't work in my case." JB: "you are fairly safe at the hospital because they expect police around an emergency room because they know criminals are brought in all cut up so that doesn't give them the advantage they want, they want things easy their cowards at heart. Let's say you're starting your day nobody has come to the emergency room yet what do you do?"

Jennifer: "we make sure that we have supplies and equipment, blankets, and bandages so were ready." JB: "that is your information phase you make sure that you have everything you need so when it hits the fan you can take care of everything that needs to be taken care of does that make sense." Jennifer: "I never quite thought of it that way but that does makes a lot of sense, I guess it's your perspective."

JB: "if you are not prepared you cannot do as good a job as if you are prepared and basically were doing the same thing you do, only your saving people and were eliminating them." JB: "you're upset because I got shot, had I been a split second quicker the bullet would've missed me entirely but that's what the vest was for, even if I had passed out LJ would have killed the other seal our bullets were so close together neither one of us knows which one of us shot first so if I had hit my head on something and passed out it wouldn't have made any difference you understand that." Jennifer: "I guess when you explain it that way it doesn't make me as nervous but you are taking risks."

JB said "more people in this country are killed in automobile accidents, than are shot and killed." Jennifer: "are you sure about that?" JB: "yes I looked it up on the Internet and I think you should do the same, I think the figures will surprise you." Jennifer: "let's go to bed I want to be close to you so you come with me." JB got up and followed Jennifer into the bedroom, they hugged and kissed and fell asleep in each other's arms. JB woke up Jennifer was gone he could hear the shower running so he got up and went out and sat on the couch. Jennifer came out of the bathroom wrapped in a towel and came over kissed him on the cheek smiled and went into the bedroom, JB got up grabbed his clothes and he went into the bathroom took a shower shaved was ready for the day.

Jennifer was in the kitchen she had gotten Ben ready for school and she was fixing breakfast. They sat down together; Jennifer said Grace and they ate their breakfast. Jennifer said "what are we doing today?" JB: "we are staying home I'm going to take you up on the range and you're going to shoot some more I want to make sure you can hit the two inner circles all the time." JB's phone rang it was LJ. JB: "how is class going?" LJ: "real good these dogs are awesome it's amazing what they can do." JB: "that's good we got friends up on the hill again but there's only two this time." LJ "Do I need to come back?" JB: "No and I am back to 95%, it is really fairly quiet so you guys continue and learn all you can, JR said he'd be here on Wednesday and Hank has surveillance going on the Arabs in town. The construction crew from the dog people will put the compound up starting tomorrow and that will be done when you get back"

LJ: "the training people have a dog that the guy's wife didn't like, the dog. pasted every test at 95% or better on all the training tests but the dog is small weighs about 25 to 30 pounds so they said we can have the dog at half price so I told him to send it to you if you don't like it send it back but they thought this would be a good asset as he can get into places the bigger dogs can't and he does not look like a dog sniffer." JB: "when is this dog supposed to show up?"

LJ said "they said you should get it today in the morning." JB asked "what am I supposed to do with this dog?" LJ: "they have instructional videos and instructions when you first get the dog they said don't let the dog out of the house without a leash on for at least the first week and let the dog have free run of the house and let him come and pick you, don't chase after him, if he has to go he'll go to the door and if you don't come over he will whine so you need to hook his leash on and take him outside other than that they are fairly easy to take care of, the local police here use their dogs all the time and from what I have seen I think they're quite good, I will check back with you and see how you're doing with the dog bye."

JB looked at Jennifer and said "LJ said hi and we're getting a dog today." Jennifer with surprise on her face said "A dog?" "yes somebody sent a dog back because his wife didn't like the dog and the dog never scored lower than 95% on all his tests but he's not very big he only weighs about 25 pounds and if we don't like him we can send him back and were getting him for half-price, so we may not make it to the range." JB informed her.

Jennifer with a stern look said "is he going to mess up the house?" JB replied "no, LJ says they're very clean and when they have to go, they go to the door and they whine we have to make sure he's on the leash for at least a week before we start letting him loose outside so Ben will have to be careful not to let him out without a leash; so for this first week I will be the only one to handle him, so if I go to the office I will take him with me."

JB called Betty at the office. Betty answered. And JB said "will you see if you can get rechargeable external battery packs for the cameras and if you can order 2 for every camera, and we are supposed to get a delivery of a dog, send him down here when he comes, thank you goodbye." JB called Hank and told him about the new dog coming in and then said "are you ready to receive the download for this morning?" Hank: "yes go ahead." JB started the download. JB said "I'm going to change the cameras from video to single pictures on movement that way the downloads will not be so big and I think we will get what we want anyway and the batteries will last longer." Hank agreed, the download finished so JB said "goodbye" and they hung up. JB's CO called about twenty minutes later and said "a Sgt. will call you in about ten minutes and walk you through the upload." JB said "thanks Sir I will be waiting for the call goodbye." ten minutes later JB's phone rang: "hello this is JB." This is Sgt. James the CO told me to call you about an upload." JB said "yes Sgt. I have my laptop here and it is already to go."

The Sgt. walked JB through the codes and instructions he had to put in, five minutes later the upload was done; JB thanked the Sgt. and hung up. A half hour later the front doorbell rang, JB went over and opened the door there was a delivery guy with the dog. JB took the crate and set it on the floor and then signed for the dog, he thanked the deliveryman and shut the door. There was a packet strapped to the crate and JB opened the packet and there were the videos and instructions on how to handle the dog, plus a 10 foot leash.

JB read the instructions, and then opened the front door on the crate and out came the dog. He shook himself looked around came over and smelled him, then he went out in the kitchen and smelled Jennifer then he saw Ben on the couch and smelled him. Jennifer walked over and closed the bedroom doors so the dog couldn't go in there and then she sat down on the couch, JB went over and sat beside her and read through the instructions. JB told the dog to come and the dog came over and sat in front of him JB put his hand out and let the dog smell it, then he patted the dog on the head and the dog seem to like that then he went over and sat in front of the closet look to JB looked at the closet looked to JB looked at the closet.

JB: "I just think he showed me where my guns are." JB said I think we need to watch the videos he handed the instructions over to Jennifer and said "read these so we both know what they are." She read while BJ took the video that said basic instructions, he took it over to the player pushed it in turned on the TV and waited for the screen to come up. The first thing the video said "we try to make our commands very simple for the dogs and the people so when you want the dog to look for guns and rifles you just say gun and the dog will look for guns and rifles. You want to look for explosives you say bomb the dog will then look for any kind of explosive he can find. If you want to find somebody you let the dog smell some of their clothing or if you know where they have walked take them to the area and say search and let them look for scent and then they will follow it on the ground until they find the person or lose the scent. JB patted the dog for finding the gun and rifle and put them back in the closet and came over and sat on the couch and watched the rest of the video. The dog came over and lay by JB's feet according to the video that was a good thing.

JB said "do you have anything you need to get at the store?" Jennifer: "yes a few things." JB: "Okay we will go now as the dog will need to be fed he hasn't eaten since yesterday, and he probably needs to go to the bathroom so I will take him outside and let him relieve himself. JB put the leash on the dog got up walked to the door, opened it and went quickly outside, to the left where he was under the shade of the tree. Then he carefully went from position to position where he could not be seen until he got to a spot where the dog could go. He waited as the dog looked at everything smelled it and then relieved himself.

JB thought so far it's going pretty good. JB re-traced his steps back to the house put the dog in his crate. Then JB, Jennifer, and Ben got in the car and left for the store. Jennifer and JB both grabbed carts. She went for groceries, he went for dogs supplies. Following the recommendations that he had gotten, he went for the dog food that would be best suited; as well as some dog toys, and a bed. That way he could quickly acclimate the dog to his new home. Once he had everything he needed he headed to the checkout counter to meet Jennifer. Shortly after he had reached the checkout he saw Jennifer approaching with all the groceries they needed. They checked out together and left for home. As soon as they arrived she began putting the groceries away. JB took care of the dog and got him situated and fed.

JB said "Jennifer should we have some fun with the dog?" Jennifer: "what do you mean?" JB: "I'll take the dog outside, you tell Ben to hide anywhere in the house get one of his old shirts that he's worn and I'll bring the dog in, and we'll see how long it takes him to find Ben." Jennifer: "that might be fun and Ben will love it." JB: "tell Ben he can't come out until the dog finds him and we holler for him." Jennifer: "okay I'll go get an old shirt and have him hide, and I'll call you when he is hid." JB got the leash and took the dog outside. ten minutes later Jennifer called out.

JB went back in the house and closed the door and locked it. Jennifer gave JB the shirt. JB held the shirt down to the dog and said "search." The dog started going around the room into the kitchen out of the kitchen around behind the couch in the first bedroom, then the second, then he went down the basement, Jennifer and JB followed. They watched the dog from the stairs as he started going around the basement he ran around and then backtracked and stopped in front of the hidden door. The dog looked at them then looked at the hidden door. JB said okay Ben come out. The hidden door opened and there was Ben. JB looked at his watch and said it took him just a little over 13 minutes to find Ben I think that's pretty good. Jennifer: "he may be little but he sure did a good job." JB: "If he keeps this up he'll be worth every penny we paid for him. If he's as good with explosives as he is with gun and search he could walk the park and nobody would know he's really a bomb sniffing dog." JB patted the dog and praised him, the dog seemed really happy. Ben patted the dog and said "Good dog, I like him he's going to be fun."

JB smiled and said "when the guys check in I will have to tell him what this little guy did when he first got here." Jennifer: "where is he going to sleep?" JB: "what did the instructions say?" Jennifer: "you know what they said right next to the bed." JB "I will call the dog trainers and see why the wife did not like the dog." JB went back to the paperwork to get the phone number and called support, their phone rang four times and then somebody answered. JB said "this is JB from the park; I have the dog so far we like him very much, and why did the wife not like him?"

The trainer said " hang on a minute and I will check the file, a minute later he was back he said "the dog wanted to sleep on the bed not beside the bed." JB said "why didn't they just put him in the crate beside the bed?" The trainer: "they said he whined." JB: "we took him out of the crate and let him loose in the house and he went right to the closet set down in front of it looked at me look at the closet looked at me look at the closet in 30 seconds he found my guns." The trainer: "yes according to the notes he's a fantastic little dog and at the time we didn't have a dog in here that was better than he was." JB: "what if we left the dog sleep with our son will the dog still work good for me?" The trainer said "I would put him near you for at least the first week if you are the one that is going to work the dog." The trainer said "we think the wife just didn't like the looks of the dog kind of an ugly looking dog because they only had the dog for three days, and they didn't even take him out and work him.

The trainer said "I see you're putting up a training facility why don't you work the dog out there as soon as that is done the following week and get him used to you doing all the things that he has to do and then make a decision. And after that time period he may be just fine as he's the type of breed that is a family dog the others are more one person dogs." JB: "how long is our time period on the dog?" The trainer said "I will give you five or six weeks that should be enough time."

JB said "that sounds reasonable thank you very much and I'll let you know our progress." Jennifer: "I don't know if I want the dog sleeping with Ben." JB: "well I think a boy should have a dog, and I think even though the dog is small he will try to protect Ben, and Ben could have a chore to take care of the dog, make sure he has food and water." Jennifer: "I agree that would probably be good to have something he's responsible for." JB: "we will get the dog through the first week, and then we'll see how that goes." JB watched the video a second time.

JB looked at Jennifer and said "Jennifer it says the dog will get between you and somebody else if they're armed without you having to tell him to look for a gun I think that sounds pretty good, forewarned is forearmed." Jennifer said "what does he do?" JB: "he gets between you and the other person and gives a low growl." Jennifer: "that sounds neat your own little personal burglar alarm." JB: "I think I'll take him out for a walk before we have lunch and see if he has to go I'll be back in a little while." JB went to the closet and got out his vest put it on, then his holster and pistol slipped on his outer jacket, the dog came over to the door, JB clipped the leash on the dog, opened the door, shut the door and went quickly to the left. Then JB headed toward the office, he walked around the bend and a stranger was walking right toward him JB thought what is he doing here, he'd never seen the man before, and nobody should be in this area. The dog crossed over in front of him and growled the man stopped, JB stopped and said "can I help you?" The man said "no I walk here all the time I live just a few blocks down the road and it's a nice place to exercise." JB: "yes it is, I have only been here a couple days, I'm with the construction up on the hill and they let me stay in this little house but they told me nobody was here in this residential area but me." The man said "they probably don't know I'm here I just walk in walk around and walk out." JB: "which way are you going?" The man said "I walk here a little farther then go left and go out by the road." JB said "then I will walk with you as I've never been this way." The man said "no you don't have to; I don't want to put you out of your way."

"I'm just walking the dog so it's not really out of my way and I haven't seen everything here, it is such a pretty place." JB explained to the man. The man said "yes it is it must be nice to live here?" JB said with a smile "it probably is, my job here will be done in a couple days and I'll be gone." The Man said "what do you do here?" JB: "I'm with a construction company up on the hill we are putting up some buildings for the park, a local gun club wanted a shooting range and I guess they're renting some space from the park, at least that's what they told me when we started." The man said "that's interesting; I will have to see about joining."

"They said they were going to have their grand opening next week, you should stop in and look the place over, you have a nice day." JB stopped quickly and the man walked two paces ahead of him, JB already had his gun out and the man was reaching for what appeared to be a gun in a shoulder holster, JB said "I wouldn't do that you'll never get it out." The man said "whoa I don't mean any trouble I was just going to say goodbye." JB: "I never saw somebody say goodbye and reach for their shoulder, if I were you I would not move I'm a nervous guy." JB got his phone from his pocket and called Betty and said "get the police out here we have a slight problem."

Betty said "there's one in the parking lot where are you.

"I'm on the south edge of the parking lot south of you, and send a security guard down here." JB said as he put the phone back in his pocket. JB looked at the man and said "I am a real nervous type you better lay down on the ground and spread eagle your hands as I might shoot you by accident." The man said "are you serious?" JB: "always and I'm getting impatient you either get down on the ground now or I will shoot you." The man got down on the ground and spread-eagled and said "are you crazy?"

"No just paranoid." JB said with a serious look on his face. Just then a security guard came running down the side of the parking lot and shadow pulled up with his lights blinking." The Man on the ground started screaming: "this man threatened to shoot me do something about it." Shadow said "Sir you are on private property you had no business being in this area of the park, they can have you arrested, are you aware of that?" The man said "no I didn't know that I'm new around here."

"That's interesting you told me you came here all the time you really need to make up your mind." JB said and then looked at David "you might want to check his left side I think he was reaching for a pistol." Shadow came up knelt down put a handcuff on the man's right arm pulled it down behind him and then pulled the other hand down and handcuffed it. JB told the dog to stay and moved to the end of the leash and helped shadow flip the man over, and took the gun out of the shoulder holster. Shadow: "Sir, Do you have a permit for this gun." The man said "I want a lawyer." Shadow said "You haven't been charged with anything why would you want a lawyer have you done something wrong?" The man shut up. Shadow and JB walked over to the squad car. JB motioned for the security guard to come over to the squad car. JB called Betty and said "put the security guard that is manning the screens on the phone." A minute later security guard said "can I help you sir?" JB: "did you see the man that we have detained on your screens?" The security guard said that section doesn't have any cameras." JB: "give Betty the phone." Betty said 'what can I do?"

"Call the security people and get somebody out here we need more cameras and why hadn't that been mentioned before I'll be up to the office shortly." JB called Hank. Hank answered: "you have a problem?"

"Yes I was walking in the home area and I walked into a man, I talked and walked to the edge of the residential area I stopped he took two steps realized I wasn't beside him I drew my gun then he turned quickly and started to draw but changed his mind, so I got the drop on him, shadow has him handcuffed he screaming for a lawyer but we told him we haven't charged him with anything why would he need a lawyer, he hasn't said a word since I believe shadow has ran his license and when asked did he have a permit he said nothing other than he wanted a lawyer. Did shadow send you a picture?"

Hank: "yes and we are running the license through DMV, and the picture through the database." Has his picture shown up in any of your other photos from surveillance?" Hank: "no he seems to be a new face." JB: "call me if you find out who or what he is." Hank said "Okay, I will let you know bye." Hank called back" I am sending a squad over with a form for you to fill out and you are going to be the head of our SWAT department as of Friday so you are a legal cop." JB: "okay tell him to go to the office and I'll have shadow put this gentleman in the back of the squad car and your man can pick him up and do what you want with him." Shadow put the man in the back of the squad car.

JB said "I will walk over to the office as I was exercising the dog and I will meet you there in a few minutes if you want leave him parked in the sun it is all right with me." Shadow laughed and said "that would be great but they would probably get after me for that." JB said "I can see were going to need a temporary holding area, there just seems to be way too much going on here." JB knelt down and patted his little dog and rubbed him all over he was really proud of him, he thought you saved my butt today."

He and the little dog walked over to the office and went in." Betty said "is that your new dog?" JB: "yes it is and he warned me that the gentleman out there in the squad car had a gun before I had any idea he had one. I am learning to love this little dog." Betty said "the surveillance camera people said somebody would be over within a half hour." 15 minutes later the squad car pulled up the Sgt. Came in. "I'm here to see JB." JB said "I'm right here. They went in to the conference room, the Sgt. followed JB into the room, and JB shut the door. The Sgt. said "fill this out and sign near the bottom of the form and date it last Friday." JB filled out the form, dated it, signed it, and gave it back to the Sgt. The Sgt. got up and went into the office said "thank you" JB shook hands with the Sgt. and he went out got in his squad car and left. Five minutes later another squad car pulled up and they loaded the man from shadow's squad car into the new one and it left. Five minutes later another van pulled up it was a surveillance guy.

He came into the office and said "I am from the surveillance office what can I help you with?" JB: 'we seem to have had a breakdown in communication we had some dead spots where a gentleman was over in the housing area and he was not picked up on surveillance so we have to remedy that problem." JB got out a map of the park. He showed the surveillance man the part that they had walked down and the man on the screen said we don't have any of those paths on screen; if they do I don't know which windows they are in." The surveillance man pulled out the map they made when they installed the cameras and which camera was at which location. He says "I don't have those paths on my map; I don't think we knew they existed." JB: "I don't care about that, I just want it fixed and then I want somebody to walk around every path and make sure we have cameras that cover 100% of this park so we can go back and spot something that was left that shouldn't have been, what time it was left, and hopefully the face of who left it." The surveillance guy said "I can have more people out here in an hour and what we don't get done when it gets real dark we will get finished tomorrow is that acceptable." JB: "that is acceptable but if you don't get it done tomorrow you don't leave until it's finished, there will be three children and two wives here Wednesday and I want surveillance on them." The surveillance man said "that should be doable, as we free up people from other jobs I will bring them out here so it will be faster as time goes on." JB: "I want overlapping in the residential area so we can start to see them coming into the new area as they are leaving the old." The surveillance man: "we have some cameras they cost twice as much but when they sense movement they inform the software and the window on the screen blinks and draws attention to that window that there is somebody in this area then the man on the screen can telephoto in from here." JB: "right off the top of your head how many cameras do you think that is?" The surveillance man: "without exact measurements I will guess 10 to 15 and we will have to bring in a bigger screen or have twin screens." This will give a better picture to the guard on the screens." A second screen same size as the one you have now." JB: "that sounds fine do it, and if we need to expand this room let me know now and I'll have them working on it all night." I think if you could expand this wall out six more feet that would do it." JB: "I will get them on it, Betty get a hold of maintenance to tell them we want to bring this wall out 8 feet and we need it done by tomorrow afternoon I don't care how and tell him they get double time if they finish it on time, and I don't care if they put what else they're doing on hold."

JBs phone rang it was Hank. JB said "what you got?" Hank: "well that guy we just got from you has three outstanding warrants, and we are running his gun through ballistics." JB: "thanks for the info, I sure am learning to like this little dog, he probably saved my life, thanks Hank, talk at you later." JB's phone rang it was LJ. JB; said "how is the dog training going?" LJ: "great I'm impressed with these animals more every day, how is yours doing?"

JB proudly said "well we brought him in the house first thing he did was go over to the closet and told me there was guns there and then a little later we had Ben hide, took him 13 minutes to find Ben in the basement behind the secret door, today there was a guy walking down the path in the residential section and he told me he was packing and I walked this guy out to where he was going into one of the big parking lots I stopped he took two steps and realized I was not with him and he spun around reaching for a gun and now he's in Hanks Jail got three outstanding warrants and there doing ballistic tests on his pistol then he told me that the surveillance guy was packing, I am learning to love this little dog."

LJ said "I know what you mean the more I work with this dog the more I wished we had him over in Afghanistan, they really are quite remarkable." LJ: "anything else going on?"

"Yes the guy that we had arrested was walking around the residential section and he never showed up on the surveillance screens so I got them working right now to put in 10 to 15 more cameras, we will probably put another watcher on as we will have 2 screens to watch, how are the other dogs doing ?" LJ: "we should be able to sweep the park with the three dogs we have and the city should be able to cover most of what they're going to want to cover with the two they got in a pinch we can go down there and get them done in half the time so I think it was a really good idea to get all these animals." JB: "how is CR doing?" LJ: "he loves his dog, the dog sleeps right beside his bed and I wouldn't want to sneak up on him, that dog will be on you so quick, he says he's never felt this protected at night, we sure have a good crew and I think these two policemen that are here with us in the way they have been working we are going to have a super SWAT squad." JB: "well I sure miss you two I'm getting excited about us starting a SWAT team next week, when are you leaving there?" LJ they liked the way were taking to the dogs and they have done some other things to increase the dogs training and we will probably leave here Thursday morning and get back Thursday evening so I will let you know when you need to come and pick us up." JB: "all right see you Thursday."

JB hung up, he thought Wow things are really coming together, and I will have the whole crew here Friday. The four of us will really get things done, I have to talk to Hank about this rank thing LJ was a lieutenant, CR is a master sergeant, and JR is a warrant officer and I don't think anyone of us including me is a better leader than any of the others, we are all as good as each other if you gave us a target and told us all to shoot without a high-speed camera you couldn't tell who shot first. JB: "I'm going down to the Springhouse I think we got everything done here that needs to be done if you need me that's where I will be." JB grabbed the leash and he and the dog went out the back door and walked from tree to Bush, and stayed out of sight until he got to the place where the dog could relieve himself and he put the dog on the long leash and let him sniff around and go. When he was done JB said: "come and the dog came, and walked with him and they went to the Springhouse from cover to cover.

JB went in the house locked the door and took his jacket off and put it in the closet, took off his holster put it in the closet, clip out of his pistol and the bullet out of the chamber, put them on the top shelf, took his vest off hung it in the closet shut the door and went in to visit with Jennifer.

Jennifer said "how did your day go? Did you get along with the little dog?" JB smiled and said "yes I did, he saved my life today." Jennifer's eyes got real big: "what do you mean." JB well as I was walking around the path in this residential area some guy I never saw before came up so I chatted with him a bit the dog, like the video said he would, went over in front and growled at him so I knew he was armed otherwise I would've never known so I chatted with him and walked him out of the area and I stopped quickly and he got two steps away and spun and started to draw his gun but I had mine out and that was the end of that he froze I spread-eagled him on the ground and called Betty and told her to call the police, shadow came over quickly we cuffed him and I guess he has three outstanding warrants on murder charges and they are running ballistics on his gun to see if they find any other things that match that gun so that was the first thing he did that probably saved my life because the guy probably would've caught me flat-footed, as he was moving pretty quick and I wasn't expecting it. The other is he told me that the surveillance guy was packing or had a pistol concealed that little dog can be my best friend he senses things I don't."

Jennifer looking at the dog said "then you keep the dog." JB: "are you sure?" Jennifer: "if you think he saved your life today why would we want to get rid of him." JB: "that's what I thought to." I was talking to LJ and he says CR loves his dog and it sleeps beside his bed and he says he's never felt so safe sleeping before." And from the way LJ talks he seems kind of smitten with his dog to, he figures they were one of the best investments we've made so far in our welfare and safety." Jennifer: "then I don't have to worry about you so much, you have a guardian angel."

JB smiling said "you might say that, and the full crew will be here by Thursday evening, JR and his wife and kids should be here Wednesday afternoon, Ben will have a couple of boys to play with, and you will have a woman you can talk to, she is really a nice lady so I think you both will get along." JB called his dad and said "2 o'clock in the morning we're going up on the hill see you then." His dad said "okay have a good night."

CHAPTER 18

TUESDAY WEEK THREE

JB woke up at 1:45 AM and put on his cloths, and then his vest, his holster and pistol, and then the jacket over that, put two clips in the pockets. Grabbed his laptop opened the door slipped out locked the door and headed up to the big house he could hear the van running. 12 minutes later they were up on the hill, his dad stopped 300 feet from site two JB got out 30 feet in front of the van turned left and disappeared into the woods, his night vision was working quite well and he had no trouble finding the camera the batteries were at 75% so JB set the camera for motion single pictures downloaded and went back to the van.

Then they went to site three JB replaced both sets of batteries changed the camera to single pictures on motion, downloaded then went back to the van. They went to the last site repeated the operation and were on their way home. They would be home by three he was getting pretty good at this. He looked through all videos did not see any new people closed the laptop and they had just arrived home. They got out of the van dad locked the van.

JB said "thanks dad see you in the morning." Dad went in the big house, JB went to the Springhouse opened the door he heard the dog moving in the crate. JB opened the crate put the leash on the dog and took the dog out so he could go to the bathroom. ten minutes later they were back JB opened the door they went in. JB took the leash off

163

the dog. He put his gear in the closet, went over got on the couch he could hear the dog come over and lay down on his bed JB scratched his head and they both went to sleep.

JB got up at 5:30 AM put on his running shoes, put the leash on the dog went to the door and they started to run they were back in 22 minutes, they came back in the house shut and locked the door took the leash off the dog and then proceeded to do his push-ups and crunches. JB thought Jennifer might as well be at work, she will be as safe there as here till these cameras are up. Jennifer came out of the bathroom and JB said "I'm going to have to be in and out most of the day without the security cameras in this area you could be as safe at work as you are here so if you want to go to work I will drop you and Ben off."

Jennifer: "you seem to be in pretty good shape and I assume your bruises are gone so okay I will get dressed for work and get Ben ready for school." She came over pulled up his shirt and checked his kidney there was no sign of a bruise, she said "I have never seen a bruise kidney heal this fast it's a shame we can't tell people about this they would recuperate so much quicker." JB: "that's the trouble with the world today all anybody cares about is money not about each other." Jennifer: "I believe you're right about that."

JB: "I was curious have you thought about where you want to live when this is over, the big house, or build one for ourselves?" Jennifer: "there's that gigantic master bedroom and two smaller bedrooms, then there's three guest bedrooms, a dining room, living room, kitchen, and then the game room in the basement that's a big house." JB: "I thought if we were in the big house there is plenty of room for your parents to come over and stay a week or two if they wanted." Jennifer: "I never thought of that if we have another child the two mothers could help take care of it and I know they both would love that."

"Mom said that they wanted a smaller place so it is not like we are going to run them out, I don't care what we do as long as we're together I am happy." JB replied. Jennifer said "so far you've been real easy to live with." JB: "well you know me what you see is what you get, but I won't argue, but I will discuss and there is a difference." Jennifer: "I have noticed that" and she smiled. She said "I will think about the house, that's a lot to clean up."

JB: "you won't have to clean up, the park pays for the cleanup of both houses that's a perk, and we never had anything stolen, and once a year we close the park, and have a big picnic for them and their families and they can come to the park free anytime they want." Jennifer: "you treat the employees quite well." JB: "our employees work hard for us, they don't steal from us so we treat them well, most employees have worked here all their lives, most of them are members of other employees families that they have recommended so it's hard for an outsider to get in because they've already got one of their family applying for the job before anybody else knows."

JB: "we have had employees come and tell us to fire one of their family members because they are not working like they should; they figure it's a bad reflection on them." Jennifer said "breakfast is ready." JB, Jennifer, and Ben sat down Jennifer said a prayer and they ate breakfast together. JB jumped in the shower shaved got dressed was ready for the day. He put the leash on the little dog and they all left he locked the door Jennifer made sure Ben had his seatbelt on she got in the front she let the little dog in the back he got in the back seat with Ben, and they left.

JB: "today I'm going to drop Ben at school first and then take you to the hospital. Jennifer: "why are you doing that?" JB: "we are mixing the routine up so they never know which one we are going to do first, and if I see somebody following us I will just drive around we will tell Hank and he'll pick them up and follow them, and when they know they're being followed we will just come back home."

JB dropped Ben off at school then took Jennifer to the hospital and dropped her off at the emergency room exit. The little dog jumped up in the front laid on the seat beside JB as they went back to the park. JB grabbed the leash put it on the little dog, went into the office. Betty said "good morning, a semi-truck just took a load of material up to the site." JB: "I'll have to go up later and check that out." JB called Hank: "Get ready for the download", Hank said "okay start." JB started the download ten minutes later it was finished. JB: "Betty what did you find out about the battery packs?" Betty: "We should have them Thursday", "Betty I want you to order a vest for the little dog, 25 to 30 pounds and the highest level they make and I think the service dogs are red in color check and see so it looks like a normal service dog not a sniffer dog and when the guys get back on Thursday get their weight, sizes and get one for each of them I guess you better get two for the two police also." Betty said "I will let you know what I find out." JB: "great, Betty I don't know what I'd do without you, I really appreciate you." Betty: "thank you very much."

JB: "I think I will go see how the surveillance crew is working and check their progress, I will probably go to lunch with dad, see you later, and call me if anything comes up." JB grabbed the leash and went looking for the surveillance people. He started where the park ended and the residential area started as he figured they would start there and work their way over. Four minutes later he came up and there were a couple of men installing a camera, JB said "where is your boss." He said "3 or four paths over." JB: "Thank you keep up the good work." JB and the little dog turned left walked a little farther and recognize that guy working on a camera, JB kept going along the path and around the corner and there was the surveillance man he had talked to yesterday. JB: "how is your schedule running?" Surveillance man said "I have two more crews that will be here in an hour and we should have everything finished by 6 o'clock if nothing unexpected happens." JB: "that is great." The surveillance man: "as you know we have our men that we have trained manning the screens we have a new guy that will start at six tonight and he is fully familiar with the software and we have two other men that will work as replacements as they work an eight hour shift as we have 24/7 surveillance."

JB said "I really like the idea that there was movement and the screen lit up to draw attention to it, snipers have the same trouble keeping from falling asleep they call that target hypnosis and I like the idea of the flashing now I realize during the day that wouldn't work, you get too many people moving, but at night once it's dark nobody should be in the park, do the cameras we have now have this feature once they go into night vision mode?" The surveillance guy: "I never thought of that, that's a great idea, I'm going to call my boss and see if he can get the programmers working on that. That would give us something that nobody else has." JB: "Tell your boss we would not mind paying extra for that; maybe that will give them a little more incentive." The surveillance man: "most of our enhancements are ideas that we have gotten from our customers."

JB: "keep up the good work I'm very pleased." JB called his dad: "dad you want to go get lunch? I will meet you at the office." Dad said "sure I'll be there in five minutes." JB hung up and he and the little dog started walking around the path they past three more surveillance guys putting up cameras JB was pleased. JB got to the office and his dad was pulling up in the van, JB opened the door the little dog jumped in, JB climbed in after him and shut the door, the little dog sat between his legs. Dad said "you and the little dog get along real good?" JB: "yes I figured he saved my life already, so he has already paid for himself, and he shows me things that I don't see." Dad said "that's good you got something that will be watching your back 24/7." JB: "that's what LJ said, CR's dog sleeps on the floor next to him and LJ said he wouldn't try to sneak up on him at night that dog will be all over you so quick it will make your head swim, CR said "he never felt this safe at night."

Dad pulled into the diner, and they went in and sat down in a different booth the one they usually sat in was full, JB found one where he could face the door. The waitress came and they ordered ten minutes later the food arrived and they begin to eat. They finished and left the diner, JB got in dad's van and headed back toward the office JB said "shall we go up and see how they're doing on the new construction?" JB's dad said "sure I been wondering what all is going on up there." JB said "There expanding the wall 8 feet out for the added camera screen in the office." JB's phone rang he answered "hello." Betty said "there is a British major here and he needs to talk to you ASAP as he has to catch a flight."

JB said "we will be there in three minutes." And hung up, JB: "dad hurry, go straight to the office there something funny going on I have a British major in my office." Dad said "okay", they pulled up in front of the office they both got out of the van and hurried into the office. JB walked in his dad behind him and said " I'm JB, what can I do for you." I am major Willoughby of the English Secret Service and I have some information for you, do you have a room where we can have some privacy?" JB: "follow me" and they went into the conference room.

The British major said "I owe a favor to a certain Commander in the Navy SEALs and I am here to execute that favor, it seems that his higher up do not want to share information with you but your Commander said he owes you too much not to, so he called me because he knew I was coming across your country and I would pass by your location so I put a layover in my flight and I'm here and I have to be back in the airport in an hour or I'm going to be in deep trouble." JB said "we will get you back; now what information do you have for me?"

The British major opened his attaché case and said "this CO said he owed you a lot and here is the information." The major took pictures out of his case and laid them on the table, the first picture was the Arab from the convenience store the major pulled out a sheet and said "this Arab is a master bomb maker." The next picture was of the other Arab this one is his apprentice so you have two bomb makers working in your city: That was the most important information I was to deliver there are a few other things in here but you can look at them later, now my debt is paid and if you could take me to the airport I would be very happy." JB: "now I owe you major Willoughby this is very valuable to know and I will get the surveillance people on him with this information immediately, if you ever need a favor call me if you ever need a place to stay call me my house is your house."

JB and the major came out of the conference room and JB gave

Betty the envelope and JB said "put this in the safe and lock the safe."
JB: "major Willoughby I want you to meet my father, dad we owe him
so if he needs anything and I'm not here take care of him and tell the
guys the same thing now we need to take him to the airport ASAP."
The three of them got in the van fifteen minutes later they were at the
airport JB got out got out with the major shook his hand again and
said you're a lifesaver thank you have a safe trip. Major Willoughby
walked into the airport; JB got back in the van, he and his dad hurried
back to the park on the way JB called Hank, said "can you get away
right now?" Hank said "yes what's up." JB: "I will tell you when you
get to the office." Hank: "I will be there in ten minutes."

JB and his dad pulled up to the office, got out of the van and
Hank pulled up. They all went into the office, JB: "Betty will you get
me the envelope out of the safe." Betty opened the safe grabbed the
envelope and handed it to JB. JB said "Hank, you and dad come into
the conference room I have something to show you." They sat down
at the table and JB opened the envelope started laying the pictures
and reports out next to each other. JB: "took the picture of the Arab
from the convenience store and said this man is a master bomb maker,
here is the report that goes with his picture, and JB handed them to
Hank." Hank: "this is not good." JB took out a picture of the other
Arab and said "this is his assistant; we have two bomb makers not
just one." Hank: "we will have to step up our surveillance they could
be planting bombs all over the city and we would've never known."
JB: "is all the material for the swat team training in?"

Hank: "yes we got it last week." JB: "basically the swat team will
be here Thursday and we will have five bomb sniffers. How close
has surveillance been on those two Arabs?" Hank: "fairly close, I
will have to check with my guys and see if they have done anything
real suspicious yet." JB: "if they have made any deliveries or visited
anywhere where they were carrying something we have to get the dogs
in there and do a thorough search and that will have to be done when
people are not there and in secrecy, this could mean late at night so
you will have to work on that schedule and we will execute." Hank: "

okay they'll be back Thursday night, let's have a meeting at 7 o'clock and start to lay out a plan."

JB said with a serious look on his face "I will get a hold of LJ and have him lay out some tentative plans with your people, LJ and CR will know better how to handle these dogs in a situation like this, your people know the area better than we do, they should pick out the buildings they think are more vulnerable and where we should start first." Hank: "I will call my people and tell them to take orders from your men and work with them however they want."

JB replied "I plan to run swat like I did the team in the Navy any plan is designed by all members of the team or we don't execute that plan until everyone agrees and has contributed something to it." Hank: "usually the people in charge lay out the plan and everyone else follows it." JB: "that's the way the Navy does it, but we were the most successful unit they had because we all agreed and usually everybody saw something that the others had missed we stayed alive for ten years designing missions together, I am not going to change that now, I want every mission a success."

Hank said "we will give you the missions and you design them however you want, you are in charge." JB: "I am going to start to sweep the park tonight after 11 o'clock, we may need someone to go through the videos for the park and see if anyone came in and seemed lighter on the way out if you understand what I'm saying?" Hank: "why don't I have a small unit of the bomb disposal squad with you tonight in case you find anything they can disarm it." JB: "are they familiar with the way the Arabs make their bombs?" Hank: "I believe they have been studying information on Arab bombs that they got from home land security." JB: "JR will be here tomorrow with his family, he has disarmed a number of Arab bombs, I will get a hold of JR and see where he wants to stay and inform him of what we are looking at." Hank: "you handle it you are in charge of this mission we will do whatever you say."

JB called LJ, LJ: "what's up boss?" JB: "I got information from our old CO, remember the convenience store guy that Arab is a master bomb maker the other Arab is his assistant." LJ: "how much information do we have?" JB: "not as much as I would like, can you leave early like tomorrow?" LJ: "we are reviewing and running searches bombs and guns, they say this is an exceptionally good class so we could leave tomorrow." JB: "you talk it over with CR and the two policemen and get back to me and you two are in charge." LJ: "we are almost done for the day so when we get done with this particular exercise I will get together and talk because I think we should come back tomorrow we can leave early in the morning, it's a little late to switch our tickets tonight so let's shoot for tomorrow."

JB: "you guys run tentative plans the four of you really know the dogs I don't, so you know the best way to use them, the two policemen know the town better than we do so have them lay out plans for the city, JR has disarmed Arab bombs so when you get back we will have the bomb squad here and he can coordinate with them how, we will do what you want to handle it, I figure we will go through buildings and the park late at night so the public doesn't know what is going on."

LJ: "that sounds good to me I will get back to you when we have set up a preplan, bye." JB: "bye." JB: "having them back a day early I think is a good plan, JR will be here, that means all my guys are here in two days, and we can spend some long nights and beef up the surveillance." JB: "Hank get with the bomb squad make sure they are up to speed on Arab type bombs and we will have a meeting tomorrow night here and have somebody from your surveillance unit fill us in on all the information they have, and remember we want input from everyone and how they think we should handle a certain situation."

Hank: "I will get on my tasks right now." Hank left the office. JB: "shall we go up on the hill dad it will help to relax us?" Dad said "yes sounds good to me." JB and dad got in his van and went up to see how the constructions were going. On the way up JB got a hold of JR and filled him in on the information about the Arabs and said "that we have two open bedrooms in the big house so you can stay there or I will set you up in a motel whatever you and your wife want, talk it over and get back to me." JR said: "we should be there in the morning, we have been making good time and the kids have been really good about not stopping all the time they're all excited about being able to ride all the rides free." JB: "I remember when I used to be the hit getting all my friends in free, you get back to me and we'll go from there." JB and his dad reached the road they drove around all the buildings and areas and they could see that almost all of the outside polls for the dog training area were almost in and they were starting to put up the fence JB was pleased they were making good progress. The walls were starting to go up in the room clearing area so everything was on schedule. JB: "shall we go check on the new surveillance cameras in the residential area."

Dad says "we better; I don't know how they got missed?" JB: "I don't know either, so much was going on, I said just get it done, and they are really working on it and that's all I can ask." Dad: 'That sounds good to me, let's go take a look and then it will be about time for you to get Jennifer and Ben." Dad turned the van around and they drove to the residential area it looked to JB as if all the cameras were close to being in. The surveillance man said we only have three cameras left to go, he says they are going to put a new server in the office that way performance will be better and with the two screens we will be able to do a better job and our backups can last longer." JB said "sounds good I will go check and see how the addition on the office is going." They got back to the office, went in and went into the room where all the surveillance screens were and the outer wall was missing and JB could see them starting to erect the panels that would enclose the new area, the floor was already completely in and just needed tiled. JB was pleased, and said "I better go get Jennifer and Ben." Dad said "you be careful." JB left and decided to pick up Ben first he was almost to school when he saw the green ford. He called Hank and said "have you got somebody in a green ford?" Hank said "no, green ford on you?" JB: "yes I'm on my way to pick up Ben." Hank: "go inside stay in their five minutes then come out and we will pick up the green ford as you leave." JB: "okay." JB slowed just a little and drove to the school found a spot parked his car and went inside. JB walked to Ben's class got Ben; and JB said to his teacher "how has he been, are his grades all right, does he get along with the other kids?" The teacher: "that would be yes to all three questions he is a very good little boy." JB: "is there anything I should help him with to catch him up on the days he missed?" The teacher said: "he's worked really hard and he has everything caught up as of today." JB: "well that's great Ben I'm proud of you." He thanked the teacher and he and Ben went up to the door JB kept Ben in the shadows and looked until he found the green ford, it was up the street about five cars in front of his, he thought well that shouldn't be too bad and he and Ben hurried out got in the car and JB pulled out into traffic. He passed the green ford, and gave a little gas to speed up to the intersection; he didn't make the green light. He slipped his pistol out of its holster and cocked the hammer and said: "Ben if I say down can you lay on the seat?" Ben: "yes I can." JB: "you have to be quick." Ben: "yes daddy." The green ford pulled up on the right. JB could see both of his hands on the steering wheel he looked up the light was still red, he looked back the man's right hand was gone. JB saw the light had turned green he gave a quick look at the green ford the man's hand was coming up and JB slammed the accelerator down and the car jumped into the intersection and JB Said "down", changed lanes to the same one, the green car was in, the green car gave chase JB waited till the car was 30 feet behind him and then slammed on his brakes the green ford hit him.

JB jumped out of the car ran back to the green ford the man was dazed he had a gun in his right hand. JB said "you move your dead." The man froze, cars were honking traffic was backing up JB heard a siren. Help was on the way three minutes later there was a police car beside his car a policeman jumped out and said "drop your gun just then another man came running up and said "don't worry about him, worry about the man in the car." The man in plain clothes reached in and unlocked the door pulled it open he put his gun to the man's head and said release your pistol" the policeman went on to the other side of the line of fire the man put his other hand up the man in plain clothes said grab your steering wheel the man complied JB moved so he was slightly behind the man and there was room for the plainclothes policeman to begin to cuff the man. JB holstered his weapon. The plainclothes policeman finished cuffing the man then put the man in the back of the policeman's car. And told the policeman to take him to the station and book him for attempted murder I will get pictures of the inside of the car and before you leave I want you to meet the man who is head of our SWAT unit, JB meet Sgt. Riley, JB held out his hand and said "it's a pleasure to meet you sir", Sgt. Riley said "it is a pleasure to meet you, I'm sorry about the mix up."

JB said "no problem things are happening pretty fast." A tow truck has been called for the green ford, will your car move, JB says let me try and got back in his car restarted the engine and pulled it forward it did disengage from the other car. JB and the plain clothes man looked at the car nothing seem to be loose enough to fall off. JB well I better go pick up my wife she'll be worried I'm running late, also check the trunk you might find some real surprises in there." The plain clothes man said ok and he would fill out a traffic report. JB thanked him and went to the hospital to pick up Jennifer.

On the way he called Jennifer and said "I had a fender bender so I am running a little late I will pick you up at the front door." She said "okay I was getting worried." A few minutes later Hank called "you sure pick up a lot of trouble they seem to be rushing this?" JB: "I think they are trying to get the bounty before the big guy gets here, I think they figure when he gets here there won't be any bounty." Hank: "you could be right." JB: "I told them to check the trunk who knows what prizes may be in there and when you find out who or what he is let me know see you tomorrow", JB hung up. Jennifer: "that sounds like more than just a fender bender?"

JB: "he looked like he was going to pull a gun on me; I told Ben to drop and I pulled in front of him quickly slammed on my brakes and he hit me and while he was dazed I got the drop on him and he couldn't get his gun up." Jennifer: "I think we may have to home school and we don't want JR's boys having the same problem." JB: "I know I think you're both going to stay home tomorrow, and see what JR and his wife think." Jennifer: "sounds good to me."

JB called his dad and said "I got rear-ended and I think we need to do some modifications on our cars, I will talk to you when I get there." JB: "Jennifer if you go to work you will have to start wearing your vest." JB: "JR and his wife and two boys should be here any time now as he said they were close." As they pulled up to the office they saw a moving van sitting in the South parking area. JB stopped in front of the office pulled out his phone and called JR. JR answered and JB said "are you here yet?" RJ: "yes we are at the big house." JB: "we will be right down." JB drove to the big house Ben and Jennifer got out JB got out locked the car and they went inside and there was JR and his family.

JR said "I hear life is getting exciting, are you a trouble magnet?" JB: "it's starting to look that way." JB: "have you decided where you want to stay?" JR: "we will stay right here, there is safety in numbers." JB: "let's have the movers pull their truck up near the office for tonight. Then we'll decide where we are going to store your stuff until you get your permanent home." Jennifer said: "are you going to introduce us?" JB: "Jennifer this is Rose, Rose this is Jennifer, Ben this is Larry, and this is John, Larry and John this is Ben." JB: "we will be back shortly." JB: "Jennifer why don't you and Ben show Rose and the boys how to work the tunnels between the two houses so they can go back and forth without being outside."

Jennifer: "we will do that and make sure each one can open and close the doors." JB and JR got in JB's car and drove out to where the truck was parked, JR got out and told them to follow them to the office and then park their truck there for the night. The movers backed the truck trailer up toward the office unhooked the trailer and said "they would be back around eight in the morning" and left. JR said "tell me what went down?" JB: "I just picked up Ben and I was in the left lane and I get stuck at the light, the green ford has been following me the last two or three days he pulled up on my right I looked over he had both hands on the steering wheel I looked at the light and it changed I look back and only one hand was on the steering wheel, so I gunned it, he gunned his but I quickly pulled in front of him and slammed on the brakes, then he ran into me I jumped out, ran to his window and pointed my gun at his head and told him to freeze. Someone must've called 911 because within three minutes, a squad car pulled up and put a gun on me then the plain clothes policeman that has been following the green car ran up and told the cop to go to the other window and put his gun on the driver he and I maneuvered then got his door open and the plain cloths man handcuffed him got the gun out of his hand put him in the back of the squad car, he introduced me to the cop from the squad car and said "this is the commander of our new swat unit and he is one of us", the cop apologized and said he didn't know. JB: "I said that's all right it's to new yet you had no way of knowing and you didn't shoot me so that's what's important and we all laughed."

JB: "I think they are getting nervous that once the main Arab gets over here they will not be able to get paid on the bounty as he's going to want to do it, so I think they're trying to get it done beforehand so they can collect the bounty." JR: "that makes sense to me." JR: "how are we going to stop this?" JB: "I don't know we will all have to brainstorm this. Let's go in the office and get Roses vest and two for the boys." JR: "sounds good to me." They got the vests, and checked up on how the surveillance installation was going. The surveillance man said "we are checking to see that all cameras are working and we've covered everything, this one will be up and fully functional before we leave, tomorrow we will be back and make sure every foot of the park is covered by the cameras."

JB: "thank you very much we appreciate your fast response to this problem you have a good night see you in the morning." JB and JR left the office got in his car and drove down to the big house. They went in and JB said "I have to go down to the spring house and let the little dog out I will be back shortly." JR said "wait a minute I'll get my pistol and come with you." Three minutes later JB and JR walked undercover to the spring house. JB unlocked the door walked in opened the crate put the leash on the little dog, the little dog jumped between him and JR and growled. JB: "he just told me you're armed, that is what saved me from the one yesterday I could not see he was armed." JR: "maybe we should get one of these little ones for my family?" JB: "that's fine with me, we will call tomorrow and see if they're going to get any more of the small ones, once he is used to me I can let him sleep with Ben."

JR "that's not a bad idea." They moved from tree to bush, bush to tree, tree to Bush until they came to the spot where he likes to go, he sniffed and then relieved himself and they went back to the house. JB put him back in the crate took the leash off. JB and JR walked out, locked the door and worked their way back to the big house, went in and rejoined the rest of the family. Ben said "I made them do it like you did me so we know they could come over when they wanted to." JB: "that's real good I am proud of you."

Mom said "supper is ready." They all set down said a prayer and then had supper." The women got up and started to clean up the table. The men and boys went down to the game room. Ben said "grandpa can you teach my brothers to play pool to?" Dad said "of course let's start, and he began to tell Larry and John how to play the game." JB and JR sat down on the couch, JB: "I think we should get a van that is bulletproof to drive around in and out of the park with our three dogs, and the four of us." JR: "that sounds like a good idea to me; you know where we can get one of those?" JB: "no but I will have Betty check on it in the morning and get a price, but I don't think price has anything to do with it, you can't put a price on us, so we will see how quick we can get one."

JR: "Do you know when LJ and CR will get here?" JB: "tomorrow afternoon, LJ said he would call as soon as he got off the plane and they should be out front by the time we get there." JR: "what is the plan for tomorrow?" JB: "we will leave here at 2 o'clock tomorrow morning and put external battery packs on the cameras so that we don't have to change batteries all the time, they are rechargeable and should last 2 to 3 days, so we don't have to get up every morning at 2:00." JB: "then we will be able to download from the car, now let's check on progress up on the hill, the 300 yard range is complete, they were putting fence up on the dog training area, they were erecting the house clearing training area, and all the new cameras should be working as they are going to walk somebody around to make sure every camera picks up where the other one leaves off that way somebody does drop something off hopefully we will get a good picture of them."

JR: "you sure have had a lot to juggle all by yourself, give me things to do that will cut your load in half." JB said "I didn't know how quickly you wanted to start and have you made a decision on where you want to live?" JR: "yes we decided to build a house in here next to you so we are all still together, I don't know what I would do not having you all around." JB: "I feel the same way, even with Jennifer and Ben I had an empty place and I was not as happy as I could have been, now that's all changed I feel everything is complete."

JB stood up and said "Jennifer and Ben time to go home two o'clock comes pretty early." They all said goodbye and JB: "Ben opened the door and we will go through the tunnel." Ben opened the door JB waved goodbye and Ben closed the door and they went to the spring house. Jennifer put Ben to bed and came out and sat next to him on the couch. JB: "how did you like Rose?" Jennifer: "she is really nice I believe were going to be really good friends." JB pulled her over close and hugged her and kissed her and said "two o'clock comes awful early see you in the morning." Jennifer got up and went to bed JB went over grabbed the leash put it on the little dog and they went out for a walk ten minutes later they were back JB lay down on the couch and the little dog came and laid on his pad.

CHAPTER 19

WEDNESDAY WEEK 3

1:45 JB got up dressed snapped the leash on the little dog and they slipped out the front door he locked it and they went toward the big house. JR and his dad were just coming out the front door. JB: "I'm going to let the dog relieve himself and then we will leave." The little dog crossed over between him and JR, JR smiled: "always doing his job", JB nodded and said "JR sit in the front with dad, I will sit in the back with the dog." twelve minutes later they were on the hill. JR said I will do this one you do the next and then come back and get me, we will get done twice as fast."

JR got out took his laptop and two of the new batteries and vanished into the woods. Dad pulled up to the third site, JB grabbed two new batteries took his laptop and the little dog and vanished into the woods. Dad drove up to a turnaround went back past the second site turned around again and pulled up and waited for JR. Three minutes later JR jumped in, dad drove the van to the next site. Five minutes later JB jumped in the van and said "JR we both will do this one and get done quicker."

Dad stopped at the forth site they both got out and disappeared into the woods. JR whispered "I'll get this one you get the one on the cliff." JB went deeper into the woods toward the cliff he got to where the camera should be and it was gone he looked around. Carefully not to disturb anything and could not find the camera thought we're going have to do something different here and headed back to where JR was waiting. JR: "that was quick, was there a problem."

JB with a disgusted voice said "camera was gone they must've found it, I think we'll have to get a real covert camera and stick in their maybe two." JR: "why don't we look a bit we can go up and back the trail and see if maybe there trying to spy on us with our own cameras we should get a flash if the cameras are set to take pictures." JB: "sounds good to me, you go all the way up to the road and then I'll meet you here, I'll go to the cliff look around there and, come back up the path."

JB walked briskly down the path thirty feet later he got a flash from the camera, he went in the direction he saw the flash and found the camera strapped to a tree he unstrapped it, slipped it in his jacket and headed back up the path JR met him shortly. JB: "I got the camera good thinking on your part what about you." JR: "I found the camera in a different place so I just picked it up and we will have to change our plans a bit." They got in the van and left. On the way back JB and JR downloaded the cameras they had retrieved into their laptops synced the files so they were the same on both machines and then viewed what they had; they were the same faces they had been getting lately. JB: "what do you think we should do?"

JR: "maybe we should interrogate them, you and I can go up capture them, and I will get all they know out of them. Hank may not like what we do but then we will know who's pulling their chain." JB: "we might check with Hank seeing as I am now officially a member of the police department, we do not want to get you in trouble and as soon as LJ and CR get back the three of you will be officially in the police department that will tie our hands a bit." JR: "you're right we should do it by the book first and if that doesn't work then we will do it our way."

JB smiling "I can live with that and I think so can the others, and they'll be back to day in the afternoon anyway." JR said "two attempted hits on you are three too many, I think we need to put a stop to this, they are just going to try to hurt our families to get at us and that is unacceptable." JB: "I agree." Dad said "I agree also, I will spend everything I have to protect you all." JR: "thanks dad, it could get messy." Dad: "then it'll get messy."

They were home, they got out of the van. JB: "I will see you in the morning I will let the little dog relieve himself and I'm going to bed." Dad locked the van and he and JR went in the big house. JB walked cautiously from cover to cover, stopped when the little dog wanted to go, went to the spring house, and locked the door. He unsnapped the little dog, he ran to his pad and lay down JB lay down on the couch and went to sleep. JB woke and heard Jennifer fixing breakfast in the kitchen. He got up walked over and hugged her and kissed her and said good morning. He said "I will take the little dog out and I will be back how much time have I got?" Jennifer: "ten minutes will do it."

JB put the leash on the little dog and they went out the door. They went from cover to cover till they got the spot the little dog used and he did his thing and he headed back to the house slipped in locked the door and took the leash off the little dog. JB: "was there anything in the instructions for the dog about his name?" Jennifer: "yes I believe they called him Benny but I don't want people to think the dog is named after our son." JB: "how about Sam?" Jennifer: "it sounds good to me", JB: "I will wait till the other dogs get here, if none of them are named Sam that'll be his name."

JB: "I like the idea of having the spring house open so your mom and dad can stay there and LJ, CR, JR, and Rose will have a place for their moms and dads to come and stay and visit." "Mom and dad have decided on their plans and construction will start sometime next week and the following week they'll be in it." Jennifer: "where do you want to stay?" JB: "I am used to living in the big house but I don't care as long as you're happy and we live together. These problems won't last forever, we will solve them, we will get rid of the Arab he's the last of their line, and the bounties will go away."

JB's phone rang, he answered "hello." The voice on the phone: "this is your old CO the Arab you missed called and he has set up a one-day visa to be in the United States and talk with you and tell you the war is over he wants peace between you and peace with the United States, the United States government has agreed to fly him over and set up your meeting next week he is going to adopt you into his family and give you their coat of arms and he is bringing his last son and another man to be in the ceremony plus there is a master bomb maker here who wants peace right along with him the bomb maker has asked for asylum and he will show your bomb squad everything he knows about bomb building. I will get a hold of your police department and have them on guard and keep out any onlookers, it will probably last less than an hour so I will get a hold of you within 24 hours of the meeting it will be in the morning." JB: "thank you sir I will tell the guys and we shall act accordingly as we still have some funny stuff going on around here, goodbye and I'll be waiting for your call."

Jennifer: "what was that all about?" JB: "remember the Arab we are waiting for." Jennifer: "yes I do." JB:"he will be here Tuesday or Wednesday next week. Not to make war but peace he has one son left and he doesn't want to lose him, so he is not the problem with the people that are spying on us, LJ, CR, JR and I will come up with a plan and capture these people and find out who they're working for and why, this could be over quicker than we think." Jennifer: "that will be wonderful; Ben and I won't have to worry anymore."

Jennifer: "I will get Ben; we will eat breakfast, and go over and tell everybody the news. They finished eating, JB: "I will take the dog out so he can take care of his business, and I will meet you over there, you go through the tunnels." JB put the leash on the little dog and quickly went out the door and went from cover to cover the dog relieved himself and they went from cover to cover to the big house. Jennifer and Ben were just coming up from the game room when JB walked in the door he turned the little dog loose and they all went in the kitchen. JB: "I have great news for everyone the Arab will be here Tuesday or Wednesday next week he wants to make peace with us not war he is going to adopt us in to his family and give us a crest to show that he is serious he doesn't want to lose his last son so he will not attack any Americans. I got off the phone with our CO and the

United States government is giving him a one-day visa." JB: "so now we got to figure out who these clowns are up on the hill so I will call Hank he can come over and we will brainstorm this a little bit either tomorrow or the next day we will take them down, because the way we have seen them in the videos we will be on them before they know what hit them."

Mom said "are you all hungry?" JB: "no thanks mom we ate before we came but you guys eat. It should be a great day." When they were finished with breakfast the women cleaned off the table and Mom said "now you men sit down and tell us what is running through your heads." JB: "well you're starting construction on your new house and you should be in that not next week but the following week, so Jennifer what are we going to do, JR and Rose need to think about what they're going to do, that is one of the things we had running through our heads." Mom: "no were talking about the people up on the hill, what is going on there?"

JB: "JR and I were discussing that and I think we should talk to Hank have a little police involvement not today but tomorrow when everybody's back we will go up and take them down and find out who they're working for. We will hit them so hard and fast they'll be in a daze and if one of them does something stupid he's gone." Jennifer said "no more goats?" JR said "no more goats, we are now the lions." JB: "we can't say much more than that until we talk to Hank and get a tentative plan going and when LJ and CR get back and the two policemen with them, they will probably be with us on the hill as they both are going to be in SWAT we will match one of them with one of us based on the pictures there isn't that many of them so we will make decisions later so there's not too many of us getting in our own way and there are two spots to hit." Jennifer: "you sound like you think this is not going to be too hard?"

JR: "no we don't think it's going to be too hard, I was up on the hill leading one of the units and this was one of the easiest takedowns I've ever had these people are not trained like we are or like the Arabs are, they are gang bangers they watched TV and then do stupid things." JB: "there was nothing in the paper or record they just vanished, their friends don't have a clue what happened so they can't plan for anything other than what they're doing now."

"Girls" dad said "when I talked to Hank after the debriefing he said he never saw anything that went as smooth as what went down up on the hill he said he has seen a lot of police takedowns and he said none of them even come close for the men being safe and the criminals taking all the punishment so I think we can safely rely that our boys will handle everything, and we don't have to worry about JB because there's no goat in this mission." They all laughed and most of the tension was gone. JB said "JR and I are going to the office we have a bulletproof van to order and Hank to call and a whole lot of things to get done before the guys come."

JB said "Rose why don't you and Jennifer look at houses. Dad said they had a lot of layouts and one of us that want to can stay here in this house so have fun." JB, JR, and dad and the little dog went out got in the van dad drove to the office and they all went in. The surveillance guy said we just got done about two hours ago with our night walk-through and every camera picked up the new entry as he left the old and we covered the whole park including the residential section. Now we are going to do the daylight walk-through should take us about three hours and then this should be a wrap." JB: "Thank you, give the bill to Betty and she will take care of it and thank you again we appreciate all your hard work." They took the cameras out of their pockets and the batteries and put them in the closet.

JB: "Betty can you make some calls and see if you can find a used bulletproof van that we can get six people and four dog crates plus places for our rifles and pistols." Betty: "I will go out on the Internet do some searching and get back to you." JB: "thanks." JB: "JR you and dad want to go up and check on the construction on the hill I will get a hold of Hank and see when he can come out." JR looked at dad and said "we're gone." They got in the van and drove up to the construction sites. JB called Hank told him about the call from the CO, Hank said "yes your C0 got a hold of me about five minutes ago and gave me the rundown, so who are these other clowns?" JB: "I don't know what time LJ and CR will get back to day, I think we should maybe make a raid on the hill as we had to look for cameras, it appears they found them and they moved them so we brought them off the hill, when you come over we will download them to you and we will make a tentative plan for tomorrow morning and we will take them down and interrogate them like terrorists, we may be able to ship them off to home land security." Hank: "I'll be over in about a half hour we will work on a tentative plan and execute it tomorrow morning." JB: "we don't know what these other people think is going on maybe they don't know the bounty is gone so we will have to interrogate them and find out." JB: "see you later bye."

Betty came over and said "I found two places that seem to be reasonable and both have very good reputations one has a pretty large truck that would probably work for your swat moving headquarters, the other one has a van that sounds just like what you want." JB said "what kind of prices?" Betty: "the large van they want 50,000, the other one is 35,000. If you want all the electronics you will need in the big van they want another 15,000 for that, I priced a new smaller van and they were up over 60,000 the big one was up over 100,000. The cheaper ones the motor has been rebuilt on both of them brand-new tires brand-new shocks the frames have been beefed up each one will warranty the vehicle for 50,000 miles." JB: "can you get them to send pictures and descriptions and the prices and see if you can get them before Hank gets here in a half hour." Betty got back on the phone.

JB got the leash and took the little dog out so he could relieve himself. JB called Jennifer and ask her how things were going, she said "great everybody thinks we should take the big house since you lived there most of your life so I agreed. Rose picked out a couple plans she likes and plans to show them to JR and they will get their house on order, she thinks LJ and CR will want to stay in the big house until they find somebody they really like, which is fine with me." JB: "that is great, I'm walking the little dog, and Hank just pulled into the office so I'll have to go back I will see you later bye-bye."

Hank grabbed his laptop, JB grabbed his and they went into the conference room set everything on the table JB started the download to Hank's laptop." Hank: "who do you think these people are?"

"JR and I were discussing that this morning and after the CO called we think their just gang bangers that got wind that there was bounties out and they don't even know the bounties have been pulled and they think all they have to do is find an Arab and he'll tell them how to get the money, so JR and I don't think they're too bright I think we should do just about what we did last time one of my guys and one of your guys that's going to be on the swat team, and we will set up and take them down if they go to shoot we will shoot, if any are left, then we will interrogate them and try to find out what they think they're going to accomplish and if they think they're getting a bounty we will just turn them over to homeland security and they vanish, if they were after the bounty then their terrorist." JB replied.

Hank: "I guess we could get away with that." Hank: "shadow told me you have a whole bunch of the security cameras going up in the park, and you got construction going on up the hill?" JB: "Yes the dog training area should be finished today, and they are putting up the building for House clearing and Betty's going to bring in some pictures and pricing on two vans one we will buy here at the park and it will be used here and swat and there is a big one for swats control center that she got a pretty good price on so we will look at those as soon as she gets them." Hank I see you went to two big screens on security cameras?" JB: "yes somehow the whole residential area got missed for cameras so I have had them install zoom cameras so they can actually zoom in on what's going on in that area."

"Also the Arab that runs the convenience store, he does not want to make bombs anymore, he is here on asylum and he will be here when the Arab comes Tuesday or Wednesday and he will sit down with us and the bomb squad and build a bomb show how to take it apart and also a couple of Navy SEALs will be here to go through that class as well so he is not a problem we just have to find out about the other Arab." JB also "I've been thinking when we are doing the raid up on the hill your guys may take out the Arab in the first apartment building and in the other apartment building just to make sure they're not doing bomb building in one something else in the other."

Hank: "that sounds doable, I will see about getting search warrants good for tomorrow or Friday." Hank: "I better get back to the office; I got a lot of work to do here see you tonight." Hank left, and JR and dad came back and we went back into the conference room they looked at the pictures for the vans Hank had taken a copy of the large van to start paperwork on that before they lost it. Dad said "have you ordered it yet?" JB: "No but we will." JB called Betty in and said order the van and find out how quick we can get it." JB's phone rang it was Jennifer she said lunch was ready and they should come over so the three of them got in the van and went to the big house. They ate lunch JR said "Rose has picked out a house plan, so we will get it on order." JB: "JR you and Rose get your house on order and dad and I will pick up the guys when they get in, they should be due in shortly." JR: "I will see you later after we get this taken care of." JB and dad went from cover to cover back to the office. Betty said "they will get the changes done to the van and it should be here Tuesday of next week."

JB's phone rang, he answered it and it was LJ "we're down on the runway come and get us we're homesick." JB said "dad they are on the runway let's go." JB and dad jumped in the van and headed for the airport, fifteen minutes later they were in the pickup zone dad opened the back, JB opened the side door. Five minutes later LJ and CR came out along with the two police and 4 dogs. The dogs were in crates the van was about 6 feet wide so it took three across the back LJ took his dog out of the crate CR and JB turned the crate long ways and laid it on top of the other three it fit they closed the back, CR and Mary took the back seat. LJ said "JB sit in the back with Curt and I will sit in front." LJ took his dog and loaded him in front of the front seat and he got in next to dad. They started to leave the terminal and JB's phone rang. JB answered "and said hello."

Mom said "JR's been shot, came from the hill." JB: "is he dead?" Mom: "no we have an ambulance coming Jennifer has him stabilized and Hank is on his way to the hill shadow is blocking the road right now." JB: "I will call Hank thanks mom by." JB: "JR got shot." Jennifer has him stabilized and an ambulance is on the way to take him to surgery there and skip the ER altogether. LJ and CR do you have your pistols on you, both said yes Curt and Mary said yes." JB: "we do not need rifles in the woods we can't shoot more than 20 feet, so our pistols will be fine we have the dogs we can find them as they are probably hiding out there somewhere."

JB: "I will call Hank and see where he is and what he's doing." JB called Hank, "hello this is Hank", JB: "this is JB where are you?" Hank: "we are at the bottom of the hill." JB: "stay there we are on our way, we will be there in eight minutes." They pulled up to the bottom of the hill got out of the van and went over to talk to Hank. JB looked at LJ and CR said "how far away from somebody hidden do they pick up".

CR said "5 to 10 feet sometimes longer, we all have our vests, and our pistols and two clips." Mary and Curt both nodded that they had their pistols and clips." JB and Curt looked at Mary and Curt and said "how good are you in the woods, can you walk without making noise?"

Mary said "I am not sure I've never really hunted."

Curt: "I think I can be quiet I've Stalked Deer."

LJ you take Curt go to the first site, pickup sent and then follow it try to take them alive if possible but don't endanger yourselves" CR you want to take Mary and cover the right side of the road 5 feet deep and show her how to walk and go slow we are not sure if they have communicated off the hill or not the biggest thing is I want you to keep them from crossing the road if you can and if they do you take them."

JB: "are you good with that?"

CR: "Mary are you comfortable with that?"

Mary: "yes and I'm a good marksman and I will shoot."

JB: "Will your dogs attack on command." LJ: "no we never did any of that but if they run they will take them down we did do that." JB: "The pictures we been getting were the same people and the last set of pictures only had two in site three none in four none in two and nobody went down the path into site one." JB: "Curt if you were them and knowing the way things are situated and you just shot somebody would you go deeper or would you go down the hill?"

Curt: "I would go down." LJ: "I would go down the hill but I don't think they're that bright I think they're going to be out toward the road on the path to site three." CR: I agree with LJ." JB: 'Mary what do you think and look at it this way, you just shot somebody and you're kind of in a panic." Mary: "I think I would stay close to my pickup spot as they don't have to look for me." JB: "you are probably a lot smarter than they are", leave two cars down here blocking the road if anybody comes to pick them up or anybody comes you stop them put them in the squad car, and pull their car off the road nobody gets through."

Right now it's around 2 o'clock they usually get picked up at dusk they may have called there may be a car already up there or they may be gone." CR why doesn't one team start here with one dog and one of your guys Hank from here he must be a volunteer I'd rather go alone with my dog then have somebody that really doesn't want to be on my back." Shadow said I would be happy to go with you, and I'm good in the woods."

JB with a serious look on his face said "I think we should all start from down here I don't think we should send the car up, it is just a target and we don't have a bulletproof van yet" so that way we all have dogs somebody with the dog needs to go with me." CR said "Mary would you go with JB." Mary said "of course" and she and her dog went over by JB. we should each stay ten feet apart four of us will go up this side, you others go up the other side stay about five feet from the road. How does that sound?" Everybody shook their head yes. JB: "Hank can you get another man up here, so we can put one more man in LJ's team?" Hank: "sure I'll radio for one right now and you go ahead the two of us can handle this till he gets here." JB: "CR when you go past the trail for site three go a little ways farther and come back and go down to the cliff and let your dog track and they will try to find them that way hopefully they cannot squeeze in between us, just don't shoot each other, this is a hasty plan." Five on the left went into the woods CR and shadow went into the other woods they spread out 5 feet between each other and silently went up the hill." JB moved closer to Mary and said " step between the limbs; and put your feet slowly down on leaves so they don't make noise after a while it will be second nature." He moved back to his position. Took them about thirty minutes to get halfway to their destination things were going fairly smooth. All of a sudden Mary's dog growled JB stopped Mary stopped, JB pointed at Mary and held his hand up like stop then he got on the left side of the trees and slowly went forward. Fifteen feet later he saw somebody crouched down behind a tree he appeared to be unarmed but they were always armed until you know different. JB looked back and he could see that Mary had taken three or four steps closer she had her dog in one hand her pistol in the other he thought good girl. JB: "said don't move or your dead, don't move or you're dead." Fear came over the man's face. JB pointing his gun at the man's head said "do exactly like I say or I will shoot you." The man screamed "don't shoot don't shoot don't shoot."

JB said "put your hands above your head where I can see them and if you move too fast I will shoot you." JB started to walk toward the man when he saw LJ put a gun to the man's head.

The man screamed "don't shoot."

LJ said "I am only going to ask you one question at a time you don't give me an answer I will get my knife out or I will let the dog have you, your choice and nobody will ever find you in these woods the critters will dispose of you." The man was shaking he was so afraid. LJ: "were you the shooter?" The man: "no it was the other guy." LJ "Where is he?" LJ moved his hand toward the knife on his belt. The man was shaking so much with fear LJ was afraid he was going to fall down. The man said "I don't know where he is he went off the path and onto the woods."

LJ: "Was it toward the bottom of the hill or the other way?" The man: "toward the road." LJ: "right now you are considered a terrorist and now how many people are in your group?" The man: "six that I know of." LJ: "are you making bombs." The man hesitated and LJ started to pull out his knife, the man shook some more: "there is an Arab making some." LJ "do you know where he lives?" The man "yes he is my roommate." LJ: "how many bombs has he made?"

The man shaking uncontrollably said "he has made six."

LJ with a menacing voice said "are they in your apartment or are they planted in the city."

The man in a shaky voice stammered "one is in the park by a ride and other one is near the Police Department front door in the bushes."

LJ starting to pull his knife out of its sheath "which ride?"

The man blurting out "The one with the big wheel, by one of the main supports. The other four are in the apartment as far as I know." LJ: "how many are in your apartment?" The man: "me and the Arab." LJ: "where is the Arab now, up here or in the city?" The man: "in the city." JB called Hank: "Hank we got one you want to come and get him. Hank said "I'll be right there. JB said: "LJ call CR tell him we got one but not the shooter Hank is going to pick him up and we will continue on up the hill; take him and cuff him to two trees or one big one, then come back and we will proceed."

JB smiled at Mary and said "Mary you and your dog are doing great I'm proud of you."

Mary: "I have never been in a firefight from what CR said its chaos." JB: "yes it is you forget about the bullets you relax and concentrate on your target and you have a 90% chance of surviving that way." LJ was back they took their positions and slowly moved up the hill. They were almost to the top of the hill when they heard a shot sounded like a rifle. JB thought it is probably about 100 feet ahead more toward LJ. He moved closer to Mary and whispered "I thought it sounded closer to the road than we are." Mary said "the dog is telling me it's more in front of LJ and he's trying to catch the scent." They continued on slowly not hearing anything Mary's dog looked a little to the right sound was coming closer somebody was running." JB moved to the right he could see LJ moving from tree to tree getting ready. Then there was the man twenty feet ahead Mary turned the dog loose LJ turned his dog loose the man went down each dog had an arm it was over." JB took a handkerchief out of his pocket and took the rifle away from the man Mary had cuffed the man's left arm Curt had cuffed the right arm they found a couple of small trees spread him out and cuffed him to them.

LJ and CR stood in front of the man and CR said " you shot my brother I'm going to skin you right here but I'm not going to kill you I'm going to let critters do that." But first I'm going to do what the Arabs do I'm going to get a little fire going then some small sticks and I'm going to brand every inch of your body." CR started clearing a small space, gathered some small sticks and a few leaves to start a fire.

JB looked at the man in a menacing way "I think we should give him a chance to tell us who told him to do this and we will kill that guy instead." He said it's an Arab that makes bombs and lives with a friend of mine we were supposed to make a lot of money on the bounty from the Arabs." LJ: "the bounty was lifted two weeks ago and the Arab is coming over and adopting us into his family the war between us is over and because you shot one of us we can give you to him and he will take you back and you will take a long time to die."

CR: "are you alone?" The man: "no there's another guy he's probably farther down the hill you might've passed him on your way up." LJ started to reach for his knife: "are you sure there aren't any others?" The man: "not up here." LJ:"if I think you are lying' we will leave you here and we will cut you so you bleed the critters will come and chew on you, is there anything else we should know." The man: "the Arab that my friend lives with has made six bombs to be planted I don't know if anything else has been done really I don't." LJ: "how many people are in your group?" The man said "six that I know of." JB: "and you better repeat Word for Word what you've told us and if you leave anything out and the others tell the police more than you, we will not

press charges against you. And we will bring you back up on the hill."
CR: "that was our brother you shot, if he dies. You will be back up on
this hill and wish you had never been born."

The six walked off about twenty feet and whispered the man
tried to turn and look and he was scared. They came back and
unhooked him from the tree cuffed his hands behind his back and
walked toward the road. JB called Hank and told him to bring an
empty squad car up to get the shooter. JB called his dad and said
"bring up the van." Five minutes later the shooter was in the back of
the squad car the rest were in the van and they headed down the hill."

JB:"we can leave the windows cracked and the dogs will get plenty of
air and it's not that warm, let's go see how JR's doing." They all nodded
their heads yes and they went off to the hospital. JB called Jennifer:
"how is JR." Jennifer: "he's in good shape the bullet went in between
two ribs and out between two ribs so he doesn't have any broken ribs
and he should heal nicely and be as good as new."

JB asked "what room is he in."

Jennifer: "He's in recovery room 320 and tomorrow they'll move him
to a regular room." JB: "we will be there in five minutes, bye."

JB: "when we get done checking on JR we will take Mary and Curt
home and get their crates inside and situated, is that all right with you
two?" They both said yes and they pulled into the hospital parking
lot and went up to see JR. JR was still asleep and Rose and Jennifer
were sitting there Jennifer watching all the numbers on the monitor.
JB: "Rose if you want to spend the night with JR we will take care of
the children for you." Rose: "I would like that and JR told me how you
would probably take better care of us than our own family." LJ: "we
have kept each other alive for ten years were not going to stop now."

Jennifer asked "what are you doing when you leave here?"
JB replied "we are going to take Curt and Mary home help them

to unload their dogs and then we will either take LJ and CR back to the big house or swing by and pick you up and we'll all go home."

Jennifer: " pick me up."

JB: "when should JR wake up?"

Jennifer: "in about twenty minutes."

JB: "we should see you within the next hour" and they left. They drove Mary home got the dog out of the crate took the crate in the house got Mary's luggage in the house. CR said "I will call you later." JB got a hold of Hank and told him he better pick up all their suspects and there are confirmed at least four bombs in the one apartment so you should have no trouble getting your warrants and you should hit them immediately Hank said "yes we will be there in half an hour have them all in jail within an hour." JB: " we will debrief in the morning at 9 o'clock at the park." Hank "that sounds good for me I'll bring my people too." They got to Curt's house helped him unload the crate carried it in the house he said "I will figure out where to put it later, Curt introduced them to his wife and two kids and they left.

They went back to the hospital and went to visit RJ. RJ: "boss I'm sorry I made a big mistake." JB: "I made the mistake I should've given you more info about what was going on up on the hill, I should've made a bigger point of saying don't go out without your vest." JR did you get them?" JB: "yes they were easy, and not very good in the woods, and the dogs did a super job."

LJ: "we have a bomb to find at the park, and there's one at the police station, they told us where they were, but we will take the dogs and make sure." CR: "The bomb squad will take care of the one at the police department, and then come out to get the one at the park." They chatted for another ten minutes then Jennifer said "he needs to rest we need to go Rose will take good care of him and so will the nurses he is a VIP here."

They left, got in the van and drove to the big house. LJ: "CR and I will take care of the dogs in the crate and unloading JB you go up to the office and make sure everything is all right and I will come up later and then we'll go look for the bomb."

Jennifer "I will go in and help mom with the boys." JB went cover to cover to the office and went in.

Betty said "how is JR?" JB: "he is doing fine they said "he should make a complete recovery." Betty said "I saw him lying there out in front of the house and I was so worried, and Jennifer and Rose ran out and pulled him under the tree, and the policeman helped and then he came up and got supplies, and Jennifer went to work on JR, it looked like she saved his life."

JB said "it appears that they have planted a bomb about ten feet up on the Ferris wheel and the bomb squad will be here later to disarm it, we are going out now to make sure we can find it." JB went to the big house; LJ and JR were patting their dogs, and said "are you ready." JB: "yes let me get my dog and see if he can find it and then you can tell me if I'm doing it right or wrong." They both said sounds good to us. JB took his leash hanging by the door went and got his dog and out they went.

JB: "by now there should not be anyone up on the hill they all should be rounded up and in jail but I am not going to take chances and I'm going cover to cover." CR: "when we get thirty feet from the Ferris wheel we will stop you tell your dog bomb and we'll see how long it takes him to find it." They went to the Ferris wheel JB got ready; CR got his watch out and said " go."

JB told Sam "bomb." Pointed the little dog down the path the little dog went from side to side around the trees in the bushes and he got to the Ferris wheel he went around the control room they went through the gate started around the bottom of the Ferris wheel he went to the right and was going then stopped turned around came back five feet and looked up at the one support up in the air, JB saw what he thought was a package he held up his hand.

CR hit stopwatch it said seven minutes. JB came back where CR and LJ were standing. CR hit his stopwatch: "go."

LJ: "bomb." His dog started sniffing he went around the trees around the bushes side to side on the path checked each side very thoroughly went around the control room for the Ferris wheel went inside he went to the left then around and he went to the right and he went to the right then he went to the right took two steps stopped went back to the left stopped turned around and looked up in the air LJ saw the bomb he held up his hand. CR said "six minutes and 50 seconds." LJ came back. CR: "JB your dog did really well because they said the smaller dogs a lot of times missed bombs that were over ten feet high, that railing is probably about ten feet tall maybe a little higher he said I'm impressed."

JB said "thank you, he has save my life once already I'm very happy with him." JB got his watch out, CR you ready:" yes." JB pressed the stopwatch and said "go." CR's dog started going from side to side around the trees around the bushes back onto the path back and forth checking the bushes on both sides came to the control room went around it, then around the Ferris wheel went through the gate, he turned right went down made a left went down got ready to take a left stopped turnaround went back looked up in the air LJ held up his hand because he saw the bomb.

JB hit stopwatch it said six minutes and 51 seconds. LJ: "I think we have three really good dogs. ten minutes later the bomb squad pulled up and said "you guys find it?"

JB: "yes standing right here it's on the right-hand side upon that beam in the corner where the beam meets the main structure." The bomb squad brought a ladder over climbed up and carefully detached the bomb from the beam came down the ladder very carefully opened the bomb from one side reached in clipped a wire and said "that's it." We will detonate them tomorrow. JB: "thank you very much I think we are going to make this part of the world a safer place to live in, you guys have a good evening." They waved, got in their truck and left.

JB: "why don't we go back and have supper it's been a long day." They went back to the big house." They put leashes on their dogs and took them into the big house. LJ and CR introduce their dogs to the family. Jennifer said "supper is ready come and sit down." LJ sat at the corner of one side of the table CR sat at the other and their dogs sat beside them. JB sat at another corner and Sam sat beside him.

Dad asks "how did the dogs do?"

CR: "they found the bomb in a very acceptable time, we have three exceptional dogs here; it was a shame we didn't have Mary's here." JB: "maybe she went to the station and found that one." CR: "I will ask her tomorrow and see." They ate supper and then finished, mom and Jennifer started to clean off the table and loaded the dishwasher. The men went out into the living room and sat and talked about the mission.

JB: "you two will have to teach me how to really use this dog, he was showing me but I didn't realize it but Mary pointed and I got the idea without the dogs we may have gotten shot at, but they gave us ample warning. I think we should have patrols going around the park and see if the dogs pick up on anyone carrying a gun."

LJ: "I think that's a good idea, dog handler and security guard." CR: "we can't be out there all the time but once around noon and maybe another around five to start with and see what we come up with." JB: "that sounds like a good starting point what happens if the dog is checking for guns and happens to come into an area where there's an explosive will he let you know it's there?"

LJ: "they did that in training and the dog will come over and sit and look at it so then you have to figure out whether it's a gun hidden or an explosive in our case we have three dogs so one of the other dogs could be brought into the area and given the bomb command then we should know exactly what's there." JB: "that's good thinking we may have one of the safest parks in the country all because of these dogs."

Dad said "I agree they could probably even find a lost child if the parents had something that the child has worn." Dad: "I thought we should have cameras at both entrances taking pictures of each person that came through one of the gates and timestamps on the pictures and tickets, that way we could get pictures of who we are looking for sent to all the security guards that way we could cover the park area much quicker." They all thought that was a good idea. JB: "CR why don't you check with the surveillance guy tomorrow and see if they have something that will work with that?"

CR took out his phone and put it in his message app.

LJ: "when do you think we should start swat training?" JB: "I will check with Hank tomorrow, we will have to have somebody to run the command center at the police department and another to run the one in the truck I don't know if we can use the same one for either position." LJ: "since we four are part time even though you JB are commander of the swat squad, one of the full-time policeman in our SWAT team should be your second in command."

JB: "those are all good thoughts; we will have to have a sit down with Hank and see who else he plans on having in SWAT." JB: "that sounds like a good idea we have a meeting planned for tomorrow we should have Hank bring in his troops and anyone else he wants in SWAT." They all agreed and JB called Hank. Hank answered "hello." JB: "what about having a meeting on SWAT tomorrow instead of the one we had planned?" Hank: "we should meet in the morning and I will bring my people and I have ordered cars for the officers with dogs, my understanding is you have a van for all of yours?" JB: "ours will be set up to carry four dogs even though we only have three and your van will be set up for three so if we don't need our van I won't bring my dog."

Jennifer came and said "time for us to go home, Ben needs to go to school tomorrow and Rose will want to enroll her two boys, I had mom put those two boys to bed and Rose can enroll them in school when you take Ben and I will check and see how RJ is doing." JB: "okay

I'll see the rest of you in the morning have a good night." JB, Jennifer, and Ben went to the spring house. JB: "while you're putting Ben to bed I will take Sam out and let him relieve himself for the night." Jennifer: "okay be careful see you when you get back."

JB put the leash on Sam and out the door they went, eleven minutes later they were back, JB slipped in the door locked it turned Sam loose and saw Jennifer was waiting for him on the couch. Jennifer: "are we going to be safer now?" JB: "I believe we will, but we will still need to be vigilant until I know for sure, I have to check with Hank and see if he got information out of them that we had not gotten." JB: "they may try to lawyer up but that is not going to work because they're going to be turned over to homeland and we should never see them again." Jennifer leaned over and they kissed, she got up and said "I will see you in the morning it's been a long day good night." JB: "thank you for being so quick to save JR, it would break my heart to lose one of them, good night and I love you." Jennifer: "I love you too with all my heart." JB lay down on the couch and went to sleep.

CHAPTER 20

THURSDAY WEEK 3

JB woke up at 5:30 got on his running clothes put the leash on Sam went out the door locked it and ran to the big house. LJ and CR were just coming out the front door with their dogs, JB joined them and they did their run, it took a little longer than normal because the dogs had to relieve themselves but they got back in 23 minutes and they thought that was pretty good for the first time around. LJ and CR said " we will see you later and went in the big house.

JB and Sam ran to the spring house he went in and shut the door and turned Sam loose, Jennifer was fixing breakfast, she said "would you get Ben up and dressed and we will have breakfast." JB: "sure" and he went into Ben's room woke him up and got him dressed and they came out and sat down at the table and Jennifer brought breakfast over and sat down.

Jennifer said grace and they ate in silence. Jennifer: "would you clean up the table and I'll take Ben and go to the big house and make sure the boys are ready to go and have had something to eat." JB: "sure I'll see you in about ten minutes." JB cleaned off the table, put the dishes in the dishwasher and started it. He put the leash on Sam and they headed for the big house. JB went into the big house Jennifer had the three boys ready to go.

JB said "LJ and CR get those things we talked about last night checked on and I'll see you in about an hour at the office." LJ and CR said "will do and be careful we think things should be quiet now for a while but you never know." JB: "that's what I'm hoping but we will still be careful. Jennifer put Ben and JR's two boys in the back seat, JB put Sam on the floor and Jennifer got in the front and then he got in and drove to the hospital. He pulled up at the front door Jennifer got out turned and said "I will send Rose out" twelve minutes later Rose came out and got in the front seat. JB drove to the school parked in front and they all went into the school.

JB took Ben to his class, asked the teacher where to take Rose so she can enroll her two boys in school? She said take the next left down the hall and it will be halfway down on your right." JB said "thank you" and he and Rose took the boys to the main office. It took about fifteen minutes for Rose to get the boys enrolled they said "they would get the boys in their rooms", so JB and Rose left. Rose got in the back because Sam was sitting in the front seat, JB got in and they drove back to the hospital.

JB parked in the visitors lot and he and Rose went in. Rose said "they have him in room 210; Jennifer said "she'd meet us there." They got in the elevator, went up to the second floor got out and checked directions and headed toward room 210 it was just a short way down the hall, they found it and went in JR was eating breakfast Jennifer was sitting in the chair beside the bed. JB: "how do you feel this morning?" JR: "tired but I guess they got enough pain pills in me that I don't feel a lot of pain right now."

Jennifer: "you will be taking antibiotics and pain pills for a week, and then the antibiotics for another week, and I brought everything to do a castor oil pack on you twice a day in the morning and in the afternoon, the hospital said "I could do that as they can see it could cause no harm, they say it will take you at least six weeks to recover and they plan to keep you here for three. So if it helps you heal as fast as it did JB we will have you out of here in less than two."

JR and Rose both said "we hope so." JR: "where are LJ and CR?" JB: "they are checking things out up on the hill and we got a good idea to help us find children that get lost in the park and they will be checking on that with the surveillance people so I got them working, but they will come over later and visit, we will kind of do it in shifts as we're going to try to speed up getting swat going and a couple of other things, you just relax and get well, we can't get along without you." JR: "we will have to get furniture and appliances and beds, do they have any thrift stores around?" JB: "the park will furnish the house and two days after it's completed all of that should be in the house and ready to go all Rose has to do is pick out the styles and things she wants." Rose looked at JB and said "how can we ever thank you?"

JB: "when I said we were all family I meant that and because he'll be working at the park and when my dad dies we four will own the park, JR, LJ, CR and me. I believe that dad has already gotten a hold of the lawyers so when he and mom are gone it is divided equally among the four of us." Rose got up and came over and hugged him and kissed him on the cheek. JR: "Rose I told you JB will take care of everything and not to worry."

Jennifer: "it's time for you to go now I want to give JR his castor oil pack and then redo his bandages." JB: "JR you listen to her she'll take really good care of you, Rose I'll be back later to pick you and Jennifer up and we will get the kids." JB got in the car and thought to himself I think we need three, might as well get four minivans with built-in crates for the dogs through the park and cancel the bigger one. JB pulled up to the office went inside said "good morning Betty I need you to do something for me see what kind of a deal you can get on four minivans for the park and all of them have crates installed for the dogs", Betty: "okay, what about the bigger van we ordered, and how is JR?" JB: "He seems to be doing real well Jennifer and Rose were taking care of him when I left." JB called Hank and Hank answered: "good morning, how is JR?" JB: "he's pretty good all in all they say 4 to 6 weeks he should be as good as new, he was pretty lucky, Betty cancel the medium van?" Betty: "okay" Hank: "that's good, let me fill you in we raided the two apartment buildings the one that we knew about first where the Arab was staying we got four completed bombs and it looked like he had three more that he was building, the other apartment they had plans where they were going to set bombs it looked like based on the map they had, they were going to rob a bank set off a bomb. Hit a second bank set off a bomb, hit a third bank set off a bomb, and they figured with all the commotion they could get away Scott free and be gone before we found them." JB: "does that look like we've got this all cleaned up?" Hank: "I'm not sure yet but right now we don't have any evidence otherwise and the Arab at the convenience store says he likes America he wants to stay here and he will inform us of any cells that he finds out about, but he doesn't want to get involved so they come after him?" JB: "I can't blame him for that, and the captives come up with any more information than what we got from them on the hill?" Hank: "no and the new ones when they found out they were being charged as terrorists and what was in store for them told us everything they knew and that's how we found out about the bombs, they don't want to be put in with the Arabs."

JB: "I am in the process of ordering four minivans with crates for the dogs and I'm getting them through the park so we have a way of hauling the dogs to swat."

Hank: "I should have enough money in the grant to pay half on them, we will put swat on them that way if you don't have time to come down here you can go straight to the location of the call." JB: "as soon as Betty gets back to me with a price she is negotiating for the four right now and I will call and let you know what the total is." Hank: "sounds good if I hear anything I will let you know bye."

Five minutes later Betty came in and said "the people we got the other vehicles from say they have three minivans ready to go that somebody else ordered but they don't need them for four weeks they can ship them immediately as I said they can have the crates installed in a couple of hours and ship the three of them and they can have them on their way by early this afternoon we should have them by Saturday, and we can have them for 30,000 each and they will have another one done by Wednesday next week and we will have it on Friday and they have plenty of time to refill the other order."

JB: "let me call Hank and run it by him and I'll get back to you." JB called Hank. Hank answered, JB told him "I got the price for the four of them, it is 120,000. So that 60,000 for each of us." Hank: "that'll work into the budget go ahead and order." JB: "as good as done, bye."

JB: "Betty go ahead and order Hank said it's a go, also see if you can get another small dog for JR." Betty: "I will give them our card and I will call Hank and give him the number and the name of the man I have been talking to and he can set up his half and it will be done, and I will call about another small dog." JB heard a car pull up; he thought I hope that's LJ and CR. A few minutes more and LJ and CR came in and sat down beside him.

JB told them about the vans, and that JR was doing well and about getting a small dog for JR. LJ said "the dog training area is complete, house clearing building is up they are running the electricity and hooking up the control panel and then it will be done, and I think the dog for JR is a good idea." CR: "I have a call into surveillance and they said their man was out but he would get back to me as soon as he got back, and I think JR should have a dog." JB send a text to Hank to call him when he was free.

JB: "LJ I want you to go up on the hill take some of the rechargeable batteries in case any of them need changed otherwise just drive by and download you should be able to reach all cameras from the road, and go heavily armed with rifle, and pistol, were not having any more accidents, if you want to take a security guard to drive for you, then all you have to do is download and if necessary shoot." LJ: "not a bad idea I'll grab one and get it done." Hank called, JB said "how good is Curt?" Hank: "he's real good he's getting ready for his Sergeants test and we feel he'll pass." JB: "how about you make him my second-in-command." Hank: "I was going to put him in command of the dog division, I have a couple others that I will send over to talk to you and just pick one."

JB: "I was going to put CR and Mary in charge of dog training, CR will set bombs and guns for your people and Mary would do it for ours." Hank: "I never thought of that, but she is an exceptional officer and quite capable, let me think about that I'll get back to you." Hank: "okay, anything else." JB: "yes, they recommend 4 communication people for the command center, 2 mobile 2 in the station command center, and during the mission you will have the command center at the police department and we will have the mobile on site, what do you have for a budget?" Hank: "I will have to check and get back to you, bye."

CR came into the room and said "the surveillance man said we would need cameras at both entrances and they would feed a separate computer that would access the hard drive on the regular surveillance cameras and what was on its hard drive and they have facial recognition software and the pictures are tied to the ticket numbers, example a family of five would have five tickets all having consecutive numbers, he said depending on how many people are in the park you should have an answer within 5 to 10 minutes, it will continue to track those pictures until told to stop; it sounds to me like it will do what we want it to do." JB: "sounds good to me how much is it going to cost." CR: "20,000 installed and you will have to have an operator trained to use it, the surveillance man thought the operator of the cameras in the residence area should be able to handle that and what he's currently doing."

JB: "I think we start finding lost children, people will keep coming back to the park, if you agree order it." CR: "the 20,000 was a completion date three weeks from now which I thought should be fine as attendance should be light until after four weeks, the price was 30,000 done in the next week and a half, so I will get a hold of them and tell them it's a go at 20,000."

JB: "CR I know it's your personal life but have you and Mary got something going?" CR: "I think we might, we spent a lot of time together during dog training, we really enjoyed being together she and

I both want a lot of the same things from life and our goals are very similar, she wants to do SWAT for at least two years and then come in as needed, she wants a couple of kids, and so do I, she says she feels happy when I'm around and I feel the same way when she's around, she said "if the relationship keeps going like it's going we could get married and save money to put down on a house, I said that was fine with me I didn't tell her the park would give us one, if we get married then I'll tell her, but I have enjoyed being around her more than I have with any other woman I have met so far."

JB: "I think if the two of you can sit down and discuss anything you should have a wonderful relationship, I think that's what gets most marriages in trouble, they don't discuss things early enough, no discussion no resolution like our planning if we don't all agree we do something different." CR: "that is kind of what I thought, I told her I don't drink, she said "she drinks very little just to be sociable but never where it impairs her control, I like that, when she's around I just feel better, happier. She asked if I dated much, I said no because you are around and then you vanish two days, five days, two months, and you can't say why or where and I felt that was not fair in a relationship." She said "that's one of the most considerate things I've ever heard a man say and she hugged me."

JB: "you may have found what you're looking for, I know we are all at the place in life where I think we want to start a family, when I watched JR and Rose and the kids I would always felt a little empty." CR: "I had that same feeling." JB: "I'm really happy for you and hope it works out." CR: "me too she just grows on me every time I'm with her. She needs to do her monthly shooting requirements so we are going to go tomorrow and get her qualification for this month. I think I might be able to tweak her and improve her score." JB: "well if she wants improvement you are the best I've ever seen." JB: "if I could only take one person going into a firefight with pistols, you are the one I would pick, I would rather have all four of us." CR: "I like the four number, too all sides are covered."

Betty came in and said "A man just called and said he needed to talk to Mr. JB and he would be over in fifteen minutes, his name is Siham and he owns a convenience store, I told him you would be here, should I be worried?" JB: "no he is on our side now, I think he is going to warn us of something, bring him in as soon as he gets here."

Betty: "okay, I never dreamed this job was going to get so exciting" she turned and went back out front. CR: "looks like we have another good and bad situation." JB: "well we have more resources now than we had before, I think we will get better with each mission and depending on what it is we may have Hank put an arm guard on JR's door." CR: "good otherwise I would be over there with my dog." JB: "yes I know, Sam sure saved me all right and I really didn't know how to use him. Twenty minutes later Betty came in: "a Mr. Siham is here to see you."

JB: "bring him right in." Betty went out and told Mr. Siam to go on in." JB and CR both stood up and said "hello '. JB: "Sir would you like to sit down?" Mr. Siam: "that would be fine", and he sat down across from them. JB and CR sat down. JB: "what can we do for you?" Mr. Siam: "I have news for you, three people came into my store looking for me they are from Afghanistan, I said "I no longer make bombs, and they said "you make bombs or we kill you." I said: "come back tomorrow at three and we will talk, I said I was just leaving to make a delivery." They said "fine 3 o'clock tomorrow."

JB: "were you followed?" Siham: "I don't think so but I brought sandwiches and drinks and left them out front that way it looked like a real delivery, have your woman bring the box in and I will show you who they are." JB: "Betty would you bring the box in." Siham opened the box and took out 4 drinks and 4 sandwiches and laid them aside and 4 other containers and beneath them he pulled out an envelope. He opened the envelope and pulled out three photographs. He said "can I have a marker." JB opened a drawer took a red marker and gave it to Siham. Siham circled a face on each of the pictures, they looked and each was a different man and they were from Afghanistan. JB said "you tell them that you will make the bombs for them and you will charge them whatever you normally charge them we will have plain clothes police in your establishment they should be 6 to 8 feet away from you; do you have an area in the back with quick access to the front?" Siham: "yes and they can see out but the men cannot see in."

JB: "The police will come early slip you a listening device that we used to record the conversation, if everything goes well you tell them you will make the bombs and however you normally would do it if you get money up front or whatever do what you normally do. Five or ten minutes later they will come up to the counter to pay the bill and they will act like they want to buy something there you give it to them in a bag slip the recorder in the bag then they will pay their bill and leave. The men in the back will stay there a while; can you trust all your employees?"

Siham: "yes they are loyal to me they will say nothing to anybody because they know if I found out I would send them back." JB: "is there a backdoor?" Siham: "yes." JB: "I will have them dropped off at 2:30, they will knock 3 times 2 times 1 one time, then you will know they are the police and I will have them not show their badge and scare your employees unless you want them to." Siham: "just have them say they came for a package."

JB: "do you think they might hurt you in the store?" Siham: "I am not sure but if they did it would be with a knife and they would cut my throat and run?" JB: "if you want I will have CR there he can be sitting six to eight feet away, he can shoot them before they hurt you." Siham: "thank you thank you, but that would hurt my business, I will take the chance."

JB: "then know the police will shoot them before they get out the door, you are helping us we must protect you." Siham: "they would carry the knife in their sleeve in a second my throat will be cut." CR: "would you show me how they would do that?" Siham: took his right hand went across to his left wrist and then slashed in front of him it took about a second." CR: "would you do that again." Siham looked at CR and moved quickly to do the slash again" his arm was just starting to make the slashing movement when CRs pistol was right in Siham's face "bang." CR: "my shot at that range would knock him out of his chair I don't think he could cut you." Siham: "I have never seen such speed; I think you could stop him."

CR: "there were three which one of the three would pull the knife?" Siham: "the middle one." CR: "would the other 3 be armed?" Siham: "I don't think so they would not carry a rifle and they may have knives." CR: "the choice is yours I think I can get all 3 of them before they can hurt you." CR: "you are helping us, in a way you are protecting us, so one of our jobs is to protect you." Siham: "I have never seen such honor as you display." CR: "you decide and let me know because they will not worry about me at all, I will have on dark classes and my dog looks like a seeing-eye dog, they will think I am a blind man having a drink and a sandwich, and if one of them is armed the dog will let me know." Siham: "I have heard of these dogs they must be worth their weight in gold." Siham: I must go now or I will have been gone too long, and the bombs will not explode I will hide a flaw." JB: "I must pay you for the delivery you need to make money I have a business you have a business." Siham: "this talk with you is payment enough, I have friends I didn't know about, thank you." Siham got up bowed and left."

JB looked at CR and said "I really think he is on our side what about you." CR: "it sure looked like it from where I was sitting." JB: "but we might as well try the sandwich, bowl, and the drink they smell pretty good." CR: "I was thinking the same thing." They started to eat and LJ came in: "was that the Arab from the convenience store?" CR: "yes some people are trying to force him to make bombs and he came and told us and delivered the sandwiches as a cover if he was followed." LJ: "are they good?" JB: "yes take one and some kind of a salad in this bowl or is it soup take a drink."

JB: "Betty you want some lunch there's one left." Betty came in and took the fourth one and went back to her desk. LJ: "this is really good I could have this for lunch every day." CR: "me too." JB: "I haven't quite figured out what it is yet but I'll agree it's good." CR: "Betty how do you like lunch?" Betty: "I wasn't sure if I was going to like what it was, then I heard you guys just chomping away so I tried it and you're all right its really good." JB: "what kind of videos do we have?" LJ: "Just a few critters." JB: "then I will call Hank and fill him in and have him have men in place at 2:30, you two do whatever you want, you might need to take the dogs for a walk, I am going to go in and see Hank, and pick up the girls and the boys, see you later."

JB: "Betty where are the keys to the van?" Betty: "top left hook." JB: "bye I probably won't see you again until tomorrow." JB got in the van and drove to the police department, he went in filled Hank in on everything that transpired with the Arab, gave him the signals times and how it was laid out then left to go to school and pick up the boys." JB drove to the school did not see anyone following him parked out front, went in and got all three boys came back loaded them in the van and left for the hospital, he still did not see anybody following him, he parked in the visitors lot, he and the boys got out locked the van and went into see JR." LJ and CR were there talking to him. JR's boys went over and said "how are you dad?" JR: "I'm doing pretty well thanks to Jennifer and Mom." JR: "how was your first full day in school?" It was fine a couple of boys were going to pick on us but we told him our dad was a navy seal and he would beat them up and then go beat their dads up so they left us alone we are friends now."

Jennifer: "where did you get that from?" Larry said "from Ben he said it worked real well for him, and it worked real well for us, we got friends and didn't have to fight." JB: "I think we will have to go over to the school and talk to each one of their classes, or were going to have the whole school afraid of us." They all laughed and CR said "you really have to say they're doing it the nonviolent way and it appears to be working, don't mess with a plan that works."

They all laughed again and JR said "we have to stop this laughing it's starting to hurt." JR said: "I'm glad you didn't fight, you would probably have hurt them." Larry: "John and I talked about that and we thought Ben's way might be easier." Jennifer: "Rose I'm sorry Ben has put words in your boy's mouth." Rose: "I'm not. That was really the simplest thing to do nobody got hurt and everybody's happy, I don't know what better outcome you could have." JB: "when you deal with bullies you have no choice in most cases they are going to pick on you until you hurt them so bad they don't want anything to do with you ever again that is the mentality of a bully."

JB: "while I'm thinking about it we will have three armored minivans delivered Saturday for LJ, CR, and me they will have SWAT written on them that way you don't have to go to the police station but straight to the problem site, they will have built-in crates for our dogs. A week from this Saturday JR's van will be in same as the others they will also have compartments for weapons and equipment. And since the park paid half for them they will become your personal van for your personal use and park use, we will have a way to cover the SWAT sign when not on SWAT business."

Jennifer: "it's time we went and got the boys home and fed, Rose do you want to stay here or come with us." Rose: "I'm going to spend the night here and I'll see you in the morning." LJ and CR: "we need to go back and take care of our dogs; we will see you when you get home." Jennifer: "let's go it's getting late." JB and Jennifer went and got in the van Sam was sitting in the front seat next to JB, Jennifer and JR's boys got in the back Ben sat in the front with Sam. JB pulled out of the lot and they drove to the big house. JB snapped the leash on Sam opened the door for Jennifer, she and the boys got out, shut the side door he locked the van and said "you take the boys inside I will walk the dog and be back in about ten minutes" Jennifer squeezed his arm and took the boys inside.

JB went from cover to cover till he found a nice spot Sam relieved himself and he went back to the big house went in put the leash by the door and let Sam loose. Sam went to be with the boys and JB went out in the kitchen, Jennifer and mom were busy fixing food. Dad heard them talking and joined them in the kitchen. JB said "let's go down to the game room and play a game of pool I'm getting out of practice again, he got up headed toward the game room and dad followed. They got down there and dad said "were not here to play pool are we?"

JB: "not really but in case they look we will make it look good. I ordered four vans for us Hank is paying half so they will have a SWAT sign and it can be changed to a park sign so each of us will have our own bulletproof van we can haul our families in and the vans will be equipped so we can go straight to a SWAT site operation without having to go to the police station first." Dad: "that sounds like over 100,000, may be 140,000." JB: "Betty got a price of 120,000; Hank is paying half, so we are only paying 60,000." Dad: "that's not so bad, why did we have to come down here for that?"

JB: "the Arab from the convenience store stopped by, three Arabs came to him to make bombs, he said he didn't want to make the bombs, they threatened to kill him if he didn't, so he said he would and they are to come back tomorrow and they left." Dad: "that doesn't sound good." JB: "the Arab waited a while after they left made up a box of sandwiches and drinks and a bowl of something and brought it to the park like it was a delivery and he told us everything and he said he will make the bombs but he will hide a flaw so they will not explode he gave me pictures which I sent to Hank, and Hanks men will be in the convenience store having lunch while they talk. They will record what is said even though they won't understand a word of it the Arab will translate later.

CR and I think he's on the level and he is on our side he does not want to make bombs anymore, Hank will have plain clothes policeman there so the Arab should be safe, CR said he would pose as a blind man with his dog because Siham said if they got upset with him they would probably cut his throat right there and run, CR gave him an example of how he could draw and shoot before they could cut his throat he was amazed but he said he would pass on that this time." Dad: "CR is that fast?" JB: "CR can draw shoot three times in less than a second and he will hit the middle of the bull's-eye, he is the fastest of the 4 of us, we are over a second."

When we go 4 abreast I am on the left CR is on my right JR is on his right LJ is on the end, JR is married so I want him protected and CR protects me and JR and it has worked quite well." Dad: "you figured that out pretty good." JB: "no we all decided that, JR balked at first but we said you have a family we have to protect you first so he relented. I have no doubt CR could shoot the three Arabs in less than a second." Dad: "I bet you have some real stories to tell but we will never hear them will we."

JB: "no we will never tell and we will honor Siham's wishes." "I told Hank to shoot them if anything goes wrong, we will send the recording to my CO and he will get a transcript and sent it to us." JB: "Siham put in some surveillance cameras just so he could give us pictures of people that wanted his bomb making skills. Since he volunteered this we are very sure he is on our side." Jennifer came down and said "it's time that we went home mom is going to put the two boys to sleep and we need to get Ben in bed." JB: "okay see you tomorrow dad." JB, Jennifer, and Ben left and went to the spring house. Jennifer had Ben take a bath and got him ready for bed and read to him a little bit and he fell asleep.

She came out and sat next to JB, he put his arm around her and they sat like that for a while. Jennifer said "I wish I was strong like Rose." JB: "Jennifer they told me how you rushed out grabbed RJ and started to drag him to cover and Rose helped you then you gave orders on what she should do and you started to work on him, Betty said "she'd never seen anybody handle somebody hurt like that, that sounds pretty tough to me, you didn't think, you did what you were trained to do, that's tough"; that's how the seals operate you do and then you think about it when it's all done."

Jennifer: "I wasn't really thinking I was just doing what I needed to do to save JR's life." JB: "you are just not used to being in a situation where you can't worry before it happens because you know it's going to happen, does that make sense?" Jennifer: "I guess it does, but I will get through it." JB: "the difference between the special forces soldier and a regular soldier is the special forces soldier will not quit until he dies or collapses." Jennifer: "how many missions have you been on?" "Over 300." JB replied. "The four of you?" Jennifer asks. "Yes, we've been together on every mission." JB informed her. "I'm changing the subject, the more I think about the big house, and the more I'm starting to like the idea." Jennifer said with a shiver.

JB: "I like that, I grew up there it's home to me, and right now with you and Ben in the spring house this feels like home to me but I think we do need a little more room." Jennifer smiled: "I think so too."

"I need to take Sam out for his nightly walk would you like to come along." JB said.

"Sure let's go." Jennifer replied.

JB put the leash on Sam and he and Jennifer and Sam went out the front door. JB led them from tree to bush, bush to tree, tree to Bush until they reached Sam's favorite spot, he finished his business and they went back to the spring house. They hurried in the house locked the door, took the leash off Sam, Sam went and got on his bed, JB kiss Jennifer good night, Jennifer went into the bedroom, JB crawled into his sleeping bag on the couch and went to sleep.

CHAPTER 21

FRIDAY WEEK 3

JB woke up at 5:30 put on his running clothes put the leash on Sam went outside locked the door and went to the big house LJ and CR were waiting there for him with their dogs. They started their run and were back in 22 minutes. CR: "at 9 o'clock Mary and I are going up to the pistol range so she can qualify I'll be back to the office after lunch." JB: "see you then, LJ:"I will cover the office till you get back from taking Jennifer to work and the boys to school." LJ: "have fun."

JB took Sam and went to the spring house went in locked the door turned Sam loose. Jennifer had just got done cooking pancakes, Ben was already at the table, JB went over and sat down, they ate breakfast and JB said: "that was delicious thank you very much I will get cleaned up and we will leave." Jennifer: "hurry please as I have a meeting fifteen minutes before my shift starts." JB: "I will make it quick." JB shaved and showered and got dressed, put his vest on, holster and gun then jacket, put the leash on Sam and said "let's go." They left the spring house, got in the car and drove to the big house, got JR's boys, and went to the hospital; Jennifer got out and went to work. JB drove the boys to school, parked the car and walked them to their classrooms, told them have a good day and I'll see you later." He left got in the car and drove to the park, he watched all the way and did not see anyone following him, and he thought this is nice for a change. He went in and said "hi to Betty and LJ." JB: "tomorrow

we should be getting our three vans; we will have to check them out."
LJ: "it will be nice to have my own vehicle; I haven't had one of them
since I was a kid." JB: "I know what you mean, when we get rid of all
the crap we've had lately, it should settle down, and so far the city
has not had any major problems that a SWAT team would have to
deal with." LJ: "I will grab a security guard, and go up on the hill and
download, I should be back in half hour to 45 minutes." LJ went to the
first security guard he could find said: "come with me" and they went
up on the hill. The down loads all went quick; as they drove back all
he saw was critters on all the videos. LJ went into the office. JB: "shall
we go up and check the house clearing that should be done, and who
will be in charge of setting up the dog training facility." LJ: "it should
be one of us that have gone to school, Curt or Mary could take turns
for the police or I could do it for everybody and somebody could do
it for me." JB: "I think eventually Hank will get a third dog, we will
see the city has been pretty quiet lately, but wait till it gets warmer
people get to drinking more and start being stupid." JB grabbed the
keys got in the van and they went up to check out the room clearing
building. They got there and the man in charge of setting up the
building pulled up. JB got out introduced himself and the man said
"we were short a couple pieces I had them overnight them and they
were delivered to the motel and now I will put them in and then I
want to go through how to run the house with you, it will only take
five minutes." JB and LJ watched as he installed the last two pieces and
then he spent the next twenty minutes showing them how to work the
computer and the different scenarios that were built into the house
and then he showed them how they could make their own programs
and routines. He shook their hands and left. LJ: "I think it might not
be a bad idea if the entire police force goes through this house at least
four times a year or every three months."

JB I think that's a good idea, I plan on all our SWAT people
going through once a month, and the four of us will make up different
routines, shall we put RJ in charge of this." LJ: "he will love it, he likes
gadgets and I bet he'll come up with some real interesting routines,
we could even slip some in that were similar to ones we have done in
the past." JB: "I will have to tell him next time we see him that will

give him something to think about, and we will take the manual in so he can go through it."

LJ: "that will make time go faster for him."

JB: "why don't I put CR and Mary in charge of the dog training facility that way they get to spend a lot of time together and learn to get along with each other she can set it up for our dogs he can set up for theirs." LJ: "I think that's a real good idea." JB: "why don't we go see how CR and Mary are doing at the pistol range?" LJ: "sounds like a good idea to me."

They got back in the car and drove to the pistol range. Mary was in the process of doing her last fire for her pistol qualification." The range operator pulled her target back, marked it and entered it on her qualification sheet." He looked at it opened his book and checked what everyone else had done, Curt usually got the highest score, Mary and he were tied for this month.

Mary got real excited grab CR and kissed him. Mary: "you did this for me you showed me the simple mistakes I was making that nobody has bothered to tell me, thank you; I knew I really liked you." CR blushed and JB and LJ both smiled. JB: "CR and Mary you two are in charge of the dog training facility, Mary you will set up the tests for our dogs and CR you will set up the tests for the police." CR and Mary said "thank you they would like that very much." JB: "LJ and I will see you at the office when you get done here."

CR; "I should be down in twenty minutes." JB: "congratulations Mary, you'll have more fun when we start house clearing." Mary: "I'm looking forward to it." JB and LJ left and drove to the office. They got out JB locked the car and they went in the office." Betty said "good morning so far it's been quiet." JB: "Betty call the dog people and order another small dog." Betty: "Ok." CR came in twenty minutes later and the three of them went into the conference room set around the table and the phone rang. Betty answered the phone got up came in and said "a Mr. Siham is on the phone, and wants to talk to Mr.

CR." CR picked up the phone and said "CR here are you in trouble."
Siham: 'the three Arabs came into my store at 10 o'clock this morning
and wanted me to talk with them, I told them I was busy this was my
busy time I said 3:00 because that was my slow time. They were very
unhappy and stayed around for a half hour I kept busy because I am
busy during that time of day, and I have a lot of customers that start
coming in, they finally got the idea and left, but it has made me very
nervous. Mr. CR can you come to my store before three I would feel
safer?" CR: "I will come at 2:55and I will walk in if they are there I
will stumble around and get a table within 6 to 8 feet from yours, I
will order a sandwich and some tea as they watch me eat they will
believe I am blind and if I have to I will shoot all three." Siham: "I
hope it doesn't come to that, but when they don't come when they're
supposed to it makes me nervous."

CR: 'I will see you later, bye." CR put the phone down and looked at
JB and LJ and said "the blind man will have to go to work; we better
discuss this a bit and proceed from there." JB said "let me call Hank
so he knows we are coming and his people are prepared just in case."

LJ: "I will run over get a layout of the room and ask Siham where he
is going to set them, and have him put reserved on the table where
they are sitting, and the tables around them and make sure nobody
can get behind them in case CR has to shoot." JB: "sounds good to
me hurry we don't have much time to plan."

LJ grabbed the keys for the car and left.

JB called Hank. Hank answered "is there a problem?"JB: "yes
there is, Siham called, the three Arabs showed up at 10 o'clock, and
he told them this was his busy time and that is why he had their
appointment for 3 o'clock, he could not talk now he was running his
business they hung around for a half hour and then left. CR is going
to take his dog and do his blind man routine and sit within six to eight
feet of the Arabs and if they pull a weapon and try to hurt Siham he
will take them out. We cannot lose Siham he is a valuable asset and
we are sure he's on our side so he must be protected."

Hank: "I agree he is our only link to the Arabs, we need him to keep us informed." JB: "you might want to go in a little earlier to get a table that you can see what's going on, CR is going to get a table where the Arabs are going to sit so he can see if they pull a weapon." Hank: "I will talk to you after this is all over, bye." JB hung up the phone. CR: "I better go get my kit out of my bags and why I didn't put that in storage I don't know, that would've been a real pain, I will have a mustache and a small beard, dark glasses, a stocking cap, and a loose coat. The dog will have the Seeing Eye harness which we worked with in class for just such a thing, CR got up and left for the big house.

Thirty minutes later LJ was back, got a flash drive put it in his laptop downloaded the pictures and gave it to Betty, she put it in the computer and printed them out. LJ took them into the conference room and spread them out. LJ then taped them together so he had one big picture of the room, CR could then see the layout of the room, LJ had talked to Siham and told him what table to use for the meeting and what table to make sure was open for CR. LJ marked them on the map so CR would know what table to use. About 1:30 they heard a vehicle pull up CR looked out the window and it was Siham. He got out of the van went to the back pulled out a box and came into the office, Betty brought him into the conference room he put the box on the table and looked and said "Mr. CR is that you?" CR: "yes it is me." CR got up holding the harness on his dog and started to walk around the room. Siham looked at JB and said "is the dog leading him." CR: "no I am guiding the dog but he is trained so it looks like he is leading me."

Siham: "Allah has put me in good hands I'm not afraid anymore, thank you my friends." They had Siham look at the pictures they had taped together and showed him the marked tables where he should set and where the other Arab should set so CR could see all three of them, they showed him where to put reserve signs and told him to use a roundtable where he should sit and if he had pictures of his bombs put them where he is going to sit ahead of time with something covering them up and holding them down. Siham: "what if they come over to look at you?"

CR: "Siham come over and look at me." Siham walked around the table and started toward CR he was about 4 feet away the dog got up and growled CR turned his head so his ear was pointed at Siham. Siham: "forgive me for doubting you to act like your blind, I will not worry now." JB: "let me pay you for this stuff and go back and do what we have told you to do." Siham: "no, no this is my gift for saving my life."

CR: "we haven't saved your life yet." Siham: "but I know you will; now I can do my part without fear." Siham got up and left the office got in his van and drove off. JB: "I'm glad he came now he knows what he needs to do, and is not afraid anymore, and if things go south CR will just have to take them out, save at least one if you can. CR: "I will do my best." LJ: "we know you will, you are always the best." They heard another car pull up and CR said "that must be Mary we were going to lunch, I completely forgot with all this." LJ: "this is a good test to see how she takes sudden changes of plans."

Mary walked in and said: "I thought CR was here?" LJ: "well if she does not recognize him in disguise, then the dog stood up. Mary: "CR what's happening?"CR: "now we know nobody else will either." CR: "we got an unexpected mission and I am going in undercover as a blind man." Mary: "should I go to back you up." JB said "CR she's a keeper, but no Mary in this scenario he goes solo." Mary: "will he be safe?"JB: "yes he will be safe there will be two hidden plainclothes in the back and three on the table not more than 6 feet away from him, anymore we are getting too many people to have a good mission." Mary: "that makes me feel better, I guess lunch is off."

CR: "Mary open the box there on the table and see what we are going to eat for lunch." Mary took a knife out of her pocket and opened the box she pulled out 4 sandwiches, 4 bowls and 4 drinks. LJ: "ladies first you pick and we will take what's left and if it's anything like what we had yesterday it's really good." Mary picked a sandwich, a bowl, and a drink and set it across from CR. Then she passed sandwiches and bowls and drinks to the rest of them. They ate in silence and when they were done. Mary: "that was really good, where did you get this." CR: "from the Arabs convenience store and sandwich shop he used to be a bomb maker." Three Arabs came over here and want him to make bombs so he came and told us, we are going to protect him and hopefully he can lead them down the path, then we can take them before they can do any damage."

LJ: "so far we've done real well except for RJ." When he gets out of the hospital we will start doing house clearing he is going to be in charge of that." Mary: "I am looking forward to that, I had better get back to work, and CR would you walk me to the car." CR got up and followed her out to the car. She put her arms around him kissed him and told him you be careful I don't want to lose you, she got in her car and drove off. CR came back in set down and said "I guess I'm in a real serious relationship, and it feels pretty good." JB laughed and said "welcome to the club." They ran through the plan three or more times and thought of scenarios that might happen and thought the plan was pretty solid and it would work right in with the plan that Hank was going to use.

JB and LJ put a bullet in the chamber of their pistols and put them in their holsters they decided they would drop him off a block from where he needed to be and he would have ten minutes to walk there before his mission was to start. They would position themselves so if everything was quiet and they saw the Arabs coming out they would walk a step and go into one of the shops along the street and they figured they would never be seen. LJ took his dog down to the big house JB took his dog to the spring house and they went back, got in the van and left.

They arrived at 2:45 and let CR and his dog got out, LJ drove a little farther up the block and found a place to park the van. They got out LJ cut down the alley to get on the other side of the building JB would be on the side opposite LJ that way they could only get away by going across the street in the middle of the block. They got to their places and saw CR go in to the Arab shop. The clock was ticking.

CR walked in and guided his dog down the walkway through the tables and then the dog seem to take him to the right and went to a table and stopped CR took his hand and patted over the table until he found the chair then he patted until he found another chair and then he went around to the left and patted till he found the third chair then he went back pulled out the middle chair and sat down. He sat there for a while and somebody came over and said "Sir could I help you?" CR: "yes it smelled so good when I was walking by I thought I would come in and eat something what do you have, the man said "we have sandwiches, soup, and beverages?" CR: "what sandwich is your bestseller and do you have ice tea?" The man: "our bestseller is the Lamb sandwich and we do have ice tea, sweet and tea with no sugar." CR: "I will take the Lamb and could you mix the teas half and half." The man: "yes I will be back in a little bit with your food." CR sat staring in front of the three Arabs, and they kept looking at him. At 3 o'clock Siham came in and sat in front of the three Arabs. They started to talk and the Arab closest CR got up and started walking toward CR's table, CR kept staring in the direction he was staring like the man did not exist.

CR's dog was lying next to him on the floor the Arab got real close to the table and the dog got up in a sitting position and growled CR turned his head away from the man like he wasn't sure which way to listen the Arab waved his hand the dog stood up and growled, CR: "told the dog quiet, he does not like strangers if there is somebody there May I help you, would you say something so I know where you are, some people don't like it when you don't face them." The Arab turned and went back to his table and sat down.

CR: "can I help you I cannot see, you will have to talk or I don't know where you are still looking in the same direction he had been before the man turned. The man that had taken his order brought his sandwich and drink. CR: "Sir would you show me where you put my drink the man grabbed CRs hand put it touching the drink, thank you now would you put my hand on the sandwich, the man moved his hand to the sandwich, thank you now I can eat." CR patted his hand on the table around the drink, then around the sandwich and he found the straw and tore the paper off and then searched for the glass and put the straw in the glass. Then he felt all over for the sandwich took both hands picked up the sandwich and took a bite all the while staring between the three Arabs and Siham.

They watched as CR took another bite of the sandwich and then put it down and chewed then he patted around till he found the glass put his fingers around the top of the glass so his finger was by the straw and then brought it up and hit his face until it went into his mouth. The three Arabs quit watching and started to talk to Siham, they were talking in Arabic so no one could understand a word they said. Siham would talk and pass a picture, talk and pass a picture. This went on for ten minutes with CR staring and slowly eating his sandwich and drinking his drink, CR had only half a sandwich left but he was slowly eating and drinking his drink like he was the only one in the world.

The Arabs got up walked out to the main aisle turned and looked at CR who was still staring where he had always stared since he had sat down. One of the Arabs picked up a napkin container and acted like he was going to throw it, only he never let it out of his hand. CR's dog growled. CR: "told the dog quiet and said is anyone there." No one answered and the Arabs turned and left.

JB saw the Arabs come out get in a car he took his phone snapped pictures of the car and license plate and watched them drive off into the distance. CR finished the sandwich at the same speed as he had the whole time and his drink, then held up his hand and said "can someone help me I need to pay for my food?" The waiter: "that will be 6.95" CR reached in his pocket and pulled out a clip took the money out of the clip and unfolded it counted five bills laid them to his left counted two bills laid them to the right of the first stack then he laid the last bill next to the second stack. CR said to the waiter "the stack on the left is one dollar bills correct." The waiter said "yes." CR said "the middle stack is fives?" The waiter said "yes." CR put his hand on the ones from the first stack then he took the two fives from the second stack and handed them up and said to the waiter "here this is for my bill" the waiter took them and left. CR picked up the four ones laid them on top of the 20 folded them up, put them in to the clip and put them in his pocket he got up, told the dog door and then guided the dog to the door like he was being pulled there, the door opened automatically and he went out turned left and started down the street, he went to the end of the block turned left and kept walking.

JB followed him and caught up opened the van and CR got in the back seat closed the door JB got in the van drove up a little bit cut through the alley, picked up LJ and they headed back to the park. Siham told the men in the back that he would go to the park and give the information to JB and to have his boss come there in half an hour they said fine and left. JB pulled up at the park office and LJ and CR got out of the van and LJ went into the office.

CR said "I'm going to get out of this and then I'll be back'. JB: "I'm going to pick up Jennifer and the boys and he left. He called Jennifer and told her they'd had a mission and he was running late but he'd be there in ten minutes, be at the front door. He pulled up Jennifer saw that Sam was not in the car so she jumped in the front with him, and JB took off and headed for the school and parked and Jennifer ran in to get the boys.

Five minutes later she was out with the boys loaded them in the van jumped in the front and they headed for the park. Jennifer: "why were you late?"JB: "The Arab from the convenience store called up somebody wanted him to make bombs and we had a quick mission CR went undercover as a blind man and I was on watch and I couldn't call. I apologize I should've had Betty call you it won't happen again."

Jennifer said "how did it go?"JB: "I guess pretty well, he took a little longer than usual to make sure nobody thought he wasn't blind." JB: "these are hard-core terrorists; so far we are a step ahead of them thanks to Siham." Jennifer: "can you trust him?"JB: "yes we feel we can trust him and he even put in surveillance cameras so he could give us pictures when he found out this was happening. And his store makes an awful good sandwich we've had them twice now I may have to get some and bring them home for you to taste."

JB pulled into the parking lot saw Siham's van and stopped at the office got out and told Jennifer you drive down to the big house I'll come down later." Jennifer pulled out and left, JB went into the office, then into the conference room. LJ, CR and Siham were sitting around the table; JB heard a car pull up and figured that must be Hank. He sat down next to CR. JB looked at Siham said "how did CR look as a blind man?"

Siham: "I knew he wasn't blind and I believed he was blind, I have never felt safer in my life." Hank came in caught the end of that and said "what blind man?" LJ: "you know what blind man, what did your men think of the blind man." Hank: "they wanted to know how a blind man could protect the Arab or was it the dog that was to do that." JB: "well I guess CR did a pretty good job, and we knew your men would backup a blind man shooting a terrorist with a knife trying to cut off Siham's head, I didn't know how fast your men can draw and I knew CR could shoot all three in a second if necessary."

Hank: "you mean that." LJ: "he's that fast takes the three of us almost a second and a half to get three off, but not CR." Siham: "I tried to draw a knife from my arm like I would if I had my knife there and he had his gun in my face before I could draw, I have never seen anyone so fast. And the three Arabs came early in the morning to demand I meet then, when I had set it up for three and I told them I was too busy and they hung around and then left, I was afraid they might come back and kill me and I knew if he could be a blind man, they could not hurt me' and when they left they acted like they were going to throw a napkin container at him and he never moved, I would have ducked. These men are beyond belief."

Hank: "what did these Arabs want?" Siham: "they want me to make ten bombs that they can plant throughout the city. Then they will call up the newspaper and demand their brother's return or they will set off a bomb every day until he is returned. I can make the bombs, and I can make them so they can never find out they won't blow up until they actually try to set them off, because they will not explode."

Hank: "you sure of that?" Siham: "yes I take the explosive out of the detonator and replace it with pepper they look the same and they are not going to stick their tongue on it."

JB: "I took pictures of their van so I have a license number just in case, where your men able to follow them Hank?" Hank: "yes we know where they're staying, and we have the number, it is a rental." We can even follow the car on a side street controlling a drone; my men are practicing that right now." JB: "how soon do they want the bombs?"

Siham: "five days and I told them it would take 10 because I have a business to run, I don't have enough supplies to make 10, and I would do it right or not at all." Hank: "Siham do you hire women to work in your store." Siham: "no, none of my women speak English." Hank: "what about an Englishwoman, I could put an undercover policewoman in your store." Siham: "let me pray about that." Hank: "what is above your store?" Siham: "I think somebody was going to make an apartment to live in, now the only way up is through the store, the previous owner said the city would not give a permit for an outside entrance."

Hank: "I think I could fix it so you would have an outside entrance just let us use it for a while to monitor your surveillance and help us protect you." Siham: "I would be happy to do that." JB: "Siham where are these Arabs from?" Siham: "from the east a hundred miles from Ahmad Emir Zafir, they are enemies; they killed one of Ahmad's sons, he would be in your debt if you killed one of them or all three, I have called him and told him they are here."

JB: "Siham when do you expect them to contact you again?" Siham: "next Wednesday at 3 o'clock." JB: "how many bombs do they expect you to have done by then?" Siham: "I will have five done, I told them they could have none until all are done and payment is made." LJ: "smart man, how can we protect you on Wednesday?" Siham: "I will pray about that, and then I will call you and tell you what I have decided." Siham: "Mr. CR I must return your money, you cannot pay when you are protecting me." And he handed CR his money." LJ: "we like your food can we order and have you deliver here two or three times a week, and let us pay for it?" Siham: "for what you do I cannot tell you no I must tell you yes?"

Siham: "Mr. CR for what you did today I give you this video from my surveillance system, now I must leave." Siham got up and left and they heard his van leaving the lot.

Hank: "May I see the video?"

CR: "sure" and he handed over the flash drive. Hank opened his laptop stuck the flash drive in a USB port brought up a video program and played the clip. Hank: "now I know what Siham meant, after watching this I would think he was blind too." Hank gave CR back his flash drive" and left.

JB: "I bet mom and Jennifer has fixed supper at the big house so I think we better lockup and go over there." LJ: "bring your flash drive mom and dad and Jennifer might find it interesting, and be sure to show it to Mary." They got up locked up the office and went to the big house."

Mom said "you have about 11 minutes to take your dogs out and let them relieve themselves then come in and wash up and supper will be ready", JB went to the spring house and got his dog, LJ and CR put a leash on their dogs and went out the door. The three of them were back in nine minutes turned the dogs loose again and then they took turns washing their hands in the bathroom. They sat down at the kitchen table Jennifer said Grace and they all started to eat.

Jennifer said:" boys you clean up the dishes and put them in the dishwasher." , LJ, and CR got up and started to pick up the plates. Jennifer: "no I mean Ben, Larry, and John it's time you learned to have some chores." They got up and started to clean up the plates from the table scraped off what was left into the garbage and put them in the dishwasher. When they got done Jennifer said "I will put the soap in thank you boys you did a good job."

JB: "I think we should all go down to the game room and CR is going to play a video clip." They all went down to the game room, CR took out his laptop hooked it to the cable on the TV, and stuck in the flash drive.

CR: "I went undercover as a blind man today this is what people saw." They watched the video for twenty minutes. The three young boys said "is that really you uncle CR?"

"Yes I was protecting the Arab that was by himself against the three across from him, the three bad guys had to think I was really blind so whatever they did I could not move to protect myself the dog was there for that." Ben: "he is like dad's Sam he will protect you right?" CR: "yes they will tell us when people have guns, they find bombs, they find lost people, but you can't tell people at school about the dogs and what you saw here tonight, do you understand?

The three boys all said yes. Dad looked at CR and said "that was an amazing piece of work I'm proud of you." CR: "thank you." Dad: "do you know why these three are here?"

LJ: "it appears that they are related to the first bunch of Arabs we took out they think they're being held somewhere and they're going to set off bombs in the city until they are returned to them." Dad: "will they have to set off one before we can get them?"JB: "the bomb maker is going to make duds. so when they try to set them off they won't explode, you three little boys can't say a word about this in school if you do I'm going to punish you severely, you can cause people to get killed, there are things that you boys will know that you cannot tell to anyone else outside of this family, do you understand?" The boys all said "yes."

Jennifer: "you boys have time for one more game and then it will be time for bed." The Boys went back to the pool table and started playing. Jennifer said "we should all go back upstairs to the living room." The adults went up to the living room and sat down. Jennifer: "Mom and Dad, JB and I decided we will move into the big house when you move into your new one." Jennifer: "LJ and CR would you want to move into the spring house so you don't have to put up with kids?" LJ and CR said "that will be fine, but the kids do not bother us, but they might like it that all three of them are together here." Jennifer: "okay, Ben lets go we need to get you in bed, and mom can you put the other two boys to bed?" Mom: "yes I can take care of that."

JB, Jennifer, and Ben left and went to the spring house. JB opened the door and they went in shut the door and said "I will take Sam for a walk and be right back" he put the leash on Sam and went out the door. In eight minutes he was back unleashed Sam locked the door; put the leash by the door." Sam ran to his pad and lay down, Jennifer was sitting on the couch JB went over and sat down next to her, and put his arm around her and she snuggled up to him.

Jennifer: "CR sure looked blind; he is really good isn't he." JB:"yes he is, he is the fastest of the three of us." Jennifer kissed JB and he kissed her back, she got up: "I will see you in the morning and I love you." JB: "I love you too with all my heart, good night." Jennifer went in to her bedroom JB crawled in to his sleeping bag and went to sleep.

CHAPTER 22

SATURDAY WEEK 3

JB woke up at 5:30 put on his running suit grabbed the leash by the door hooked up Sam and went out and went to the big house. LJ and CR were waiting and they did their run in 22 minutes; JB said "I will see you later" and went to the spring house. He went in the door, closed it unhooked Sam put the leash by the door and went in the kitchen and sat down and said "good morning sweetheart." Jennifer:"good morning love of my life, how was your run?"JB: "it felt really good I believe I'm getting closer to 100%."

Jennifer: "what is your plan for today?"JB smiled and said "grab you hug you and kiss you and carry you off." Jennifer laughed said "I would really enjoy that one, what are we going to do with the Ben?" "I can dream can't I; but really we have three bulletproof minivans coming in; one for each of the three of us, JR's will be in next week. They are equipped with a dog box and places for weapons, and we should be able to use them to get around in."

Jennifer: "you mean you're going to drive me around in a tank like thing?"

JB: "no they're supposed to look like regular minivans other than they have plates in the sides and doors and the roof plus bullet proof glass

230

in the windows, and there is supposed to be a sign that is switchable from SWAT to the park, and next week JR's will come in. When things get normal you will be able to take Ben to school and yourself to work, then my schedule will not be interfering with yours."

Jennifer: "I don't mind, but I know it would free you up for other things." JB: "I will have to talk to dad about installing movable gates to make it harder for people to get in after hours."

Jennifer: "would you get Ben up so he can eat breakfast?"

JB: "sure" and he went and got Ben up. He and Ben sat down at the kitchen table with Jennifer and had breakfast.

Jennifer: "I have to go to work today to make up for some of the days I have missed."

JB: "okay that's fine with me and I would like us to get married before we move into the big house?" Jennifer: "that is fine with me as I don't want a big wedding, I just want my family and yours, and that includes your brothers and their family, and I understand CR is sweet on the policewoman named Mary?"JB: "I would say that is so, she is already worrying about him." Jennifer: "that does sound serious, so she would be invited also." JB: "well you better tell your parents and mine and figure out who's going to marry us, set a date, and I'll be the happiest man in the world." Jennifer: "I will call mine from work, and I will tell your mom and dad when we drop Ben off at the big house."

JB: "are we going to take the two boys in to see their father?" Jennifer: "let me call Rose and see what her plans are for the day?"JB: "okay why don't you call her now?" Jennifer called Rose talked for two minutes then hung up. Jennifer: "Rose thought she should come home and watch the boys since I have to work, she also said JR got up and walked around the room."

JB: "that sounds like JR he doesn't like to be inactive, we are going to put him in charge of the house clearing building so I'll have LJ run up there and get the manual, and he can start to study it and that will keep him busy." They got in the car drove to the big house, JB: "you go in I'll let Sam relieved himself and then I'll be in." Five minutes later JB went in the big house. LJ and CR were sitting at the kitchen table their dogs right beside them JR's boys were just finishing breakfast Jennifer was talking to mom and JB thought I'm the luckiest man in the world. JB looked at LJ and CR: "did Jennifer tell you that JR was up and walking around."

CR: "no she didn't but that sounds like him." LJ: "CR we better go up to the housecleaning building and get the manual to keep him busy." CR: "sounds good to me, we don't want him doing too much too soon." JB: "Jennifer what is Rose doing." Jennifer: "she said she was coming home to watch the three boys so mom wouldn't be overworked since I was going to be there to watch over JR, she said that they got real excited about him walking around and they did some checks and they said he should not be that far along in the healing process, he is ahead of schedule."

LJ: "he got hurt once before and they had to strap him down a couple days as they were afraid he would pull everything loose." CR: "I remember that he was a bear." LJ: "when are you leaving?" JB: "as soon as Jennifer is done talking to mom." CR: "LJ lets go get the manual and we can meet them at the hospital" LJ and CR got up and left. Jennifer said "let's go mom is all excited about the wedding, I'll call my parents while you are taking me to the hospital." Jennifer said "goodbye to mom and dad." JB: "goodbye mom, and dad I have something to talk over with you when I get back."

Dad said "okay, I will be right here." They left boys with mom and dad they went out got in the car and JB started to drive to the hospital. Jennifer called her mom and dad told them the news and said "she would get back and give them the exact date when she figured it out." JB dropped her off at the front door and parked the car. He went up to the room and Jennifer was talking to a doctor so he went in and sat down and talked to JR. Jennifer came in: "the doctor can't believe how fast JR is healing, but we know it's the castor oil pack's."

JB: "they probably won't believe it anyway, so I will just say he's always been a fast healer." JB said "the park and the police department are buying us minivans that will say Park and they can be switched to say SWAT and then we will be able to drive them right to a SWAT operation without having to go to the main police station first, there will be a crate for the dog and a place where you can store your weapons, the vests I would leave at home so we can wear them every day until things change."

JR: "I'm sorry I can't help you on this latest mission, I feel like I'm letting you all down." JB: "you have never in your life let us down; it was my fault I didn't talk to you more about the vest, if I had you wouldn't be in this situation." JR: 'no we have to look at it as every once in a while an accident will happen and there's nothing we can do about it, except try to make sure it never happens again."

JB: "three of the minivans will be in today yours will be in toward the end of next week." JR: "can Rose drive that back and forth to the hospital." JB: "yes she can and it's armored." JR: "that makes me feel a little better I was worried about the trip back and forth but I knew you were there."

JB: "does Rose have her pistol where she can get at it." JR: "I think it's packed in a box in storage." JB: "I bought one for Jennifer, and I think Roses hands are about the same size as Jennifer's, we will have them compare hands, and if they are the same I will buy her another one, it never hurts to have a spare." JB: "have you two decided on a house." JR: "Rose picked out one she liked the layout on so I guess we can order that, she can tell dad when we get back and he will call the company and get it on order and it should be done in two weeks." JB: "mom and dad are moving in to their new house next week, Jennifer and I are moving into the big house and we are getting married next week, so we will get the hospital to let you out for the ceremony."

JR: "That will be nice I can move around." JB: "no you'll be sitting in a wheelchair, and that's an order." JR: "that is the first time he ever said that to me." JB: "I can't lose you now because you rush things take your time LJ and CR are bringing you something I think will keep you busy, so you will not be so bored." Jennifer and Rose came in, and went to talk to JR.

JB said "I told JR about the wedding, and I told him he could be there but he had to be in a wheelchair, he said he would comply." Jennifer: "by looking at the charts he's going to be somewhere around what we expect in the 2nd to 3rd week by next week, so it should be all right for him to be out for a while as long as he stays in the chair except to go to the bathroom."

JB: "Rose JR said you had picked out the house you wanted built?" Rose: "yes I have." JB: "when we get back to the house, you tell dad and he will get it on order and they will start to build it next week and in two weeks you should be able to move in." Rose: "I don't know how we can ever thank you." JB: "you and JR being here with me is all the thanks I will ever need; Rose what did you do before you married JR?"

Rose: "I worked as the assistant to a manager and I helped him get things done, filed papers called on orders why."

JB: "when the boys are in school would you like a job at the park being Betty's assistant, because in the next 2 to 3 years I think she's going to retire, you could then take over her job, and we would get you an assistant so when you had to do things with the boys you could take off."

Rose: "I was kind of thinking of getting a part-time job when I found out that I wouldn't have the house to clean and the boys were in school I thought I can make a little extra money, when would you want me to start." JB: "whenever you want." Rose: "let me see how JR is coming along and we'll talk it over and I'll let you know."

JB: "sounds good to me, because I know I can trust you." JB: "JR I have the dog company looking for a dog similar to mine which is more of a family dog and they're supposed to get back to me if they have one that they think will work, because I told them how much I liked mine. And so far he's been really good with Ben, Ben pets him, but I told him he couldn't play with him yet until I've had him a little longer. They told me that the little dogs were more family oriented and the big ones were more one person dogs."

LJ and CR came in and they went over to JR and gave him a manual. CR: "this is going to be one of your new jobs, so that should keep you occupied." JR looked at the manual it read user's manual for room clearing, how to operate the control computer and program it. JR: "I think I will like this job, thank you guys." Rose said "we better go mom is home with three boys, she might need some help."

JB: "I'll see you guys later" and he and Rose left. They went down to the car got in and drove to the big house, JB let Rose out and he went to the spring house to get Sam. He went in put the leash on Sam got in the car and drove up to the office. There was the girl that worked weekends and she was out talking to a truck driver with three minivans on the truck. JB pulled up went over and she said "I didn't know what I was supposed to do; I didn't know these things were coming." JB said "Sir would you start unloading those." The driver said "sure would you sign this receipt?" JB: "sure" and he took the pen and signed the receipt."

The man put the receipt book in his truck pulled out three sets of keys and said "we will unload one at a time; there are two keys for each vehicle so I would separate them so you don't lose both at the same time." JB: "I bet you say that a lot." The driver laughed: "more than I'd like to think about." He got up and drove off the first van, said "would you like to park this where you want it?"

JB: "sure" he took the key and drove the van over by the office took the keys out of the ignition and locked it up." Then he put the key in his right pocket. The driver had the second vehicle off, JB went over took the keys parked that one beside the other one. Got out locked the door and put those keys in his left pocket." The driver had the third van off the truck and JB came over and said "my understanding is that the sign here in the back that says SWAT should be changeable to the park name do you know how to work that'? The driver: "I'm not sure let us take a look." Driver: "come here look at this little ring, pull it and this top comes off, he put his hands on both sides of the sign and pushed up sign came up and out they turned it around and it said 'Lincoln Park', they went around to the other side and JB pulled the ring and pushed the sign up turned it around and it said 'Lincoln Park' and he pushed the slider back in locked it in place and said "my vans ready to go." The driver said "I hope you enjoy your vans I have a long way to go, goodbye."

JB went into the office laid three pieces of paper out on Betty's desk wrote on the left piece of paper LJ van he took one key off the key ring from his right pocket and laid it on the left piece of paper with a single key on top, the key ring and spare key toward the bottom. He took the key out of his left pocket took one off the ring wrote on this paper CR, put the single key up near the top, the key on the ring near the bottom he put the third paper and put JB on it, put the ring with the spare key on the bottom he took the other key and put it in his pocket. went to the spring house let Sam out of his crate put the leash on and walked him to let him relieve himself they went back to his van opened the back opened the crate Sam jumped up in the back went into the crate and lay down, JB put the leash in the grove shut the gate it fit perfectly, he thought nice idea. JB drove to the office shut off the van and got out.

LJ and CR pulled up. JB: "your keys are in the office on Betty's desk they went and grabbed their keys and came out. LJ went to the van next to JB's tried the key it wouldn't work CR came over and stuck his key in opened the door LJ went to the other van and opened the door they looked all through the van opened the back looked at the crate shut it up locked up the back and they both said "nice." We have got to go down and get our dogs out and let them relieve themselves; we will be right back. LJ and CR finished with their dogs took them back to the big house and put them in their crates, and then they headed back toward the office. Just then they saw a van pulling into the parking lot toward the office.

CR: "I don't like that, looks like Siham's van, something tells me I better go back to the big house. Get dad, and have Rose, the boys, and mom get in the tunnel, and wait there until one of us comes and gets them." JB saw the van pulling toward him, and thought what could be the problem now. He relaxed and got ready for action if it was needed. The van stopped thirty feet from him, the door opened and a new Arab he saw at Siham's store got out and walked toward him.

The Arab said "Sir I was told a blind man lived here?"JB: "yes he lives in one of the houses why?" The Arab: "I was told he sees visions, and I need to ask him if he can see a vision for me." LJ: "he is usually asleep at this time but I will go wake him and have him come up here." The Arab: "thank you kind sir we will wait." LJ turned and headed for the big house, he got there as CR was coming out the door with dad. LJ: "they want the blind man; they were told he sees visions?" CR: "Siham is in trouble again." LJ: "I did not see him but it is his van."

CR: "we should go back in the big house; I will get on my disguise. CR said "Dad I will show you how to work the recorder, as soon as I get in front of the Arab turn it on." I'm going to put my mike and video camera on; I don't think they will see it." CR put on his mustache, beard, and stocking cap he took his coat off and put on the one he wore to the convenience store, put his seeing-eye harness on his dog, and put on his sunglasses. CR: "dad you go around about where they can't see you and sneak in the back door of the office, they are standing within 150 feet so the recorder should pick up everything that it sees and hears when you turn on the recorder with this switch if it picks up the camera the light will come on you push this button for record and just let it run."

Dad said "okay" and left.

LJ and CR walked back to where JB was. LJ took CR by the arm and walked him over to JB, CR: "someone would like to talk to me." JB: "yes there is an Arab man here and he said "he heard about your visions." CR: "have you lost someone?" The Arab: "my brother has disappeared and Siham said you have found people before." CR: "I have been blessed a few times and have been able to help people. Would someone get me a chair?"LJ: "I will get you one and be right back." LJ went to the office opened the door went in a minute later he was back with a folding chair. He opened it up helped CR set down and stepped back.

CR: "let me tell you how the visions comes to me, I set down and relax I meditate it's like a prayer someone who has been with the person who vanished needs to relax along with me and his memories will come to me in a vision he must be relaxed and in good spirits if he loves the person that is missing it is much easier. Do you have someone that was with him just before he disappeared?"

The Arab: "I have someone that was with him but not the same day he disappeared."

CR: "I don't know usually it is the same day only hours from when they vanished; let me explain, a man was with his son, he told me that he looked away for a little while his son was kicking a ball he turned around the son was gone he looked and looked and could not find him. So we both sat down in chairs facing each other and within a few minutes I saw the little boy playing with his ball then I saw the man turn and walk away and the vision stopped, the man had lied to me, he had not just turned away he had left his son, I told him you must think about loving your son and you must tell me the truth or the vision stops, the man told me he was ashamed that he had went inside and left the little boy alone so I said continue and think about what you did and when you came back outside now I can go back to the little boy and see if I can see where he goes so I backed up the memory and there was a little boy I joined the little boy and watched him walk and kick his ball and he kicked his ball off the path it was on to his left over a hill he ran to get his ball and it went into a hole and he fell in after it. The man said there was no hole he could fall into. I said yes there was a hole I see it, the man said there is an old well there but it is covered, the man called his neighbor told him to quick check and see if the cover for the well was missing the man ran over to the well and looked and called him back and said the cover is gone and someone is crying inside the hole. He told the man to call the 911 and tell them your neighbor's son has fallen into an old well. Now do you understand how the vision works?" The Arab said "I think so."

CR: "is there a 2nd chair?" LJ: "I will run to the office and get another one" he was back quickly with a second chair. CR: "the man that saw the missing person should now sit in this chair." The Arab said something in a foreign language, and the van door opened, and another Arab brought Siham over and sat him in the chair and stood behind him in a menacing way." CR: "I will now relax and the person who was with your brother should now relax and we both need to think loving thoughts toward the brother."

CR sat there for about three minutes said "something is wrong I am cold there is fear here I cannot get a vision with fear or hate since I feel both I must have love or no vision, the fear and hate seem to be very close together and is kind of almost overwhelming me what is wrong?"

LJ said "Sir I think you need to stand about four or five feet away from the chair and think of your God so you don't have hate on your mind." CR said "that is better, now person in the chair think loving thoughts about your friend let the fear go away. CR: "what were you and your friend talking about?" Siham: "he wanted me to help him build some things." CR: "I see you now, you seem to be arguing this is not good, you are not happy this is angry the vision is blurring, I see demons there is evil here and my vision is blurring what is wrong?"

The Arab behind Siham drew a knife from his sleeve and moved forward and CR shot him and he fell to the ground, the other Arab started to move toward Siham CR shot him in the leg he went down

JB had his gun out running toward the van screaming get out of the van with your hands up the man in the van got out with a gun in his hand JB shot him he went down. It was all over in two seconds.

Policeman started coming across the parking lot in police cars that came through the entrance to the parking lot and raced over to where they were. JB went over to the Arab on the ground pointed his gun at him and said: "don't move a muscle." The Arab: "I am hurt I want a lawyer." JB said "why would you want a lawyer you have not been charged with anything?"

JB looked at Siham and ask: "what did he want?" Siham replied "he wanted any bombs I had done, I told him he had to wait until all were done, he got mad and I said remember the blind man in my store, he has found people that are lost from visions. Then he put me in the van and made me bring us here, I knew CR would save me."

Hank got out of his police car, policemen got out of their cars and tried to talk to the Arab on the ground; and Siham said "he doesn't speak English if you want I can talk to him and translate." He said something in a foreign language and at the end said "lawyer." JB laughed: "so you want a lawyer well I don't think you're going to get a lawyer because you are trying to purchase bombs you just tried to kill this man in front of me you are terrorists homeland will take care of you and there are no lawyers there."

LJ looked at Hank and said "Hank would you mind if I talked to the man lying on the ground wanting a doctor?" Hank replied "no go ahead." LJ asked "Hank would you and your men move away about forty feet while I talked to this gentleman?" Hank shook his head yes and said "sure", they moved way out into the parking lot. LJ went over to the Arab on the ground and ask: "do you want to see your God?" The Arab: "kill me then I am martyred and I will go and be with Allah." LJ: "you tell me all your plans and I will let homeland security have you and then you eventually can meet your God if you don't we're going to take you up into the woods strap you to trees cut you so you bleed and let the animals of the forest kill you; it will be very slow and painful you will not meet your God."

The Arab said "you cannot do that this is America I can have a lawyer." LJ turned looked at Hank and yelled "Hank come here."

Hank came over by himself. LJ talking in a low voice "tell your people that there are only two Arabs and get your corner out here after we leave to take care of the two on the ground, this other one doesn't exist were taking him up on the hill he doesn't want to talk."

Hank: "okay, there are only two Arabs I don't see any others." Hank walked away back to his men and they got in their cars. They all turned around and left. The Arab started screaming: "you can't do this, you can't do this, you can't do this." LJ with a determined look said "they're gone yes we can do this." JB stated "there is some black bags in the office we need to put them down in the van so there's no blood and let's head up on the hill and get this man set up and leave." LJ turned and headed for the office and he came back with 4 black bags took one and wrapped the Arab's leg tied the bag on so it wouldn't come off handed the other bags to CR. CR said "dad quit recording."

LJ came back with his van opened the door and tied black bags to the seat. JB got some rope and tied the Arab to the back seat so he couldn't move and I will use his knife, I'll get some plastic gloves, and we will be ready to go. JB went into the office grabbed some rope, rubber gloves and came back out and the Arab said "I will tell you anything you want to know." LJ took out a recorder and said" what is your name?" The Arab: "my name is Dowana Emir." LJ: "why are you here?" The Arab: "to find my brother he came over here and has vanished." LJ: "what were you going to do to find him?"

The Arab: "we were going to call the paper and say we needed to know where he is and to give him back or we would set bombs off one every day in your city until we had him." LJ: "what else are you going to do?" The Arab: "we were going to kill Siham for not telling us what happened to my brother." LJ: "then what were you going to do?" The Arab: "get my brother or if he was dead go back to Afghanistan." LJ: "what else." The Arab: "that is everything." LJ untied the Arab helped him out of the van and set him in a chair. JB called Hank and told him to come back two minutes later they were loading the Arab into a squad car. Hank said "the corner will be here in about fifteen minutes and take care of the bodies then you can have your people clean up this area. JB: "I hope you are putting him where he cannot talk to anyone else, we don't want other prisoners talking to him and then talking to somebody else." We have been keeping them in interrogation rooms cuffed to chairs and only let one arm loose to eat and they are escorted into an out of the restroom and nobody else is there, until homeland comes and picks them up which was usually just a few hours." LJ: "we recorded this whole thing we are going to delete a little of the end and we will upload a copy to you within the next twenty minutes so then you will have a recording of everything that transpired."

Siham: "one of my employees was beaten by them, if I give you a copy from my surveillance, can you send that with him so he can be charged with that to." LJ: "sure go back to your store make a copy quick and bring it back to us and we will upload it to the police." Siham: "how many of you are there here today?" : "7 Adults and 3 children, why?" Siham: "I must bring you lunch and I think I have something special for your children." JB: "you do not have to do that you know." Siham: "yes I must, that is about the only way I can repay your kindness." JB: "we do appreciate your gifts." CR: "Siham could you add one more adult to that list?" Siham: "for you Mr. CR I will do anything, you have been sent from Allah to protect me."

Siham turned got in his van and left.
JB said "Mary coming to visit."
CR replied "she texted me that she heard that the police had come to the park and she is on her way, she should be here shortly." JB said "CR you better go in and get that tape doctored so we can upload it to Hank when Siham comes back." CR and his dog went to the office. Dad came out and said "I will go get the family out of the tunnel now that everything is over and not fix any lunch as it will be coming later, maybe we'll have a picnic in the office." Dad left for the big house. CR: "I am going down and take off my disguise and put my dog in the crate." LJ: "I'll go with you my dogs running loose in

the house I'll crate him to." They left together, five minutes later a car pulled up and Mary came into the office. Mary asks "where is CR?"JB replied "sit down Mary; he will be here in a few minutes." Mary in a worried voice "what happened I heard the police were dispatched here to the park?"JB in a calming voice "we had some excitement wait for a little while and I will show you the video CR was blind again." Mary with a worried look "CR's all right isn't he?"JB though *I love that one*: "he is fine not a scratch on him." CR and LJ came in five minutes later. Mary scolding "why are you doing all these dangerous things?" CR smiling said "because I'm the only blind guy we got."

Mary slapped him on the shoulder and shook her head. JB and LJ laughed. Five minutes later Dad, Mom, Rose, and the three boys came in the office; they all sat down around the table. About eight minutes later a vehicle pulled up, JB went out into the outer office and Siham came in carrying a box larger than the others he had brought. They walked in to the conference room Siham set the box on the table looked at CR and said "Mr. CR I am your servant forever." CR looking at him said "Siham you are my friend that's better than being a servant."

Siham opened the box and handed out sandwiches to everybody then he handed out bowls then drinks, he pulled out three sticks that were wrapped gave one to each child and said "this is what you call desert" the boys all said "thank you we appreciate this." Siham walked over to CR and handed him a flash drive, here are all the recordings I have of today."

CR asks "Siham you think we will have more problems like this?" Siham: "I think we should have not many visitors like them for a while, but you never know if I hear I will tell you." CR replies "we thank you for lunch; and you could've brought another and ate with us." Siham: "I must get back I have employees to oversee; you have a saying when the cat is away the mice will play." Siham turned and left they heard the van start up and drive away.

They passed around the sandwiches, the bowls, and the drinks; they all ate in silence and enjoyed their lunch. The boys started to suck on their desserts; and Rose said "you boys had a pretty big lunch why don't you save those for supper." The boys shook their head yes and rewrapped the sticks. Mom, Dad, and Rose said "those were delicious what was in there LJ: "Lamb, we are not sure about the bowls." CR: "we will see you later Mary and I are going to check out my new minivan." They got up and left. JB: "we should go to the big house and I will lock up the office."

They all left and went to the big house. JB said "I have to let the little dog out of my van I will take him to the spring house I'll be back: He opened the back and got Sam out, and he walked him around until he relieved himself, then took him to the spring house and put him in his crate, put the leash by the door opened the door locked the door on the way out and headed for the big house. JB entered the house closed the door, and found Mom, Dad, Rose, and LJ they were sitting in the living room chatting. JB: "Rose are you going with me when I go in to pick up Jennifer?" Rose: "yes I am going to spend the night there." JB: "are we taking your boys?" Rose: "yes I would like them to visit with their father, and then you can bring them back with you and Jennifer." JB: "Rose do you have furniture in storage, like beds tables and things that you wanted in your new house or do you want all new things?" Rose: "JR and I have been talking about that and we like our old stuff but we didn't bring any appliances we thought we would get new." JB: "Rose when would you like to start at the office." Rose: "Monday would be fine." JB: "we will leave in a little bit as I want to visit a little with JR too." Rose: "I'll get the boys ready then we can leave whenever you want."

JB: "Dad I was thinking we should put rolling gates on the entrance to the parking lots so after hours people can't drive in easily they will have to climb the fence if they want in." Dad: "I think that's a good idea, we will get Betty to check on that on Monday." JB said "Rose it is time to leave." They all got in to JB's minivan and left for the hospital. JB parked in the visitor's lot, and they went up to JR's room. Jennifer was sitting next to JR's bed and they were talking. Rose went in and kissed JR, Jennifer got up and went over and hugged JB.

Jennifer: "I heard via the grapevine that you three tangled with three Arabs this morning." JB: "there was only three of them that means we outnumbered them 3 to 1 so it was really easy, and CR did most of the work, the Arabs didn't know a blind man could shoot that well." JR chuckled: "so he did the thing with a dark glasses and the stick?"JB: "no he used dark glasses and the dog, he looked more like a blind man than ever, even the Arab that owns the convenience store said he knew he wasn't blind and said he was convinced he was blind."

JR: "I didn't know he could use a sniffer dog?"JB: "they have taught them to turn right and left and to keep tension on the handle of the Seeing Eye harness, it looks like the dog is pulling him but really it is CR telling the dog when to turn and where to go." JR: "Rose told me there were videos, put them on a flash drive and bring them to me next time you come and your laptop." JB: "will do, how are you doing with the manual for House clearing?" JR: "I'm going to like that; I have some ideas on things we ran up against in some of our clearings." JB: "Jennifer how is he coming along?" Jennifer: "he is ahead of the curve he's almost were somebody would be at the end of the second week, this keeps going he'll be able to leave here in another week or week and a half." JB: "that's good, we really miss him." The boys got done visiting with their dad and Jennifer said: "Time to go boys."

They left and went and got in the minivan and headed home. JB parked by the big house, let everybody out and said "I have to let Sam out and will be back in about 12 minutes, he drove to the spring house got out opened the door closed it, let Sam loose called him put the leash on and they went out for a walk, and five minutes later he was back put Sam back in the crate patted the dog and praised him, closed the crate. Opened the door closed it made sure it was locked jumped in his van and drove back to the big house. He went in dad, mom, LJ, and Jennifer were sitting around the kitchen table talking. JB sat down and listened to them talk.

Dad: "you know Betty will be retiring in a couple years she has worked awful hard and deserves it, so you might want to start looking for somebody to replace her." JB: "I talked to Rose and ask her if she wanted to work in the office and she said yes. She will start Monday and then Betty can start having some days off as soon as Rose gets up to speed." Dad: "Betty has been one of the best employees I've ever had so she will train Rose right." JB: "Jennifer I would like us to be married when we move into the big house." Jennifer: "I was thinking the same thing."

LJ: "I'll be back in a half hour to forty-five minutes, for some reason I have this urge to go to the diner." JB: "is it that cute blonde waitress that works there?" LJ: "yes can't get her out of my mind, and everybody hits on her and I don't want to be like everybody." Mom: "that's a good idea maybe it will not be so busy its afternoon and you two might get to talk." LJ: "I hope so, see you later", he went out got in his van and left.

JB: "I hope it works out, I think he feels left out because the rest of us all have somebody." Jennifer: "well everything seems to happen in its time I've been praying for him." JB: "dad let us go down to the game room with the boys let the women get their planning done." Dad: "good idea", they both got up and went to the game room.

LJ pulled up to the diner and it looked kind of empty, got out of the van locked it and went inside and headed for the table toward the back where they usually sat it was empty and he got in and faced the door. The older waitress came out saw him and turned around and went back into the kitchen. LJ thought that was kind of funny but then the cute blonde came out picked up a menu and a glass of water and came over. She put a glass of water and the menu down in front of LJ and said: "May I ask you a question?" LJ: "you may ask me anything you want."

She said: "of all the people that come in here everyone hits on me but you, are you gay?" LJ: "no I'm not gay, and I think you are quite attractive, and I don't want to hit on you like everybody else, I'm not looking for a quick affair, and I'm looking for a lasting relationship." She said "my name is Peggy, I am single, no children, and I am looking for a lasting relationship." LJ: "I've had this urge all afternoon to come to the diner, so I decided I would come down and see if you worked on

Saturday." Peggy: "no I usually don't work on Saturday and Sunday but one of the girls had a family emergency so I told her I would work for her and I've been thinking about you all afternoon." LJ: "so you don't get into trouble I would like a cup of coffee, and what kind of pie do you have?" Peggy: "we have Apple, Peach, Lemon meringue, Coconut." LJ: "that last one sounds good." Peggy: "I'll be right back." She was gone about three minutes and came back with two cups of coffee and pie. She put the pie and one coffee in front of him, put the other one across from him and sat down. Peggy: "can I ask you another question?" LJ: "you may ask me anything you want; there are some things in my life I cannot tell you about because of national security anything else I will tell you." Peggy: "you sure get right to the point don't you?" LJ: "I will never lie to you, I will never intentionally hurt you mentally or physically, God put us on this earth to help each other and get along with each other, so I try to do that as much as I can." Peggy: "I think people just selfishly care about themselves me, me, me, and don't think about anyone else." LJ: "everyone is my friend till they prove me wrong." Peggy: "you are different than anyone I have ever met." LJ: "I hope so; I don't particularly want to be like everybody else." A large man came into the diner and sat down closer to the door. Peggy: "I will get him a glass of water and a menu and tell Alice he's here so we can continue talking." Peggy got up, got a glass of water, grabbed a menu, and walked over to the man and put it in front of him. He reached out and grabbed her arm and said: "could you sit and talk to me a while?" She tried to pull away but he was holding on quite tight, she looked at LJ with a help me look. LJ got up and walked over and said "Sir Excuse me this is my fiancé would you please let go of her arm." The man said "are you a tough guy?" LJ: "can I ask you a question, if I had grabbed a hold of your fiancé would you ask me to let her arm go?" The man looked at LJ, and let go of Peggy, and said "I am sorry I didn't know ma'am would you forgive me I didn't see a ring." LJ: "the reason she's not wearing a ring is she can't make up her mind which one she likes and she will have one as soon as she makes her decision." The man: "I'm surprised you just didn't hit me." LJ: "if I hit you we would be enemies, there are too many enemies in this world, if we discuss with each other we would have more friends this way maybe we can become friends instead of enemies."

The man said "that's a good philosophy I guess I would rather be your friend than your enemy my name is George." LJ held out his hand and said "they call me LJ; it's a pleasure to meet you." Peggy: "let me get you a cup of coffee on the house and Alice will come out and wait on you shortly." The man said "thank you." Peggy stuck her head in the kitchen and said Alice you have a customer, she and LJ went back to the table.

Peggy looked at LJ and said:"wow this is the fastest relationship I ever had I just know your name and were engaged." LJ chuckled: "I really didn't want to hurt the man so I thought why come over unless I had a reason and I would rather solve a problem peacefully he's probably just a lonely man and doesn't really know how to communicate with people, and as I said earlier I don't like to hurt people." Peggy: "what kind of a relationship are you looking for?" LJ: "I'm looking for a long-term relationship, the rest of my life, where we plan things together and until we agree we don't make a decision."

Peggy: "you mean you're not the boss, I'm not boss?" LJ: "yes I think marriage should be a partnership or team where everyone works together instead of against each other." Peggy: "you are probably the nicest man I have ever met." LJ: "thank you, what kind of a relationship are you looking for?" Peggy: "the same thing you are, a loving relationship where we both treat each other with love and respect." LJ: "I would like at least two children what about you?" Peggy: "you do get to the point; I would like at least two also." LJ: "do you have plans for tonight?" Peggy: "no I get off at 4:30." LJ: "do you have your own car?" Peggy: "yes." LJ: "how about coming out and meeting my family." Peggy: "I would need to go home and change clothes." LJ: "my family doesn't care how you are dressed they are more interested in what's on the inside." Peggy: "where do you live?" LJ: "I live in what they call the big house at the park and I'll explain that later here is my number pull up to the office and call and I will come and get you." Peggy got up and went back into the kitchen. LJ finished his pie left a $10 bill on the table and left. Peggy was talking to Alice in the kitchen and told Alice how he had calmed the man down that had grabbed her arm, and that he had asked her to come and meet his family. Alice said "he must be serious." Peggy: "yes he said right off he was looking for a long-term relationship." Alice: "why don't you go home and change I can finish here by myself, we got hardly any people." Peggy said "thank you I'll see you on Monday." Peggy left got in her car and went home. LJ went back to the big house went in and the adults were in the living room. JB: "how did it go?"

LJ: "she'll be over here later to meet all of you. Mom: "you are throwing her in the water to see if she can swim." LJ: "well if we are going to start dating, we do a lot of things together; she might as well meet the family." Jennifer: "did you tell her you were direct and to the point." LJ: "she's already figured that out." They all laughed and mom said "we will just put another plate on the table." JB: "shall we all get dressed up." LJ: "no I told her to just come as she was."

Mom looked at LJ and said "LJ if you think she's going to come in as she was at the diner you got a big surprise coming." LJ: "maybe I better go shave and shower and put on some nicer clothes." LJ left to change clothes. JB: "I really hope this works out for him." The rest of them all agreed. Forty-five minutes later LJ got a phone call, it lasted about twenty seconds and he hung up. LJ: "Peggy is at the office, I'm going to walk up and bring her down." LJ was back with Peggy in eight minutes. LJ opened the door and they came into the big house.

He took her into the living room and everybody stood up. LJ said "this is JB and his fiancée Jennifer." Peggy said "hi I'm Peggy." LJ said "this is mom and dad." Peggy said "I'm Peggy." LJ said "my other brother CR is out with his girlfriend Mary you will have to meet them later and JR got shot last week and he's in the hospital and his wife Rose is there with him, there are three boys in the basement one is JB's and the other two are JR's and Roses, that's the whole lot." Peggy: "you were all in the Navy together as I've seen five of you in the diner together?" Dad: "they were Navy SEALs and I guess they were together for ten years they are probably closer than brothers." Peggy said "what did you all do in the Navy?" JB: "we saved good people and eliminated bad people." Peggy: "that sounds dangerous?"JB: "at times it was, and times it wasn't for most of that is classified so we can never tell you that." Peggy: "LJ said there were things he couldn't talk about." JB: "it's time for me to walk Sam you might as well introduce Peggy to your dog and the three of us can walk them, unless Jennifer wants to come along to." LJ said "why don't you get Sam, I'll get Mike." JB went to the spring house to get Sam. LJ said "Peggy come with me." They went into a workroom and there were two crates sitting there one had a dog in it and one was empty.

LJ said "CR went over to visit his girlfriend Mary and he took spot with him she also has a dog they got together in dog training school." He got his leash opened the crate snapped it on Mike he came out looked at Peggy and moved beside LJ and sat down. LJ: "these dogs are what we call sniffer dogs, we give him a command and he will look for guns, explosives, and people, they are not attack dogs but they will protect you." LJ took two treats out-of-the-box on top of the crate, rolled one around in his hand and then gave it to Peggy and said roll it around in your hand so your scent is mixed with mine." Peggy said "how is that." LJ: 'looks good now hand the treat to him." She tentatively reached out her hand the dog very politely took the treat. LJ: "hold your hand out and let him smell it." She did as he said the dog smelled her hand. LJ: "now rub his head slowly." She reached out and slowly rubbed the dog's head, spot wagged his tail and sat beside LJ. LJ: "you're good to go he likes you." Peggy: "he's a tougher test than the rest of the family." LJ: "you passed with flying colors" he reached over and squeezed her arm. They went outside JB, Jennifer and Sam were waiting on them.

They made small talk while they were walking, the dogs relieved themselves. JB took Sam into the spring house and they went back to the big house. LJ put Mike away and mom called out supper is ready. They ate supper when they were finished LJ and JB got up and cleared the table put the dishes in the dishwasher Jennifer threw in some soap and they went back in the living room to visit. Peggy thanked mom for supper and mom said "dad and I are going down with the three boys and you young folks enjoy yourself." Peggy said "this is the nicest evening I've had in a long time, you make me feel like I belong." JB:

"we rely on the judgment of each other and if the dog likes you, you got to be all right." Peggy laughed and said "thank you" Jennifer said "JB and I are getting married next Wednesday; you're invited if you want to come, and it's going to be a very small wedding just family." Peggy: "thank you very much I will be happy to come." They chatted and talked and had a really good time then Jennifer said "it's time I got Ben in bed and the other two boys need to go to bed so LJ it's time for us to go home."

Peggy said 'goodbye, it was nice to meet you." Jennifer: "it was nice to meet you too, and I hope we see more of you." Peggy: "I hope so too but that's up to LJ." LJ: "as far as I'm concerned she's welcome all the time." LJ: "I guess I should let you go home too, I have to get up early in the morning, we take the dogs out, and we run and we exercise to keep in shape." Peggy: "it's probably a good idea as I'm working all weekend for one of the other girls she had a family emergency." LJ: "I will walk you out to the car shall we go." Peggy got up and she and LJ walked out the door, as they were walking she reached down and took LJ's hand he closed his around her and they walked to the car. Peggy: "this is one of the nicest evening's I've ever had; I felt like I was in another family and belonged." She put her arms around LJ and kissed him and he kissed her back." LJ said "this has also been one of the best nights I've had in a long time, when do you get off tomorrow?" Peggy: "I get off at four." LJ: "I would like to spend some more time with you, so we can get to know each other better." Peggy: "I would really like that." She got in the car and drove off. LJ went back in the big house.

JB and Jennifer went to the spring house, and went in. Jennifer: "I'm going to put Ben to bed while you're walking the dog I'll see you when you get back." JB grabbed the leash took Sam out of the crate went out the door they came back in seven minutes. JB let Sam loose and he went over and lay down on his bed. Jennifer: "I think Peggy likes LJ, and he likes her." JB: "I think they been secretly looking at each other every time he's gone into the diner." Jennifer: "you're probably right." She leaned over kissed him and said: "I am tired and we need to go over to the hospital in the morning and get Rose." JB: "gave her a kiss", and she got up and went to bed. JB got his sleeping bag out lay down on the couch patted his dog and went to sleep.

CHAPTER 23

SUNDAY WEEK 4

JB woke up at 5:30 got dressed grabbed Sam and went to the big house LJ and CR were waiting for him with their dogs. They took off running and were back in twenty-two minutes. JB went back to the spring house turned Sam loose did his fifty push-ups and one hundred crunches, went to the bathroom showered and shaved, got dressed and went to the kitchen. He sat down at the table looked at Jennifer and started to sing: "you are my sunshine my only sunshine you make me happy when I am blue and I love you."

Jennifer: "that is the first time anyone has ever sang good morning to me and I love it." She came over and kissed him. Jennifer said "would you get Ben up and dressed?"JB: "sure I will" he got up and went into Ben's room. Ten minutes later he and Ben came out and sat at the table. Jennifer had cooked pancakes and that made Ben really happy as they were his favorite. They ate and cleaned off the table and they went outside got in JB's van he put Sam in his crate and they were off to take Jennifer to the hospital

JB parked in the visitor's lot and they all went in and they went up to JR's room. He was in good spirits and eating his breakfast, Rose was sitting in the chair and she looked a little tired. JB: "Rose when I take you back I want you to go to bed and get some good rest. Mom can watch the boys until you wake up. Rose: "thank you I didn't sleep good last night; this chair is not the most comfortable." JB talked a little with JR and said "are you ready to go Rose?"

Rose: "yes I am", she went over and kissed JR, and she and JB left. JB dropped her off at the big house and went in with her to talk to his dad. JB: "dad did you get JR and Rose's house on order?" Dad: "that's on my agenda for this morning I will call it in and then check Monday morning because they said they would start immediately." JB: "thank you now I won't have to worry about that." JB: "I think we all deserve a day off because it will be long weeks in the park when we are open seven days a week and we won't get any days off, and I think we will start having swat work."

CR: "Mary and I were thinking that we were going to go up to the dog training area and go through some of the information and then maybe get some tests ready to set up, to keep our dogs sharp." JB: "it's your day do whatever you want, but take some time for R&R." JB: "LJ, I figured you'd be spending some time with Peggy?"

LJ: "yes I was going to pick her up when she got off at 4:00, actually I was going to follow her home so she could clean up and then I was going to take her out to supper, then I told her she can ask me anything she wants but I would not tell her anything about missions."

JB: "Jennifer is going to check on JR and give him a castor oil pack and then she going to call me and I'm going to go pick her up so we can spend some time together." 30 minutes later Jennifer called and said "bring Ben and we will go visit with my folks I haven't seen them since we moved down here." JB: "sure but we will have to take Sam with us, and I will go armed."

Jennifer: "do you really have to?"

JB: "yes a SWAT team member must be ready to answer a call at any time 24/7." Jennifer: "well I guess I'll just have to live with that." JB:

"I will get Ben and Sam and meet you in about twenty-five minutes."
He hung up. JB got Ben put him in the van and drove down to the
spring house. He went in put a leash on Sam and he and Ben walked
Sam. Nine minutes later they came back loaded Sam into his crate,
Ben got in the back seat and they went to pick up Jennifer. On the
way he called LJ and told him that he and Jennifer and Ben were going
to visit her parents and if anything happened call him there and run
swat until he got back, and I will be back by five at the latest and not
ruin your date with Peggy.

JB called Jennifer: "we are almost there; I will pick you up at the
emergency room exit." He pulled up so her door was facing the exit
she came out jumped in buckled up, and they were on there way to
see her parents. They arrived at Jennifer's parents and her dad and
mom came out and hugged her and Ben. Her dad came over and
shook hands with JB and said: "we are really glad you two got back
together, we thought you two belonged together, but we didn't want
to interfere with your lives."

JB: "I think God put us back together, that's what he wanted and we
will never be apart again as long as I live." Jennifer's mom came over
and hugged him and said "we are so happy for you two and Ben, we
thought this is how it should have been all along." JB: "you might as
well meet the rest of the family he went around to the back opened up
his van and got Sam out. Jennifer's mom and dad looked and said "oh
you guys bought a dog." JB: "this dog is not a family pet I've had him
a little over a week and he's already saved my life, he is what is called
a sniffer dog he finds guns, and bombs, and people. He is already
found one bomb in the park. When we first got him we told Ben to
hide while I had the dog outside and Ben hid behind the secret panel
in the house the dog found him in 13 minutes, and they say he is a
breed that makes a good family dog, so he can help protect Ben also."

Jennifer's dad: "you mean if I had my gun on myself your dog would
tell you I'm armed?"JB: "that's what he's done so far, if you want to go
get a gun put it in your pocket come back out." Jennifer: "Dad forget

that." Jennifer's dad: "I have heard about dogs like this and I would like to see it." JB: "Jennifer let's just see how the dog does." Jennifer's dad went into the house was gone about five minutes and came back. He got within 4 feet of JB and Sam got in front of JB and growled. Jennifer's dad: "that is amazing because he sure didn't do that when I came up to you the first time.

JB: "I was walking in the residential area where people are not supposed to be, but a man came walking down the path Sam did the same thing to him that he did to you so we walked a little bit and then I stopped and he took a couple steps realized that I wasn't there and he turned and reached for a gun, had I not known he had one he probably would've shot me before I could have reacted, and that's how Sam saved my life." Jennifer's dad: "I think I'd have that dog with me all the time." JB: "he will be with me in the park and when I have to go on a SWAT run, he will be with me then too." They went into the house and JB brought Sam in too. Jennifer's mother said "is he house broke?"JB: "yes if he has to go he'll go to the door and whine so you know he has to go outside." Jennifer's mom: "wow, he has a built-in alarm." Jennifer: "yes at home he goes and lays on his bed and watches us I believe he is on guard all the time, I have felt much safer since we got him, and he and Ben get along real good."

Dad showed Ben a computer game that they got for him to play when he was there and he had fun playing while the adults talked. JB looked at his watch and said "Jennifer we need to leave, LJ is in charge of SWAT and I told him we would be back by 4:30 so he could go on his date with Peggy, and I have to be in charge again." They told Jennifer's parents to call and come over and visit anytime, but in four weeks he was going to be busy 14/7 when the park was opened full-time, but Jennifer and Ben will still be available. They got in the van and headed back toward the park. They were five minutes from the park JB called LJ and told him he was back have a good time. LJ said "thanks I'll see you later." JB pulled up to the big house they all got out and went in unhooked Sam and hung the leash on the hook on the wall. Dad was in the game room with the two boys and Ben ran down there. JB and Jennifer went into the living room CR, Mary, and JBs Mom were in there talking, and Jennifer sat down and joined in.

LJ drove to the diner went in to get Peggy; she was sitting by the door. LJ: "I will follow you'. Peggy went and got in her car LJ got in his van and he followed her to her house. She said I'll be ready shortly and she went into the other room. Twenty minutes later she came out and LJ looked at her and said "you look really nice." Peggy: "thank you." LJ: "I'm not sure what kind of food you like and don't like, so why don't you tell me where you would like to go." Peggy: "the Olive Garden sounds good."

LJ: "let's go hop in my van." He opened the door for Peggy she got in the front seat he went over got in the driver's side and said "I am new to this town would you like to give me direction so we can get there?" Peggy: "sure I will." She gave LJ directions and they parked and went in to the Olive Garden. They said "we would like a booth if that's possible?" The waiter said "come this way." When they got to the booth LJ had Peggy sit with her back to the door and he sat facing it. Peggy: "do you do this all the time?" LJ: "yes, it makes it easier for me to protect you, I can see things coming. Remember that's how I saw the gentleman in the diner grab you and came to your rescue." Peggy: "yes you did, I guess it is a good thing." The waiter left the menus and said "do you want the soup and salad", they both said "yes they wanted that with their meal." The waiter said I will be back with that while you look through the menu and see what you want."

Five minutes later the waiter was back with their salads and breadsticks. He asks: "are you ready to order?" Peggy said "I will have Parmesan-Crusted Fresh Tilapia mashed potatoes and green peas." LJ: "Cajun Chicken Linguini Alfredo." They ate their meal, ask for more salad and breadsticks then ask for containers and a bag to put this in so they could take it home." The waiter took their stuff and was back in three minutes with the bag full of their food he handed LJ the bill, LJ gave him enough cash to pay the bill and cover a nice tip they thanked him and left.

Peggy said "I would like to go back to my place so we can talk."

LJ: "that is fine with me; now give me directions to your place." They got to Peggy's and went in. Peggy took the bag and said "I will put this in the refrigerator and we can have it for supper tomorrow." LJ said "that's fine with me." She went into the kitchen he heard the refrigerator door open close and she came back sat beside him and kissed him he kissed her back and then he said "why don't we get the question and answer period over with, it will make me feel better." Peggy: "what were you in the Navy and what did you do?"

LJ: "the simplest answer is I was a navy seal, our job was to rescue good people and eliminate bad people." Peggy: "does eliminate mean what I think it does?" LJ: "yes it does, remember I told you I would not lie to you." LJ: "our job the last four years in Afghanistan was to eliminate terrorists, I don't know if you know much about them or not but they blow up their own innocent people just to kill a couple of us. They do not think like we do, they cut off people's heads and the four of us had bounties on our heads of over $1 million dollars that has since been lifted, the man that had the bounties on us is coming to America on Tuesday to make peace with us and the United States."

Peggy: "you must be very important?" LJ: "he decided he wanted no more trouble with us as he only had one son left and he knew the government could take him and his son out if they chose and that would be the end of their line, that's as much as I can tell you until after Tuesday." LJ: "if we get married, there are a couple things more I could tell you that I can't tell you right now, I hope that is all right with you?" Peggy: "that is fine with me; I think you might have told me a little more than you should." LJ: "I did, because I think I can trust you."

Peggy: "and you really didn't date?" LJ: "no, I didn't and neither did JB or CR, RJ the fourth man in our group is married and has two children." Peggy: "are your parents still alive?" LJ: "yes I try to visit them at least twice a year, though this year I'm not sure in four weeks the park goes on 14/7, and I'll be working there and the four of us are running the swat team for the city on an as-needed basis." Peggy: "is that why you have the dog?" LJ: "yes, the park sent us to school, to learn how to handle the dogs we have already found one bomb in the park and the bomb squad dismantled it we will be checking the park constantly for things like that, the dogs also tell us when somebody is armed and nobody should be caring arms in the park except for the police and the four of us."

Peggy: "you said you each have specialties what are yours I am a sniper and a medic I also could take you out into the woods and we can live off the land for as long as necessary." Peggy: "we may have to do that sometime my folks used to take us camping and I really enjoyed it." LJ: "surviving is like camping, with no tent, no food, and maybe just a knife." LJ: "one of the plans we have is we want to take kids that are in gangs and try to get them out of the gangs take them out and teach them some survival skills teach them there a lot of things better than being in gangs."

Peggy: "that sounds like a good idea I hope it works." LJ: "you could volunteer and help with girls because we are going to teach both and you can learn right along with them and then help them." Peggy: "I think I would like to help with that and we would be together more that way" LJ: "yes but we could not stay in the same tent, you would have to be with the girls I would have to be with the boys, but other than that we would see a lot of each other that would make me very happy." Peggy: "me too." Peggy: "you said you would like 2 children, how soon would that be."

LJ: "that would be a decision we would make together." Peggy: "well if we were married we can move into my apartment." LJ: "no we wouldn't have to do that, the park will build me a house anytime I want one, and we would live in the park." Peggy: "I don't know much about the rest of them but they must be really nice people." LJ: "the best, if my parents wanted to live here they would build a house for them if they wanted it." Peggy: "if I got mad at you and tried to hit you what would you do?" LJ: "I would not let you hit me but I would not hurt you, I might make you mad but it will not be intentional and I will never abuse you mentally or physically, men and women don't think alike and that's why we need to sit down and discuss things so we don't have problems like that."

Peggy: "I think that's enough heavy stuff for one night, and by the way you scored a plus." LJ: "well that makes me very happy." Peggy: "do you know how to dance?" LJ: "not very good but I am a quick learner and if it involves holding you I'm all for it." Peggy smiled and said "I will put some music on and we will start to dance." She put on some slow music, he got up she came over and she said you move your foot here then you move it over here and before long they were dancing and holding each other tight. They danced to two or three songs then Peggy said let's go sit on the couch. They sat down he put his arm around her she leaned over and put her arms around him and they kissed again and again.

LJ: "I can do this all night but I have to get up early in the morning the three of us go out early and we run and then we do some other exercises before we start our day, to keep us in shape that's something we don't miss." LJ: "the four of us do lots of things together JR's wife is usually involved with a lot of them Jennifer will be too, CR has a girlfriend Mary and she is included in all our stuff you can be included also if you would like." Peggy: "I like you enough that I think that I would enjoy that." LJ stood up pulled her up off the couch held her tight and kissed her and said "I guess the plan is we are having supper tomorrow night together?" Peggy: "I thought you would figure that out real quick, I really enjoy it every time we're together." LJ: "I do too, I hope it never ends." She walked him to the door kissed him again locked the door behind him and got herself ready for bed. LJ left got in his van and headed for the big house, and he was very happy.

CHAPTER 24

MONDAY WEEK 4

JB got up at 5:30 put on his running clothes put the leash on Sam and headed for the big house. LJ and CR were waiting for him and they started there run this morning they did it in twenty-one minutes they were pleased and JB said "I will see you later" and he headed for the Springhouse. He went in closed the door put the leash on the hook Sam ran over and visited Ben eating his breakfast; JB gave him fresh water and fed him. He sat down said "good morning" to Jennifer, they ate in silence, and when they finished. JB: "you don't seem happy this morning?"

Jennifer said "I feel like something bad is going to happen today, don't know why." JB replied "then I will be extra watchful, I think we get these things to warn us most of the time we pay no attention, and then bad things usually happen." JB: "you don't think anything's wrong with JR do you?" Jennifer: "no Rose says he walked around a little bit in his room again, and after she got done giving him his castor oil pack and cleaned him off the nurse said his wounds are almost healed, he seems to be doing great just like you did."

JB look at her and said "will you be careful, and be observant take no chances, the police bring anybody in you have the policeman stay in with you while you're working on them and asked the police if they got all the weapons from them."

Jennifer looking serious said "you be extra careful to, though I

260

think you're always on the lookout for something out of the ordinary." JB replied "that's how I stayed alive for ten years." Jennifer: "let's go up to the big house and get the two boys and you can take me to work and drop them off to school." JB put the leash on Sam and they all went out got in the van and drove to the big house. Jennifer went in got the three boys and was back in seven minutes. Jennifer: "Rose said she would meet you at the office later." Rose's two boys sat in the second bench because Sam was sitting beside Ben on the front bench. JB turned and took the three boys to school, Jennifer got out and Sam jumped in the front seat she opened the side door three boys got out and closed the door and she took them in the school and came back.

JB pointed to the back and Sam got on the front bench, Jennifer got in and they drove toward the hospital. He dropped her off at the emergency room entrance kissed her goodbye and said I'll see you later today." Sam got in the front seat and they headed for the park. JB pulled up and saw that LJ and CR's vans were already there. He went in and said "hi to Betty and Rose, "they were sitting next to LJ and CR, they had brought a couple of folding chairs from the conference room and were sitting there talking to each other. LJ look at JB and said: "we need to expand this office and maybe make some more rooms, but we like it better open, that way I don't feel caged up." JB: "that thought has crossed my mind what do you think Betty?" Betty: "I agree and I don't like to be caged up either." JB: "we will have to use somebody other than our maintenance crew because today they start taking all the rides out of mothballs and they're going to be extremely busy for the next four weeks."

Betty: "we had some work done on our house by a couple of guys, they were brothers from somebody I went to school with and we were very pleased with the price and in the work they did for us why don't I call them and see what kind of a bid they can give us, just figure out what we want to do." JB: "there is room outside for us to expand away from the conference room we should be able to go out there at least 15 maybe 18 feet and not run into the walkway." We could put another desk to the left of the conference room door and that should give us 4 more desks." Betty that will give us seven desks that should work as I think we need a spare desk that way if your dad comes in he has a place."

JB asks "Betty who put the bid in on the first aid Station, and do you have the drawings to build it?" Betty answered "yes, I do and they work in hospitals, and doctors' offices and they are familiar with the regulations and what they need to do." JB replied "then we will stick with them as I think they did give us a pretty good price." We are going to need a block building to hold unruly people until the police can get here and haul them away. Why don't you see if your two guys can do that also?"

Betty said "I will get a hold of them and have them come out and look at things." JB on another note "Betty, Rose is going to be your assistant, give her things to do, so you can start taking some time off and with all the things that are going on I think you're going to need help. When do you plan on retiring, we hope never but you have a life to, dad said he could've never ran this place without you and mom, and she retired. If I lost you this place would go down."

Betty: "I was thinking in a year or two, as we wanted to travel to see more of this country." JB's phone rang and he answered, two minutes later he hung up. Swat is needed, two gangs have taken some hostages threatened to shoot each other in the plaza downtown, Mary and Curt will meet us there and remember we are going to use our radios that we used on the hill so if they have scanners they won't know what we are doing."

JB ask them "where are your dogs?"
LJ replied "There in the big house."
JB said "from now on we will have to have them with us at all times Sam is in my van and I will just bring him in here that'll be more protection for Betty and Rose." LJ and CR ran to the big house. JB got Sam out of the van and took him into the office and turned him loose and went to his van pulled out a ways from the office and as soon as LJ and CR got there, he headed for the plaza.

Police already had the area roped off JB stopped, got out went back and changed the sign on his van to swat, LJ and CR did the same thing. They parked, got their weapons, and walked their dogs toward the sergeant in charge he was talking to his men over his car radio. He stopped and said: "we have them surrounded so far it's quiet. JB: "We are not going to use regular police channels sergeant hand out radios like we used up on the hill do you have them with you?"

The Sgt. said "No, they're back at the department."

JB replied "you call and get somebody to rush them here so everyone of you has one, and get them here as quick as possible, they may have scanners and we don't want them to know what we're saying and what we are going to do; we are going to call this stealth mode, call on your cell phone so it stays private." JB looked at LJ and said "LJ you and Curt station yourself on the building on the left CR you and Mary station yourself on the right-hand building; Sgt. how are the gangs laid out, he said your men will be on their sides so you should have a good view."

JB said "keep vigilant Mary and Curt you watch their backs and keep track of your back Sgt. I'm going up on this building behind us and set the radios to 90 that's where ours are set and when they get here you keep one and get somebody to deliver one to each one of your men because that's how we are going to communicate and you do not tell anybody back at department about stealth mode." JB went up to his point of view; he could see the whole thing."

JB on the radio: "LJ, CR this looks funny I think it's some kind of a set up watch your six and stay vigilant. A minute later JB heard bang, then bang, bang, bang it was coming from CR's direction. JB hit the radio send button "LJ can you see CR?"

LJ replied "I don't see Mary but CR is running away from the wall."

JB said "Sgt., Get an ambulance here right away."

Sgt. replied "I already did, it's on its way I did that as soon as I heard the shots."

Davison had snuck up on CR and Mary, her dog turns quickly to look behind and growls, he is aiming at CR, Mary draws her weapon and moves in front of CR and the man fires and hits her in the chest she goes down CR turns draws and shoots him twice in the chest and a third shot to the head as he falls CR looks down, he looks at Mary her eyes are blinking he says "stay where you are, don't move, I'll be right back I got to make sure he's done", and he ran over, the man is not moving and he did not have a vest on, his blood was spreading all over CR checked for a pulse there wasn't any, he ran back to see how Mary was, she is getting up slowly, CR tells her not to move and he opens her shirt, there is a bullet in the front of her vest

CR with a worried look said "are you all right?" Mary says "yes that really hurt she stuck her hand up under the vest, well I don't feel any blood so just bruised I guess." CR helped Mary up she said "he's one of us why was he going to shoot you?" CR replied "I don't know I've never seen him before in my life."

CR with a serious look said "Mary why did you move in front of me I don't want you getting killed." Mary replied "I didn't want you shot, and I knew if I went down you would take him out and I figured my vest would save me." CR shaking his head said "I love you, don't ever do that again just holler and shove me out of the way and shoot at them that way neither one of us should be hit, I thank your dog for warning us, and without them we might both be dead."

The police were closing in on the gang members and the police are on the bullhorns telling them to lay down their weapons and stop fighting they both turned and started shooting at the police. JB: "CR take out the gang leader on your right, LJ take out the gang leader on your right you are authorized to shoot, wound them if possible, two seconds later both gang members went down. CR radioed and said "we have an officer down up here my rooftop he tried to kill me and Mary, his name is Davison, get some detectives up here."

JB radioed the policeman on the horn and told him to tell the gang members to lay down their weapons or they were going to start to die. The policeman on the foghorn: "your leaders are down stop fighting lay down your weapons or the rest of you will be shot." They slowly started to lay down their weapons and held their hands in the air; the police came in and cuffed them till they were all in custody.

JB said "I need the corner and detectives Billy and Carl up here on the rooftop where CR is; there is a policeman down up there. JB got on his phone and text Hank 911 one of your policemen tried to shoot CR, call me quick. Three minutes later JB got a return call from Hank. Hank said "what do you know?"JB: "CR said Mary jumped up, a shot was fired she went down, CR spun drew his pistol and shot three times and the man went down, he checked Mary she was dazed but her vest stopped the bullet. He checked the man, he was a cop he had a nameplate that said Davison he was dead." Hank: "are you sure Mary is all right?"

"CR said she was, the bullet didn't go through her vest, so she's probably just bruised. JB replied"

"What else have you done?"Hank asked.

"I've asked the sergeant on the bullhorn to have Billy and Carl to go to CR's location and start to investigate immediately and take statements from Mary and him. And I assume we must get search warrants to go to Davison's house and see if we can find anything that says why he did this."

Hank replied "I will leave here and head back immediately." JB said "let me know what your ETA is and I will have somebody at the airport to pick you up, sorry I had to call you."

"You did the right thing as you don't know all the procedures, I will call Billy and tell him he's in charge of the investigation, he and Carl are the best two detectives I have, goodbye and I'll call you with flight information as soon as I get it." Hank replied hurriedly.

JB said "LJ you and Curt go over to CRs position and Billy and Carl will take possession of your weapons until the shooting is investigated and they are going to go over and check this man's house to see what information they can find the only gun you should have to give is your rifle we will have to get a spare gun for CR as they will take his rifle and pistol, I will see you over there shortly."

JB left his position and went down to see the Sgt. Sam got in front of him and growled. Sgt. Said "why did he do that." JB replied "he is trained to do that to warn me that somebody in front of me is armed." The Sgt.: "I wish I had one of those." JB: "he's already saved my life once by doing that; Sgt. better get a second ambulance over here and do you need more police to put in the ambulance to take the wounded and as you're going to have two different gang members and I don't want them talking." Sgt.: "Hank called and told me to handle everything for you since you don't know all the procedures and he is now trying to get a flight back."

JB asks "what do you know about a policeman named Davison?"

The Sgt. replied "He is not liked by too many people, he's a strange man but he has appeared to do his job like he should why?"JB: "he is the policeman that is down, he shot Mary and CR took him out." Sgt.: "That must've been the following three shots; did he miss, is that why it took three shots?"JB: "I doubt it, my guess is he figured the man had a vest, so I think your corner is going to tell us there was two shots to the chest and one to the head."

The Sgt. asked "He's that good." JB replied "He's that good, you get a chance watch him on the range, and you want him on your side." JB pushed send on the walkie-talkie and he said "LJ and Curt to go over where CR and Mary are, as they would collect their guns until the investigation is over." Sgt. said "I will tell the investigator to go up there and take their statements and their weapons."

JB went up to the rooftop LJ and Curt were there along with CR and Mary, and an EMT was checking Mary out." JB: "does she have any broken ribs." The medic said "it really doesn't look like it, but she's probably going to have a nasty bruise." JB went over to the corner and ask "where was he hit?" Corner: "two in the chest one in the head, he was dead before he hit the ground, I've never seen shooting like that before." A few minutes later Carl came and started taking statements first from Mary then from CR. Then Carl said "who did the shooting on the other building." LJ told his story and then Curt told his."

JB: "where is Bill?"

Carl: "he is getting a search warrant to go to Davison's house."

JB: "is he picking you up here or you meeting them over at the house."

Carl replied "he is going to call me when he gets a warrant and I'm going to meet him over there." JB said "I will follow you over; I would like to know why a policeman we've never met was trying to shoot one of us." Carl: "it doesn't make much sense to us either, so far none of the gang members are talking." JB: "Have you charged them with anything yet?" Carl: "not yet that way we can hold them longer, before they can lawyer up."

Carl's phone rang, it was Bill he had the search warrant, Carl said "we will meet you over there", and hung up. JB: "LJ and CR you two go wherever you want I'm going over to the Davison's house and see what I can find out." LJ: "I'm going to go with JB, CR I think you should spend some time with Mary, make sure she's mentally all right, and I doubt she's been shot before. "JB, LJ, and his dog, followed Carl, got in their vans, and followed Carl to Davison's house.

They went into the house, no one was there, and they looked around and couldn't find anything. LJ: "let me try something they mentioned at school I'll be right back as soon as I get Mike." LJ and Mike came back and LJ said: "let's find his dirty clothes and let Mike smell them." They found a cloths hamper and pulled something out for Mike to smell." They let him smell then LJ said "search" and Mike started looking fifteen minutes later they were in the basement and Mike was sitting in front of the wall and scratching."

LJ said "they told us in school that somebody had their dogs search and he stopped in front of a wall it had a secret door and they found a large room behind it." Let's look and see if we can find some way to open this wall. JB looked on one side LJ on the other. LJ pushed on a section of the wall and a door popped open. They went in and there were pictures on the wall of JB, LJ, CR, and JR. There were pictures of the plaza, the park, there was a mark where JB got shot, and there was a mark where JR got shot.

There were ledgers, and in there it looked like they were payments to the two gangs that had been arrested, it looked like Davison had some criminal activities going on the side, there was a safe beside the table, Carl said "we should get a locksmith over here to open that?" Bill I know one I can call, he is good with safes." LJ was looking at a picture on the wall. LJ: "JB come and look at this picture." JB looked at the picture and said "he looks familiar." LJ: "that's Henry, Davison knew Henry."

JB replied "Davison must've been the brains of all of this, were they friends, related; Bill and Carl you'll have to figure this out, he was the man who wanted to shoot me, this may shed a lot of light on what's happened the last two weeks." Bill: "I'm glad you two came along we didn't know who this Henry was, we would've missed that, and we will look for how they were connected." JB's phone rang; he talked for a minute then hung up. JB: "that was Hank he just landed at the airport I'm going to go pick him up." LJ: "I'm going to go back to the park, when the others get there I'll fill them in." It took 14 minutes to get to the airport he parked in the pickup zone eight minutes later Hank came out loaded his stuff in the van. And they pulled out of the airport JB filled Hank in on what they had learned so far.

Hank: "I never particularly liked Davison but he always seemed to get his work done." JB: "so far it looks like he was the brains behind what has been happening here the last couple of weeks and it appears like he's running some illegal operations with the gang members we picked up today." Hank asked "how is Mary?"

JB replied "her vest worked real well but she's going to be bruised, I told CR to talk to her as I doubt she's ever been shot before." Hank: "90% of my police department hasn't been shot at let alone hit." JB: "CR said Mary's dog growled he started to turn she got in front of him he heard the bang she went down so he drew and eliminated the threat while he was shooting before he realized it was a policeman and he was baffled why a policeman would be shooting at them, the third shot was in case he had a vest and stopped the first two, he was not going to let somebody kill Mary."

Hank says "I believe I would've done the same thing in his place." JB: "where do you want to go?" Hank: "Let me call the Sgt. and see if they've wrapped up at the plaza." Sgt. Said "most everybody is gone they are roping off the plaza but there's nobody up there anymore Bill and Carl are still over at Davison's they've got a locksmith coming in to open a safe."

Hank replied "thank you, I will see you when you get back to the station." They pulled up at the station Hank got his luggage out of the back, and JB and Hank went in the station." Hank told the Sgt.

in front to send the crime scene investigator to his office. He and JB went into Hank's office and waited. Five minutes later the crime scene investigator came in he had two papers with him he sat down in front of Hank and said "we found the body of Davison laying in a pool of blood he had two bullet wounds in the chest and one in the head all three had traveled from a distance there was light explosive residue on the body, so he had been shot with all three from a distance which was quite amazing.

A female police officer Mary had a slug in her vest we extracted the slug and we will be able to get rifling's from it we assume it was from Davison's gun which we found lying on the roof. Based on what we found their testimony seems to be accurate about what happened." CSI investigator: "Based on my experience that CR must be quite a marksman." We looked for the slugs that went through the legs of the gang members but they ricocheted off the concrete and at this point in time we have not found them, I have a couple of men looking for them but by now if they haven't found them, we won't ever find them." Hank: "thank you very much, let me know if you find any information that changes what you told me." The CSI man: "I will do that", and he got up and left. Hank: "I hope things calm down after this."

JB: "I have Betty setting up a first-aid Station in the park she is looking for an outside contractor to put it up and also we are building a block building that we can use as a holding station for your police to pick people up who get into bad trouble." Hank: "based on what I've seen your men will have their weapons back tomorrow this looks about as clean as it can get, those dogs have saved one of us again, they were really a good investment and they found two bombs one at your place one at ours as we had to call Mary in to find it, so I think they've paid for themselves." JB: "I agree, and I'm even looking for one for JR, a small one like mine".

Hank: "well I shouldn't of gone in the first place but you did a top-notch job from what I can see, it just went smooth outside of Davison it was a flawless mission, but with the information we are getting it's going to turn out to be a fantastic flawless mission." JB said "I better go pick up Jennifer and the boys it's getting about that time, who are you sending out tomorrow when the Arab arrives?"

"The Sgt., Mary, Curt and shadow, I think with what the government is going to provide that should be more than enough." Hank replied.

JB said "I think so, and I don't think we are going to have any trouble with the Arab because it is his last son he will not want his line to die; see you tomorrow have a good evening." JB said as he headed for his van to go to the school. He parked the van went in and got the three boys they got in the van and left. He called Jennifer told her he would pick her up at the emergency exit five minutes later she got in the van and they headed for the park.

Jennifer with a sarcastic voice said "you kept me busy today with these nasty children." JB smiled and replied "we didn't want you bored with nothing to do, aren't we nice to you." Jennifer laughed: "I guess I didn't look at this in the proper perspective." JB asked "did Mary come in." Jennifer: "no, why?"JB: "she was shot this morning, and the EMTs checked her out, but if she's at the park I want you to check her out, CR took out the man that did it." Jennifer: "the police just told me that swat snipers shot the two that were brought in."

Jennifer: "it was kind of different how they brought them in first one then once he was gone they brought the second one in." JB: "we didn't want them talking to each other so we kept them separate so that they cannot get their stories identical unless that's the way it really happened." JB: "how is JR?" Jennifer: "at the rate he's healing we will release him at the end of the week, you guys must be really tough." JB pulled into the park and he saw LJ and CR's vans he pulled in next to them told the boys to run to the big house and he and Jennifer went inside.

Betty said "I got the quote for the two buildings they quoted 6000 to 7000 to expand what we have here and the block house would be 15,000." JB: "when can they start?" Betty: "they said they could start in two days, finish the office then build the larger structure, they thought they would have everything done in 2 ½ to 3 weeks." JB: "that sounds good to me, based on what we've done on some of these other buildings it sounds reasonable to me."

Betty said "I'll have Rose call them and tell them they got the job." Betty handed Rose the quote and she made the call. Betty: "the dog people say they have a dog like yours, and he will be finished Wednesday, they will ship him Wednesday and we will have him Thursday morning, he will cost 2000." JB: "tell them we will take him." Betty said "Rose got them to knock 500 off the price." JB looked at Rose "Rose thank you and you know that's going to be JR's dog." Rose: "yes but we have to get the best price we can." JB went over and sat in front of Mary. JB: "Mary how do you feel." Mary: "sore." JB: "tell me what happened."

Mary: "CR said you would quiz me, nip moved and growled I looked up and there was a man with a gun pointed at CR I moved so he couldn't hit CR the bullet hit me and I went down, the next thing I know CR is shooting the man, and he went down, CR asked me if I was all right and he opened my shirt and we could see the bullet in my vest, he said are you all right, I felt underneath my vest but felt no blood and I said yes I'm just hurt he said he'd be right back then he went to look at the man. A minute later he was back and helped me up to make sure I was all right."

JB: "Would you do it again?" Mary: "to protect CR, of course." JB: "Mary I'm really proud of you, welcome to swat, and thank you for saving my brother." He got up and said "Jennifer would you take Mary in the conference room shut the door and check her out make sure she's all right."

Jennifer replied "yes I will." She and Mary went into the conference room. JB looked at CR: "you think she's good." CR: "yes I do, when you asked her would she do it again she didn't even hesitate, as far as I am concerned you can pair me up with her anytime and I hope it is all the time." JB: "unless the dynamic is entirely different she will be your partner on all SWAT missions, and you might give serious thought to marrying her."

LJ: "I've been thinking we need to set up something to teach them repelling and I thought the cliff on the side of the hill might be a really good place to do that." JB: "sounds good to me, CR." CR: "sounds good to me to, better put it on the list." Jennifer and Mary came out of the conference room and Jennifer said "she has a real bad bruise, other than that she looks good, I told her how to do the castor oil and we will see how fast it works for her."

LJ got up and said "I have a dinner date so I will see you later." He left got in his van and headed for the diner. He got there a little early; he went to the back and sat facing the door. Peggy saw him and came over and said "were you involved in what went on at the plaza this morning?"

LJ: "yes I was." LJ: "come closer you can't repeat this, it was a policeman that was shot, he turned out to be a criminal, he shot Mary." Peggy: "is she alright." LJ: "yes as I was saying she jumped in the way to protect CR she got hit in the chest but her vest saved her, CR shot the man." Peggy: "at least you didn't get shot at, did you?" LJ: "no, I was safe on a rooftop."

Peggy: "is Mary a good shot." LJ: "she qualified in a tie with the man that usually gets the highest score every month." Peggy: "when are you going to teach me how to shoot?" LJ: "we can go up to the range on the weekend if you'd like, but you don't have to shoot for me to like you." Peggy: "I thought it might be a good skill to have when you're not around." LJ: "you say the word and we will go shoot." Peggy: "I guess when you told that man we were engaged, I think he must have spread the word and it must have got around, not near as many people are hitting on me now, that's kind of nice." LJ: "I am glad I could make you happy." Peggy: "you just being around makes me happy." LJ: "how soon do you get off?" Peggy: "fifteen minutes." LJ: "would you get me a cup of coffee while I am waiting." Peggy: "brought him a cup and said I'll be back."

LJ leaned back and enjoyed his drink, he gazed around there was an old man and an old lady at the other end and partially up toward the middle there were four men sitting around the table having pie and something to drink. LJ laid two dollars on the table for the coffee; he looked at Peggy and said "I will be walking the dog while I'm outside."

LJ got up walked out opened the back of the van and saw that two men from the table were coming out the door and he took spot out of his crate shut the van and turned, the men had walked down the walk and were about eleven feet away from him staring right at him. LJ: "can I help you gentlemen?" The biggest one said "are you the one who is supposed to be engaged to Peggy?"

LJ: "what if I am, what if I'm not, what business is it of yours, one of you her brother, no you're too ugly." The big one took another step forward, Mike growled. LJ: "before we get started here, can I ask you a question?" The big guy said "sure go ahead." LJ: "how long can you afford to be out of work?" The big guy: "what do you mean?" LJ: "exactly what I said, I really don't know you, and I have nothing against you, and I don't really want to hurt you, but if you pursue it, I will try not to hurt you anymore than you can afford to be out of work I'd rather not cause you hardship and do use your feet or your hands?" The big guy: "why do you want to know that?" LJ: "Because if you use your hands I will break your legs, if you use your legs, I will break your arms and fingers." The big guy: "so you think your real tuff."

LJ: "no, I know I am, I've been busting guys like you for over ten years, how much experience have you got I put so many people in the hospital I've lost count." The other two from the table just came out, and one said "you talk big for one guy." LJ: "well I'm going to cripple three of you really bad the dog is going to tear up the fourth one, so if you want to be first come right on over." LJ took a step forward; spot also took a step forward. LJ: "you said that Peggy was yours which one of you is her brother, husband, cousin." Then the new guy said "why." LJ: "Because I won't hurt you so bad I don't want her mad at me as I cripple one of her family members." The new guy took one more step forward the others didn't move Mike took a step forward and growled. The new guy: "maybe I'll stab your dog." LJ: "that's even worse he is trained to rip the muscles in your arm so you cannot use the arm anymore and then you automatically drop your weapon you'll have three or four surgeries in six to 7 months before you can even move a finger, and you can't say I didn't warn you." LJ: "I'm tired of talking, either turn around and go back in the diner and I will forget the whole thing as I have work to do"

LJ took a step forward. The first two turned around and walked back inside, the second two realized that they were the only two left, they went over got in a car and drove away. LJ took Mike walked him around the back he relieved himself, he came back out to the front Peggy was there. Peggy: "Alice came back and told me that the four of them had come outside so I ran out to see what they were doing, I was going to call 911 if they were bothering you." LJ: "is that why you're dating me?"

Peggy: "no, because you treated me nice every time I waited on you, you didn't act like you owned me after you left a tip."

LJ: "okay I will stop this nonsense right now, were going back inside." LJ went inside with Peggy by the arm; he went over to the two and said "what makes you think you own Peggy?" One of the men started to scoot his chair back LJ said "you get up I will break both your arms, and you sit there and answer the question." The man stammered and finally said "we saw her first." LJ: "well I saw her last and she's mine and if I even think you are bothering her you're going to spend the rest of your life in a chair sucking food through a straw, you understand me."

Both men got white as a sheet and one stammered "we are sorry it won't happen again." LJ: "and I never want to see you in this diner again, do you understand?" They both said yes, dropped money on the table and left. LJ looked at Peggy said "is there a backdoor?" Peggy: "yes, follow me." They went out the back door LJ went cautiously around the diner looking for anybody that was hiding he got to the front and told her to stay back and he went to the car he got Mike out and took him to where the men were standing and said search, spot walked around a little bit went to a spot where a car had been parked and sat.

LJ: "good dog and petted him and he put him back in his crate. He called Peggy come on over. LJ: "do they know where you live?" Peggy: "I don't think so unless they followed me, and I didn't know it." LJ said "you get in your car and don't drive over the limit, I will follow you and if anybody's following us, I will take care of it.

Peggy got in her car and drove out of the lot with LJ following her. They got to her house and parked. She got out of her car LJ got out of his van, went around to the back and got Mike. They walked up and went in Mike never growled so LJ knew they were safe. She opened the apartment door and they went in. LJ took the leash off, Mike walked around checked every room came back and sat down next to LJ. Peggy: "what did he do?" LJ: "he checked to see that nobody else was here." Peggy: "you didn't trust me?" LJ: "after something like that they may have busted into your house and waited until we got back to jump us where they have the advantage because we are confined to a narrow area, I have stayed alive ten years by not making mistakes, people like those four aren't too bright and they do stupid things, I really don't like to hurt people, but if they force me I will hurt them so bad they will never come near me again."

Peggy: "they have ruined our evening, you probably think I'm a really a bad person and might date terrible guys." LJ: "I do not know you well enough to judge you, and I can't hold anything against you, this looks to me like it's out of your control, now forget it ever happened and let's have a nice supper, you haven't eaten it all have you?" She smiled and said "no that was to be our special dinner." LJ: "it still is."

She reached over and squeezed his hand got up and said let's go out to the kitchen." They went into the kitchen and she had a tablecloth on the table candles plates and glasses, she was having a special dinner." She lit the candles, and then got the food out of the refrigerator, put the salad on the table put the breadsticks in the microwave and heated them up for a few seconds and put them on the table and sat down. They ate the salad and bread sticks. Peggy said "now for the next course." She opened the two containers put his Alfredo on the plate put it in the microwave heated it up put it in front of him, then she put hers on the plate heated it up, and put it where she was sitting sat down and they started eating.

When they got done she got up went to the fridge and brought out two slices of coconut pie. She took his plate and put pie down in its place, she picked up her plate and put them both in the sink took a piece of pie and put it down where she was sitting and they had dessert. When they were done she cleaned off the table blew out the candles she led him out into the other room turned on her record player and said "I would like this dance."

LJ smiled "you can have them all." They danced a while she held him tight he held her tight and they had a great time. She put her arms around his neck, and kissed him and he kissed her, they kissed and kissed and kissed. LJ: "I could stay here forever but I have an important meeting tomorrow and I have to be there so I need to go home and get some sleep." She walked LJ to the door kissed him hard again he said I'm not sure what my schedule is but I will try to see you tomorrow if I can."

He turned grabbed a hold of Mike's leash and said "as soon as were out the door shut it and lock it." And out the door he went. He walked down the steps walked to the back of the van, opened it Mike growled he whipped around a man was running at him with the club in his hand LJ shot him in the leg down he went screaming the other shadow turned and ran. LJ called 911, 911 answered LJ said "I need an ambulance and a squad car this is LJ from SWAT A man tried to hit me with a club and I shot him in the leg so get them out here quickly." Nine minutes later an ambulance and the squad car pulled up.

LJ shined the light on the man, he was holding his leg, the club that was lying beside him was a ball bat, and LJ said "I warned you and you didn't listen now you are going to spend some time in jail." The man said "it's my word against yours." LJ: "how stupid are you the club's right beside you with your fingerprints on it." Shadow got out of the squad car and EMT got out of the ambulance.

Shadow came up and said "LJ, you have trouble with this idiot." LJ: "yeah he and another man came at me with this bat if you want we can have Mike track the other one down, it is up to you, I will cuff this one around the light pole and we'll go look for the other one." Shadow said "sure", shadow got on his radio called for backup explained the situation and said "were going after the other one, get somebody here, I got this one cuffed to a light pole."

LJ went got on the side where the other one had been and told spot to search. They went down the street to an alley around the corner LJ stopped and said "see the man in the car across the street you stay here and I'm going to walk down this side of the street crossover and come back with the dog he will think I'm someone from the neighborhood." Shadow said "sure", LJ came out of the alley turned left, walked to the corner, turned right went across the street and turned right slowly walked up to the car tapped on the window and said keep your hands on the steering wheel or I will shoot you."

Shadow ran across the street flashed his badge and said "open the door slowly and get out." Shadow shined the light in the man's face and said "this look like the other one?" LJ: "yeah he was one from the diner so he had to be the other one." Shadow cuffed the man and they walked him back to Peggy's apartment building. Peggy was out front asking: "was there a man with a dog?"

The other cops said "I don't know I just got here." Then she saw LJ, shadow, and Mike coming around the corner pushing a man. LJ: "told shadow about the confrontation at the diner, shadow took pictures of both men sent them to the station and said "are there any papers or open warrants on these men. Five minutes later the printer in shadows squad car started printing out the records of the two men. Both had warrants of domestic violence and many complaints that were dropped before trial." LJ: "you two picked the wrong guy this time, Peggy is going to put a restraining order against you and if you're within hundred feet of this building and I see you I will turn the dog loose and I'll have you arrested, the same goes for the diner." The EMT got in the ambulance and it left. Shadow put the wounded one in his squad car the other cop put the other one in his squad car shadow said "have a nice evening" and both squad cars left.

Peggy went over and grabbed LJ and said "I was so scared when I came out and that guy was laying on the ground shot and you and spot were nowhere to be seen, I don't want to lose you now that I found you." LJ: "they may get the idea that they don't want to mess with me, the next time I'll take them up on the hill put the fear of God into them, I have no use for people like this, from the record they just do this to other people and then scare them so they drop their lawsuit, I don't scare."

LJ kissed her again and told her to go in the house so he could leave." She kissed him again ran up the stairs went into the apartment locked the door. LJ put Mike in his crate, then he got in and drove to the big house. LJ took Mike out walked him around so he could relieve himself, they went into the big house closed the door, he put the leash by the door, turned spot lose, CR and dad were in the living room talking. CR said "did you have a good evening."

LJ gave him a blow by blow on the evening from the diner, the nice dinner he had with Peggy and then the altercation when he was leaving." Dad said "are you sure this girl's all right or is she trouble?" LJ: "well she had a tablecloth on the table and candles I think she really planned for us to have a really nice evening without all this, and both men have records of beating people up and then scarring them to death so they drop their law suits before trial; I think she's a victim here."

Dad: "next time I go to the diner I will talk to Alice, she knows everything about everybody." LJ: "I do like the girl and she seems to like me, I do really enjoy being with her, but if I have to I can walk away, I don't need drama, and I don't like to have to hurt people."

CR: "you said the dog liked her?" LJ: "yes I had him in her apartment, he just sat down by me, she would sit down next to me, he never growled, and he let her pet him." CR: "sounds to me like the dog likes her, listen to the dog they pick up things we don't, next time you see her, we will double date, and let Mary talk to her, they tell each other things they would never tell us." LJ: "sounds like a plan, I think I'm going to bed, morning comes early." CR: "I think I will do the same we are going to have a big day tomorrow, the Arab is supposed to be here between 10:00 and 11:00."

CHAPTER 25

TUESDAY WEEK 4

JB woke up at 5:30 put on his running clothes got the leash, hooked up Sam and headed for the big house. LJ and CR were waiting for him they took off and were back in twenty-one minutes. JB: "LJ tell Rose to get clothes for JR and to get him ready I will drop her and Jennifer off, then I will take the kids to school, then I will be back to pick them up, he must be here for the ceremony."

LJ: "will do, see you later." JB went to the spring house turned Sam loose put the leash on the hook and went in and gave Jennifer a hug and a kiss. He said "I will drop you and Rose off at the hospital, Rose can get JR dressed and we will borrow one of the hospitals wheelchairs, so we must get back to the park by at least 9:30, so we are ready for the ceremony." They arrived at the hospital; he dropped Rose and Jennifer off. He told Jennifer: "I will pick you up out front in twelve minutes."

Jennifer: "we will be ready and we should be out front waiting for you." JB pulled up to the front door got out and opened the side door and waited for them to come down. They came down eight minutes later and JB helped JR onto the seat, Rose climbed in beside him and shut the door. JB took the wheelchair around to the back opened the back and slipped it in next to the crate. Jennifer got into the front seat he came around got in and they headed for the park.

Maintenance was erecting a canopy in the parking lot; there were three police cars, and a military vehicle. JB: "called Betty and said "Betty when they're building the addition to the office will you have them also build wheelchair access into the office." Betty: "will do." JB grabbed the wheelchair and pushed JR over to the canopy it was 20' x 20', he thought that should work. He heard somebody call his name and turned around and there came his old CO and four of the seals he recognized. His CO grabbed his hand shook it and said "your chief of police thinks you walk on water."

JB: "he just doesn't have the experience we do." The CO: "not many people do, I sure miss you, after talking to the police chief, in the last four weeks you have shutdown more terrorists than we have." JB: "we just happen to be in the right place, at the right time and they were amateurs." The CO: "JR how are you doing?"JR: "they said the way I am recuperating they should let me out at the end of the week." JB: "we miss him he took out a mortar site no rounds were fired and the guy that was left sang like a bird." The CO: "JR and LJ were probably the best interrogators we had."

The CO do you know what a coup this has been, when you got Ahmad Emir Zafir to declare peace with you and the United States. JB: "I actually think it is because of Siham, CR saved his life and he says Allah has sent us to save him." The CO: "he told us that he will tell you whenever he learns of a terrorist's cell, as he owes you his life." JB: "yes and so far he has been quite helpful."

CO: "Ahmad should be touching down at your airport in the next twenty minutes, the limousines and the escorts are already there, he should get here a little after 10:00." LJ and CR came out and said hello to the CO and shook his hand. CO: "yes I miss you, you guys made me look so good, you really spoiled me, and you did all my work for me." CO's phone rang; he talked for thirty seconds and hung up. The

CO: "the plane has touched down and is taxing to the pickup zone he should be here in twenty minutes."

LJ: "I will check with maintenance, tell them we need the chairs here quickly." Five minutes later a Gator Utility Vehicle with five folding chairs in the back. LJ: "set up 4 chairs in the front pointing toward the back set up one chair pointing toward the other 4 chairs between the middle in the back." LJ thanked them and after they had left, he rearranged them slightly, five minutes later dad pulled up and he and Peggy got out of the van. They started walking toward LJ, and he started walking toward them.

They met and dad said "I've been in talking to Alice and I thought Peggy should be here to see you get adopted." LJ smiled and said "this makes me very happy." And Jennifer should be back soon with all the boys, as we think they should see this too. Peggy looked at LJ and said "this is going to be one of the happiest days of my life", and she hugged him. CR: "Mary will be here soon and I think we should get some more chairs for the women and the three boys."

JB: "I'll call Betty and have maintenance get 7more chairs out here quickly", he dialed the phone told Betty they needed 7 more chairs out here in five minutes and hung up. Five minutes later 7 more chairs were lined up at the very end of the canopy. Five minutes later Rose and the boys showed up. JB: "went over to the boys and said "you boys cannot talk, if the adults' clap you can clap, no talking and watch this as it is a very important ceremony, do you know what a ceremony is?" The boys all shook their heads no.

JB: "the four of us are going to receive a very high honor from a Sheikh; do you know what he is?" The boys shook their head no. JB: "he is the leader of his tribe, a very powerful man and we must show him great respect." ten minutes later the limousine with its police escort showed up. LJ had Mary sit on the end, then Peggy, then Jennifer, then Ben Rose, next Larry, then John. JB sat on the chair that would put him on the right-hand side of the Sheikh, next LJ sat down, CR helped JR out of his wheelchair and sat him in the next seat CR put the wheelchair and laid it flat on the ground and then CR sat in his chair, and they waited for the Sheikh to come.

The first Arab came in and stood on the left side of the Arabs chair, next Ahmad came in and sat down, the next Arab came in on the right of the chair. Two Navy SEALs with automatic rifles came in and stood behind one on each side of the Sheikh's party four feet back from them, at attention. Next came Siham he stood on the far right next came the CO he stood on the right of Siham. All parties were now present. The Sheikh spoke in Arabic.

Siham: "I now speak for the Sheikh, he does not speak English, I am now the ruler of my tribe, my brother hated Americans and he was the leader, he is dead now I am the leader I do not hate Americans, so now I will adopt these four honorable men into my tribe to finalize peace with America." Siham said something in Arabic. The Sheikh spoke again the man to his left opened the box and the Sheikh took an object from it. The Sheikh spoke again. Siham: "I have only one son left, now I adopt four new sons into my family, the first is James Benjamin Jones, please step forward."

JB got up and walked to the Sheikh. This dagger is the symbol of our tribe on one side of the handle is 5 sapphires, on the other side 5 rubies around the sapphires is silver around the rubies is gold the blade is the finest sword blade we have and he put the blade back in its sheath came forward and handed it to JB you are now my adopted son."

The Sheikh went to the box took out another one, and JB went back to his chair and sat down. The Sheikh turned and motioned him back and pointed to where he had been standing, JB went back and stood where he had received the knife. Siham: "Larry John Nelson come forward, LJ went forward stood next to JB, and the Sheikh then gave him a knife. He went back to the box got another knife and came back. Siham: "José Rodriguez come forward, JR came forward the Sheikh handed him a knife. The Sheikh went back to the box retrieved another knife came back. Siham: "Charles Robert Young come forward, CR came and stood beside JR. The Sheikh handed him his knife.

The Sheikh said more things in Arabic. Siham: "the Sheikh thanks you personally for eliminating three of his deadly enemies and saving my life and you were not even adopted yet; by adopting these four I now declare my declaration of peace with the United States and I will welcome these four into my family. JB: "we appreciate your gifts and becoming your son's May I ask you a question?" Siham spoke Arabic to the Sheikh. Siham: "yes you may."

JB: "do you still raise horses?" Siham spoke in Arabic. The Sheikh spoke back. Siham: "yes besides my sons they are the light of my life." JB: "I knew a man who raised horses and he told me how he could get stallions when he wanted and mares when he wanted out of his horses, would you like to know his secret." Siham spoke Arabic to the Sheikh again. The Sheikh moved right over in front of JB spoke in Arabic and grabbed JB's hand. Siham: "he will be indebted to you forever if you can give him the secret."

JB: "the man said if you want stallions, the mare must face magnetic north, she must stay that way during the breeding, when the breeding is done she must continue to face north for at least fifteen minutes, you may walk her but she must still face magnetic north. If you want mares she must face magnetic south, the same she must be that way for at least fifteen minutes after breeding is done. He said "he wanted sons to help with his ranch, so he had the head of his bed facing magnetic North he got four sons, his wife wanted a girl so he turned the head of the bed south and she had a girl. This man was noted for guaranteeing the sex to people who bread to his stallion and if the wrong sex came out he gave them their money back but he controlled the breeding he told me he never gave any money back. I hope this might help you in your breeding program and getting grandsons."

The Sheikh squeezed JB's hand and said something in Arabic to Siham. Siham: "the Sheikh said he is well pleased with his new sons he will do as you say he wants me to write it down in Arabic word for word." The Sheikh looked at everybody and said "peace to America." The Sheikh spoke Arabic again. Siham: "the Sheikh thanks Mr. Jones for sharing his sons with him, he wishes more of his people would understand and be at peace with America." Siham: "could you give me that in writing?"

JB: "took two sheets of paper out of his pocket and gave it to Siham, it is written out here and hopefully there is enough room underneath for you to write it out for the Sheikh, there is also a drawing of the breeding stall he built." JB handed Siham a pen."

JB's dad walked over to the Sheikh pointed at JB, then pointed at himself and stuck out his hand. The Sheikh understood and they shook hands. The CO came over and said "Siham is there anything more we must do." Siham: "as soon as I get this written down it will be over and you can take him back to the airport he realizes his time is up." Siham handed the papers to the Sheikh; the Sheikh had it put in the box they turned and went back to the limousines got in and drove off.

JB's dad came over and looked at JB's knife and said "that knife must be worth 10,000 to 15,000." JB: "did you notice the blade has my name engraved on it, its one-of-a-kind." Jennifer, Mary, Rose, and Peggy came over and looked at the knives." Mary: "the Arab that translated, he was the one you saved right?" CR: "yes, he's the one, he says Allah has blessed me and I will always save him." Mary: "I saw the video and I thought you were blind, I can't blame him." And she hugged CR.

Peggy looked at LJ and said "thank you for having me; I thought I had lost you." LJ: "no, I thought what happened last night was completely out of your control, the police department said there was outstanding warrants for those men, they beat up people then people swear out warrants on them, then they scare them so they cancel the warrants before they ever get to court, this one's going to court they can't scare me, and if the others come they'll go to jail also." Peggy put her arm around LJ and he leaned over and kissed her on the cheek.

Mary said "CR and I are going out to supper tonight; would you and LJ like to go with us?" Peggy said "I would if LJ wants to go." LJ: "of course I'll go, why would I not want to go somewhere with you" and squeezed her. Mary said "CR, I have to go back to work but I will get off around 4:30." CR: "fine I will pick you up at your place at five." LJ: "Peggy do you have to go back to the diner?" Peggy: "no my boss gave me the day off with pay, so I'm yours until you're tired of me."

LJ: "I don't think I could ever get tired of you." Peggy: "that makes me very happy" and she hugged him then said "could you teach me how to shoot." LJ: "sure let me see if we can borrow Jennifer's pistol." He went over to JB and said "could we borrow Jennifer's pistol, so I can teach Peggy how to shoot." JB: "sure Peggy come with me, we will see if it'll fit." LJ and Peggy started to go with JB when JB's dad said "LJ I need you here for a little bit JB will take care of Peggy and we will get the park business out of the way and then your free to go."

LJ said "fine" and came back over to dad. They sat down in the chairs. Dad said "I went to the diner this morning and talked to Alice about Peggy because I knew you liked her and I found out about those jokers. They have been harassing her for months anybody that shows an interest in her they would catch him outside and beat him up, she has had nothing to do with them but they have made her life miserable. Alice said she had been watching you for a while and didn't know whether you were gay or just shy because she thought you showed an interest in her, and she thought you were awful nice, she was hoping she could get to know you and those clowns would not know, she had no idea you were a bad ass."

LJ: "only when I have to be, she was kind of shook up when she came out of the apartment and there was a guy shot laying on the ground and I was nowhere around, she didn't know what to think, and she seemed real happy when I came back with the other one, and to have them hauled off in squad cars; I didn't know if she was using me to get rid of them or was she just a victim." Dad: "that's what I thought and I knew Alice knows about everybody that comes to that diner and she's a good judge of character and she would not make anything up, she will tell me the truth, so I thought if you two are going to develop a relationship she should be here to see what goes on in your life."

LJ: "I'm really glad you did, I think our relationship might get real serious she may be the girl I've been looking for to be my wife." Dad: "I kind of thought that, and Alice said that Peggy has been looking for somebody to spend the rest of her life with." LJ: "CR decided that he and I and Mary and Peggy should start spending time together and hopefully they'll go away, but if they don't, we will make them wish they had."

Dad: "JR's dog came in so I think JR is in the office getting acquainted with him, so I will leave you here, so you and Peggy can go shoot." LJ: "thanks dad that really helped." JB and Peggy came back and JB said "Jennifer's gun fits her pretty good so they have ammo up at the range, check her wrist at 50 rounds but I wouldn't go over 100 she has delicate wrists."

LJ: "I will take it slow that'll make a good excuse for her to spend more time with me." Peggy: "I love the sound of that." JB: "we'll see you later I got to go in and get JR and his dog back to the hospital." Peggy: "you all have dogs" LJ: "yes JB's and JR's are smaller dogs and they are more family oriented than a dog like mine, but he sure seems to like you, and if he likes you, you can't be all bad, I figured you were a victim, and I was going to stop that, because I do like you and I think a little more than just like." She grabbed him and gave him a kiss.

LJ: "let's go get my van." They got in the van he went to the big house got the dog loaded in the crate and they went up to the range." Ten minutes later they were at the range. LJ started her out on dry fire they did that for five minutes, then he rubbed her forearms and said "now we are going to put a bullet in the gun, he took all the bullets out of the clip, he put one in the clip, the rest in his pocket, then he put the ear protectors on her and ask how they fit. She said "fine." There was a target twenty feet down the range, he told her to aim the gun at the target like she'd been doing and squeeze the trigger, she squeezed and nothing happened.

He said that was really good, now were going to cock the hammer, he showed her how to put the bullet in the chamber she did it and he said aim down the sites squeeze the trigger, she squeezed and the gun went off and kicked back. She looked slightly scared and he said "give me the gun take these binoculars and look at your target, do you see a hole"; she said "yes" he said "where is the hole" she says "near the bottom of the second ring toward the right, he said "not too bad for the first shot."

LJ hit the lever and had the target come to them unhooked it and took a pen out and wrote across the top Peggy first shot. He set it down put a new target up and sent it down to the twenty foot mark. He put two bullets in the clip gave her the clip and had her put it in the gun, then he showed her how to release the slide and the bullet went into the chamber and he showed her the gun was cocked it was live never point that at anybody less you intend to shoot them.

LJ: "now I want you to aim at the center put your left hand over your right and hold the gun steady aim for the center of the target and squeeze. Bang. Aim and squeeze again bang. He reeled in the target there were two holes, one hole was touching the bottom of the middle ring the other hole was half way above the middle and second ring, LJ: "the one at the bottom was your first shot, the one at the top was your second, you anticipated the kick and moved your gun up as you were squeezing the trigger, that will take a little practice to get rid of that, so you don't develop a bad habit." LJ brought the target back grabbed some little stickers covered up the holes and wrote A1 on the bottom A2 on the top put the target back up and sent it back to the twenty foot mark. LJ gave her five bullets and told her load the clip, she loaded the clip, and he said insert the clip in the weapon, and release the slide, you are live, aim and shoot. She fired the first round, he said relax, she fired the second, relax, the third, fourth, fifth, the gun was empty. He brought the target back and the bullets were in the cluster in the second and third rings where the circle line was. LJ: "I am proud of you; you are doing very well for a first time shooter." She said "I'm trying real hard, so you're happy with me'. LJ: "the way you have put the bullets in the target if one of those men from the diner was coming at you, he would go down with the little bit of training you've had here today, the trick is being able to pull the trigger when you have a live human in front of you, you must picture the target not the human and pull the trigger, it's called training.

LJ: "how do you wrists feel?" Peggy: "they are tingling a little." LJ: "we are going to quit for today, and I will make an exercise for you to help strengthen your wrists." He took a blank target send it down to the twenty foot Mark and gave her the empty gun said hold this." He said "stand back", and he fired repeatedly until the pistol is empty. He brought the target back and she looked at the center it was all shot out. LJ: "in four or five months I will have you shooting almost as good." He gave her the target and said "look at that from time to time, and picture it in your mind it will help you make your grouping better, as you are telling your mind what you want your body to do."

She put her arms around him and squeezed and said "you are a good teacher; I thought maybe you would yell at me." LJ: "the only time I would yell at you would be to get you to drop down move left or right so you didn't get hurt, I can think of no other reason to yell at you." They took the targets got in the van and went down to the big house. They went in and CR was sitting in the living room, and he said "let me see the targets." Peggy handed them to him. He looked at them one at a time looked at her and said that is very good for your first time shooting; you paid attention, which is half the battle."

LJ: "where is JB?" CR: "he's at the office we will take my van and drop off Jennifer's gun and then we'll go pick up Mary." They got in the van drove to the office, LJ ran the gun in and came back and they headed for Mary's house. CR went in and was back a few minutes later with Mary they climbed in the front. Mary: "I know a nice quiet little place where we can visit and get to know each other." They went into the restaurant ordered chatted ate chatted, Mary asked Peggy questions and Peggy asked Mary questions and they got a little history about themselves. It was getting later CR took Mary home, then they took Peggy home and LJ said "I will pick you up at 12:30 to go to JB and Jennifer's wedding. He walked her up to the door kissed her good night, waited until she got inside, he got in the van and they headed back to the big house.

Jennifer and Ben left mom and dad's, went to the spring house, and went to bed, tomorrow they were getting married.

CHAPTER 26

WEDNESDAY WEEK 4

JB woke up at 5:30 got up put on his running clothes put the leash on Sam and headed for the big house. LJ and CR were waiting and away they went, 21 minutes later they were back, LJ and CR said "we will help your mom and dad move stuff in to their new house, we will move your stuff over here, move our stuff to the spring house, and when the girls get done cleaning the house we will help you get your stuff where you want. JB: "sounds like a plan, thanks a lot, my life will make a big change today, hope I'm ready."

CR: "you're always ready, just enjoy." JB went in the spring house shut the door, turned Sam loose, walked in the kitchen and gave Jennifer a big hug and kiss, and said "good morning light of my life." Jennifer: "good morning, husband to be." Today was the day they had both dreamed of for a long time. Jennifer: "your dad said it was such a nice day that he thought we should have the wedding under the canopy, I thought that sounded nice and I said okay, is that all right with you?"

JB: "it's fine with me; if you're happy I'm happy." Your dad said since he adopted me he told my father he had to pay half of the cost, he is having it catered, so we don't have to worry about that, and the caterers clean up afterwards and whatever's left of the food they send over to the big house. JB: "I guess I will have to adopt Ben to make him legally my son." Jennifer: "no, I listed you as the father on the birth certificate, and told my parents if anything happened to me they could decide whether to tell you or not."

JB: "well I'm glad nothing happen to you, because I like having you both." JB: "when we get done with breakfast I will box stuff up and have it out here close to the door, LJ and CR will come over later and take it over to the big house, then bring their stuff back. Jennifer: "when we visited my parent's do you remember mom made me put on the wedding dress, she let it out so it would fit and she wants me to wear it, is that all right?"JB: "of course it's all right, it's a special day for us, and I want you to be as happy as you can be, and just being married to you will make me extremely happy."

Ben came out of his room dressed for the day or so he thought and sat down at the table. Jennifer had made pancakes; she put them on the table. They all set down she said grace and they began to eat. When they were finished JB cleaned off the table put the dishes in the dishwasher, Jennifer put in the soap and started them going. She got the boxes out and started putting all her stuff back in to move to the big house. JB dressed for the day Jennifer said leave your running clothes on the couch and I'll put that in one of the boxes and get out of the closet what you want and take it with you over to the big house." He put his holster on checked the gun to make sure there was a bullet in the chamber put his jacket on put the leash on Sam and walked to the big house.

There were three dogs running around and Sam made four. Dad said "I will go get the park van and bring it down here and we will load your two crates and take them down to the spring house and we will bring Sam's crate back." LJ and CR carried the two crates out to the front for the waiting van. JB: "Jennifer is packing right now she will call when she's done, then we'll take your stuff down and bring our stuff back that way we don't make as many trips."

CR laid his stuff on the back seat LJ laid his on the front seat their weapons were already loaded in their vans so they didn't have to worry about them, and they loaded the two dog crates in the back.

Ben, Larry, and John were in the game room having a good time. JB thought well that will keep them out of our hair. Jennifer called and said "boxes are ready come and get them."

JB said "LJ, CR take your load down." They went out got in the van drove to the spring house. Dad said "how many people are going to be here?"JB: "you and mom that's two, the four of us makes six, four girls that's ten, Jennifer's parents makes twelve, Hank and his wife that's fourteen, Betty fifteen, the three little boys eighteen, I think Curt and shadow who were up on the hill with us may come, so that makes twenty."

Dad: "I wasn't sure so just in case I told the caterer thirty people, and I told the Baker the cake should feed thirty." JB: "I think that should cover it. Dad: "you and Jennifer got the license the other day the preacher is supposed to get here about 12:40, the wedding will start at 1:00, maintenance will be here at 12 o'clock and start setting up the seats, I had 1:30 as the time to set up the tables, and 1:45 the caterers and the Baker should arrive and we should be eating by 2:00." LJ and CR got back with the van got up and they all three started carrying stuff in Jennifer oversaw where her things were being put, they put Sam's crate next to JR's dog's crate, and the van was empty.

Mary was on her way, she had picked up Peggy, and was coming to pick up Rose and they were all going to buy some new dresses. The two girls came in and hollered for Rose. LJ went over to Peggy grabbed her hand took her over to the other side of the room and gave her $200, and said "let me buy the dress and use the rest to get whatever you want." Peggy: "I can't take this." LJ: "are you my girlfriend?" Peggy: "I hope you know I am." LJ: "can't I buy my girlfriend something?" Peggy: "I can't answer that and win."

LJ: "it would really make me happy if I could buy your dress, and remember you're already my fiancé." Peggy: "will I ever be able to win an argument?" LJ: "I didn't know we were arguing, I thought we were discussing there's a difference." Peggy: "I've never known anybody like you", she kissed him and went back to Mary. Rose came and the three of them left.

CR: "have your first disagreement?" LJ: "I figure she didn't make much at the diner so I gave her $200 to get her dress, and I told her we weren't having a disagreement, we were having a discussion, and wasn't I allowed to buy my girlfriend something." CR: "the government should have you on all their deal making discussions." CR: "where does all this stuff come from that you come up with?" LJ: "I don't know; it just pops in my head." LJ: "you should have heard what I said at the diner to those four clowns I didn't even know where it was coming from but it seemed to work really well, I really didn't want to fight at the diner and get Peggy in trouble."

LJ: "I figure I will see them one more time because they're going to try to scare me into dropping the charges, and I won't, I figure they'll do something stupid and I'm going to wreck them, they all have warrants against all four of them. I told them I would put them in wheelchairs, they would be eating through straws their hands wouldn't work their legs wouldn't work and that's why they went back inside, it was too much for them to think about all at once."

At 11 o'clock Jennifer's mom and dad came, JB went over and gave them directions to get to the big house; they took the road and drove down. At 11:30 the three girls came back, with boxes under their arms. JB: "I will go get JR, and pick up our clothes for the wedding." He got in his van and left for the hospital, he was back a little after 12, and he drove down to the big house. JR got out of the van sat down in his wheelchair and said give me Shorty's leash and I'll take him into the house.

JB: "okay here you are." JR headed for the big house. JB: "grabbed the four boxes locked the van and headed for the big house." The girls headed up to mom and Dad's bedroom to see how Jennifer and her mom and JB's mom were doing, and to change into their new dresses. LJ looked at CR and said "I think we should have a couple security guards out there where we can't see." CR: "LJ that one of your premonition's?" LJ: "I kind of checked out for a second and I saw two bozos coming across the parking lot where we couldn't see them, and the canopy was up."

CR: "you finish getting dressed I'm going to walk up to the office and will get a hold of a couple guards, I felt something doesn't feel right too." CR went to the office, Betty was still there, he said "Betty get me two security guards and send them to the canopy." Betty you think there's going to be trouble?" CR: "LJ has premonitions, and they are right 99 times out of 100, we don't question it anymore, it saved us I don't know how many times, so we are not going to take any chances, tell them I will meet them at the canopy in ten minutes."

He reached in and pulled out his pistol checked to make sure there was a round in the chamber and put it back in its holster." Betty: "you always carry that?" CR: "lately with all that's going on, there is going to be a lot of people here today who I care about, and in cases like this the four of us are always armed, that's how we stayed alive for ten years, if it works don't change it." CR: "has JB said anything more about putting gates on these entrances?"JB walked into the office and said "LJ told me about his premonition."

CR: "I'm going to meet two security guards in about eight minutes out at the canopy and they're going to be there were we can't see, if they see someone coming they will let LJ and me know and we will take care of it, and you continue with the ceremony, and I asked Betty about the gates for the entrances, she said 5000 for the two and I think you should do it and there should be surveillance cameras on each gate." JB thought a few seconds: "Betty call them it's a go and get them up as quick as they can, and get a hold of the surveillance guy and tell him were going to want cameras on those gates and security here should be able to open the gates if necessary and we need to have badges for all the employees."

Betty took down notes and she said "I will call the gate people and tell them it's a go and I will leave a message for the security guy to call tomorrow because I will know when the gates can be put in and will schedule them together." JB: "let's go talk to the security guards", and they left the office and walked to the canopy. They both walked around to the back side of the canopy, they each came up a side stepped inside the canopy and walked backwards to see where the field of vision was, they got to the end of the canopy, went back to the front.

JB: "what do you think?" CR: 'I would post them one on each side of the canopy where they're not seen by the people inside, one looking at the left gate one looking at the right." JB: "I like that, will they let us know?" CR: "if the one on the right see something he can walk over to the one on the left and if he comes around the corner I will see him and know something is wrong, if the one on the left sees something all he has to do is come around the corner. LJ and I will disengage and if you're not married yet he can give RJ the ring and we'll go around and take care of it."

I'm going to tell maintenance to bring some straw out here stack it up 8 foot high and to bring enough plywood to make 1 inch thick wall leaning up against the hay we are going to park our vans rear end away from the canopy against the plywood as our rifles will be in the front back seat so we can open the door and have easy access, I will talk to Hank when he gets here and run the scenario as if we see one of them carrying a rifle we need to shoot first and ask questions later, so all of these people here are safe." JB: "I agree nobody's going to hurt my family or my friends." CR: "if they're just caring clubs I will give them the option, lay face down on the ground and wait for the patrol car to get here or another step we shoot."

JB: "I like the plan." CR: "the plan is a go I will explain it to the security guards." Just then the two guards walked up. One said "sir you wanted to see us." CR: "give me your names because during the wedding you are going to be getting double time, and you had better be alert and not miss anything in the directions you are going to be watching do you understand?" They both said yes CR explained to them what they were to do then he had each one repeat it twice; then he said men coming up on the right side facing out what do you do, the guard went over to the second guard showed him the man coming he came around and either touched you or LJ. CR: "guard on the left you see a men coming from your direction, what do you do I come around and touch you or LJ.

JB: "if you do that just like you did just now, and do that while they're still quite a way to the canopy I will give each of you a $100.00 dollar bill." CR had been giving the guards instructions JB called maintenance and they pulled up with hay and was stacking it five minutes later plywood came and they were screwing the panels together so they crisscrossed and made quite a sturdy wall LJ came up got the plan and the three of them went and got their vans his dad came out saw what was going on and got his van and brought it out and drove the van up to the plywood, maintenance now had propped up the panel and tied it to the hay.

CR had them take ropes and they rolled down the windows in the vans strung the rope through and had it fixed so if a bullet did hit the plywood the ropes would hold it from pushing the hay down upon the canopy the bullets would hit the vans. CR: "I think that will be sufficient for something done on the spur of the moment JB and LJ agreed. JB: "once Hank gets here I'll give him a heads up." JR pulled up in his wheelchair and said." What's up?"

CR ran through the whole scenario and why they were doing it. JR: "I will get my pistol." LJ said "no you're still a patient and we have more than enough weapons to take care of anything that should come our way, you're on vacation till the hospital releases you." JR: "I've sure been missing all the fun." The preacher pulled up and JB asked him to park farther away from the canopy, he told the security guard to have everybody go over and park by the preacher's car. LJ looked at CR and said "the clock is ticking." People started pulling in, Hank and his wife got there and came walking over JB pulled Hank aside as Hank was eyeing the vans the wall and he told him about LJ's premonition and how accurate they had been in the past."

Hank said "do what you got to do I don't want my wife hurt, but it looks like you thought this through." JB:"if they come I think they'll come through the left gate as were facing out because there's the most cover there." Hank: "I agree, and congratulations on your marriage." JB and the preacher went in; the preacher faced out and stood by his right hand. His dad and mom were sitting in the front row. LJ and Peggy started walking up the aisle, they parted and Peggy stood leaving a space next to the preacher LJ stood next to JB. CR and Mary came next and did the same routine RJ and Rose came next RJ stood next to CR JB's dad brought the wheelchair and JR set down. Jennifer and her dad came down the aisle Jennifer's dad handed her to JB. And he sat down next to Jennifer's mother everybody else sat down and the preacher started to go through the vows, LJ gave JB the ring and he put it on Jennifer's finger the preacher said now I pronounce you man and wife you may now kiss the bride. LJ and CR felt a tap they quietly backed up walked around the corner with the security guard and saw the two men coming, LJ opened his van door pulled out his rifle, and looked down the scope, he said "yeah they are the other two. CR: "what weapons do they seem to have?" The one on the rights got a ball bat; I'm not sure about the one on the left, looks like he's got a knife." CR: "well let's go take them out."

LJ put the rifle back in the car shut the door hit the lock button thought better and hit the unlock button and they walked toward the two. twenty feet out LJ and CR stopped. LJ: "do you two have a death wish." The mouthy one said "we are on public property; we have a right to be here." LJ: "no you're on private property, and there is no trespassing when the park is closed, you are now breaking the law, and you can leave now or suffer the consequences." The mouthy one said "you're going to drop the warrant or we are going to beat you up." LJ: "drop your weapons lay down on the ground you're under arrest for terroristic threats." The one with the bat started to run toward them CR shot him in the leg, he went down the other one looked in disbelief dropped his knife and said "don't shoot, don't shoot." And hit the pavement.

They heard a siren and the black-and-white showed up pulled up stopped near them handcuff the one spread eagled the other one who was screaming for a Dr. no one seem to show him any sympathy people poured out from underneath the canopy, they all walked over. JB: "nice work." Hank came up: "did you get that on tape." LJ pulled his recorder out of his pocket, hit the stop button backed it up played it through. Hank: "do you wish to press charges against these men?" LJ and CR both said "yes." Pretty soon they heard another siren and the ambulance rolled up.

Hank looked at LJ and CR and said do we call home land security to get rid of these terrorists." Both of the men on the ground said what you mean terrorists we were just having fun with them." Hank: "you two must be the dimmest lights on the tree we've got your threats on tape we have your weapons on the ground all we have to do is call homeland security and we will never see you again because you threatened over twenty people you can scream a lawyer all you want but homeland security throws you a way there are no lawyers you will never be seen again."

LJ: "I would just as soon homeland security take them, I don't need this hassle." CR: "I agree take the tape call homeland security, the world will be a better place." LJ looked at CR and said "you never let me shoot first." JB, Hank, and CR started to laugh." CR: "well next time I will try to let you shoot first." And they all laughed. Mary came up looked at CR and said "I'm going to marry you; I need some way to keep you out of trouble."

JB laughed so hard tears came to his eyes and LJ was laughing RJ had come up and he was laughing and he said "you guys got to quit making me laugh, it hurts my ribs. Hank said "you swat guys, did you notice he assessed the situation that I can take this man out by taking out his leg and down he went, and the other brave man couldn't get to the ground fast enough I would call this a very good takedown."

Peggy came up put her arms around LJ and said "I love you, I know you will protect me the rest of my life she kissed him on the cheek." The EMT put a bandage around the man's leg said we will take him to the hospital it looked like the slug went clean through who knows where it is and then you can take them down and do whatever you want with them." The policeman got out of the other squad car came and helped the EMT pick the man up put him in the ambulance they both got in the other man was put in the other squad car and the squads left. JR: "ladies and gentlemen there is no extra charge for the entertainment." And everybody laughed, they all went back into the canopy, and proceeded to have a good time, the caterers were doing their work, and so was the Baker, it was time to eat everyone sat down and the rest of the wedding progressed.

Everyone was having a good time, some were dancing some were talking it was a great reception. About 4 o'clock people started to leave JB and Jennifer said goodbye and thanked everyone for coming. CR:"Mary and I are going to her house I will see you tomorrow." LJ said "Peggy and I are going to go to her house'. Maintenance had already unhooked the ropes and hauled away the wood and the hay, the canopy was coming down chairs were being loaded and stacked; table legs are being folded under and loaded.

Rose said "I have to get JR back to the hospital." JB: "Rose take my van here are the keys." I will put the wheelchair in the back after JR gets in the front." Rose said "boys you are coming with me and spending some time with your father." They all got in the van and left. The caterers took the food to the big house. Mom and dad said "we will take Ben with us and he can sleep at our house tonight." Jennifer's mom and dad came over and said "we are so glad you two have finally gotten married", and they left. JB and Jennifer walked to the big house hand-in-hand, this is the first time they would be alone together. JB opened the door to the big house; he picked Jennifer up and carried her across the threshold, Mrs. Jones I wanted to do this for the last 12 years." Jennifer: "me too." They went upstairs she took off her dress he took off his suit. Jennifer went over to the bed unstrapped her bra dropped her panties on the floor and lay on the bed. JB took all his clothes off went over and lay on the bed beside her. They kissed and hugged and explored each other's bodies and made mad passionate love.

CR and Mary, LJ and Peggy went to the spring house got CR

and LJ's dogs took them for a walk so they can relieve themselves. CR: "Mary and I must go and let her dog out so he can go, I will see you when you get back. LJ and Peggy went into the spring house LJ let his dog loose Hung the leash by the door. LJ: "I am going to hang my cloths up in my bedroom and put stuff in the drawers so I am ready to go in the morning, do you mind helping me." Peggy: "I would be happy to help you."

They went into his room; she started hanging his shirts and pants in the closet while he put his underwear and socks in the dresser drawers. In five minutes they were done. Peggy: "you and CR are living in this house?" LJ: "yes we will probably stay here until we get married, then the Park will build us a house, this is like our private village, we like that because for ten years we have all lived together in the same building, except when we were stateside, JR would live with his family in another section of the base, but when we were in Afghanistan we were in the same barracks, those deployments usually lasted for a year, we would be in the states for six months, and then they would send us back to Afghanistan, the last six years four years were in Afghanistan, that was tough on JR and his family, Rose was real happy when we all decided to get out."

When JB's dad had his heart trouble, JB said he had to go back and run the park, and if we got out we would all work in the park just as we had in the Navy, and the city here wanted him to head up a SWAT unit, all four of us are qualified to start and train a SWAT unit." Peggy: "are you a sniper?" LJ: "all four of us are snipers, JB and I are rated at 1200 yards, CR and JR are rated up to 600 yards, most of the shots that we did were within the 300 to 600 yard range."

Peggy: "was it hard shooting people?" LJ: "if you had a child and somebody was hurting that child what would you do?"Peggy: "I would grab something and hit them and hit them until they quit." LJ: "then you would do the same thing I would, if somebody is going to hurt one of my fellow soldiers or somebody I care about, you point and squeeze and eliminate the threat." Peggy: "when you explain it that way, I understand and it is not such a terrible thing." LJ: "if you had gone out to stop those men today, and he started to come at you with his bat raised, and you have a gun, what would you do?"

Peggy thought for a minute and said "I guess I would've shot him but not in the leg." LJ: "most people make judgments of others without thinking the situation completely through and what would they do under the same circumstances." LJ: "the news media does not show Arabs cutting people's heads off, and when they blow themselves up and kill and hurt a lot of people there misguided, to me those people are idiots and if they were in one of those explosions they would never say that again." Peggy: "when you left my apartment last night and those two men came after you, what were you thinking?" LJ: "if they get past me there's nothing to stop them from going in and hurting you, and for me that was not an option, I didn't want you hurt because I care for you deeply."

Peggy: "I have never felt this safe my whole life, I'm glad you're not in the service anymore, I would feel so lonely if you were gone for a year, but I would wait faithfully until you came back." LJ put his arm around her pulled her near and kissed her and she kissed him again and again. LJ: "I could do this the rest of my life, but we have to slow down, I want us to get married because we want to not because we have to, because if you got pregnant I would not want you with someone else and him raising my child." Peggy: "I would not like that situation either, but I have never felt like I do about you ever in my life." LJ: "I feel the same way, but I want us to be friends too, I want a rest of our life relationship with you."

Peggy: "for what I know about you so far, you must have a plan about how we're going to go about this?" LJ: "is there something in your life you wish you would have done but didn't do it?" Peggy: "I didn't want to be a waitress, but all I have is a high school diploma and no real trade." LJ: "if you could go to school, what would you want to learn?" Peggy: "I would like to learn to cook better and maybe learn baking, I would love to cook pies and cakes, like they have at the diner, he buys them from somebody else."

LJ: "all right you look up a school where you can learn some basic skills and then go into baking." Peggy: "I don't have time I have to work to pay my bills; I don't want to spend all my nights going to school and not be able to be with you, you're more important than anything else in my life." LJ: "the park gives me free lodging, the service gave me free lodging, we didn't go out and drink and blow money, I have a chunk in the bank I will have no problem paying your bills for you and paying for your school, and we can still spend nights together when you don't have things to study; ten years from now I don't want you thinking I sure missed something because I didn't do it, does that make sense."

Peggy: "that could be expensive; I can't have you spending that kind of money on me." LJ: "now are we back to the dress, let me tell you how I look at this, it's a present from me to you, because it will make you feel better which will make me happy; if it makes you happy and it makes me happy how could it not be a good thing?" Peggy: "there you go a question which I can't really answer, why do you do that." LJ: "here's the way I look at that, you just told me you couldn't cook very good so if you're going to feed me every night I think it's an investment in my future for you to learn to cook better, and if you learn to bake and wanted to have a business you now have a skill that you are lacking, that's also an investment in our future, so to me the money is not being thrown away."

Peggy: "do you always get your way?" LJ: "no I don't, let's say I didn't work at the park, we are married you're working at the diner, I have a job you got pregnant now you can't work and now instead of living on two incomes we are only living on one, now it's hard to keep all the bills paid because we have extra expenses, and only one income. Now had you gone to school and had your skill and we got married and you got pregnant even with the baby you can still make your pies and sell them and we would still have two incomes and a baby. Which scenario do you think is better?" Peggy: "you know it's the second one." LJ: "do you see why I look at it as an investment?" Peggy: "where did you learn to think things like this out?"

LJ: "working out missions were our lives dependent on the output of our actions, do you understand what I'm saying?" Peggy thought for a while then said "it really makes a lot of sense when you put it that way." LJ: "if you wanted to work at the diner I'm sure your boss would work something out where you could work on the weekend, there's always a solution if you just get all the facts before you make a decision." I have a lot of money in the bank that I was going to use for a down payment on a house when I found somebody I wanted to spend the rest of my life with, but because dad has adopted me as a son the same as CR and JR, the park will provide us with a house whenever we want one at no cost to us, so that money I had saved for a house to me would be better spent helping you feel better about yourself, and making you happy."

Peggy: "I will try to check during break to see what I can find out." LJ: "why don't I have Rose research it for you and find out which of the local schools here have what you want, and you can pick the one that you think best fits what you want, she will have more time and can get on the Internet at the park and I don't think you have access to that." Peggy: "how can I ever thank you?" LJ: "seeing you learn something and it makes you happy is all the payment I want." LJ: "it's time for me to go I have to take care of my child Mike, as he will probably have to relieve himself again and he's missed me today because we haven't spent much time together." He got up she got up they hugged and kissed, she walked him out the door he kissed her again and left, she locked the door went back to her apartment. LJ got in his van and headed for the Springhouse, life was good.

CR and Mary went to Mary's house she went in and got nip CR got spot and they went for a walk around the neighborhood for the dogs to relieve themselves, they picked up after the dogs put it all in a sack tightened it up so you could not smell it, put it in the garbage, and went to her apartment. Mary: "when I heard that shot, I was afraid, I didn't know you were armed."

CR: "we are always armed, you never know when somebody is going to do something stupid, and the way the four of us looked at it we were responsible for the lives of everyone under and around that canopy." Mary: "I'm still not use to the way you think." CR: "here's what went through my mind, I was on the side of the man with the bat, LJ was on the side of the man with a knife, he takes care of his side I take care of my side, it just that simple I didn't have to kill a man I just disabled him, he's out of the picture LJ scared the other so bad he was out of the picture it was all over in three seconds what more could you ask for."

Mary: "I guess I just don't have the experience yet." CR: "you have the instincts, you took a bullet so I didn't have to and I think you figured that your vest was going to save you and you knew that I would take the man out, when you get more training you will start doing things a little different, it's all about training and practice, I've had over 300 missions and ten years' experience, that is my edge over you."

Mary: "you just keep teaching me and I'll be the best partner you ever had." CR: "and the prettiest to." Mary: "do you always joke." CR: "that's not a joke, that's a fact." Mary leaned over put her arms around him and kissed him and he kissed her back. CR: "and if I'm feeling a little sad I can kiss you, I could not do that with my other partners, and that's a fact." Mary: "when are you going to ask me to marry you?" CR: "in a few more months, when I know you can really put up with me, and I know you can cook." Mary laughing said "I love you and I've never felt this comfortable, and safe, ever in my life."

CR: "I love you too, I have never been this happy in my life." They snuggled up hugging each other and fell asleep on the couch. CR woke up and said "I've got to get back 5:30 comes pretty quick", he kissed her went out the door got in his van and headed for the Springhouse.

CHAPTER 27

THURSDAY WEEK 4

JB, LJ, and CR did their morning run, came back and exercised, and Jennifer said "Rose and I are making breakfast for all of us, so be back in twenty minutes." LJ and CR said "yes, we will be back", and they went to the spring house. When they came back dad and mom had joined them. And everyone was sitting at the table. When they were finished Jennifer and Rose had the three boys clean off the table and put the dishes in the dishwasher.

LJ: "I told Rose about finding out about a school for Peggy." JB: "I will take Jennifer, and the three boys to school, Rose, this afternoon, take my van and pick up the boys and Jennifer, use the front door I am dropping Jennifer off at the front door." I think things will be quiet for a while but I don't want to take any chances." Rose: "I understand JR told me about how pickups were modified so they were never the same."

CR: "Mary is supposed to come up and we are going to run through and set up some tests for the dogs JB: "LJ will you check with maintenance and see how they're doing with getting rides ready to go and take this $200 and give one to each of the guards that were at the canopy yesterday." LJ: "will do and I'll meet you at the office when you get back." JB took Sam put him in his crate, Jennifer and the boys got in the van, and they drove off. Dad said "I'll go with you." LJ and Dad left." CR and Rose went to the office and Betty just pulled up and got out of her car, the three of them went into the office. Rose started to do her search for LJ. LJ and dad went to the maintenance building, and looked down their list, Monday they did three rides, Tuesday one ride, Wednesday they got one done, today they had two scheduled which made by the end of day they should have seven, dad said "that's not bad with everything that's gone on, I'm pleased."

Dad and LJ went back to the office. Rose said "there is only one school in town, the class started on Monday, she could start tomorrow and they would catch her up and by the end of next week she would be at the same level as everyone else in class, the total class will run for two months, then they run two months of cooking and two months of baking and then there is six months of cooking or baking depending on which way she'd like to go." LJ: "you got that down on paper, and what is the cost." Rose: "the two-month classes are $1000.00 the six-month classes are $5000.00, yes and here is the sheet, and I have another sheet that I will keep here just in case that one gets lost."

LJ: "thanks very much Rose I'm going to the diner and have coffee and pie with Peggy I will go over the school with her and we will plan on having her go tomorrow, unless she changes her mind." They heard a car pull up and Mary came in with them, and said "hello'. CR: "Mary and I are going up and we are going to set up some tests for this afternoon for Curt, and my dog, Mary's dog, and LJ's dog to go through tomorrow, if JR is up to it he can run his dog through a training session, on how to use him." JB came in. CR: "It would be good for you to do a training session." JB: "yes it would, I'm sure he can tell me things that I would miss at this point, put me down for a session tomorrow." LJ: "maintenance by the end of today will have seven rides up and running, I will give Betty a list, so she can mark them on the chart."

JB: "what about the First-aid building, when are they supposed to start building?" Betty: "they are coming tomorrow to rough out where the building is going, then Monday they will start excavation and pour the footers, their plan is to have it completely done by the end of the week and stocked up on Saturday." LJ: "I'll be back in 45 minutes", and he left for the diner. LJ got to the diner, and picked a table with his back to the wall and facing the door. Peggy saw him and came over and he said "coffee and a piece of that coconut pie, and can you take a break right now?"

Peggy: "yes I will be right back, with your coffee and pie." She was back in a minute, with his coffee and pie. She sat down, and LJ pulled out the papers about the school. Peggy: "when does the school start?" LJ: "it started Monday, but you can start tomorrow, and they will catch you up by the end of next week, they will have you at the same level as the ones that started Monday, the class runs for two months. Then there are two months of cooking and two months of baking, and then there are six months of cooking or six months of baking, your choice." Peggy: "how much are the classes?"

LJ: "right here at the bottom of the paper $1000.00 for the two months classes and $5000.00 for the six-month classes." Peggy: "that is too much money." LJ: "I thought we already discussed this, it's not too much money, and if you walk away from me, it's worth every penny because I helped you fulfill one of your dreams in life." Peggy; "I don't ever plan on leaving you." LJ: "well then that settles that, I'm sending my fiancé to school."

He started to eat his pie. She started to cry. Alice saw her crying, and came over and started to chew LJ out, for making Peggy cry. Peggy said "he's putting me through cooking school, and Baker or chef school, that's why I'm crying." Alice looked at LJ and said "I am sorry, she's right you are the nicest man we've ever met." Alice: "are you going to quit?"

Peggy: "see if Jenny can work my shift tomorrow, and then she could start working during the week and I'll work weekends, I'll give her everything I make this weekend so she will not be short of money." Alice: "won't you be short of money?" LJ: "no she will not be short of money, I will pay all her bills for her, all she needs to worry about is learning." Alice put her arms around LJ and hugged him and said "Peggy you better never let him go." Peggy: "I won't." LJ: "I have to get back to work, I already told rose to set it up, call her, and she will give you all the information, and where you should go, and the times." He got up to leave she grabbed him and kissed him and said "I love you." He smiled and said "I love you too." He left $10 on the table and got in his van and headed back to the park.

One of the security operators for the screens stuck his head out the door and said "I think I have a couple guys casing the place?" LJ and JB quickly came in, and looked at the screen. They watched two men were pointing and looking at things, and looked like they were trying to stay out of the cameras that were hidden and they kept their faces so they could not be seen.

LJ: "I'll go out and tell them the Park is closed and see what they do." JB: "I will back you up from cover." LJ walked out of the office and down the stairs and said "can I help you gentlemen, the park is closed right now." One man said "we were thinking about bringing a group of children here and we were just kind of looking at the place, and it looks like a really nice park." LJ: "come with me to the office and I'll give you a brochure, which should tell you everything you want to know." They followed LJ to the office; he said "wait here and I'll get you a brochure, because we have discounted rates if you have over twenty children."

LJ went to the office, grabbed some brochures, and came back and handed one to each one of the men. JB came up and said "I hope my assistant has answered all your questions?" The two men answered "yes, we will take it back to our group, and get back to you." They turned and left. LJ: "I will follow them from cover and

309

see where they go." JB: "we better go up on the hill, and check our cameras, make sure nobody spying on us from up there, we've been a little lax lately on that."

LJ shook his head yes, and went after the two men. They went over and out the north entrance to the park LJ looked through the foliage, and saw them get in a car with two other men, it looked like they were looking at the map of the park on the back of the brochure, after five minutes they drove off. LJ went back to the office, he told JB what they did, and said "I don't believe that's why they were here." JB: "me either, usually they call us for pricing tell the number of people and asked for two or three brochures, I've never had them come to the park before."

JB called CR and said "you and Mary, down here for lunch, I will have Siham bring lunch for five. CR: "we will see you at noon." JB gave Betty $60 and said "call Siham and order five lunches, and ask him if he could have them here by noon." Betty grabbed the phone and called, she put the order in and hung up the phone, and said "a Mr. Siham answered and said they would be here at noon, he seemed very pleased." CR and Mary showed up at 11:30. They sat down with JB and LJ and JB said "security called and said he thought two men were casing the place LJ talked to them and he thought they were fishy so you two go in and look at the video and come back and tell me what you think."

They were gone for ten minutes and came back in the room. CR said "I don't think they're very good but I would bet a hundred dollars that's what they were doing: Mary: "I thought it looked like they were looking at things, like someone wants to know where they're going for the next time." JB: "I think we're going to have to set up an area where we teach SWAT how to be invisible." LJ and CR nodded agreement. JB: "I thought they kind of looked like military or X military, which means they may be mercenaries.

LJ: "I figure 4:00 in the morning within a day or two. CR: "it looked like they came in through the north entrance and were coming toward the office." LJ: "I gave them brochures but I didn't take them in the office, and with the hidden cameras surveillance should be able warn us, I'm going to sleep with my camouflage on tonight and every night until they come." CR: "me too." Mary: "is this a SWAT mission." JB: "I guess it is." JB called Hank told him the situation, said "he was going to make this a SWAT on-the-job training mission and he wants Curt and Quincy who volunteered Mary was already here, tell them to bring black clothes and have enough for three days have them here by 3 o'clock this afternoon."

Hank said "they'll be there." They heard a van pull up, two minutes later Siham came in with a box gave it to Betty she gave him the $60.00 and he gave her six dollars change. JB: "Siham have you heard anything lately, we think some mercenaries were checking us out." Siham: "I have heard nothing I am sorry, if I hear of anything I will call immediately." JB: "thank you, we appreciate all your help, and we love your food."

Siham smiled, and said "thank you" and left. They started eating their sandwiches, CR made a rough map and said "put Curt and Mary on the office roof with our rifles, we will take them up to the gun range and site them in for 50 yards, I guess they'll either have them spread out or in a group LJ and I will come in take the second two and stop them we saw four in the car, but to my thinking there must be a head guy because I don't think the two we saw were really head guys" JB: "I will stay back and take the head guy and if he tries to shoot one of you, I will take him out. We will set our night vision to not send out light just receive." That way they won't know we are there until we have them surrounded game over, they do what we tell them, or we shoot them." JB, LJ, and CR agreed on the plan.

JB called Hank and said "can you get Curt over here at 2 o'clock, we have to get the rifle he will use sited in at 50 yards, and he and Mary are going to be on the roof of the office during this mission. Hank: "he will be there at 2:00, if not before." JB: "I was looking at scopes for SWAT and I really like this one it is ATN X-Sight II 5–20 X Day and Night Rifle Scope, check it out let me know." JB hung up the phone. He showed the scope data to LJ, CR, and Mary. LJ and CR said "well we can show them this is what we saw and why we shot, that should cover our buts." JB: "Betty I want you to order one scope with the extra 64 RAM, tell them I want one to look at and if we like it were going to get 6 more for our SWAT team and see what kind of a price you can get." Five minutes later Betty "they will ship one at the retail price they will not charge the card they will give you five days to try it out and if you have not talked to them in that time they will bill your card for the one, if you put in the order the price goes down to 600 each, that includes two day shipping." JB: "tell him to ship one, overnight I will pay for the extra shipping, we need to see this tomorrow." They heard two cars pull up, Mary looked out the window and said "Curt and Quincy just pulled up." JB: "Rose you need to go get the boys and pick up Jennifer." Curt and Quincy came into the office and LJ said "Curt, Mary, CR and I are going up and site in the rifles for 50 yards, we will be back by three", and they got in LJ's van and left.

JB: "Quincy I remember you saying you been in a firefight?" Quincy: "yes, I did a year tour in Afghanistan, probably forty maybe fifty missions, why?"JB: "I need a second in command, and you have firefight experience but I can't use one of my men, even though they are more qualified, because the rest of you need to be paired up with them to learn, how they handle different situations." JB: "the Navy way is one of the highest ranking man makes the plan for the mission. I think that one man could not think of everything that could go wrong or right on a mission, every man in the team has different skills so they look at things differently, the reason that we were so successful was we all planned our missions and we all contributed to it and if we didn't all agree we made another plan until we did. The only missions we didn't complete, the information was bad for some reason, or the target didn't show, so we never had a failed mission. I will plan the SWAT missions the same way, if I'm not around, you plan the missions the same way if you're my number two. LJ, CR, and JR have as much experience, as I do, no one person can think of everything, remember that it may save your life."

LJ and CR sited in the rifles for 50 yards, CR gave his to Mary LJ gave his to Curt and they proceeded to teach them the best ways to shoot in twenty minutes they had them hitting dead center in the target. They packed up went back to the office, LJ and CR were confident they could back them up. JB: "we think they're going to try to get into the office, they will come in two different configurations, we know there are four, we think totally there will be five or six, and anymore they get in their own way." So basic configurations could be four abreast, the 2nd row will be one or two; the next configuration would be to first row, two second row, one or two third row. Curt and Mary will be on the office roof, on a four across they will concentrate on the middle, LJ and CR will take the outside, Quincy and I will take the next row. CR: 'they come in four across, Mary which one do you shoot?" Mary: "from my left second one in." CR: "Curt which one do you shoot?" Curt: "from my right second one in." CR: "Very good." JB: "Quincy will be with me, I will take the one I feel is the leader Quincy will take the other." JB: "any questions?" Quincy: "do we shoot to kill or wound?"JB: "we will tell them not to move, if they look like they are going for a weapon or to use one you are authorized to kill, the team is more important than they are." JB: "is everybody comfortable with four across?" They all shook their head yes. JB: "now we will take the three row scenario." LJ: "Mary which one will you shoot." Mary: "the one on the left front." Curt: "which one will you shoot" Curt: "the one on the right front." LJ: "CR and I will take the next row and we will come at an angle which will ensure no bullets will go toward Mary or Curt. JB: "we don't think we will have trouble with the last one or two especially with the other four down, if we have to shoot them we will shoot in a downward direction so the bullet should go downward in a 45° angle. JB: "based on our interface with the two, we don't think they will want to engage with us, they do not appear to have the experience that we have, whoever is leading this is not too bright to do a military mission on a civilian target."

LJ: "we think they will infiltrate within the next three days, we expect it to be 4 o'clock in the morning, based on experience. JB: "we are going to get up at 3:30 and we will be behind the office, Mary and Curt will go up on the roof, CR and I will go to the right side and we will station ourselves about fifty yards from the office thirty feet from where we think they will come, LJ and Quincy will go to the left and do the same thing, we will lay upon the ground, they should not be able to see us. If at any time we think they look like they're going to engage we take them out, the minute you see them move their weapons you are authorized to shoot, but only if they do not do as instructed, LJ will make first contact, telling them not to move or they will be shot."

JB: "any questions?" They shook their heads no. JB: "we will go to bed at 7:30 and wake up at 3:30, that will give you seven hours of sleep, as you are probably not used to working on one to two hours sleep." JB: "any questions?" They shook their heads no. JB: "Betty find the best price on seven Remington 700 rifles, have them shipped today second day, so we will have them Saturday."

Betty: "okay I will get right on it." JB: "let's go to the big house, as we have plenty of food there." When they got to the big house, Jennifer said "come in the kitchen, grab a paper plate, take what you want and grab a drink, there is also left over cake, please finish the cake as the boys don't need all that sugar. They ate chatted a bit; when they got done eating they dumped everything in a trash can so cleanup was a breeze. JB: "there's a game room downstairs Ping-Pong, pool, and the hockey table, TV and if you're interested there is a twenty minute video on an undercover blind man, ask CR and he will run it for you. Have a good night, lights out at 7:30, up at 3:30 meet at the big house at 3:40 you have each been given a radio, set it to channel 77 and you have a new set of batteries put them in, you will hear everything that goes on over your radio only speak when spoken to, and the best way to get to sleep do not think about tomorrow clear your mind and go to sleep.

Mary and Curt there are two cots set up in the spring house, Quincy and I have two cots set up in the living room, and we will be quiet as to not to wake Jennifer, Rose and the boys. At 7:00, Jennifer came over kissed JB, Ben hugged him, and they went upstairs. Rose took her two boys and went upstairs. Quincy went in and lay down on one of the cots JB turned off the light he got in the other cot and in three minutes he was asleep.

CHAPTER 28

FRIDAY MORNING WEEK 4, SWAT FIRST WEEK

At 3:30, JB and Quincy got up, turned on the light and JB showed Quincy how to set the night vision to receive only they put them on and quietly left the house. They went from cover to cover until he got to the office, LJ, CR, Mary, and Curt came up the walk. JB sent Mary and Curt up on top of the office he didn't hear movement he said "are you set?" They both answered yes. JB, Quincy, CR, and LJ headed out to the parking lot at around fifty yards CR and LJ separated about the distance of thirty feet on each side of the path they assumed the intruders would take, JB and Quincy went ten to fifteen feet farther and did the same, they all lay down almost impossible to see unless you looked right at them. The clock was running, would they come today, or would it be tomorrow, set up and wait the name of the game.

15 minutes later they heard a vehicle pull up. Five minutes later security beeped their pagers that there were people moving in the lot. Eight minutes later four-men two abreast started to spread out in a fan as they passed LJ and CR closed in ten feet farther back were two more and Quincy closed in LJ said "don't move or your dead." The six men froze right where they stood, they could see no one. LJ: "you have two options you move you die, second option you do exactly

316

what we say and you live, do you understand?" The left front man said "men freeze do exactly what they say or they will kill us they are the devil ghosts.

LJ: "first two men slowly to the ground. JB: "you two in the back you move you die."

LJ: "first man on the left how many weapons do you have." Man on the left "I have a pistol and two knives, "LJ: "slowly with your left hand using first finger and thumb pull your pistol up and extend your left arm out to your left and don't move any more than that. CR: "front right do the same only hold yours in front of you." LJ: "show the man your target on his chest", the man looked down and there was a red dot the center of his chest. LJ: "you two are covered there is a rifle on each one of you we have advanced night vision, that's why you cannot see us, their rifles have advanced night vision they can target you and you can't see, it you move your dead, do you understand." The man on the left said "yes men do not move or you will get us all killed, do exactly what they say." LJ moved and put his pistol to the man's head and said "very slowly reach over with your left hand and take your pistol out of its holster and very slowly bring it to your left side arm stretched out", the man complied LJ took the revolver dropped the clip from the gun pulled the lever back ejected the bullet from the gun and dropped it and then told the man take one step back two steps to your left lay spread-eagled on the ground, what other weapons do you have?" The man said "left boot knife." LJ: "took the knife tossed it ten feet away.

CR: "where is your pistol?" Man: "Right side holster", CR put his pistol to the man's head, took his left hand retrieved the pistol, stepped back dropped the clip from the pistol, pulled the lever to eject the bullet and thru the gun away, and said "take one step back two steps to your right, spread eagle on the ground, do you have any other weapons?"The man said "knife outside right boot." They heard two cars pull up outside. CR: "front row I want you to put your hands palms down on the ground slowly walk back from the push-up position until you can stand, and remember slowly. They complied and their butts were up in the air, CR: "now stand up." LJ repeated the same scenario on the front man and got rid of all his weapons. CR did the same on his side. They complied, CR: "2nd row, now put your hands flat on the ground, and do what the first row just got done doing." LJ: "walk over to your two friends, form a single line side-by-side and separate hold your arms up in the air like a cross then grab the hand of the man next to you now start walking toward the entrance, any move to escape and I will shoot you, snipers come forward."

Curt and Mary quickly got off the roof and came running. LJ: "Curt you get behind the man on the left 2 feet back, Mary same on the right I will be in the middle 4 feet back we will now walk toward the entrance you two on the left and right do anything funny they will shoot you and then I will shoot the two in the middle your life depends on you walking carefully forward." They started for the entrance. JB: "Quincy pat the man down and see if he has any weapons." Quincy complied, and said "he is clean." JB: "to the right of the others, take him to the entrance if he acts funny shoot him." Quincy left for the entrance. JB: "idiot mastermind who are you?" The idiot: "I am Lieut. Jamieson, and you better not hurt me my father is a senator." JB gave him a gentle slap to the back of his head, he fell to the ground. JB: "I don't know who you are, and I don't care, you are trespassing on private property, you are illegally performing a military operation in the United States, I can shoot you right now and there are no consequences, now get up."

Jamieson slowly picked himself up, he was visibly shaken. From out of nowhere a shadow figure dressed as an Arab came up and spoke words in a foreign language and waved a knife in front of Jamieson's face he took a step back and JB grabbed his collar said you move again and I'll shoot you." Jamieson: "he has a knife." JB: "this is a master assassin, he taught us how to become invisible, how do you think we all of a sudden were able to capture you, we were invisible that's why it was so easy for us to disarm you; and he just told me to kill you in Arabic.

Jamieson said "my father will pay you lots of money if you let me live." JB: "the Arab just said "you are a worthless individual and liar, he hates liars, and he has killed everybody who has ever lied to him." All of a sudden the Arab was back with his knife, and he stuck the point under Jamieson's chin, Jamieson started shaking so bad JB thought he was going to fall, the Arab vanished. Jamieson started sobbing, JB thought to himself we keep this up he'll have a stroke. JB spoke in Arabic and the Arab appeared with his knife raised JB held up his hand spoke in Arabic, and said "I have asked the Arab to spare you, as you are too stupid to even understand what you have done, and I think you may be crazy, and he has complied with my wishes and he has gone back to Afghanistan." JB: "I am going to take you to the police, I'm going to tell the Navy you should be court marshaled, and we will all testify at your trial, how you attacked civilians in the United States, we also have video and sound of everything that went on here and that will be shown at your court-martial."

JB grabbed Jamieson by the collar aimed him toward the entrance stuck his gun in his back and said walk. Jamieson had trouble walking stumbled a lot and they finally got to the entrance, and Hank was there, the other five were gone they hauled them off in their big van. JB: "Jamieson if that's your name, put your hands behind your back, Hank cuffed him another officer put him in the back of the squad car and left. Hank: "what took you so long?" JB: "Well people like him should not be in the military, the Navy will never court-martial him because of his father's position, so we filled his mind with fantasy and I think when you get back to the station, he will be talking about an Arab that vanishes and appears and vanishes and appears, and went back to Afghanistan and you will not see that in the video, which will let the father say he's had a nervous breakdown, and he will put him in a sanitarium for a while, and the Navy can give him a standard discharge for medical reasons, and get rid of him, the video should be uploaded in twenty to thirty minutes, and there will be no Arab."

Hank said "I will find out who his CO is and call him in the morning and tell him, we have men that say they belong to him who attacked a civilian property early this morning and we are holding them as terrorists, if they are really his, he should get here as quick as possible otherwise we are going to turn them over to homeland, and we think this Jamieson is out of his mind he keeps talking about an Arab that vanishes and appears, and that should make all this go away." JB: "thank you, and expect your video." JB went back to the office. They were all there. JB: "well what did you think of your first training mission?" Mary: "I thought it went very smooth, they had no idea we were there, and it looked like they were taking an early morning stroll." Curt: "I thought they weren't too happy about being here in the first place." Quincy: "the two in the back really need somebody to tell them what to do, they were both idiots."

LJ: "there will be two video versions of this mission, the one the government will get, and the real one that you get to see, how we set their leader up so the Navy can discharge him. JB: "you all did a wonderful job, you performed up to par I am looking forward to other missions with you, this mission never happened as there are four good people that were put in a situation they should never have been in and there's no reason to ruin their careers because of some idiot of a higher rank." They all agreed. LJ: "this was a simulated night mission where we just deployed acted like there were enemies and went through the exercise, and that is the version that will go on the books." JB: "JR should be released from the hospital tomorrow and Monday morning you will do your first exercise in house clearing; Curt, Mary, Quincy, and there was a Samuel that was going to volunteer for SWAT, if he is still interested he should be here Monday."

JB: "we have a mobile command center that is on order and will be here in a few weeks until then we will work out of our four vans, also next week we will go through shooting at the pistol range, I'm going to talk to Hank and I want your rifles here by Friday or Saturday depending on which day they come the following day we will go to the long range and we will start at hundred yard targets, unless we don't get them till Saturday, sometime within the next two weeks I want to do some repelling practices and we may have to set up a stand to practice repelling on, also the dogs will go through exercises and one of you will be paired up with a dog team as backup so you all become familiar with things the dogs can do and how they can save your life." CR came into the room and said "here is the actual video of the mission."

He hooked it up to the big screen and they watched the video during the part where the Arab appeared and disappeared they laughed, and said "who is that?" LJ: "that is CR, alias blind man alias Arab assassin." Somebody said "he should be in the movies." They all laughed. CR: "this next version is the official version, so watch it and this is the one you can talk about." CR ran the version. JB: "Each one of you needs to write your report without the Arab, and get it to me by tomorrow, and thank you again for the good work you did this morning."

Curt, LJ, CR, Mary, and Quincy all decided to go to the diner for breakfast. They all got in their vehicles and headed out. JB locked the door and went to the big house. He went in got Sam took him for a walk, came back unleashed him by the door hung his leash on the hook, he could hear the women in the kitchen, and went in and joined them. Jennifer: "I didn't know if you'd be coming or not but we made enough just in case." JB: "the rest of them went to the diner so we will just have what's left for breakfast tomorrow if there is still some left; I am really hungry I've already worked half a day." Jennifer they usually don't let people out till noon, but I think they will make an exception in JR's case as they are having trouble keeping him in bed."

Rose laughed and said "I can appreciate that, he likes action." JB: "Jennifer and Rose I will drop you off at the hospital, I'll take the kids to school, and come back and pick Rose and JR up." They ate breakfast; JB had two plates of pancakes and some sausage. Rose had the three boys put the dishes in the dishwasher she had already loaded the soap they started the dishes washing they went out got in JB's van and left. JB dropped Rose and Jennifer at the emergency entrance, and then took the boys to school. He parked out front, went in the school and people were looking at him in his strange dress, he drop Ben off at his class, then dropped the other two kids in their classes and as he went to go out the front door the principal said "you should not be carrying a gun in the school, I should call the police." JB: "I'm the police", and showed him his badge. The principal: "oh I'm sorry I didn't know." JB: "now if you have need of SWAT you will know what we look like as we come to save you, if you had people in here that were armed they wouldn't come in to shoot defenseless children, because they would know somebody could shoot them." He walked out got in his van and went back to the hospital to pick up JR and Rose.

He called Jennifer and said "front door or emergency exit?" She said "emergency, we will be there in ten minutes." JB pulled up parked where he would not be in the way of the ambulances. He got out opened the side door and waited for Rose and Jennifer to come. Five minutes later Jennifer and Rose were pushing JR in a wheelchair and Shorty was walking beside him, and he could tell JR would rather walk himself. Rose pushed him to the van he got out he hugged JB and said "thank you for getting me out of prison." They all laughed, he and Rose went in and sat in front seats, JB closed the front passenger door and went to the back opened up the rear put all his stuff on the floor beside the crate, and put JR's dog Shorty in the crate with Sam, and closed the door. JB kissed Jennifer good bye, and she went back to work he got in the van and they headed toward the park.

JR: "you look like you're ready for a mission, or just got off from one." JB: "got off from one, you can see the videos when we get to the office, we saved the Navy a lot of embarrassment; from an idiot son that daddy the Senator hoped would make a name for himself in the Navy." JR: "sorry I missed it, it will be fun watching." JB: "you'll love the part where CR becomes a 300-year-old vanishing and appearing Arab assassin." JR: "now I really want to see the video." Rose: "JR now you can only run half the distance you normally run for the next week, and half the push-ups and half the crunches until next Friday then you can do the whole thing, if Jennifer finds out your cheating, you will be back in the hospital strapped to a bed." JB: "and I will help hold you down while they are strapping you in, I need you, we have got to start swat training and getting these rookies to where we can depend on them; they did good last night, but this was easy, and I hope you don't hurt yourself from laughing at the Arab."

They went in the office, LJ and CR and JR hugged each other, JR said "really good to be back." CR: "I will now run the videos of this morning's mission for JR first the version that didn't happen, and then the official version, if you see something that you thought we might have done better now is the time to bring it up so we can make sure it never happens again." When they got to the part of the Arab JR started laughing and laughing and tears came to his eyes and he said "he was appearing and disappearing right before my eyes I would not have believed this was possible. I can see his whole world has changed and the idiot is about to collapse, if I could have been there to see it with my own eyes, you guys were great." CR: "this is the version the police got, with him ranting and raving about an Arab appearing and disappearing he will be on the funny farm for a while." JR: "I wish we could weed out more of those idiots, the Navy would be a much better place." JB: "we have a new scope coming in to try out, it has a built-in rangefinder built-in calculators you give it wind speed and direction it figures the distance and adjusts the crosshairs on your target you squeeze the trigger." JR: "I will love to see that."

Betty: "I did a tracking five minutes ago and it is scheduled for delivery at 10 o'clock, it should be coming soon." JR: "A lot has been happening since I've been gone." CR: "we know you; you'll be caught up in no time." They heard a vehicle pull up, and the driver came in with an overnight delivery the scope had arrived Betty signed, and the deliveryman left. JB opened the box pulled everything out, there was a DVD that said watch me first. JB handed the DVD to CR, and he put it in his laptop, and they proceeded to watch a demonstration on how the scope worked, how to site in the top of the target the bottom of the target and it set the crosshairs where you should shoot, now all you had to do was line up with the spot you wanted to hit and squeeze the trigger. The next video on the DVD was how to take off your old scope and put on the new one, how to put the batteries in, and where to put the auxiliary memory chip. JB went out to his van brought in his rifle took his scope off put the new one on and said "there is a second video here", and he handed the next DVD to CR, he pulled out the first DVD and stuck in the second. That showed how to transfer files from the scope to a laptop via Wi-Fi or Bluetooth how to delete files and all the different features of day and night usage. LJ, CR, and JR, and Mary jumped in LJ's van and left, Curt, and Quincy got in JB's van, Sam jumped in the front seat, JB gave Curt his rifle, shut the door, got in and they drove up to the shooting range, it was time to test out the scope. JB did the things he saw on the DVD and was pleased, I am going to order one for myself. LJ did the same things JB did and he said "I want one for my rifle." JR took the rifle did the same thing that JB did and he wanted one also. CR did the tests and agreed he wanted one too. Mary tried it next, then Curt, and Quincy. They were all impressed.

JB: "shall we go to the diner and have lunch. They got in the vans and went to the diner. They went and sat JB, LJ, JR, and CR sat with their back to the wall, the rest sat with their backs to the door. Alice brought water and menus and said she would be back later. Five minutes later she came back took their orders and left. Fifteen minutes later the food started coming, and they started to eat and talk about how things were going, what was coming. Life is always good after a good mission.

They went back to the office and told Betty to order twelve total of the new scopes, and he called Hank and told him about the scopes and he had ordered eight for SWAT and five for the park. Hank asks why they were so expensive and JB told him what they did and that the scope would record the mission from that rifle's point of view. Hank said "if it will do that, order me one too."

JB: "Betty will you make that fourteen scopes, and see if we get a better break." JB: "Yours is on order, bye." JB: "JR I only want you working half days for the next week, then you can do full days. JR: "Ok I am not at 100% maybe 65%. JB: "Rose why don't you go with him, and give him a castor oil pack, and let him rest for an hour, I will get Jennifer and the boys." Rose: "thank you, I will take care of him right away." JB: "Rose put him in my van and take him that way, and I will walk the dog when I get back." Rose: "I've been walking him; I can do it in one of the twenty minute intervals, thanks anyway." JB: "remember your family, I will do anything for you, we might take you up to the dog training area and run you through an exercise so you know better how to understand the dog, and if he gives you a sign you'll know what it means."

Rose: "that sounds like fun, I'll have to do that." She and JR left. JB: "I'm going to go pick up Jennifer and the boys see you later." JB went out got in the parks van and headed for the school. He picked the boys up as they came out of school they went back to the van and he headed for the hospital. He thought he saw a car following him, went a little farther he turned left went two blocks, turn left at the next intersection went down turned right, and the car was still there. He called Hank. Hank answered: "this is JB, you got somebody following me?"Hank: "yes, he's a rookie he thinks he can follow people, I told him you'd spot him in four blocks." JB: "make it 3, he was too close." Hank: "I'll tell him the bad news." JB: "bye." He turned back and headed for the hospital. He called Jennifer: "up front." Five minutes later he picked her up in front and they headed home.

JB called LJ and said "I am going back to the house and make sure RJ is all right." LJ: "I am going to Peggy's, She thought she would be home at 6:30, I told her I would take her out to supper." JB: "have fun see you tomorrow", he hung up pulled into the park and went to the big house.

Jennifer went upstairs to check on Rose and JR. Rose was cleaning him up as his hour was up, Rose said "he fell asleep through the whole thing; I think he pushed it a little hard today." Jennifer: "have him go to bed early, and I'll have him turn back after half of a mile, he's doing so well we don't want a setback." Jennifer checked JR's pulse, it was normal, we need to put him in bed and let him sleep a little." They got him up, and put him in bed covered him up turned off the light and went downstairs.

Jennifer looked at Rose, and Rose looked at Jennifer, Jennifer said "you're thinking the same thing I am." Rose: "yes we have all those pancakes we made this morning, we have some fruit left, we can put that in the blender, then pour that over the pancakes and the kids will think they're having dessert for supper." Jennifer: "we make a good pair; I never had friends like this since high school." Rose: "me either", and they hugged each other, got the pancakes and the fruit out. Rose put the fruit in the blender, a little vanilla and some honey, and blended. Jennifer put the pancakes in the oven and turned it on the low setting in ten minutes they were warm.

LJ left the office went to the spring house showered and shaved put on some nice clothes and went to the big house. He went in they were eating supper. Jennifer: "have some pancakes?" LJ: "I'm taking Peggy out to supper, so I'll have to pass, but thanks any way they look really good." JB: "you have a good time and we'll see you tomorrow. LJ left got in his van and drove to Peggy's house. He was listening to the radio and fifteen minutes later she pulled up, he got out and walked over to her, she put her arms around him and kissed him, I had a really good day, and I'm going to love this." LJ: "I am happy for you, what did you learn today?" Peggy: "I learned how to make flowers out of radishes, and how to slice vegetables to make them more appealing, and how to use a chef knife, and paring knife more efficiently." LJ: "do you want to change or go like you are?" Peggy: "do you mind if I go like I am."

LJ: "of course not, I love you just as you are." Peggy: "do you mind if we have Chinese?" LJ: "no, I eat anything." Peggy: "I'm hungry, let's go." They went out got in LJ's van and she gave directions to the Chinese restaurant. They went in ordered, ate their meal, LJ paid the bill and they went back to Peggy's house." They went in, she shut locked the door led him over to the couch sat him down she put her legs up on the couch and turned so she was facing him, put her arms around him and kissed him hard, he kissed her hard. Peggy stood up grabbed him by the hand, let him into the bedroom, she took his shoes off, undid his belt, unzipped his pants, and pulled them off, crawled up on the bed with him and she started to undo his shirt, he undid hers at the same time, the shirts came off she had no bra on, he kissed her neck, kissed her breasts, she quivered with ecstasy, he reached down pulled her skirt off, pulled her pants off, she pulled his off, they fondled each other and he could wait no longer, they made mad passionate love, over and over and over until they were exhausted. She curled up next to him and said I will marry you whenever you want. LJ: "let's wait a little longer, until you get through your first course, that'll give us time to plan. She said "okay whatever you want, I love you with all my heart." LJ: "and I love you with all my heart" and he rolled over and kissed her gently, they made love again this time soft gentle and loving, it was wonderful, and they both fell asleep.

CHAPTER 28

SATURDAY WEEK 4

LJ woke up at 5:00 and thought I'm not going to make this run. He got up went into the bathroom cleaned himself up, Peggy came in cleaned herself up grabbed him by the hand and they went back to bed. They caressed each other made love again and went back to sleep. LJ woke up at six, Peggy was in the shower, he got in with her they soaped each other up, rinsed off went in got dressed. Peggy said "will you drop me off at the diner, and pick me up this evening?"

LJ: "of course, I want you to have a list of all your expenses, and your account number, so I can put money in your account, so you can pay your bills." She said "sure, I will have it for you tonight." They left the apartment got in his van and he took her to the diner. She kissed him goodbye and ran in the building. He headed for the park. LJ went to the spring house, went in changed clothes, the leash for his dog was gone, he thought I better go face the music. He drove to the office got out of his van and went in to the office.

JB: "good morning; how was your evening?" LJ: "the best in my life, I'm engaged." CR: "congratulations I'm happy for you, when's the wedding?" LJ: "we haven't set a date yet, we are going to pick out a ring next week." JR: "how does she like school?" LJ: "she loved it; she told me all about the things she learned yesterday." Betty: "the scope company called, they left last night, they gave me a tracking number, and it should be here tomorrow morning, I will check its progress during the day and let you know."

JR: "I have a simple house clearing program set up for swat, LJ and CR would you run through it, I think it's basic enough for the police." They said "sure we can run through it." JR: "they will be using rubber bullets so they don't destroy the building." JB: "why don't the three of you go up and run through it and see what kind of times you're getting, what kind of times does manual say?" JR: "ten minutes with no errors is excellent, twelve minutes with no errors for less than five times through is a pass go to program two, any hit of a civilian is a fail." JB: "when you get back give me the numbers."

The three left got in LJ's van and headed up to the hill." JB: "what is the timeframe on the rifles?" Rose: "their due in tomorrow morning also." JB though *if it's not raining, we will do a fifty yard shoot in the afternoon.* Rose hung up the phone "a security guard named Jimmy, wants to talk to you, I told him come in ten minutes, is that okay?" JB: "sure, we will go in the conference room." Ten minutes later Jimmy came in, JB thought *that's mouth, wonder what this is about.* JB: "Jimmy let us go in the conference room." Jimmy followed him as they went in JB pointed at a chair and said sit down there please he sat down on the other side, JB opened a drawer and pulled out a yellow pad. Across the top of the sheet he wrote Jimmy – security guard. JB: "is this personal or professional?" Jimmy: "both Sir." JB: "go ahead, tell me what's on your mind, and then we will go from there."

Jimmy: "I know I made some terrible mistakes when you had your first day, and I got to looking at my life and I'm not happy with it, it's probably not put me in the best position with my job here at the park." JB: "remember I told you that you all started with a clean slate, that's behind us, it does not count against you, what you do from now on makes or breaks you."

Jimmy: "I want to get myself in better shape, I want to be the best security guard you have, and I want to learn all the skills I can and may be qualify as a policeman or maybe even swat." JB: "I am always open to somebody trying to improve themselves" JB; the four of us run and exercise every morning we are now running 3 miles in 21 minutes with the dogs, without the dogs we usually did it in 20 we are not trying to be fast but steady and not be winded when we are done." "You start out with a mile and a half at eight to ten minutes take your blood pressure and pulse before you start and after you finish that should be on a sheet where you can put the day of the week and how you feel when you get done, when your pulse rate is less or the same as when you started, then it is time to jump the distance by half a mile until you are up to 3 miles, and if you can get that in twenty minutes, we will have you come and run with us."

Jimmy: "you would do that?"JB: "I never say anything I don't mean." Jimmy: "I will work really hard." JB: "that's good now the second part we do fifty push-ups, your back is perfectly straight like a board, JB stood up when around and did five push-ups for Jimmy so he knew exactly how to do them, I want you to start out and try to do ten when you can do ten in less than five minutes jump to twenty and when you can do them in less than ten minutes jump to thirty, we do fifty in less than ten minutes", Then we do one hundred crunches, they're different than setups, he came around the table and did ten crunches when you can do hundred crunches in four minutes, you can come and do your work out every morning with us. If you do not make those goals, it will not be held against you, as long as you are performing your duties in an acceptable manner, and I wouldn't mind seeing your progress."

Jimmy: "can I have that in writing so that I have it right?" JB: "yes I have written the routine down on the yellow sheet I will give it to Rose she will type it up and you should be able to pick it up after lunch." Jimmy stood up and said "thank you, my father is a drunk and he doesn't care what I do, I want you to be proud of me and happy that I work for you."

JB: "so far you are starting down the right road, it's not easy the difference between a Seal and the rest is a Seal or a Delta force will not quit, they will go till they pass out or die to finish a mission." JB: "once you complete this to where you can work out with us you can then go up to the shooting range and we will teach you how to shoot the pistol correctly when you're done with that, we will let you learn other things and if there are any of your fellow security guards that want to do this same routine, they may join us also when they achieve the goals." JB: "I am going to tell you about the 80/20 rule, have you heard of that?" Jimmy: "no." 80% of the work is done by 20% of the people, let's take seal training 100 men start out at the beginning of seal training, by the end of the first week 20% have dropped out that leaves 80 at the end of the second week there is sixty at the end of the third week there is 10 at the end of the fourth week there is 10 at the end of the course there is probably five or six. Think about that." The security guards are not expected to do what we do, they will have to be in decent shape and good in self-defense and rendering a person ineffective, do you know what I mean by ineffective?"

Jimmy: "they can't cause any more trouble?" JB: "that's good enough you understand." JB: "is there anything else?" Jimmy: "no I really appreciate that you have given me a chance to continue my employment here." JB: "I will be waiting for your results and you have a good day." They left the conference room JB took the sheet off the pad and gave it to Rose and said would you type this up for him and if you can make it in some kind of a chart to make it easier for him to fill out that would be nice."

Rose: "JR has one of these I'll make it like that one looks like." JB: "can you have it done today or do you need until tomorrow?" Rose: "no I can do it today because I just did one for JR for his rehabilitation." JB turned and said "it will be done this afternoon." Jimmy said "thanks" and left. JB: "I hope he makes it, we will see what he is really made of."

They heard a van pull up. JB: "that must be the boys; we will see what their records are." JR, LJ, and CR came into the office. JB:

"what were the scores?" JR: "CR went through nine minutes and 15 seconds no civilians hit, LJ went through in nine minutes 45 seconds no civilians hit." JB: "how do you think our police brothers are going to do?" CR: "first time through I think Curt and Mary will get the best scores but I think they'll be 12 or 13 minutes." LJ: "we don't know about Quincy as we've never seen him shoot and were not sure what his scores are at the pistol range, Samuel has never showed up for anything after that first mission so if he doesn't show up for this I think we need to look at somebody else."

JB: "I will have to check with Hank and see what's going on with him, we worked with shadow his name is David, and his work has always been excellent I wouldn't mind if we got him in SWAT, though I think he has not volunteered because of his wife." LJ: "when you get a hold of Hank, and find out what's going on as I don't want to have to catch up people because they can't make a decision, it would be hard for me to trust them, shadow I worked with him I have no problem with him and I really understand the wife thing."

JB: "I'll give Hank a call and see what he's got to say." JB called Hank. Hank: "what's up?" JB: "Samuel, he has never been in anything we have done so far, what is his problem?" Hank: "I don't think his wife likes the idea of him being in SWAT, I think he's trying to save his marriage." JB: "you tell him he's off the list and hopefully that'll fix up things at home." Hank: "I can do that." JB: "what about David, everything he's done with us we been more than pleased with, we would love to have him in SWAT we think he's quite competent." Hank: "I think he's got the same problem, but maybe not as bad." JB: "what if we invited him out here with his wife to dinner and we could talk to them." Hank: "I don't know, but if you don't try you'll never know." JB: "do you have anyone else that is interested?" Hank: "another one of the women was interested but when Samuel volunteered, I think she thought she couldn't compete with him."

JB: "We seals on average are bigger than the guys in Delta force, but I think that's because they have us carrying boats and doing stuff in the water the Delta force is basically land guys and most of them are small and wiry and I wouldn't mess with them, they are fast and deadly, just like CR." Hank: "I'll talk to David and let you know, and I'll put up a sign again for volunteers." JB: "we don't want anybody but a volunteer; I would rather be short one, than have one that doesn't want to be here."

Hank: "I'll agree with that, we want to have people we know we can count on." JB: "CR and LJ just went through the first house clearing program." Hank: "CR did it in nine minutes and 15 seconds LJ did at nine minutes and 45 seconds, they've had hundreds of real house clearing there's no way I'm going to put your guys up to that standard, though once we get going I would think you should have all your policeman go through the house clearing every three months minimum, once a month would be better; SWAT is going to go through the house clearing once a week." Hank: "I think that's a real good idea, the next couple months we will start them, let's get swat going first."

JB: "I plan on running Curt, Mary, and Quincy through after lunch, so if you could have them out here at 1:00 that would be fine, if you have them out at 12:00 they can go to lunch with us, they need to start physical training and shooting on the pistol range and the rifle range, in four weeks I want them to have put 1000 rounds through their weapons." Hank: "I was surprised when Mary tied with Curt; he is usually our top marksman."

JB: "CR spent a half hour with her before her test." Hank: "can he do that with the rest of my men?" JB: "anyone of my guys can improve yours if they will listen." Hank: "maybe I'll start sending the low scores out for training, that should give the rest of them incentive to come." JB: "fine with me, but my guy's salary will come out of your budget while they're working with your people." Hank: "that's fine I expected that." JB: "that's all I have for now goodbye." Hank: "goodbye."

LJ: "one of the seals that we worked with on a few missions, that we liked and used a number of times on missions, he knew we were going to set up a SWAT team and he wondered if there was an opening." JB: "how many missions has he been on?" LJ: "I'm sure it's over 100, and he liked our system much better, and I remember he was good on house clearing."

JB: "when would he be available?" LJ: "Six weeks." JB: "call him and tell him he's got a job if he can't get in the swat unit I will put him in charge of security that'll be one less thing we got to mess with." LJ: "will do." LJ called and left him a message. They heard three cars pull up outside, and Curt, Mary, and Quincy came in." They said "we heard were going to do some house clearing." JR: "yes, you are going to run through the first program, you will be firing rubber bullets, so flip a coin draw straws, on who goes first, second, and third." JB called Hank and said 'we just got a call from a seal that we worked with in the past he was wondering if he can get into our SWAT unit and I told him yes but if one of your people volunteers I will put him in charge of my security guards, so that will take the pressure off of you if your guys aren't interested." Hank: "yes it will take the pressure off, is he as good as your guys?" JB: "close enough, we didn't mind when he came on missions with us and he pulled his weight every time."

Hank: "it's fine with me then, if you're happy I'm happy bye." JB hung up. JB: "LJ get a hold of him and see if he has leave he can take and get here sooner." LJ: "called and left a message for the seal to call him back, he had a job." JB: "let's go to lunch, Rose should we bring you something back for lunch?" Rose: "a fish sandwich and a salad."

They got into two vans and went to the diner, JB, LJ, CR, and JR sat with their backs to the wall the rest sat with their backs to the door, a new waitress came gave them water and menus and said I'll be back in five minutes. They decided what they were going to get, the waitress came back took their order and JB said "we have an order to go, would you bring it after we're done eating so it'll still be warm when we get back", the waitress said "yes she would" and put the two separate orders in. They finished and paid their bill, JB paid for the order to go and they all got in the vans and headed back to the park. JB took the food in to Rose, and went back got in the van and they went up to the hill to do the house clearing.

JR: "this is how the house clearing goes you try to get through as fast as you can they say the best time is 10 minutes 12 is acceptable, you shoot a civilians you fail, the secret is don't shoot the civilians and good luck." JR: "have the three of you picked who is to go first?" Curt: "I am they both voted for me" JR put Curt at the starting line at the buzzer, Curt started his run, and he finished 13 minutes and shot no civilians. Mary got to be next, JR put her at the starting line hit the buzzer, and she started her run. She finished in 13 minutes and 10 seconds she shot no civilians. Quincy stood at the starting line JR hit the button he started his run. He finished in 13 minutes and 20 seconds and shot no civilians.

LJ: "I think you all did extremely well as this is your first time seeing this, I'm very pleased." JR: "over the next week you will run again three times and the following week twice you should decrease your time but you don't want to shoot the civilians. Mary: "can we know how fast CR and LJ went through?" JB: "it would not be fair as they have had over 150 real house clearings under war conditions." LJ: "let's just say we did it faster than you did, and we don't want you rushing and failing one of your runs, we want you to learn so you can get use to what you're looking at." JB: "when you finish running this five more times, then you go to the second program then we will tell you what they did." The three of them said "that sounds like a good idea."

LJ's phone rang he answered it, it was the new seal, LJ talked for a minute and a half and said "he'd like to talk to you." JB took the phone and said "JB here, what do you want to know?" The seal: "I have a month of leave, and I really wanted to have some money in reserve so I can pay until I find a reasonable place to live." JB: "I am asking you to come in two weeks and I will pay you what you lost by taking your leave, and we will make sure you have a place to stay until you find what you're looking for." The seal said "LJ said that you would make sure I had no hardships and you were fair, so I will take the leave get out four weeks early and I'll see you in two weeks, and I'm looking forward to a long relationship, I will tell LJ when I leave here and when I should arrive, or do I need to only talk to you?" JB: "LJ is fine CR is fine RJ is fine and I'm fine, the four of us are equal, and be careful on your trip we don't want to lose you before you get here." The Seal: "I am looking forward to it, see you in two weeks." JB handed the phone back to LJ; he talked another two minutes and hung up. LJ: "he could have my room and I could go stay with Peggy."

JB: "that's fine with me as long as you get here by 5:30 every morning for our run." LJ: "I won't miss it again." JB: 'I am going to get Jennifer and i will be back." When they got back to the office JB gave Jennifer the keys so she could drive straight to the big house. He went in and Rose said "the guns and scopes will be in tomorrow around 10:00." JB: "we might as well call it quits for the day be here at 9:30 tomorrow, and when the guns and scopes arrive, we will get them set up and go up on the Hill and site them in for fifty yards, have a nice evening." CR and Mary followed each other out of the lot and were gone. Curt and Quincy got in their cars and left. LJ headed to the diner to pick up Peggy.

JB went to the big house, he walked with Rose and JR. Rose went in the kitchen to help Jennifer. JB and JR went in the living room sat down and JB said "what did your manual say about the times the rookies put in today." JR: "they were all a little ahead of the average time for first timers, so I thought they did pretty good for a first time."

LJ got in his van drove to the diner and picked Peggy up. LJ: "are you hungry?" Peggy said "yes shall we get Chinese carry out?" LJ: "sounds good give me directions." Peggy gave him directions and they got to the Chinese restaurant." He told her what he wanted and she went in, ten minutes later she was back out, she got in the van, they drove to the apartment. LJ went around to the back got Mike out and they went up to her apartment. They sat down and ate and Mike sat next to LJ. Peggy cleaned off the table; LJ pulled out his notepad and said "let's go over your expenses." She said "okay the apartment is 700.00 a month, the electric bill is running about 50.00 a month, my insurance on the car and the renters is 85.00 a month, my phone is 87.00 a month and that's it." LJ: "that comes in 922.00; I will just put 1000 in your account." Peggy: "you don't have to put that much in, 922 will be fine." LJ: "I will give you the 1000.00 as you will have gas and let me tell you something else that's going on." LJ: "in two weeks another seal is coming, so I thought if I moved in here with you he could have my room in the spring house, and we will pick out a house plan and get it built and just move in there." Peggy: "then you could take me and pick me up every day for school." LJ: "I have to be at the park at 5:30 every morning for our work out and I doubt if you can get in the school at that time of the day, I will have to leave here at 4:50 in the morning, so you will have to drive yourself to school." Peggy: "when will you be moving in?" LJ: "in two weeks, and next week one night after school we will pick out your engagement ring, you will marry me won't you?" Peggy: "yes I will." LJ kissed her good night went out got in his van and headed for the park. He got to the park he drove to the spring house got Mike out of the back of the van took him for a walk and then went back to the spring house and he went to bed.

CR and Mary went to her apartment and she changed clothes, CR said "I've been doing a lot of thinking since you took that bullet for me, I have never felt, like I feel for you, I would like you to be my wife, and will you marry me?" Mary: "yes I will, I want to spend the rest of my life with you." Mary put her arms around his neck and they kissed and kissed and kissed." CR: "if you want we can go out and look at rings tonight, and if you find one, we will get it." Mary: "I would like that very much", and kissed him very hard. Mary put nip in his crate and CR put his leash on spot and they left the apartment, he put spot in his crate and they drove off.

The first jewelry store they stopped at Mary didn't see anything she really liked, they thanked the salesman and left. They went to the second jewelry store, 15 minutes later Mary found one she liked, the salesman said he would get it set to the right size and they could pick it up tomorrow, CR and Mary left.

Mary: "how soon do you want to get married?"

CR: "I would marry you tomorrow, but you set the date and that's when we will get married."

Mary: "I had a goal to qualify for SWAT."

CR: "when you took the bullet for me you qualified for SWAT, the rest is just academic, your time for a first time through a building clearing was very good, I think with two or three more times through instead of thinking you will get to where your reflexes will let you shoot quicker and your times will go down, and I've been around you enough that I don't think you'll have trouble meeting all the physical requirements."

Mary: "what about children?"

CR: "like you I would like at least two, and I'll make enough that you really don't need to work." Mary: "I guess being a full-time mother would be another challenge." CR: "yes it is, you can do something men cannot do; you can bring a new life into the world, men can't, so I think yes it's a big challenge." Mary: "well neither one of us are getting any younger, we should probably try to have our first child within the next year and a half."

CR: "even if you're pregnant you can still control your dog, shoot your rifle and your pistol though I think when you get about six months along you might want to hold off on that for a while until after the baby is born." Mary: "I will have to talk to Jennifer and see what she thinks, and see what their plans are as you said "JB wanted to have at least one more child, maybe she'll want to become a stay-at-home mom; I was so wrapped up in my career, I didn't give it much thought until I met you." CR: "we will work it out, we will make our plan and both agree and it will be fine, I need to get back to the park to get up early in the morning, our guns and scopes should be in around ten, we will go to the range and site them in."

CR put his arms around her and kissed her good night and he left for the park. He drove to the spring house got spot out and went for a walk, came back to the spring house and went to bed.

CHAPTER 30

SUNDAY WEEK 5

LJ got up got dressed put his leash on Mike and headed for the door. CR was right behind him with Spot and LJ opened the door CR closed it, and they headed for the big house. one minute later JB and JR came out and they started there run. They came back JB and JR went in to the big house LJ and CR ran on to the spring house.

JB went and did his push-ups and crunches then went up shaved showered and went down to the kitchen Jennifer was making breakfast. Jennifer: "mom said she was going to feed Ben breakfast and bring him over later and right now it's just you and me, Rose and JR should be down soon." JB: "do you want any more children?" Jennifer: "yes, we should start the rest of our family within this next year."

JB: "I agree let's wait a couple months until things settle down." Jennifer: "I was thinking the same thing, so we will try after a couple months; I started the pill a week ago." JB: "it is all right with me you stop the pills when you feel it's time and we'll go from there." Rose and JR came down; they said good morning, Jennifer said "I made enough for you two if you want." They said "yes thank you very much." JB: "JR how was your run?" JR: "I can tell my lungs aren't hundred percent yet, but I'll get there, you just keep climbing the hill." JB: "I know what you mean."

LJ: "I think I am going to go to the diner and have breakfast you coming along?" CR: "sure, get your dog and let's go." They opened the side door put the dogs in told them to sit, shut the door they both got in the van and headed to the diner. They went in found a table by the back wall where they could sit and face the door and sat down. Peggy came over and gave them water and menus and said "do you both want coffee?" They shook their head yes, she went and got two cups, and said I'll be back in a minute to take your order.

Three minutes later Mary came over and sat across from CR. CR: "how's my sweetheart this morning?" Mary: "great now I'm having breakfast with you." Peggy saw Mary and brought a glass of water and a menu and said "would you like coffee?" Mary said "yes, and if you want my order I would like scrambled eggs with veggies and sausage." CR and LJ gave her their orders also and Peggy left. Peggy said "I get off at 4:30, you want to eat out or my place?"

LJ: "your choice I think you're going to be tired, why don't we grab something and eat at your place." Peggy: "okay, I will see you at 4:30." Peggy brought their food and hurried back, the diner was busy this morning. They ate and left enough money on the table and they all gave Peggy a nice tip, LJ winked at Peggy, she smiled and got back to work. LJ and CR got in the van Mary got in her car and they headed for the park.

Quincy, JB, and RJ were there and said "hi" to LJ and CR and Mary as they came in, 9:15, JB liked people early. At 9:20 Curt came in, they all said "hi", and they heard another vehicle pull up. Hank came in; they all said "hi." Hank: "I just had to see these new scopes."

JB: "pull up a chair; they should be here around 10:00." At 9:35 another vehicle pulled up, and JB's dad came in and said "I came to see the new scopes too." JB: "they're supposed to be here around 10:00." They made small talk at 9:50 another vehicle pulled in and then there was a knock at the door, Sherry the weekend receptionist answered the door it was the UPS man, he came in she signed for the package and he left.

JB got up brought the package to his desk opened it and said "here are the scopes", and he started handing them out; he gave Hank his, then Mary, Curt, Quincy, LJ, CR, JR, and one to his dad, CR put the disc that said run me first in his laptop and they ran through setting up the scope. Hank said "I'm going out bring my rifle in and put the scope on." He went out and was back in two minutes. He took his old scope off put the new one on. They put in the second DVD and Hank went through the setup. Hank said "what are all those extra scopes for?" : "they are for our personal rifles, and spares in case one goes down I do not want a rifle out of commission because of the scope." Hank: "I didn't think of that, good plan." twenty minutes later another vehicle pulled up, it was FedEx. They heard a thump, thump, thump coming up the stairs and FedEx man wheeled the dolly in with a wooden box and said "one of you give me a hand in putting this on the table."

LJ said sure went over and they put it on the table. FedEx man said "could one of you sign for this?" LJ said "give me the pen", and he signed and the FedEx man left. JB: "Sherry could you call maintenance and have them bring a pry bar and hammer?" Sherry: "yes", and she dialed maintenance talked for 20 seconds and hung up the phone. Sherry: "it's on its way he said they'd be here in three minutes." JB: "thank you." Three minutes later a maintenance man came in with pry bar and the hammer. He walked over slipped pry Bar between the top and side at the end of the case and started to open it, he went down the side prying it up and down until the lid came off. JB: "thank you very much, that's all we needed, JB hope we didn't interrupt you." Maintenance man said "we were just starting to go to the next ride so it was no big deal."

JB: "well you tell everybody we appreciate all the good work you do." The man said "thank you" and left. LJ: "I'll go down to the spring house and get my cleaning kit so we can clean these rifles get all the packing grease off." CR: "I'll go with you with all these rifles one Kit will take forever." Mary went to the bathroom got some paper towels and came back and they took the first gun out of the box and started to clean it off. Curt took another one out of the box and started to clean it off. Quincy took one out of the box and started cleaning it off. JB took one out of the box, started cleaning it off. JR grabbed one out of the box started cleaning it off.

JB: "each one of us will use this rifle on any SWAT mission we will not use our personal rifles anymore, we have been lucky so far none of the bullets have been found from our rifles, and the pistol fired on the hill they couldn't find any bullets so our guns are clean. I will order pistols on Monday and have them here in two days; you will keep your weapons in your cars so you have them when you go on a mission. In the next month between your rifle and your pistol I want you firing 1000 rounds. With the old scope Curt and Mary shred the bull's-eye after 20 minutes of training. All shooting with our rifles, with the new scopes you will record how you sited in and then the results, then you can play it back and hopefully it will help you increase your accuracy as you can see where you thought the bullet should go and the scope will show you where it went."

LJ:"we are using subsonic ammo on all missions." LJ: "the ASA put out a report about ammo; this is what they had to say about the old preferred round, **168-grain Match King: over penetration. Nearly 90 percent of the snipers who had used the ammo in an engagement told ASA that it had passed through the target.**" "At some point, this is going to cause an inadvertent injury or death to a hostage or team member, ammunition makers, including Hornady and Black Hills, are now offering alternative sniper rounds that use **ballistic tips for less penetration and offer similar or better ballistic performance than the 168-grain Match King**.

LJ: "they also said the average distance for a shot is 51 yards." The ASA also said "the precision rifle used most often by police snipers is the **Remington 700,** which you are now holding in your hands." CR: "one of us will be paired up with you to help you get to be the best rifle shooter you can be, the scope can't do it all, you are the one that squeezes the trigger, and you must be steady and control your breath." You will also be shooting standing, kneeling, moving, and you will have to hit a moving target at 50 and 100 yards from different positions, we do not get to pick the location, it picks us."

CR looked at Mary's rifle and said "looks ok." JR looked at Quincy's rifle and said "looks okay." LJ looked at Curt's and said "looks okay." JB looked at Hank's rifle and said "looks okay." JB then looked at his dad's rifle and said "looks okay."

JB: "well let's go up on the hill and try them out." CR, Mary, Curt, and JR climbed into CR's van and headed up to the rifle range. JB, Dad, Quincy, and Hank got in JB's van and headed for the rifle range. LJ said "let's have the police up on the line 1st Mary, Curt, Quincy, and Hank. Put your rifle on the table and each of you take a target and take it out to the 50 yard marker, and slip it in the stand. LJ said "CR you take Mary, I can take Curt, JR you take Quincy, and JB you want to take Hank. They all said "sure that sounds good." 10 minutes later they were all destroying their targets. Then LJ, CR, JR, and JB had their rifles sited in and destroying their targets five minutes later. JB: "you all did so good take these new targets and go out to the hundred yard mark. While the policeman were taking their targets out JB said "when they get fairly good with this we will have them do prone and then kneeling, 20 shots, then we'll have them refill their 2 10 round magazines, so far they have each shot 30 rounds, we can do 10 prone and 10 kneeling, and see how they do, then we will quit. They all had done pretty good there were a few beginning shots scattered around target and then the other shots were in the bull's-eye and in the next ring

LJ said "you all have done a fine job, I'm proud of you; fill your clips full and were going to do 10 in the prone and 10 in the kneeling." They filled their clips got up to the line in front of their tables lay on the pads. LJ: "t his is not a time test but try to fire as fast as you can, and still be accurate." LJ: "are you all in the prone position?" Each one said yes right down the line. LJ: "ready, fire." They started firing, Curt got done first Mary second Quincy third and Hank fourth. LJ said take these red stickers and go out and put them over the holes and hurry back. In five minutes they were back. LJ: "back in the prone position." The three of them lay down.

JB: "Hank I would like you to do this exercise also so you know how difficult this is." Hank: "that is a good idea I should know what they go through otherwise I can't understand what they are going through." Hank lay down in the prone position. LJ: "I am going to say ready and you will quickly get up on your knee and I may say shoot before you get there, but do not shoot until you are on your knee and make sure you hold your rifle tight to your shoulder as you have nothing to support the weapon but your arms."

LJ: "ready a second later shoot." Curt did the first shot, Mary the second, Hank the third, Quincy the fourth. From then on it was hard to say who was doing what Curt got done first, Hank second Mary third and Quincy last. LJ: "you all finished in 15 seconds, that's a second and a half per shot average, time wise that's pretty good, now go out and get your targets and bring them back. When they got back, LJ said "Curt you notice how the spread is not as tight as before I don't think you got your strap tight enough for your arm and elbow to lock it down better as you wobbled a bit but not bad for the first time."

CR looked at Mary's target and said "did your knee bother you?" Mary: "I wasn't used to the hard ground, it's very uncomfortable." CR: "if you're good at sewing you could put some extra padding inside your pants where your knees hit, or I will make you a board and you can hit them every night for 10 minutes and they will get to where they don't hurt anymore." Mary: "I will try doing the pads first."

JR: "Quincy you did very well, you were slower than the others but you have a much tighter group so your shooting is excellent on all the targets but try to work it a little quicker as you may have to hit your targets in a shorter period of time, but this was good shooting." JB:

"Hank you need to slow down a bit because you were trying to fire too fast you weren't letting the scope do its job for you, I think you tried to revert back to your other scope as your shots were toward the middle I think the later shots was the scope finally got it set for you." But you all did quite well for the first round, you keep this up and we will have the best SWAT team in the state." JB: "you all got 50 rounds today, Monday you'll do 50 more as I want you all to do 1000 rounds by the end of the month; LJ, CR, and JR will be with you to make improvements, so your times and your accuracy will increase, I'm going to get maintenance when they're done getting the Park rides done. They are going to make a moving target that we can control the speed going back and forth so you learn to shoot moving targets but that's a month away."

JB: "that's enough for today; we will go back to the office and clean your rifles." They all got back in the vans and headed back to the office. They got back they all cleaned the rifles JB asked dad how he liked his scope. His dad said "it's going to improve my hunting; I've always been a little off in distance and wind." Hank: "I will write out a check for this scope, since we have to keep everything clean for accounting otherwise they'll be on us where we can't breathe." I bought enough rifles for SWAT and ourselves to use for SWAT missions, if or when any of us quit technically the rifle belongs to the park as it came out of our funds." Hank: "yes they are not listed as police property, the vans we own 50-50, so two are yours and two belong to the police department. JB: "what do you think of the shooting at the range today?" Hank: "I think you're doing a really good job, within 2 to 3 months I think we are going to have the best SWAT team in the state, if it isn't already."

Hank: "I forgot to tell you, two of the smaller towns want to know if they can call our SWAT team if they have problems, they heard what you did at the plaza and how it was handled, they said, they would've had more casualties than you did, they would've shot to kill the two gang leaders, they thought you did it cleaner than they would have."

JB: "well my old CO said we have taken out more terrorists this month than they have, and wished we were back."

Hank: "I bet he did, his loss is our gain, have a good weekend, I have to go home, the wife has things for me to do; bye." JB: "talk at you next week, bye." JB: "Mary, Curt, and Quincy I am very proud of you, you are doing fine work have a good weekend." Curt and Quincy left and headed for home. JB: "CR looks like your wife has got plans for you have a good weekend; and everybody laughed; LJ you have a good weekend, I'm going to see what Peggy is up to." JB: "let us go see what the girls are up to", he and JR headed for the big house. They got to the big house and walked in and there were Jennifer and Rose and the three boys sitting in the living room, JB thought they have a plan.

Jennifer said "we thought we should all go out to supper, we've had such a hectic week, you two get cleaned up, were already to go. JB looked at JR and said "I guess we better get cleaned up", and up the stairs they went. 20 minutes later they came back and JB says we have to walk the dogs before we go. Jennifer said "Rose and I already did that so you wouldn't have to, they are in their crates, they are good for the night." JB: "get in our van and we will go, what would you like to eat." Jennifer: "Rose and I are hungry for shrimp and the boys all want fish and chips and your dad told us there was a good fish place and you know where it is."

JB: "well if they have not moved it I know where it is", they all went out locked the door got in the van and off they went."

CR and Mary went to the jewelry store, and picked up her ring. Mary slipped it on her finger and said "it fits perfectly" she grabbed CR and hugged him, and they left the jewelry store. They went to Mary's house he got spot out of his van and went to her apartment. Mary got her dog and they went back outside took the dogs for a walk, 10 minutes later they were back. They went up to the apartment, turned the dogs loose and Mary grabbed him by the hand, and let him into the bedroom. She sat on the bed and took off her shoes and then her pants. CR said "I thought we were not going to have children for a while." She said "when I decided I was going to marry you I started to take the pill two weeks ago, I am yours forever." CR sat down beside her and took off his shoes, and took off his pants and leaned over and kissed her and she kissed him and he undid her shirt and took it off. She took off his shirt. He undid her bra and kissed her breasts tickled her neck with his tongue, she giggled and she pulled his underwear off and he pulled off hers and they fondled each other until they could not stand it any longer and made love passionately over and over again until they collapsed in each other's arms. And they fell asleep.

LJ got in his van and went to the diner. The diner was empty and Peggy came over and sat down. LJ: "Have a busy day?" Peggy: "Yes earlier it was a zoo and then it just slowed down and I got a lot of tips, Jeannie will be happy. The evening shift will be here soon, I've already swept the floor and cleaned the counter so we can leave at 4:30. LJ: "are you real hungry, and want to eat now or later?" Peggy: "I'm not that hungry," why?" LJ: "I thought we might go look at rings." Peggy: "I thought you said next week?" LJ: "I did but I looked at you and change my mind, your finger looked a little lonely." Peggy put her arms around his neck and kissed him.

LJ: "I hope you don't do that with all your customers." Peggy: "only the one I'm going to marry." Five minutes later the evening waitress came in and Peggy said "here are the tips and have a good evening." LJ and Peggy left and went to Peggy's house. They went in, Peggy quickly changed and they headed for the mall. The first jewelry store they came to was closed and said would be back at six. So they looked for another one, this one was open. The salesman said "what are you looking for necklaces, bracelets, or rings?" Peggy: "rings and wedding bands." The salesman brought out a box and there was one that was a set engagement ring a wedding band for the bride and the groom; it had a diamond in the center and two small blue sapphires on each side, the wedding bands each had three blue sapphires." Peggy asks "how much is this one?" LJ said "put it on first." Peggy put it on and said "that's really pretty."

LJ: "would you like that one?" Peggy: "yes, but I have to know how much it's going to cost first." Salesman said "it's 1500.00" LJ: "sounds good to me let's get them sized and we will take it." The salesman said "the jeweler that sizes the rings won't be in now until tomorrow morning, you could pick it up tomorrow afternoon." Peggy: "LJ that is too expensive." LJ: "let me ask you a question, how long are we going to stay married?" Peggy: "the rest of my life." LJ: "how long are you going to live?" Peggy: "here we go again, 70, 80, I'm not sure." LJ: "pick a number." Peggy: "70." LJ: "how old are you now?" Peggy: "25." LJ: "over 45 years in $1500 that's only $33 a year, I think I will more than get my money's worth." Peggy: "you and your logic, I love you." LJ: "write it up, I will pay you, and what time tomorrow do you recommend we pick it up." Salesman: "any time after 12:00." Salesman got the sizes for the rings, and filled out the invoice. LJ paid the man and they left.

Peggy: "you said we would discuss things we both had to agree." LJ: "we did, you said yes you liked it, and I like it, we both agreed." Peggy: "not on the price." LJ: "well we really didn't agree on that, I think you're worth more than that, I was thinking about spending 3000.00 because I think you're worth it." Peggy: "are you made of money?" LJ: "I have been looking for the girl of my dreams for 12 years, and when I find her, I want to spend a little money on her."

Peggy: "I would like us to live in a house instead of an apartment, and houses cost money, and you're spending all the money on my school and a ring, it scares me." LJ: "Peggy I have been saving money for 12 years, we are going to build the house based on the plans you pick out, and with the money I have saved I am going to invest in things to make us more money, so whatever happens I know I can take care of you, do you believe me?" Peggy: "you said you would never lie to me and yes I believe you."

LJ: "do you think I have your best interests at heart?" Peggy: "yes, you're giving me a skill that I can make a living with, whether you're around or not." LJ: "I live at the park for nothing, I make a very good income, and I can pay for your ring and give you the thousand dollars and still have money left over this month." Peggy: "I didn't know." LJ: "and that's my fault, I apologize for that, when I went over your expenses, I should've told you what my expenses are and how much I make and we wouldn't be having this conversation."

LJ: "I wanted you to marry me for me, not for how much money I had, is that wrong." Peggy: "no, it's just I've been scraping by barely making ends meet and it scared me when you are spending all this money on me." LJ: "if you want I will go in and cancel the ring, but if you really love that ring please let me buy it for you." Peggy: "you can because I love you and I want to make you happy, and if it makes you happy it's all right with me, I love you so much I want to make you happy as much as you want to make me happy." They hugged and kissed each other and LJ said "where do you want to have supper?"

Peggy: "I've been looking at regular food all day, how about Chinese?" LJ: "sounds good to me, love of my life." Peggy smiled, LJ opened the door she got in, LJ went around got in and they went to have Chinese. They took the buffet, laughed went back for seconds just had an all around good time. LJ paid the waiter and gave him a nice tip and he gave his fortune cookie to Peggy. She said "don't you want your fortune cookie?" LJ: "I don't need a fortune cookie I got you."

Peggy smiled gave LJ a big hug they went out got in the van and went to Peggy's house. LJ went over and sat on the couch Peggy locked the door and came over and sat beside him. LJ: "now that our relationship has gone a step farther, there are things that I haven't told you: I have been saving money for 11 years, so I would have enough money to start a business, build a house, or do something else with my life: I have a large sum of money in the bank, so let me handle the money okay?" Peggy: "okay." LJ: "JBs dad has adopted the three of us, as his sons, when he dies all four of us will own the park, I have no expenses other than eating, ammunition, and things I want, so until we get married will you let me handle the finances?"

Peggy: "yes, hold me and kiss me, I've missed you all day long." They hugged and kissed for a while and then LJ said "I have to go back to the park, I have to get up early and run, I will see you later tomorrow, they said goodbye and he went back to the park.

CHAPTER 31

MONDAY WEEK 5

JB got up put on his running clothes and went downstairs and JR was going for the door they went out together and waited for LJ and CR. JR said "I've had a lot of time to think I was in looking at the surveillance screens and I didn't see anything on the outside fence; there could be holes, or people could have cut a hole in places; I was going to take Shorty and go around all the fences." JB: "I don't want you to go alone, take a security guard with you, that way if you get too tired you got somebody to help you: when had you planned on doing this?"

JR: "either today or tomorrow." JB: "I think it's wide enough that you could go around on one of the gators, I think they mow back there so the weeds don't get too tall, let me check with maintenance because right now they're not using them, but still take a security guard with you; and maybe we should have covert cameras and have them checking for movement 24 seven because people shouldn't be back there, and I never even thought about that, you may not be 100% physically but you're still valuable, the three of us missed that."

LJ and CR came up from the spring house and JB said "JR said we should have cameras on the outside fence people could be cutting them and getting into the park and we would miss that." LJ and CR shook their heads yes in agreement. JR: "another thing I thought actually the kids gave me the idea we don't have any of the new fancy rides, I know it's too late for this year why don't we put out a box where people come in and give them some names of new rides they would like and see what the people want, a little survey."

JB: "we would have to raise the admission price, a day pass 25.00 and a season-ticket is100.00, a family season-ticket is 150.00." JR: "I did some checking on the Internet the cheapest I found was $35 most of them a single ticket is close to 50.00 and up, now they have newer rides than we do, I think we need to start upgrading a new ride or two every year for the next few years, and charge more for the tickets."

LJ: "is there room for us to expand?" JB: "I don't know, we need to talk to dad, we should talk to him later this morning, say around 9 o'clock." CR: "sounds good to me, let's run." They took off and started their run. They got back from their run and JR was sitting on the step, he said "I have a good job for the three kids, why don't we give them some paint and have them paint numbers on each fence post, so if there is a hole in the fence we know right where to go to fix it." LJ: "that's a great idea, it will give the kids responsibility and we can pay them a little money, and one of us will inspect them and get after them if they don't do a good job."

CR: "I will give one of them one of our radios so they can call security guards or us if necessary." JB: "Ben can take Sam along and that will give them some protection." JR: "I will see if I can get a gator and I will ride around and take some strips of cloth and if I find any tears or holes I will mark them and we will get them fixed." JB: "if you do go armed, have your vest on and I don't want you getting hurt anymore." LJ: "I think I'll go with him, he's got me curious." LJ and CR headed for the Springhouse, JB and JR went into the big house. Jennifer and Rose had breakfast ready and said "go get the kids and call LJ and CR and tell them we made enough for them." JR called LJ and said "Jennifer and Rose said they made enough breakfast for you and CR and come on up." LJ: "we will be up in five minutes." LJ and CR came in and sat down and three minutes later JB, JR, and the three boys came down and sat around the table.

Jennifer and Rose finished putting the food on the table and sat down. Jennifer said grace and they all begin to eat. They finished their breakfast and the three small boys cleared the table and the two women put what was left in the fridge. LJ said "JR when do you plan to go around the fence?" JR: "after we talked to dad." Rose: "upstairs I'm going to give you your castor oil pack before you do anything else." JB: "JR you got to look at it this way every time you get a castor oil pack that heals you a day sooner, that's what it did for me."

JR: "yes I know, the hospital said the earliest they thought I might leave is 3 ½ weeks, so Rose let's go upstairs and get it done." LJ: "I've been concentrating so much on the hill and the front gates that I completely forgot about the fence; at least one of us saw the whole picture."

CR: "that's a real good example of why we all brainstorm a mission and we are still alive." JB: "Amen to that, I'll call dad and have him come over in an hour and a half, if we are not growing we are dying and I don't think there's been a new ride in here for five or six years." CR: "it is too late for this year, but we could have one or two new ones by next year couldn't we?" JB: "Dad would know that better than I would, I just think he couldn't handle anything new, we are supposed to take the Park to the next level."

LJ: "we could put in one new one, and upgrade a couple old ones." JB: "I know that engineers calculate the G stress based on what I think 300 pounds is the biggest rider we can let on, and some rides like the new roller coasters even the old ones you have to check every morning before you could put people on, someone walks the whole thing on each side." CR: "we have a lot to learn and a short period of time to learn it in."

JB: "we have Betty, I think she knows everything." CR: "I hope so, we don't want to put a lot of pressure on your dad, and we can't have anything happen to him." They talked amongst themselves about the Park, about SWAT, until JB's dad came. JB: "Dad do they mow around the outside fence?" Dad: "not until the second or third week after we've opened, there's too much going on." JB: "JR thinks we should check the fence all the way around the park, and put surveillance cameras up and see if people are getting through the fence during the day and at night."

Dad: "I thought about that from time to time but I was so busy I just never had time to follow through, but that's a good idea." LJ: "we were thinking about putting in a new ride and upgrade a couple of the old ones, and see if that would draw in more people." Dad: "I had a man come in and give me some quotes on some upgrades and a new ride I thought he called one the corkscrew, but I just didn't feel good enough to pursue it." JB: "how long did he say it would take to install it?" Dad: "nine months." CR: "so it would be done for opening next year?" Dad: "yes, and the young kids come back three or four times a year minimum to ride it, he said the parks they put it in they sold more season tickets, and condiments, snacks, and food sales increased by 30 to 40%, now that there is four of you, one of you can keep track of that and the rest of you run the park." LJ: "did he say anything about upgrading some of the old rides?" Dad: "yes he did, one would only take two to three weeks." LJ: "how much notice did he need?"

Dad: "he said one week, but that was last year, I don't know about this year, it depends on how busy he is; Betty has his number, she can call him tomorrow and find out." JB: "do we have enough money to do that?" Dad: "yes the bank has wanted me to upgrade rides and put in some new ones, and I have 2 million and a half left from last year, even with all the extra spending we can run the park for 6 to 8 weeks without touching any of the new money coming in." JB: "are we the only amusement park within 300 miles?"

Dad: "yes we are and our gross receipts are pretty good so the bank loves us, they have always given me what I've asked for." JB: "one more question do the four wheelers fit between the rides and the outside fence?" Dad: "I believe they do, you can ask anybody in maintenance, why?" LJ: "JR and I want to check the fence out, we got bad feelings." Dad: "with all that's gone on lately, it's probably a good idea, better safe than sorry, we don't want any more surprises like we've had."

JB: "that's all we wanted to run by you, meeting over, unless you have something we need to know." Dad: "No you guys are doing a real good job I'm proud of all of you." LJ and JR left for maintenance, when they got there no one was around but they saw one of the gators and the keys were in it, they put their dogs in the back and they headed for the main gate started around the fence. The fence seem to be in real good shape and they drove slowly on for 10 minutes they had passed by 4 rides and JR said "there's a hole they stopped, there's a footprint going in I don't see one coming out."

LJ called JB and said "we got a whole footprint coming in, will advise." LJ got his dog JR got his, LJ took his dog to the footprint said "search" and pointed the dog the direction he wanted to go, the dog smelled and started walking JR did the same thing and his dog started going. 20 feet later the dog growled LJ pulled his gun and said "stand up with your hands up or I am going to start to shoot, I will only say it once you got two seconds." JR moved up beside him and his gun was out. A man stood up with his hands up said "don't shoot," and four other men stood up. LJ: "you are trespassing on private property I want all of you to put your hands up the man with his hands up said something in Spanish and the other four put their hands up. JR called and said "we have five men, bring handcuffs, and do we have somebody that speaks Spanish?"

JB: "CR will get the handcuffs and I'll check with security and see if any of the guards speak Spanish." Security had been listening to his radio and said "Jimmy speaks Spanish but he's off." JB: "call him tell him to have his vest on I don't care what else just get dressed and be here in 15 minutes and he's on overtime."

Security: "right away." CR got spare keys for the vans as each one had two pairs of handcuffs he grabbed them and he and JB started into the park, security said "they are at the whirligig." JB: "thanks" and he and CR started to run. They came around the bend and saw LJ and JR with guns drawn. CR: "put your hands behind your back." The man didn't move. JR: "tell that man to put his hands behind his back. The leader said something in Spanish and the man put his hands behind his back, CR told the man:" tell him to lie down." The man knelt down and CR helped him lean forward. He went to the next man he put his hands behind his back CR cuffed him and he kneeled down and did the same thing to the other two men. CR looked at the leader and said "put your hands behind your back", he did as he was told and said "I want a lawyer." LJ: "so far you have not been charged with anything, so you don't need a lawyer, as far as I know you have either kidnapped these men, or you are smuggling illegal's into the country."

JB got out his phone and called Hank. Hank answered "hello what's up?" "I need the rest of SWAT out here and I need the patrol cars I got four illegal's and the man that brought them in, and he's probably illegal to." JB informed him.

Hank: "they'll be there as quick as I can get them there 15 minutes tops." JB: "thanks, bye."

JR said "I'll go get the gator and see if I can drive it around this ride and put a flag on the fence." JB, CR, and LJ got behind the men and JB: "start walking to your left down the path and tell the other four to do the same thing, and tell them if they start to run I will turn the dogs loose, and that won't be fun." The leader said something in Spanish, and they continued to walk. They got to the office and said "you sit down and tell the other four to do the same thing." He complied and the other four sat down. 10 minutes later Mary pulled up and got out with her dog. Five minutes later Curt pulled up, a minute later Quincy was there. JB: "I have a security guard coming who speaks Spanish; I don't think we can trust this one here."

They heard somebody running and turned and Jimmy was coming around the bend, JB noticed that he had lost some weight. Jimmy was breathing a little heavy but not bad and said "what do you want me to do." LJ grabbed the English-speaking leader and took him around the bend where he couldn't hear what was going on.

JB looked at Jimmy and said "ask them in Spanish what they're doing here." Jimmy spoke to them in Spanish, and they answered him. Jimmy: "they said they paid a lot of money, and were promised jobs here in America." JB: "tell them they were lied to and when they get home tell their friends that these men robbed them and are criminals, they must come in the right way and get green cards and they need to learn English, then I would give them jobs."

Jimmy spoke to them, and they answered back and shook their heads. Jimmy: "they said it took them two years to get the money together and now it's gone, and they want to know if you're going to put them in jail." JB: "yes they're going to jail but then they're going to be deported back to Mexico." Jimmy spoke to them again and they hung their heads. A squad and the large van pulled up. Sgt. Said "well at least you didn't shoot any of these, I'm getting tired of going to the ER" and he laughed.

JB: "they did what they were told and they did not give us any trouble, do you need Jimmy as an interpreter?"

Sgt.: "No we got one at the station so we should be all right."

JB:"take the leader, in your car and keep him separate from the other four, he has robbed them of two years of savings." Sgt.: "Okay he may have to fall down a time or two, resisting." Jimmy's spoke to the four and they started walking toward the big van. Sgt. said thank you and they loaded them up and were gone.

JR looked at Jimmy and said: "good work I'm proud of you and you've lost some weight." Jimmy: "yes I've been doing the exercises in the morning and in the evening." JB: "you keep that up and you'll be running with us in the morning." Jimmy smiled. JB: "we're going to take the dogs and were going to completely walk around the park and see if the dogs find anyone else hiding here, and we may need you to translate, is that all right with you." Jimmy: "yes that's fine, and I would do it if you didn't pay me." JB: "thank you, but you're working on your day off and I don't mind paying you double time."

JB: "JR you take Jimmy with you to keep running the fence that way if you run into any illegal's he can translate, and if we need him, we will call you." JR: "okay Jimmy up in the gator" and they headed back toward the fence. JB went into the office got a map of the park and came back out. LJ and Curt you take the first path here to the right all the way around the park until you come up to the other parking lot, CR and Mary you take the path left of them and you do the same thing I will take the third path since I could only work one side at a time I will go around all the way and come back all the way LJ and Curt you will take the path to the right of the one that I am on and you will go back and check that path CR and Mary you will take the one on the right of that and come back and run through that one that will leave one path left, the connecting paths run through them until you hit the next path and then go back we should be able to get this done in a couple hours." LJ: "Curt and I will take the last path." They left and two hours later they had covered the whole Park and JR and Jimmy were waiting for them at the office. JR: "we found one more hole in the fence and marked it with a flag."

JB: "Curt thank you very much, we appreciate the help and you can go we are done for the day unless we get a SWAT call." Curt said "bye, and have a good day" he got in his van and left. JB: "Quincy you can leave to and you have a nice day." Quincy said "goodbye and I'll see you at the pistol range tomorrow" he got in his car and left. JB hit the mike on his radio and said "CR and Mary when you get done come to the big house." JR: "Jimmy if you want you can come with us and have lunch."

Jimmy: "I would like that very much thank you." And they went to the big house.

JB: "everybody this is Jimmy he's in here today because he speaks Spanish and he was a great help today." Everybody said hi and told him their names. Jimmy went over to Jennifer and said "I was a real jerk; I hope you will forgive me?" Jennifer: "you were forgiven a long time ago." Jimmy: "thank you." Jennifer said "get another chair and plate for Jimmy." CR and Mary came in grabbed a chair and sat down at the table. Jennifer said grace and they all started to eat.

JB: "Jimmy did a good job today, I'm very pleased, I am putting you in for three hours overtime and double your normal rate, next week I am going to see about getting the police GYM where they have pads on the floor and we will start hand to hand combat, I will let you know and you can let the rest of the security guards know a week from this Friday another Navy seal is coming in and he will be in charge of all the security guards, and you will be his number two; listen to him he will teach you a lot, he's pretty good he has been on missions with us, you're free to go and thank you very much you did a good job here today."

Jimmy: "Thank you and I will keep on with my training, I will get to your morning run, and I will keep doing one in the morning, one when I get home from work and one before I go to bed." JB: "two is enough if you do one before you go to sleep you will have trouble getting to sleep so just stick with what you're doing, it is working." Jimmy: "okay, thank you very much, bye" and he went out got in his car and left.

JR: "what is his story?" JB: "he actually got Jennifer and I back together, he and a couple of his buddies were being real jerks and I straighten them out, a week ago he came into the office told me he wanted to turn his life around, he had been a real jerk and he wanted to improve himself and get in better shape; so I gave him our exercise routine and told him when he can do 3 miles in 20 minutes and not be completely winded he could do exercises with us in the morning and that's the goal he shooting for and the 50 push-ups, and the hundred crunches." CR: "it looks like he's losing weight and put on-muscle, we will see, I will keep my eye on him."

JB: "I told him when he got where he could run with us we would take him up to the pistol range and teach him how to shoot, he said he thinks he might like to join the police force, so we will help him along, I will call him in tomorrow and warn him, as he is very unsure of himself, his dad is a poor father figure, and is an alcoholic." CR: "Mary let's you and I go, we have things to talk about." They said "goodbye" and left. JR: "when we were out on the gator he found some twine laying on the floor and he wrapped it around the fence and pulled it back together as a temporary fix, and did the same with the other one, to me that shows promise he started to use his head."

LJ: "I've seen him out in the park, and the others are kind of wondering around, where he checks things out, he is probably the best of the bunch now." JB: "this is probably the first time in his life when he has actually had a plan and a goal in mind." They all agreed. LJ: "I think I will go and pick up Peggy's ring." JR: "over the top of the hill, getting serious." LJ: "I'm supporting her and putting her through school, so she can feel good about herself, and if something happens to me she can take care of herself." JR: "that's why I'm glad JB gave Rose a job here at the park, I know he would take care of her if something happened to me, but this way she will feel she can make her own way."

JB: "Jennifer is the same way she was supporting herself before we got back together, she can do it again." JB: "I have been thinking what if we load some of the brass, so the rubber bullets don't come out as fast and actually shoot each other with a rubber bullet, so when they make a mistake, they really know they made a mistake'. JR: "I think that has merit, we need to run that by CR." LJ : "I think that's a real good idea, we may be able to buy some already that way, which would save us a lot of time, I will check on that tomorrow, and I will see you tomorrow goodbye."

JB: "I called maintenance and told them about the fence, and they said when they could break a man free and they would send him over to fix it, and if he went into overtime we would pay over time, so the fence will be fixed today." JR: "for a day off it was sure pretty busy." JB: "we better go and spend some time with the girls and the boys." JR: "I am surprised they haven't come and got us earlier." They went to find their families.

LJ got in his van and went to the jewelers and picked up the rings. Then he went to the diner, to get a cup of coffee a piece of pie and officially give Peggy her ring and ask her to marry him. LJ called Peggy and said he was on his way to the diner. He parked in front of the diner. Went in to his normal spot, and sat facing the door. Peggy saw him grabbed a cup of coffee and came over. LJ: "could you bring me a piece of coconut pie and talk a minute." Peggy said "yes to both." She went and got the pie and came back and sat down.

LJ: "Peggy will you be my wife?" Peggy: "of course I will I thought you knew that." LJ reached into his pocket pulled out the ring case opened it up and said "give me your ring finger left hand and he put the ring on it, now its official." She went over and sat beside him and kissed him and he kissed her. Alice came out and said "what's going on over here." Peggy showed her hand and said "it's official now." And Alice said "I am so glad and happy for you." LJ: "we had a little excitement at the park today, we got four illegal's and the person that brought them, and they were hiding in the park."

Peggy: "what will happen to them?"

LJ: "right now they're in jail but they will call ice and they will be deported to Mexico and the one that brought them here will go to prison." LJ: "they broke the law to get here, what laws will they break now that they're here, every time you do something you shouldn't it keeps getting easier and easier every time you do it; they saved up for two years, and the man stole it from them, had they used that money to learn English and apply for a visa, they might've had much better luck depending on what skills they have."

Peggy: "I feel sorry for them." LJ: "let us say a pretty illegal Mexican girl came in here, and your boss gave her your job because she would work for half of what they're paying you, would you like that." Peggy: "no, I wouldn't, I never thought of that." LJ finished his pie and said "what do you want to do?"

Peggy: "take me home so I can change." LJ: "I will go out and let Mike relieve himself and wait for you in the van." LJ got up and left, Peggy went into the kitchen. LJ opened the back of the van got Mike out of his crate and walked out behind the diner, Mike relieved himself and LJ put him back in his crate got in the van and waited for Peggy. Peggy came out a couple of minutes later and said "I will get my car and meet you at my place." LJ waited for her to pull out and then he followed her." They parked in front of her apartment and LJ got Mike out and they went upstairs to Peggy's apartment. They went in and Peggy said "I'm going to change." A few minutes later she said "would you come in and shut the door." LJ: "sure", he got up went in and saw Peggy laying in bed with nothing on, he shut the door, undressed lay down next to her, and they started kissing and exploring each other's body's and then made love. LJ: "that was better than supper." Peggy: "I agree and this is a smorgasbord I want seconds." They started kissing again and again and made love again." They laid in each other's arms and LJ kissed her neck kissed her breasts kissed her stomach back to her breasts she grabbed him and they made love again, and fell asleep.

CHAPTER 32

TUESDAY WEEK 5

LJ woke up, leaned over kissed Peggy, got out of bed dressed went in the next room put the leash on Mike and headed for the park, he had 15 minutes to get there. He got there just as JB and JR came out of the house, CR was coming up the path and they all started there run, and they were back in 21 minutes. CR and LJ headed for the Springhouse, JR and JB went back in the big house. CR and LJ went to the big house and went in; Jennifer and Rose are making breakfast and said "were making enough for all, if you want to stay." LJ said "we don't want to make extra work for you, but we will be happy to." Rose: "we don't mind, and we enjoy your company."

JB and JR and the three boys came down, everyone sat down and enjoyed their breakfast. JB: "I'm going to take Jennifer to work and the boys to school and then I'll be back, then we need to get the swat team here and run them through house clearing, and JR are there some practice runs that we can let them do first?" JR: "yes, I was going to mention that when you got up there, I have a couple that we can run them through before the test program, and the manual said if they get down below 12 minutes you can start them on the next program."

JB: "we need to talk about that when I get back, Jennifer and boys to the van", JB put the leash on Sam and put him in the back of the van, the boys jumped in the back Jennifer got in the front and they left."

JB dropped the boys off, and watched till they went in the door, then headed for the hospital. JB said "LJ wasn't late, but I don't know about this relationship he has."

Jennifer: "why I think neither one of them has dated much, Peggy said she hadn't as she thought they only wanted one thing, and that's not what she wanted, I think LJ was the first guy that wanted more than just a one night stand." JB: "I know he said he wanted to find somebody that wanted a lasting relationship." Jennifer: "give them time and I think it will all work out, they'll be married in less than a year, and I think it will last."

JB: "he missed one run, but this morning he made it on time." Jennifer: "has it affected his work?" JB: "no, he's always at the top of his game." Jennifer: "just be patient and suffer through it, push comes to shove you know he'll be there no matter what." JB: "I never doubted that." She leaned over and they kissed and he dropped her off at the hospital and headed to the police station. He went in and said is Hank available?" Sgt. at the desk said "yes go on back."

JB went back knocked on Hanks door. Hank said come in and he went in. Hank: "what's up?" JB: "can we use the police stations gym as I want to start hand to hand combat training for SWAT and the security guards; we need mats so they don't get hurt." Hank: "sure can my guys come?" JB: "of course, you and your wife and kids if you want, everybody should know self-defense." Hank: "I don't know if she'd come, the kids would love it." JB: "we could pair her with Mary to start with, but then I like to pair them with men, so they don't freak out if they have to defend themselves from a male." Hank: "I'll try to talk her into it."

JB: "here I have a chart of the training I have laid out for SWAT and my security guards, in the afternoon for guards that worked nights and in the evening for guards that work during the day." Hank: "that's a pretty busy schedule." JB: "yes it is, but we have two weeks until the park opens and then the four of us can't be on the training schedules, but we will have the other seal which outside of overseeing the security guards will have more leeway on training." JB: "on Saturdays I mixed the training with police and SWAT both, so they get to know us and we will know who is serious and who isn't."

Hank: "why the security guards?" JB: "they don't get the kind of training that I want them to have in the park, and one of my guys is real serious and he is training hard and thinks he might like to join your police force." Hank: "if we steal him away from you will you be mad?"

JB: "no, I never want to interfere with somebody trying to better himself, and if he doesn't come back your gain my loss." Hank: "you're going to change the schedule in two weeks."

SWAT and police training

Hand to hand combat training

	Monday	Tuesday	Wednesday	Thursday	Friday	Saturday
SWAT						Practice
	PS 10:00 AM		10:00 AM		10:00 AM	PS 10:00 AM
Police and security guards						
	PS	10:00 AM		10:00 AM		10:00 AM
House Clearing SWAT				Practice		
	PK	9:00 AM	9:00 AM		9:00 AM	10:00 AM
House Clearing police						
	PK	9:00 AM	9:00 AM		10:00 AM	
Dog Training SWAT						
	PK	10:00AM	10:00 AM		10:00 AM	
Pistol Range Swat						
	PK	1:00 PM	1:00 PM		1:00 PM	1:00 PM
Pistol Range police						
	PK	1:00 PM	1:00 PM		1:00 PM	
Rifle Range swat						
	PK 2:00 PM	2:00 PM			2:00 PM	2:00 PM

Rifle Range police

PK   2:00 PM   2:00 PM   2:00 PM

Security guards and Hand to Hand combat training

PS 7:00 PM   7:00 PM   7:00 PM

JB: "Yes, I will know who's serious and who isn't, and I told the guards if they didn't show up they would be replaced, they were not going to sit around on their butts and do nothing, the one I told you about, his name is Jimmy, four weeks ago he was a real jerk, now he's using his head, is trying to be helpful, and is really trying to improve himself he's going to be second in command over the security guards, and he will be able to fire them from the park in the next four weeks if he keeps going like he is." Hank: "you must be high on him?" JB: "he is a different person than the one I first met, I was ready to stuff him in a trashcan, now I'm proud of him, and he gives more than is ask."

Hank: "I'm going to miss Curt, Mary, and Quincy; they are some of my better officers." JB: "you're right, we are real happy with them without the extra training they have performed outstandingly, we might lose Mary because I think she and CR will be married within the next year, if not the next six months; but we have a training facility and we should be able to re-train her dog with Quincy because, the dog knows him."

Hank: "I like the way you think, I will send the three out as I assume that chart starts today." JB: "yes it does, I want to get as much training on them as I can before the park opens; but we will all leave the park for a SWAT call no matter what we are doing." Hank: "I never thought for a minute you wouldn't, is that all we need to go over?" JB: "yes it is, I will keep in touch and stop up and watch if you want, goodbye."

JB left and went to the park. Three of the four swat vans were lined up, JB was pleased. Betty said "these are the two brothers who are going to expand our office and put up the holding building." JB shook their hand and said "do you have plans for us?" Betty said "the man on the left is William and the one on the right is John." William said "I looked your building over and based on what Betty said here is a rough sketch." JB: "have you showed this to the other three?" William said "yes." JB: "what did they say?" William: "they thought it looked good." JB: "then build it." William: "I wish you would look at it, we don't want to build it and have you unhappy." JB: "they are my partners, if they all agree I will agree now go ahead and build it, and do you have plans for the holding area." I showed them to the other three and they liked the four room plan, better than the three rooms."

JB: "did they say why?" William: "they thought it would be better to separate people to be by themselves." JB: "cell doors will not have a way of opening from the inside." William: "we were going to put deadbolts in and a separate handle on the outside, you have to have a key to get in and out." JB: "is there going to be a window in each door?" William: "yes, and there will be a security camera in the corner of the room that will be surrounded by bulletproof glass, so they should not be able to break the camera."

JB: "did the others asked the same questions?" William: "yes they did." JB: "did they tell you to build it?" William: "yes they did." JB: "I will let you get to work then." JB: "if anyone of them see something that he wants changed, we would all not have to agree, so if one of us says to change something, go ahead and do it." William said "all right we should have the lumber by 10 and we will start digging the holes now for the main supports, and thank you." William and John left and they could hear a machine starting up. Betty: "they had already staked out the plan, in case you liked it, they have had people in the past say they all had liked it and made them change, so they had to do more than they had figured or they wanted a discount for something that wasn't the way they wanted it, I told them you were not like that and that you all were in charge."

JB: "I don't blame him, there's a lot of people out there like that agree to something and then want to change it." JB:"JR you better get up there and warm up the clearinghouse; Mary, Curt, and Quincy will be there at 9:00, CR when they're done you and Mary need to set up dog training and we all need to run our dogs through, then you and Mary can run through after were done; then we'll go to the diner for lunch".

LJ: "I'm going to follow Quincy through and see if I can improve his time." JB: "Rose would you have Jimmy called to the office, I need to talk to him." Rose went to the security room a minute later she came back and said " he's on his way." A minute later Jimmy came in. JR: "noticed he wasn't breathing too hard, and said "did you run?" Jimmy: "yes sir, you said whenever we were called to run."

JB: "come over here and sit down." They went over JB sat behind a desk and Jimmy sat in front. JB: "you're doing real well, we all noticed it and you did good this weekend, so I wanted to warn you that we are going to push you, to help you get even better quicker; we may come up to you and say give me 20 push-ups, or 25, or 30; or run with me a bit and you keep up, then we can tell your rate of progression and give you some monitored exercise." JB: "do you have any thoughts on that?" Jimmy: "I hope I'm up to that." JB: "Where are you at on your running?"

Jimmy: "I have 2 miles in 11 minutes, and I was going to go up to two 2 ¼ tomorrow." JB: "how many push-ups are you doing?" Jimmy: "15." JB stood up and said "let me see you do 15." Jimmy got up dropped to the floor pushed his arms up straightened his back and went down up down up, and he reached 14, JB said "make that 20." Jimmy did six more; the last two were a little slow." JB: "That was very good and you do a nice flat back, keep up the good work." Jimmy: "thank you sir, I will do my best." JB: "Jimmy the secret is do until you drop or die, never quit and you'll get out of life what you want; that's what my dad told me, now I'm telling you." Jimmy got up said "thank you, was there anything else?" JB: "yes, you have hand-to-hand combat training tonight at 7:00 PM, tell the other guards; also get a gator and check the outside fence at least once a week; and you can go back to work and the four of us are proud of you so far." Jimmy turned and left. After

Jimmy had left Rose looked at JB and said "that was nice of you to say to him." JB: "Rose, I was not being nice, I was being factual, but we will push him because we think he has real potential." "If he doesn't quit, he will get out of life what he wants."

"I'm going up on the hill and see how things are going, call if you need me." JB got in his van and drove up to the house clearing building. JR said "Mary got to go first today and her time was 12:40; Quincy is now doing his run." Quincy got done and JR said 12:45." Now Curt's turn. Curt went to the starting line JR said go and he was off. Curt finished and JR said "12:33, there pulling up on him, I think the next times will all be under 12."

JB: "did JR tell you he has some practice runs that you could go through." They all said yes. Mary: "could I run one now then CR and I can go set up the dog training?" JR: "sure you can the program is ready, load up your gun, you'll need 20 rounds." JR said "it's ready to go." JR: "she just finished, not bad 15 minutes, the normal rookie is 16, and she may knock 30 to 45 seconds off the next run." Quincy said "he'd like to make a test run." JR set him up and away he went. CR said "Mary we better go, we have work to do." She grabbed his arm and they went to the van and drove to the dog training facility. They went inside and got to work, their manual told them where to hide for the first 10 runs from then on they could put it anywhere. They set up the first run, and they were ready to go.

CR said "JR I will walk with you on the first time through in case you have any trouble, I know you've looked at the DVDs." CR "start." JR and Shorty started down the path 10 feet down he turned right sniffed and sat down. CR: "what do you think just happened?" JR: "there's a gun here somewhere." CR: "now you need to look around for the gun." JR looked under things and quickly found the gun.

CR: "during the test, you don't retrieve the gun leave it for the next person down the path." JR started again Shorty was in front of him kind of going from left to right, right to left 15 feet farther down the trail he went over to the left and sat down. JR looked and found the gun, covered it back up and went farther down the trail 30 feet down the trail Shorty turned to the left and sat down, JR looked around on the ground and found nothing there was some boards leaning up against a wall and he moved them and there was a rifle, put the board back and started again. They went around the turn and Shorty turned right and went in a short path and sat and looked on the ground he looked behind things couldn't find anything, he looked around again and he saw a container with a box on top he took the box off of the container opened the lid and there was a gun inside, he put the lid back on, and put the box back up and continued on CR checked off another box on the scorecard.

They went all most to the front and Shorty turned right and sat down, JR found the gun wedged behind two cans. JR stood up and Shorty didn't move, JR said gun Shorty turned left and sat down. JR went over and looked in front of Shorty and he was sitting right in front of a garbage can JR looked inside it was empty so he tipped it up and there was the gun underneath. JR started Shorty down the path again and he went all the way to the end. CR came up and said "JR your dog did 100% pat him he deserves it and you should have padded him every time he found a gun, you did excellent on your first time through.

Mary said "Quincy have you seen the videos on the dogs?" Quincy no but I saw what JR's dog did." Mary: "the commands are Gun, Bomb, and search." Quincy said "Gun." Mary's dog started down the trail, he found the first gun second and third the fourth and so forth until he got to the end. CR "nip got 100%."

Quincy said "these dogs are really something, and he's already saved your life hasn't he Mary." Mary: "yes he has and CR's to."

JB: "took Sam through, and he got 100%." Then Curt went through with tuck and he got hundred percent. Then LJ went through with Mike and he got 100%. Then CR went through with spot and he got hundred percent.

CR said "JR, Quincy, this is the first test we went through with our dogs on the first day, it's to get familiar with the dog, and the dog with you." JB: "well it's time we go to lunch and then we will come back to the pistol range." They all put their dogs in their crates and went to the diner. They ordered their food and halfway through JB called Betty and Rose and gave the phone to the waitress and she took their orders. The waitress brought the take out and their bills, and they paid and left her a nice tip and left.

JB: "I will drop these off to Betty and Rose and meet you at the pistol range. They all left, JB delivered the take out to the office and went to the pistol range. CR took Mary, LJ paired up with Curt, and JB paired up with Quincy. They did dry fire drawing and aiming for 20 minutes then they did shooting, then CR, LJ, and JB went over the targets with their partners.

JB said "we need to go to the rifle range and do our shooting, 25 shots at 30 yards 15 shots at 50, and 10 at 100." They each grabbed their targets started to load up. JB's phone rang and he answered, it was Betty she said he and LJ needed to get to the office quickly. JB: "told CR and JR they were in charge of rifle shooting today LJ and I have to go to the office."

CR: "a problem?"

JB: "I'm not sure but she said it was urgent, has to do with LJ, we will be back later." LJ: "I had another vision, it was six Arab assassins, and I was going to tell you later." JB: "no I don't think it's that or Betty would have mentioned Siham's name, I think it's something else."

LJ gave JR his keys and said "I'll see you later." JB and LJ got in his van and went to the office. They went into the office and Betty said "this is John Larry Nelson; he says he is LJ's brother." LJ: "mom told me that he had remarried and had another son." John said "I have my birth certificate, if you want to see it."

LJ: "no you kind of look like him, I will take your word for it." John: "I wanted to meet you, and get to know you and I was thinking about joining the Navy." LJ: "I got out because the Navy wasn't the Navy I joined it changed; so I don't know how good I could be to help you make a decision." John: "I also came here on behalf of my father."

LJ: "we didn't part on good terms; I left him lying on the floor." JB: "would you two like to discuss this in the conference room sounds like personal business." LJ: "no this is fine, what does he want?" John: "he hasn't had a drink since that day; he checked himself into a rehab center and turned his life around." LJ: "how has he treated you?" John: "He paddled me a few times, but he never beat me, he told me how he had beaten you when he was drunk and that he was ashamed of himself."

LJ: "what does he want to tell me he's sorry, tell him you told me, and that I don't have time to go see him and I wouldn't anyway as I'm way too busy here."

John: "he thought you might say that, so I brought him with me, his liver is failing and they give him two months to live, he can't walk he is in a wheelchair and he is ashamed of himself for the way he treated you and your mother, and he hoped you might forgive him."

LJ: "has he beaten your mother." John: "no and he told her what he did to you two, and how ashamed he was for being so cruel, he called your mother last month and ask her if she would forgive him and she said yes; he ask her if she thought you would forgive him and she said she did not know, that you had never mentioned him after the two of you left, and she said how nice your stepdad treated you and you called him father.

JB: "LJ lets you and I go in the conference room." LJ: "okay, we will be right back." They went in the conference room and close the door." LJ: "I told you what happened between me and my dad and my mom, but what I didn't tell you is that I would have beaten him to death if she had not stopped me, I was ashamed as I felt I had become him, and I've been very careful never to lose my temper again."

JB: "if our positions were reversed and with what you told me I would have done what you did." LJ: "I don't know I'm too close, those feelings are welling up." JB: "I think you should go see him and tell him you forgive him, not for him but for you." LJ was quiet for three minutes then said "you may be right; it may have affected my performance."

JB: "it did in a good way, instead of killing some of these people we were after you wounded them instead and we were able to interrogate them, deep down you didn't want to cross that line unless you had to, and when you had to you did; you've always performed excellent." LJ: "you may be right, and I think for John's sake I should and it will probably be good for me also." JB: "you ready to go back out?"

LJ: "yes and I want you to come with me." JB: "I would be honored to." They went back into the other room. JB: "why don't we go to the motel, and LJ and I think you should get Peggy and we will all go to supper together, the four of us?" John: "that sounds fine to me, I will go get dad dressed and I will follow you to the restaurant. John got up and held his hand out to shake hands with LJ they shook hands and John turned and left. LJ: "I told you a little but there was a lot I left out, I just didn't want to go there." JB: "that's fine, I know who you are and what you are, my brother, I trust you with my life, and you trust me with yours, enough said."

LJ: "I better go tell Peggy what's going on, tell her to go home and change and I'll meet her at the motel." LJ drove to the spring house, called Peggy and told her to go home and change she was going to meet his half-brother he just found out about; he went in and showered shaved, changed his cloths and headed to the motel. JB called CR and told him he and JR would need to be at the police gym by 3:45 to train SWAT in hand-to-hand and 6:45 to train security guards, LJ and I have some personal business to take care of, he will fill you in later."

JB called Jennifer and told her what was going on and he would see her when he got home later and he would not be there for supper and he went to the big house and changed. He met LJ at the motel at 5:30. JB and LJ went to the second floor and looked at the arrows on the wall turned right and halfway down the hallway they came to the room LJ knocked on the door, and John came and let them in. LJ looked at the man in the wheelchair and he did not look like the man he knew, he was shriveled and was probably 125 pounds instead of the 250 he had known when he was 13.

The man in the wheelchair looked up and said "what a fine looking man you have grown up to be, thank your father for me, and I would like you to forgive the man you knew when you were younger, I am so ashamed of what I did to you and your mother, she has forgiven me and I hope you can do the same he said in a shaky voice." LJ: "I have hated you for a long time, since I have gotten older I understand you had a disease called alcoholism, and I do forgive you and I am glad to meet the brother I didn't know I had."

The man in the wheelchair started to cry and said "thank you I never thought I would hear that, now I can die in peace." John grabbed LJ's hand and thanked him and said "you don't know what this means to me and dad." LJ: "I think this was good for all of us, now I have a surprise for you; I am going to introduce you to my fiancé, she should be here any time now I will go back down and get her and bring her back up."

LJ went down and Peggy was pulling up, he went over and opened her door she got out and he filled her in on all that had transpired. I will tell you more later but right now I'm going to introduce you to my real father, and the half-brother that I didn't know existed until an hour and a half ago. They went upstairs and LJ knocked at the door and John opened it, LJ and Peggy went in John closed the door and they all stood in front of the man in the wheelchair. LJ: "father I want you to meet my fiancée Peggy, Peggy this is my father", Peggy reached out and grabbed his hand and said "I am pleased to meet you." The man in the chair started to cry.

LJ: "Peggy this is my brother John, John this is my fiancée Peggy."
John said "this meeting is beyond our wildest dreams, thank you
so much." JB: "John does your dad have a special diet or can he eat
anything?" John: "at home we feed him soup with just a little meat
mostly vegetables and we run it through a blender so it's kind of
predigested for him."

Peggy: "why don't we go to the diner and I will run his food through
the blender." John thought that would be fine, they left the room and
John took his dad to the van and he had a lift to take the wheelchair
up and the front bench seat had been removed, he backed his dad in
locked the wheels put a strap around his dad in the wheelchair. John
said "I will follow you, please don't drive too fast." JB called Jennifer
and told her to meet them at the diner and have his dad bring her and
he would bring her home."

They drove to the diner and JB said "get our seats where we can
see out and I called Jennifer as I thought it might be good to have a
trained nurse in case he has a problem." LJ: "It is probably a good idea
that is not the man I knew as a child, I am glad I came." 10 minutes
later Jennifer arrived and they went in, JB introduced Jennifer to
John and his father he got a chair for her and set her with her back to
the door and he sat on the other side John sat on the end of the table
where he could help his dad." Peggy went back into the kitchen to
see what soup was left, there was a little vegetable soup but there was
more of the potato cheese soup. She went back and told John and his
dad what the options were. John said "dad cannot have any alcohol."
Jennifer: "the alcohol is all cooked off in the cooking there is nothing
but a little beer flavor left."

John: "he will have the vegetable and if you can liquefy it that would
be better."

Peggy said "they have a Vita mix it will turn everything into a
liquid." John said "thank you." Peggy went in and mixed the vegetable
soup up and brought it out for him to eat. John took a spoon and fed

his dad. The waitress came out and she took their orders, JB said "give me the check for everything, the waitress said she would and left." John ask "LJ and JB what they did as seals?" JB: "the four of us are snipers LJ and myself are rated for 1200 yards CR and JR are rated at 600 yards we have a lot of the same skills but we all have different skills JR is good at dismantling bombs, CR is good at infiltration, LJ has medical experience and is good at interrogation, I am good at minor medical and that's all I can tell you about us, basically we rescued good people and we eliminated bad people."

John: "were all your missions classified?"

LJ: "yes that's why we can't talk about them, other than some were easy and some were quite dangerous."

John: "that sounds exciting." LJ saw the look on his father's face and he said "if I had it to do all over again I would not have joined the Navy, now it is for sure I would not join the Navy, it's not as it was when we first joined up, and that is why we all got out, other than JB's father got ill and he had to come home, we've been together for 10 years and we wanted to stay together the rest of our lives as brothers."

John: "maybe I'll have to rethink my plans."

LJ: "what do you like?"

John: "I like electronic gadgets and computers."

LJ: "have you got money for school, and what is your grade average."

John: "just a little but I think I can get a football scholarship as a wide receiver, or I was a pretty good forward on our basketball team."

LJ: "if I was in your position knowing what I know now I would get my college degree in computers, robotics, or electronic circuitry, and robots are turning up everywhere so you would be in demand."

JB: "do you take care of your father all the time or does your mother."

John: "mother was going to take care of him during the day so I could get a job to make money for college." JB: "if you want to come back I will give you a job at the park and we pay our employees pretty well."

John said "you would do that for me."

JB: "The four of us are closer than most brothers we sometimes spent months together 24/7 depending upon each other just to survive, it makes you very close; and yes I would do that for you." LJ's father started to cry again.

JB: "Sir are you all right?"

The man in the wheelchair tried to get control of himself and said "I never expected anything like this in my wildest dreams."

Jennifer: "I think you should let John's father rest he's had an awful big day."

JB: "Jennifer is an ER nurse at the hospital, if she thinks your dad should rest he should rest." JB: "Jennifer do you think the castor oil packs would help his kidneys, and make things easier for him?" Jennifer: "it won't hurt him, you got everything to gain and nothing to lose the heat will draw more blood into the area which is healing." JB what is your schedule?"

John: "we were going to spend the night and go back tomorrow, we didn't know whether you would see us or not." JB: "why don't you call your mother and tell her you're staying another couple days and Jennifer will teach you how to do the castor oil pack so you can teach your mother when you get home, I had bruised kidneys from being shot and I healed in a third of the time JR got shot through the lungs and healed in a third of the time doing castor oil pack's, we are believers, but don't tell anybody that Jennifer said to do this, I said it and I'm not a doctor." John thanked them and said they would meet at the diner at 9:30 AM. JB, Jennifer, LJ, and Peggy said goodbye and left. LJ said I'm going to follow Peggy home and I'll be back later. JB and Jennifer said goodbye and they headed back to the big house. On the way back JB explained what he learned about LJ's father when LJ was younger and the man he called dad was his stepfather and what he had done to his real father and why. Jennifer: "it's amazing he turned out the way he did." JB: "we can thank his mother and his stepfather for that."

LJ: "explain to Peggy how his real father would get drunk and beat him and his mother, and one day while he was beating his mother LJ came up behind him with a board and beat him with it until his mother stopped him, they packed up and left, that was the last they knew of him until he looked for them to ask for forgiveness as he was dying of kidney failure, and he was ashamed of himself when he quit drinking." And how John's mother was a nurse where he was doing a detoxification from the alcohol, and they ended up getting married and had John, and he turned out to be a nice man and never drank alcohol again.

Peggy: "that was awful nice what you did today."

LJ: "JB and I talked about this and he said it was as much for me as it was for him, and he was right, it took a burden off me I did not even know I was carrying."

Peggy: "I love you, and what you did today just reinforces that you are the nicest man I have ever known; and it makes me so happy that you're mine."

LJ: "I'm glad I make you happy, just having you around makes me happy"; they kissed each other and held onto each other." LJ: "I want to show you my schedule because our weeks are going to be really full from now on", he took out the training schedule that they will be on until the park opens.

Peggy: "your training the security guards at night."

LJ: "yes, we want them to have better skills than they have right now, and if John wants to work for the park, I will move in with you tomorrow night or Thursday, the rest of the days will be too busy; if John decides to come back he will take his dad home and come back the next day, I am not sure what he will do, but we will be living together before the end of the week." LJ: "The training on Saturday is open to everybody, you, Jennifer, the police, and the security guards, and if you want to quit at the diner you can, I will give you more money if you need it."

Peggy: "I will think about that, as I am not getting enough rest on the weekends, and I want to be fresh on Mondays."

LJ: "go ahead tell your boss at the diner to find a new girl and you will train her next weekend." Peggy: "there is a girl at school that wants to do the same thing I want to do, have a bakery that specializes in pies and cakes, her mother is the one that sells to the diner and she wants to quit and let Sue take over her business, she has the diner and three restaurants, she is dating this guy she says he drinks too much and he's kind of lazy, she wondered if there was any more like you out at the park?"

LJ: "we are all taken, there is another seal coming in a week from Friday, whether he is single or not I don't know." LJ: "let's talk about your bakery, how good is your friend?"

Peggy: "she helps her mother, the reason she is going to school is to learn better skills at decorating and cooking, her name is Sue." LJ: "you could call it Peggy and Sue's cakes and pies." Peggy: "that sounds catchy we will have to work on that." LJ: "I will make you a sign on paper and then see if you like it." LJ: "I need to head back to the park; I've had a long and trying day that ended better than I thought it would." They kissed goodbye and LJ left went back to the spring house and took Mike for his nightly walk. They went back in the spring house took off Mike's leash they both went in his bedroom and went to sleep.

CHAPTER 33

WEDNESDAY WEEK 5

JB came out and LJ, CR, and JR were talking and it seemed very serious. JB: "what's up I know this look." LJ: "I want to go and see Siham, about a vision of the six Arab assassins that were coming in my vision, and I want him to check." JB: "we only have training at 10:00, in hand to hand combat for the police, we can go see Siham and get lunch and we can take it back to the office." LJ said that made him feel better. JR said "I'm going up to 2 miles today, and see how I do." JR got back from his run and though the run was pretty good and decided to up my push-ups to 40 and my crunches to 70 and see how I hold up today.

JB and JR when in the big house to finish their routine; LJ and CR went to the spring house to finish there's.

LJ: "CR you want to have breakfast with me and my half brother this morning and my real father?" CR: "sure I'll be happy to." They got cleaned up and dressed put on their vest, checked their pistols and put an extra round for 18 total; put on their jacket to hide their weapons and went to the big house.

JB:"are you two armed?"

CR: "yes, and an extra round."

LJ said "we will put the dogs in my van and we will take them in with us." CR: "your vision makes me nervous too." They went to the diner and sat in their usual spot, LJ moved a chair away so his father would have a place for his wheelchair. 10 minutes later John came in pushing his father's wheelchair. John looked around and saw LJ and wheeled his dad over to the empty spot sat down in the chair. The waitress came over and gave CR, and LJ their coffee, she ask "John what he wanted to drink, he said "hot tea for both of us."

The waitress came back and gave them menus and put down the 2 cups for the tea and two small pitchers of hot water and teabags. LJ and CR gave her their orders John gave her his order and gave her a Ziploc bag of cereal and other things in it, and ask her if she could run that through a blender with 2 cups of water? She said "yes Peggy had called and told me you would be here." She took the bag and went into the kitchen, put 2 cups of water in the blender and the contents of the bag in the blender and blended it till it was smooth, and then poured it in the largest glass she had and took it back out to the table.

John said "thank you, we really appreciate this." And he handed the glass to his dad. LJ's dad asks "what are the dogs for?" LJ: "they tell us when people are armed and they will look for guns, explosives, and search for people." John: "do they attack?" LJ: "no if somebody runs to get away we can turn them loose and they will just knock them down." 10 minutes later the waitress brought their food. John said "what do you do at the park?" LJ: "the four of us are training and starting a SWAT unit for the local town we are training some of the police men and women that have volunteered for SWAT to shoot pistols and rifles better, were teaching them hand to hand combat and we have a dog training facility that we train these two dogs and four others to help protect the town and the park; they are called sniffer dogs, the four of us are on the police force and we are training three of the police that have volunteered and they've already had a few missions in the short time they've been together." At the park we have various things we do to improve the accuracy of SWAT members we have a pistol range and we have a rifle range we also have a building that they learn to go through and do what we call house clearing or how to get bad people out of good people's homes."

John: "what do you do at the park?" LJ: "Sunday we were running a check on the perimeter fencing and found a hole in the fence and found 4 people that are illegally here and the crook that stole their money to bring them over." John: "what happened to them?" LJ: "They were arrested for illegally entering the country, they could not even speak English, and we brought in one of our security guards that knew Spanish to talk to them."

John: "that is kind of cruel; they're just trying to make a living." LJ: "let's say you're working here at the park and we are paying you $15 an hour, and an the legal comes in and says I will work for eight dollars an hour and do just as good a job, then we let you go and you're out of a job, is that fair to you?" John: "no I would not like that; I guess I didn't look at the whole picture."

CR: "have you ever noticed you do something you shouldn't, second time it's easier, the third time it's even easier; they have broken the law by sneaking in what other laws will they break now that they see it's easy to do that." CR: "we don't mind them coming up here to work, but they should learn English and they should get a green card so we know there here, there are too many coming across and breaking all kinds of laws robbing, killing, and raping; we need to put a stop to this it's costing this country billions and billions of dollars."

John: "I didn't know all that was happening."

CR: "the news reporters don't report that because they're trying to destroy the United States as we know it."

LJ asks "John what kind of skills do you have?" John: "not too many I mow the grass at home, try to fix things at home, and dad talks me through it and tells me what to do so I fix it, that is all I have." LJ: "now the Navy will teach you a skill you tell them what you want and they will guarantee it but if you flunk out of what you wanted you will have two options, they will put you where they want you or they will discharge you, and now you've wasted six or eight months of your life you are right back where you started." John: 'I didn't know that: "John's dad said "remember me telling you that you have to find somebody that's been there and knows how it really works not just what the recruiter said." LJ: "go to college take classes in the different things that you're interested in, and then find which one you like the best and that is the one you will probably excel in." LJ: "check with the colleges that you said were interested in giving you a scholarship and see which one has some of the things you're looking for and take them up on the scholarship, still work in the summer to make money to help pay for what is not covered by the scholarship, you will learn more because it's your money you are spending; don't go there to play, go there to learn you can play later, and remember only 2% of the jocks make it to the pros, that is not good odds.

John: "no it's not, thank you, I will take dad back home and I will get in touch with the colleges and see what they have to say and I will be back next Monday, is that okay?" LJ: "yes it is and we will find a job for you, and I will help you anyway I can, but there are rules, pay attention to what you're doing, don't make mistakes they get you killed, we had a seal that was very careless we did not like to take him on missions but the higher-ups forced him on us for a very dangerous mission and he got one of our men killed, we had him court-martialed and kicked out of the Navy, he found out where we were and he tried to kill us and he set a bomb in the park to kill innocent people." So we don't like mistakes, if it's our fault because we didn't give you enough information that is not a mistake because you didn't know, when you know and make a mistake you only get two and then you're fired, does that sound reasonable."

John: "yes it does, helping take care of Dad has taught me you have to be real careful that we give him the right things at the right time." CR: "you do have a computer at home don't you?" John: "yes I do." CR: "Jennifer recorded Rose giving JR a castor oil pack and directions as they did it, and we think you should castor oil pack each kidney which will take two hours one hour each, JB and JR both said they felt better after getting a pack, here is the flash drive for you to play, and if there isn't a player on your machine there is one on the flash drive it's called VLC, 32-bit or a 64 bit."

John: "I understand that and thank you very much." The waitress brought the bills LJ took them and said "this is on me and have a safe trip", he gave John a piece of paper and said "here is my phone number if you have a problem call I will come and help you." John and his dad each shook hands with LJ and CR and said "thank you very much." John and his dad waved goodbye again and started their trip home." LJ and CR put their dogs in the van jumped in and headed for the park, and in a half hour the four of them would be going to the police station to teach hand to hand combat with the regular policeman, they were curious to see how many would show up."

LJ and CR went to the office and went in, JB and JR were there. JB: "LJ what did John have to say?" LJ "he is going to take his dad home and make sure his mother knows how to do the castor oil pack, and he said he would be back Monday morning to start work." JB: "what skills does he have?" LJ: "not too many, high school, he mows the grass at home, and his dad walks him through fixing stuff and that's it, he's not stupid and with taking care of his dad he had to learn to think. I think he'll work hard and I told him he only gets two mistakes."

JB: "well let's go to the police station, and see what happens." They loaded their dogs got in their vans and headed for the police station. They went to the gym and checked out the mats, they looked good enough so they sat down on the bleachers and waited, their dogs sat beside them. JB checked his watch and said "9:40 5 minutes and the clock starts." JB: "9:45 the clock starts." 9:50 the first policeman came in, LJ: "your name please." The policeman said "Henderson." JB: "thank you for coming." 9:52 2 two came in. LJ: "your names please." "Jenkins, the second man said Watkins." 9:54 another man came in. LJ: "your name please." The man said "Wilson." 9:56 two more came in. LJ: "your names please." Anderson and Clark and they sat down.

At 10:00: "I want to thank you men for coming, I want to give you a little background, four of us have been Navy SEALs for 11 years, we were in the terrorist unit our last six years most of that time was spent in Afghanistan we cleared houses we are snipers and we infiltrated and took out the enemy." CR: "we are to start you out different than your use to, we are going to have you do the moves in slow-motion, your brain will remember what you did, it is easy to do it right slowly without having done it before, you do it fast you make mistakes it takes between 5 and 10 times to unlearn the mistake and put the right movement in its place." So to start with we are going slow to get the movement right."

CR walked out on the mat, LJ followed him. CR: "What has anyone of you encountered in your everyday patrolling, did they come at you with a gun, come at you with a knife, or club?" One of the policemen sitting on the bench said "a man came at me with a club about 20 inches long." LJ: "if you would look over there on the floor there should be one very similar to what you just described would you pick it up and come over here please." The man picked it up came out on the mat. LJ how far from you was he." The man: "about 10 feet." LJ: "would you stand about 10 feet from me and attack me like you were attacked." LJ stood with his hands by his side the man bolted toward him and when he passed the 5 foot mark LJ moved at a 45° angle to his right and forward blocked and grabbed the arm with the club and hit the man in the chest hanging on to his arm and down he went LJ came down with his knee beside the man's chest and chopped just below his elbow and the man's arm went numb, LJ knocked the club out of his hand as the man yelled: "that hurt." LJ rubbed the man's forearm said can you move your fingers; the man was able to move his fingers LJ stood up still holding on to the man's arm and helped him up. LJ: "you look to me like you were really going to hit me, I had two options, I could shoot you and that's a lot of paperwork, the men on the bench laughed, or you could do what I just did, hardly any paperwork." LJ: "Let me ask you a question, what did you do in that situation?" The Man: "I took a hit on the arm and shot him, and my life was hell for four weeks."

LJ: "so my solution was better don't you think." The man shook his head yes. LJ looked at the man and then said to the men on the bench: "what would you gentlemen have done?" They all said "probably what he did." CR came out and said "can any of you men on the bench tell me exactly what LJ did in that maneuver?" They all said "it happened so fast we cannot do what he did."

CR: "he was able to do what he did, because he really didn't have to think, all he had to do was move, and his body did the rest." CR: "we would rather you did the technique 10 or 20 times slow than 200 times fast." LJ: "I want another one of you to come out here." Nobody moved LJ: "are you afraid of me, all of you outweigh me by 25 to 50 pounds." And one of them said "I didn't come here to get hurt." LJ: "did the man I demoed on walk back and sit down?"

They all said yes. LJ looked at the man he had just taken the club away from and LJ said "do you believe that will work in a real-life situation?" The man shook his head yes. LJ: "I see you are the only man here that's brave will you come back out again." The man got up and walked out. LJ walked up to the man until he was about 5 foot away and said "you are strongest when you're coming straight at me agreed?" The man said "yes I believe I would be the strongest."

LJ: "you are right you would be the strongest; now move toward me with a step like you would take when you were running only do it very slowly so the scared ones on the bench can see what we are doing." He took one step LJ took a step forward in a 45° angle and pushed the man away from him but held his shirt so he couldn't fall; by moving at a 45° angle forward I am at an angle which makes me the stronger and I am using his forward momentum against him and that's how I pushed him over I grabbed his arm and controlled how he went down guiding him where I want him to end up and I grabbed his arm so I controlled him if there had been a fence behind me something hard a wall I could just throw him into the wall and he would hit backwards at the back of his head and he would not be in good shape and for a second or two he would be slightly dazed, then I would of hit him in the throat collapsed his windpipe and he would be immobilized trying his best to breathe and he's not thinking about me, that's why I hit him in the chest because I didn't want to hurt him, but in the street you immobilize them so they don't get up on you."

Look for more in volume 2 of true love and brothers lasts forever

SOME OF WHAT IS IN
FUTURE VOLUMES

Jimmy meets Shelley

Jimmy was walking along when the call came in over his radio, and it said a man is hurting a woman with a baby near the Caterpillar. Jimmy went into a hard run and in a minute he was there. He slowed down and started walking toward the man. And the woman screamed: "he is not supposed to get within 100 feet of me, I have a restraining order." Jimmy came up and said "Sir would you please leave go of the woman's arm." The man said "go away this is none of your business." Jimmy: "Sir it is my business, and you have two options let go of the woman's arm and walk away, otherwise I will have to hurt you and you will go to jail." The man looked at him, and Jimmy pulled out his stick and said "let go now or I will assume you want option two." The man let go turned and walked away. The girl grabbed Jimmy and hugged him and said thank you I was so scared he beats me up." Jimmy: "not while I'm around." JR and JB came up out of nowhere. JB: "where is the man that was hurting the woman?" Jimmy: "I did like you did and gave him two options let her go or I hurt him, he left." JB: "over his radio security where is the man that was hurting the woman?" Security: "he's heading toward the exit you can catch him if you run take the left path." JR and JB took off, three minutes later security said "he is right in front of you in a brown jacket." JB came up behind him JR went around in front turned and said "Sir, stop where you are." The man said "get out of my way I don't have to stop for you." JR moved at a 45° angle toward the man grabbed his arm twisted and slammed him to the ground. The man said "you can't do that." JR: "yes I can see this badge you're under arrest for breaking your restraining order and we have it all recorded." Security is calling a squad car now they will give a copy of you hurting the woman and you're going to jail." They cuffed him and stood him up and JR marched him off to the holding building. JB: "I'll check with Jimmy and see you later." Jimmy took the woman to a park bench and told her to sit down and relax a little bit, she did as she was told, and she took out a piece of paper and wrote something on it, and gave it to Jimmy and said "thank you very much, this is the first time I have felt safe in a long time." Jimmy looked at the paper and said "it's against the rules to get friendly with the customers." The girl said "you have not gotten friendly with me, I'm getting friendly with you, you are the nicest man I have met in a long time, I would like to see you again and cook you supper to show my appreciation." Jimmy: "thank you very much I would love that but I will have to clear that with my boss first; and it is my job to protect you while you're here at Park." JB came up as he had been listening and said "ma'am did he ask for your number?" She said "no I gave it to him, he said he would have to ask his boss because I ask him to let me cook him dinner for what he did, and he said I didn't have to, it was his job to protect me, but I want to make dinner for him, even when he was getting my X husband to leave me alone he was polite about the whole thing he gave him two options, my X chose number one and left." JB smiled and said "Jimmy she gave you the number I think I'd call it, if you would feel better Jimmy could walk with you a little bit until you feel secure, your X is on his way to jail we have him on video, you have a restraining order, he'll be there a while." JB turned and left. Jimmy sat down beside the woman and said "my name is Jimmy Johnson, what is yours?" She said "my name is Shelley Wilson." She reached over and grabbed Jimmy's hand and said "would you hold my hand for a little while as it will make me feel safer." Jimmy squeezed her hand gently and they begin to talk." She ask him questions, he ask her questions, and they got to know each other a little better.

Read what happens in volume 2

More in volume 2and 3 true love and brothers lasts forever
THIS IS NOT THE END

Printed in the United States
by Baker & Taylor Publisher Services